Assembly Code

Book 2 of The Techxorcist
by Colin F. Barnes

Colin F. Barnes' Website: www.colinfbarnes.com
Newsletter: http://eepurl.com/rFAtL

All Rights Reserved

This edition published in 2013 by Anachron Press

Other Titles by Colin F. Barnes

Novels
Artificial Evil: Book 1 of The Techxorcist

Novellas
The Daedalus Code
Dead Five's Pass (Coming Feb, 2014)
Heart for the Ravens

Short Stories
The Shade
Dark Metaphor
The Curse of Underghast

Anthologies
City of Hell Chronicles
Crime Net

Acknowledgments

A big thanks to Krista Walsh, Sharon Ring, Dave Robison, Aaron Sikes, Jamie Stonehouse, and my mum for being wonderful and supportive people. You make doing this thing easier with all you in my corner.

Chapter 1

Petal paced the eight steps back and forth within her cell: a grey-walled block, with a shelf for a bed and a hole for a toilet. A thick steel door with only a small window and a secure flap for passing things through gave it any detail.

For two long weeks she'd ambled and shuffled to the left, to the right, all the time wondering what happened to Gerry back in City Earth. Jasper and his cronies had shot her and Len, but she'd no idea of Gerry's fate.

She thought she would have sensed something, somehow, if they had killed him off. Only a crushing Gerry-shaped void remained inside. She took some comfort in not knowing for sure. There was always hope, but still, the sickly rage crawled through her mind, constructed images of terrible vengeance. A series of circular questions ran through her mind on a constant loop: Was Gerry dead? Had the AI breached City Earth's systems? What was happening if it had? Was everyone a gibbering AI-controlled zombie? Was Gabe still a double-crossing douche?

The only thing she knew right now was that she was some distance from the Dome. After Jasper's people had shot her and taken her out of the City, she was transported away in Enna's Jaguar copter.

During the evacuation, however, a group of robed fanatics attacked the transport and killed Jasper's people. They had the glint of religious fanatics in their eyes: the fervent staring of the unhinged. For the most part they spoke Russian, or one of its sub-dialects. The group wore red scarves around their faces, and was made up entirely of women.

While Petal was bagged and thrown into the back of a truck during her recapture she heard them wail then mumble, groan and exalt, all praising their leader 'Natalya'.

Petal didn't know what to be more surprised by: that there were still fanatics of this sort, or that there were that many survivors in Russia. Enna had suggested there was an old military installation beyond the mountains that separated Mongolia and Russia. It was where she recovered and rebuilt the Jaguar from. However, the installation had faced some of the worst fighting during the Cataclysm. Clearly there were more things out there than Petal could ever know; like why the hell was she being held in a prison cell?

Each day they would come, pass a pot of barely edible swill through the door. She gagged and choked with each mouthful, but would never give them the satisfaction of beating her, despite how they laughed at her through the small glass window. They would point at her goggles, pink mohican-hair, now growing out at the sides, or her tattooed lips, and gabble in their filthy language. Occasionally a more senior robe-wearer would stand at the window and stare at her while uttering some ugly sermon. Every one of them had a plain look like the desert, she thought. Not a one of them had their own style. They were nothing but a bunch of brainwashed drones.

She would've been able to translate if the rude swines hadn't ripped out her dermal implant. The wound on her wrist still throbbed. The poorly stitched cuts scarred into brutal reminders of the 'procedure'. Without her implant she couldn't use her concealed spikes within her forearms: none of her internal modifications worked. She was lesser now, a mere human.

Those deadly retractable killing tools were of much fascination to their surgeons. Through a translator they asked how they worked, what she was, who made her. None of which she could answer. For the past five years she hadn't known anything that came before. Her mind erased like an old, unwanted hard drive. Ever since Gabe had found her wandering the desert, she'd always wanted to know where she came from. Neither Gabe nor Enna could recover her memory.

It was like she was dropped there, fully formed, from the sky one day.

One of the fanatics must have entered the cell compound as the sounds of industry rumbled into her cell. She heard the familiar sound of Jaguars and trucks, which meant she must be in either GeoCity-1 or Darkhan. Or perhaps she had been taken across the border? Wherever they were they could go back from whence they came for all she cared.

An hour later the distant sound of engines abated to be replaced by an electronic buzz and a heavy clunk.

Her cell door opened. Petal shot to the back of the room and faced the door. She crouched slightly, one foot against the wall, ready to push off. This was her chance. No one had dared come into the cell since they had operated on her and dumped her here like a piece of meat.

Her muscles tensed like knotted ropes, ready to unleash their kinetic energy into a scene of violence and escape. The door opened wider. A shadow entered the room. Petal readied her attack.

Okay you bitches. One. Two—

"Gabe? What the? Holy crap! You..." All the fight drained from her at the sight of her ex-companion dressed as one of those crazed women. He looked drastically different without his padre's hat. She could actually see his wide face and the shape of his head. Such an odd thought to be having, she considered as Gabe stared at her, freezing her to the spot. Her brain struggled to catch up with the consequences and ramifications. Where the hell had he been all this time?

A thousand questions filled her mouth so that none came out. Her heart ached for her to reach out for him, to trust him again. She ached for him to be the man that found her that hot day in the middle of nowhere and kept her alive. His face gave nothing away. It was like she looked upon a sculpture of him.

"Hey," Gabe said.

"Hey? Really? That all you got? You damned traitor! You nearly got Gez and me killed with your double-crossing act. What the hell was that all about? Paid you well did they?" She spat at his feet, shook with rage.

"Shut ya mouth, prisoner," Gabe said, his voice intentionally loud. There was a different quality to it. It didn't feel right to her somehow. "Ya comin' with me." Gabe pointed a shotgun at her chest, held out a pair of electromagnetic wrist-cuffs. "Put 'em on, girl."

"Go screw yourself."

"Language, Petal," Gabe said with a slight wink.

She was taken back to when Gabe first brought Gez to their safe house. He'd said the same thing when she got over-excited at meeting their new recruit. There was something about Gabe's face. It was too serious, dead straight as if he were acting. And she could swear he was trying to communicate something with his eyes: a warning perhaps.

She'd known him too long not to notice that subtle difference in his voice. Even his body language seemed off. Gone was the languid bravado. He was too professional now—a suit that didn't hang right on him.

She took the cuffs and put them on her wrists as requested while raising an eyebrow. Gabe shook his head and took a chain from under his robes. Keeping the shotgun aimed at her, he attached the clasp on the chain to a belt around her waist. All part of her wonderfully ugly prison outfit: a grey one-piece that chafed everywhere. She'd no idea what they'd done with her leather biker's jacket that she won in a bare-knuckle fight a few years ago. It hurt not having it more than it hurt winning it. She had few possessions that she truly cared about, and that was one of them.

"Out," he ordered as he walked behind and pushed

her out of the door.

In the dull-lit corridor, three more female guards stood with stun-batons, and a weapon she hadn't seen before: a curved sickle-like blade that hummed with electricity. The small hairs on her arms tingled as she passed by.

"They're new," she said, nodding to the sickles.

Gabe kicked her in the back, although she noticed it wasn't too hard, and tripped forward onto the rough Steelcrete floor, scraping her knees through the flimsy one-piece.

"Ya'll speak when I tell ya. Understand?"

Petal hauled herself up and nodded. What the hell was he playing at? This wasn't him, but neither was selling her and Gez out like he had. So what did he have up his sleeve this time? Whatever it was she'd bide her time, wait for an opportunity. At least she was out of that damned cell.

Petal vaguely recognised the rest of the compound as Gabe led her through various corridors and lab rooms. It seemed like Seca's place in Darkhan. She wanted to ask Gabe if it was when he pulled on the chain and dragged her through more lab rooms. A number of robed women busied themselves with assigned tasks in each room. Some worked on holoscreens, while others hunched over slates. They all wore that dark-eyed look of suspicion and piety about them: the look of the self-righteous. Each one gazed upon her with judgement, but she stuck out her chin and curled her lip in defiance.

When they entered a medical bay she noticed rows of

tanks in which bodies were maintained in a NanoStem solution. It instantly reminded her of Enna's transcendents. Were they creating their own? An army perhaps? She tried to commit every detail to memory.

A number of them turned to face Gabe as they passed through. They nodded professionally at each other. Did they know what he was going to do? Was he following orders, or giving them?

A particularly large woman, with strong, square shoulders stood hunched over a metal desk. She wore a great gold chain around her neck, clutching it in a claw-like grip, while with the other she manipulated models across a map. Petal recognised the land mass and location of Darkhan, and the borderline between old Mongolia and Russia.

The woman's eyes glowed red like OLED rubies. Clearly implants. *Curious*, Petal thought. So far all the other women were completely free of any tech. She guessed this one was the leader. Petal stopped, stared at the woman, and tried to ascertain who or what she was, but she just smirked at Petal, then turned to Gabe and said in a thick, guttural Russian accent, "This your little project, eh?"

"Yeah, Natalya, this is the one. I'm taking 'er to interrogation."

"Make sure she sings loud and clear. We need those servers. We move in three days."

"She'll sing, all right. I guarantee it."

"Good," Natalya said with a blank expression, eyeing up Petal as if analysing her.

So this woman, this Natalya, *was* the group's leader.

Like the others, she too wore that red scarf. Unlike the others, however, it didn't obscure her face. She wore it around her neck. If she didn't scowl or clench her jaw so much she might have once been pretty, but even in those upgraded OLED eyes of hers, Petal detected pain and grief. It was an expression one wore unconsciously. Petal had seen it so many times. She probably wore it herself.

Gabe pushed her forward through the lab and past the woman and her map. Petal memorised a fragment of the layout, noticed what looked like a small army somewhere in the grounds of their location. Given its westerly position beyond the great Sludge, it appeared they were indeed in the compound beneath the city of Darkhan.

Were they planning some kind of invasion on the Dome perhaps? What of the rest of Seca's security and followers? When she escaped and saved Gerry from the compound, the place still had at least fifty men and women within it. Without Seca, his life ended by Gerry, she wondered if they had melted in with the rest of the survivors and Upsiders within Darkhan. Or perhaps this mad cult had butchered them and taken the compound for their own.

Gabe kicked her again and pushed onwards past Natalya, out of the lab, and into a small room. He locked the door behind, and the foundations of the place rumbled as a group of trucks rumbled outside. Through the door, Petal heard Natalya's muffled orders and the sound of frantic steps clattering against the floor at her command.

With a heavy shove, Gabe forced Petal to sit on a chair. He sat opposite. Between them a pair of cups with a steaming black liquid inside sat on a low table next to a plate of protein rations. They looked like flat wheat biscuits: discs the size of her hands. Her stomach knotted with the thought of eating something more substantial than liquid.

Gabe regarded her with his head cocked to one side, his eyes wide and with a hint of sincerity.

"Ya have to stay calm, ya understand?" He still pointed the shotgun at her chest with one hand. He stood, unclasped the chain, and slowly released her from the EM cuffs. He sat back down opposite and said. "Please, drink, girl." And with barely a whisper added, "Ya don't have much time."

Petal eyed him with suspicion. What was his game? Was this a poison, a truth serum? Gabe picked up his cup and took a deep draw.

Not trusting him, Petal leant forward, snatched the cup from his hands, and drunk the remains. *That's damned good*, she thought. It'd been so long since she had had a good cup of coffee in her belly. She'd only ever had it twice before when she and Gabe had once stumbled on a secure ration container in one of the many abandoned shelters throughout the abandoned lands.

The hot, rich drink, freshly brewed by the taste of it, settled in her stomach. She closed her eyes, delighting in the warmth and flavour. It made such a difference to the usual dirty water they'd been giving her. Heat radiated through her body. For a short while she felt human again. *If I even am human.*

Finally Gabe spoke, his voice low and rumbling. She had to strain to hear it.

"I don't have much time. I'm s'posed to interrogate ya, but ya've gotta believe me, girl. Everything I did was for a reason."

She shook her head. "You sold us out to that crazed nutter, Seca, and for what?"

He closed his eyes, bowed his head. "I had to. I can't explain now, not fully. Just listen if ya wanna live and get outta this damned place."

Learning forward and concerned others were listening, she lowered her voice to a whisper. "What's going on? Why am I here?"

"They found something on ya implant. I managed to sneak it away." He passed it to her. "Look on the underside."

She'd never seen her wrist implant up close. It was smaller than it seemed under her skin. But now in her hands it seemed so alien, and yet it was, and presumably always was, a part of her. At thirty-millimetres square, grey, and metallic, it felt light and cold in her hand. She flipped it over. On the back, stamped into its surface, was the word CRIBORG, followed by a serial number.

A scintilla of recognition tried to bubble up from deep inside, buried somewhere inaccessible.

"What's Criborg? Is that what I am? Is it a manufacturer?"

Gabe shook his head.

"Then what?"

Checking a slate that he took from his robes, Gabe

stood and said in a hurry, "It's time to go. Follow me and do as I say. Ya might just make it outta here." He glanced back to the door, waited, and then moved towards to her.

"How the hell can I trust you after what you did?" Petal said.

"Please, Petal. It's me. Ya know me! I'm trying to help ya, girl."

Petal refused to move. "I'd rather die in this place." Which of course was ridiculous, but she could see the sweat bead on his forehead. He was definitely working against these people in some manner. Getting her out seemed important, and she'd take that opportunity to get the truth from him. She damned well deserved it after he abandoned her. He was always supposed to back her up. That's what they did for each other.

His voice was thick with sincerity, and despite every-thing, deep down she wanted to trust him again. He was Gabe, after all, her mentor, father figure, and best friend. She thought about her options: trust him and potentially escape, or trust him and what? Get captured again? They already had her captive. They could do anything they wanted with her.

"Tell me," she said. "Is Gerry alive? What happened when these bitches took me from Jasper's men?"

"I don't know if Gerry made it. I know that he defeated the AI. Trapped it inside Jasper's body. The Family took him away. Since then, everything's gone quiet, and the Meshwork's offline, or being suppressed by something. There're no communications. Enna's working on it though."

She knew in her heart Gerry could still be alive. Especially if The Family had taken him away. She had no real way of knowing for sure beyond a hunch, but while she had it, she'd cling to it until proven otherwise. Without that, she wasn't sure she could bring herself to acknowledge he was gone. The fact The Family had taken him meant something. Promised a glimmer of hope. "What happened to me? Why was I brought here? Who the hell are they?" she said.

Gabe fidgeted with impatience. He frequently turned towards the door at the slightest sound. With a sigh, realising Petal wasn't going anywhere voluntarily, he said. "This group call 'emselves the Red Widows. They took ya from the wreckage of Jasper's Jaguar, and brought ya here."

"Where's here? It's Seca's place, ain't it?"

A knowing smile stretched his wrinkled and worn face. "Yeah, we're in Darkhan. Red Widow took it over. They're slowly taking over the whole city. Wiped out all Seca's followers in a single assault. I'd have sympathy for 'em if they weren't just as brutal."

"So what's their story? What do they want from me?"

"They're fanatics," Gabe said. "Mostly an alliance of survivors from Russia and Chechnya. There's more than any of us, including The Family, ever realised. Most of 'em lived underground like bugs waiting to swarm the earth. Enna had me infiltrate their ranks, which weren't easy. Ya see, they are the descendants of the widows of the men that were killed during the war. They blame men for it all: the war, the deaths, the loss of their sons and fathers. Look, we gotta move, gotta get ya out of it. They'll kill ya eventually. Ya can't help 'em with what they want."

Petal crossed her arms defiantly. She refused to go anywhere until she knew what the hell he was talking about. And she took a degree of satisfaction seeing him panic. "And that is?"

"Their crusade. They want the servers. Old Grey, and the one Len's people were protecting. They wanna track down those who instigated the war, killed their men. Hell, they wanna eradicate all men. They're tolerating me because of the information and promises I gave. They'll kill me too, eventually, I'm sure."

"So why take me?"

Natalya's voice rose from outside, issuing some curt command in her Russian language. Gabe wiped the sweat from his forehead, flashed another glance at the door as if he were expecting someone to come bursting through any second. "I don't know the full story," he said, rushing his words out, keeping his voice low. "It's something to do with Criborg. I tried to find out, but I'm only tolerated so far. Only so much info I can get access to."

"Are you coming with me?" Petal asked as he pushed her towards another door at the rear of the room.

Gabe ignored her, checked his slate again. His face hardened. "Okay, ready?"

"For what?"

"To run!"

He gestured across the slate and pocketed it inside his long, flowing robes that matched the others. Although unlike them, he wore no red scarf.

Petal tucked her implant chip into the single breast pocket of her prison suit. Her instincts kicked in and she tried to active her internal networking transceiver hoping to connect with something, anyone. Of course, nothing happened. No implant meant no access to her systems. But before she could examine further, Gabe grabbed her by the arm and pulled her through the door.

The room was empty of Red Widows. A rack of computer screens lined the left wall. Beyond that, it was just another grey Steelcrete box lit by the dull overhead OLED bulbs.

"Behind the right wall is a tunnel," Gabe said. Sweat patches grew dark beneath his arms. "Ya have to go through it. It'll take ya out behind the city. From there follow the coordinates on this slate." He took a beat-up slate from within the folds of his robe and handed it to her. His eyes flittered, as if he were holding something back. Petal wanted to press him on it when he pushed her to the right wall.

Gabe entered some codes into one of the computer terminals. The right wall slid open revealing an escape tunnel. He took a small pistol from inside his robes. Petal recognised it. It was one similar to what Jasper and his goons had used during their attack in City Earth.

"Take this and run. Go east. Follow the coordinates on the slate. Keep ya head down. Ya a wanted girl."

Petal grabbed the pistol and held it to his head.

"Why, Gabe? Why did you hand us to Seca's men?"

Gabe clenched his teeth in irritation. "I was following orders from Enna, dammit. I had to—"

Petal smacked the gun against his face. Such a rash action against the man she used to love like a father hurt more than it'd ever hurt him. She felt like she crossed a line. "Tell me!" She already hated herself for striking him, but the question was an itch she needed to scratch. She needed to trust him again. He was her only constant.

He bowed his head, sighed deeply. "We had to make sure Gerry got to Seca directly, and you were supposed to have stayed in the cell. Stayed safe. The guard I dealt with was an insider who Enna had been working on. He was gonna get both of ya up to The Family. But ya had to go and kill him and escape. The idea was that while Gerry would deal with Seca, you'd be safe from his crazy followers. They'd have butchered ya both as soon as ya got in. We couldn't afford for that to happen. Ya would've both walked into a death trap."

"Why Gabe? Why The Family?"

"Gerry *is* one of The Family! He's one of their sons. They promised Enna they would keep you safe!"

"From what?"

"From ya self, dammit!"

Petal dropped the weapon, stared at Gabe's face. "What do you mean exactly?"

The sound of voices and a crash from outside made Gabe turn his back and frantically enter commands into the console. "Just go. Get to those coordinates and everything will make sense. For God's sake, girl, trust me, yeah?"

"What's out there? At these coordinates?"

"Ya home. Ya makers. Criborg."

"One more thing. Natalya mentioned something happening in three days, what is it?"

"A war."

Gabe pushed her through the door and closed it behind her. Petal stood trembling inside the dark tunnel. Her head buzzed with everything Gabe had said, and didn't say. She wanted to go back, get more answers, but beyond the door she heard him scream, 'run.'

So she ran.

Chapter 2

Gerry gripped his head and screamed a silent, torturous scream. A pulse of electricity ripped through his mind, stripping through the layers of security protecting his various internal systems. An insidious force probed at his mind, eating his memories.

Somewhere, out there, in the dark depths of space, an entity, a digital being had found Gerry. Snatched him up in its binary tendrils like a gargantuan squid. Gerry's brain felt like it would burst into flames at any moment under the attack. And the worst thing: he could do nothing about it. Whatever this thing was had completely incapacitated Mags, his AIA, and also the system controlling the shuttle that still hurtled away from the earth and out into the deep reaches of space.

With his heart pounding against his chest and sweat dripping from his forehead and neck, Gerry tried to collect his thoughts and push away the rising panic. Only with logical thought could he... What exactly? Fight back? This thing attacking him had no centre. It didn't respond to Gerry's shouts or thoughts, it just wanted whatever Gerry held within his mind, but for what purpose?

"What do you want?" Gerry screamed, his voice

finally sounding within the tight confines of the shuttle. The scream sounded muffled, distorted. All his senses had diminished under the attack as if his brain had tried to divert energy and resources to defend against the attack.

Gerry clenched his eyes as another pulse ripped through him, but this time he paid attention and sent his consciousness further into the nano network Jachz had repaired.

There he caught a glimpse of the data flowing to and from his attacker.

It resembled Helix++ code but had mutated to something entirely alien, something unlike anything he had seen before. It twisted into new forms, always shifting. Its logic spun around a vortex that funnelled up data and memories from Gerry's brain like a tornado.

Gerry sent his mind into it, focused as much power he could muster and conjured an attack program to break through the data-twister and destroy its connection. The program flew out into his network, but the entity saw it coming and swatted it away like it was nothing more than a bug.

Curiously, Gerry noticed that although his quick program had not damaged the entity, it did elicit a change in its behaviour. Seemingly satisfied with plundering Gerry's brain it backed off, taking pieces of code from Gerry's internal operating system with it—pieces put there by The Family to tap into Gerry's new prosthetic eye in order to receive a video feed of everything he saw. As quickly as it came upon him, it receded. Gerry rushed a suite of security programs into his network and chased the entity out, closing any vulnerable areas as it retreated. Gerry still couldn't get an accurate picture of what this thing was or where it had come from.

The thing scrambled its exit, making it impossible for Gerry to track where it came from. But as it left his mind fully, he heard the static buzz of his systems reconnecting to the network within the shuttle that connected him to Jachz and The Family.

It was the first time he ever felt thankful for that. His head still throbbed with pain and his vision hadn't returned to its usual sharpness, but at least now he could work his hands and locate the shuttle's navigation controls. He spun it round and pointed the nose back to the space station.

"Gerry, can you hear me? Please respond." The controlled, artificial voice of Jachz, Gerry's recovery manager and The Family's most prized autonomous AI, called to him over the communications channel.

"I'm here, Jachz," Gerry said between deep breaths. "What the hell happened?"

"We lost connection," Jachz said, a slight clip of concern to his usually collected voice. "I believe something blocked us. We experienced a complete blackout, communications speaking."

"Remember that thing I said I saw back in your lab? The thing in my brain?"

"I do. I couldn't find anything during the scan. It was just a glitch."

"Some glitch," Gerry said. "The damned thing near mind-raped me." He didn't tell Jachz that it also damaged the software that connected Gerry to The Family. Already his own efforts to continue to pick away at the security had fared better than his previous attempts while on the station. Despite the terrible pain in his head that felt like someone had smashed him about the skull with a sledgehammer, he was at least grateful to the entity for creating a chink in the armour of The Family's software. Whatever had happened, one thing for sure was when he got to the surface of Earth, he didn't want them seeing or hearing what he was up to.

He'd find Petal and keep her safe—from everyone, including The Family.

"I can't detect anything on the various networks," Jachz said.

"You won't, Gerry replied, sighing quietly to himself as he saw Earth hove into view. The thought of flying out into the solar system indefinitely had scared him more than the idea of his mind being opened like a can of tuna. "It covered its tracks. It's way more advanced than anything I've seen before. It..." Gerry trailed off, not wanting to give too much away.

"Go on," Jachz prompted. "I'm worried about this. I think you ought to come back to the station so we can examine you again."

"No way in hell, Jachz, old buddy. No offense. I enjoy your company to a degree, but space and me don't get on. I want gravity and an atmosphere, and I'd appreciate it if you could help me get back there."

He seemed to wait for a while. Gerry wondered if he was clearing it with Amma or Nolan—his parents, or perhaps the sneering, jealous Tyronius. Jachz came back to him. "Okay, Gerry, I'm uploading new flight instructions to the shuttle's navigation computer. Just relax and let me know if anything odd happens. I'll guide you through as you get closer."

"Thanks, Jachz."

Gerry sat back and stretched his legs to ease the tension in his muscles. A welcome sight in front of him filled the holoscreen of the shuttle and he felt himself finally relax and banish the image of that great digital beast feasting on his mind.

A blue pearl spinning on a blanket of black velvet grew larger as the background stars receded from view. The Earth filled Gerry's shuttle screen. Faint forces vibrated through the hull. The shuttle's thrusters adjusted his trajectory.

From 380 km, he started his descent. He'd spent the last two weeks up there in The Family's gigantic low-earth-orbit space station, now more than 100 km behind him, looking down at the blue marble wondering about her, about Petal. Was she still alive, was she suffering?

The numbers ticked down on his augmented visual overlay. It had taken Gerry only a few days to appreciate his new visual upgrade: an optical prosthesis to replace the eye Seca had gouged out.

"Adjusting speed of descent," Jachz said.

"Roger that," Gerry replied.

He prepared himself for entering the atmosphere. He dropped like a stone falling from outer space. His guts churned. Sweat dripped from his body into his space suit. His heart rate spiked, nearing his maximum. A red warning light flashed on his AO, his Augmented Overlay. Mags spoke to him directly in his mind.

— *Take slow deep breaths, Gerry, we're nearly there. All is fine.*

— *Easy for you to say, Mags. You don't have a fleshy body to burn up during re-entry.*

— *Well, we are one and the same thing,* Mags said, reminded Gerry of their integration.

The shuttle spun over, re-aligned to the correct path, and dropped into a thirty-degree angle.

Gerry closed his eyes hoping to avoid the nauseating feeling of seeing Earth and space and all that is in it spin around him.

"Entering the atmosphere, Gerry," Jachz said. "You'll rendezvous with the City's docking unit in T-20 minutes."

"Thanks, Jachz."

The AI's laugh resembled a small child's: innocent and high-pitched. It made Gerry wonder if it wouldn't be better for AI constructs like Jachz to stay away from Earth, stay within the safe confines of the space station. Away from fighting, pain, disappointment. They had a deeply serene nature to them. The tech integrated in them: the AIAs, the augmentations, hormonal balance controllers, and perceptive feedback enhancers, seemed to not only improved them as people, but evolved their outlook, too, despite their lack of real world knowledge and understanding. Perhaps that lack of knowledge gave them a new insight, one that wasn't poisoned by humanity's view of the universe.

"If you ever come down from your nest, I hope you find this easier than I do," Gerry said.

"Maybe one day I'll get to see your world, Gerry."

"On second thoughts, you're probably better off staying where you are."

"Oh, why do you say that?"

"It's bad news down here, Jachz, real bad news."

"I see."

Gerry detected a hint of disappointment Jachz's voice. Normally Gerry wouldn't have noticed, but since his own upgrades, he'd become more perceptive than before. Mags, his AIA, had undergone a series of new software-enhancements, integrating closer within his unique brain and the secondary neural network.

The craft shook, pulled Gerry from his philosophical thoughts. His AO streamed with speeds, velocity vectors, temperatures, and heart rate; the latter two spiking.

He tensed the muscles in his legs, pushing himself back into his seat, his hands gripping the holds attached either side of him and he tried to hide the thoughts of burning up into a fiery ball of death.

"Hey, Jachz, buddy? Holy hell! Is this normal?" Gerry said.

The shuttle rocked violently. The temperatures continued to rise.

"You're doing fine. Just breathe and relax."

"Relax. Yeah, that's good. Stay calm and relax. Oh hell, I'm going to die in this tub aren't I? It's too hot. The shuttle can't take it, surely."

"It's within tolerances. You're doing well. You'll be

through it any second now."

Gerry's stomach lurched. He leant forward, vomited into an open vacuum bin, which ensured no particulate remained within the cabin. His head throbbed. His body became damp with panic sweat. But when he raised his head and looked out of the cabin window, there in the distance, the reflective surface of the Dome shined like a welcoming beacon.

"You're through, Gerry. Engaging landing protocol."

"Well, that's something I never want to do again," Gerry said between deep breaths.

"Apparently you get used to it. Or so I'm told," Jachz replied. "You can activate your Earth surface protocols now."

He referred to Gerry's new personal scanning and recording systems. Through his optical prosthesis, Amma, Nolan, and the rest of the analysts would see what he sees, then use that information to plan their strategies. The first thing on *his* agenda, besides finding Petal, was severing that connection—which since his attack was now an easier proposition, though he did wonder if the attack had left him vulnerable.

Even now, approaching Earth, he still felt a buzz of fear in his mind as if that great black thing had left a part of itself inside his brain.

The shuttle flew within the Earth's atmosphere as it sped westwards toward the Dome. A glint of morning sunlight reflected off the surface: a tiny spark on the dawn horizon. With the sun at his back, the shuttle began to slow and dip beneath the clouds.

For the first time, Gerry got an overview of the

devastation. From his altitude he saw great acres of dark land, scorched by the nuclear bombs. Cities lay like children's building bricks. What used to be farms were now dead, poisoned lands, and rivers moved slowly, filled with radioactive sludge.

Now over the border between the Empire of China and the Republic of Mongolia, the location of the Dome, he saw how the devastation affected the forests. Although it was June and in the middle of spring, there were still no leaves or greenery. Even now, over forty years since those fatal bombs fell, the nuclear winter still had the seasons within its cold grasp.

Gerry closed his eyes, not wanting to see anymore of the rubble, or the dead, empty, charred buildings that used to be home to tens of millions of people. He wondered what had happened to all the bodies. Had their bones vaporised and got sucked up into the atmosphere only to rain down later in the fallout? Or were they still there, buried under Steelcrete tombs?

No matter the circumstances of the war, he found it difficult to side with The Family's justification for ending it like this. *It was more than war they ended*, he thought. *It was nearly everything*. So much loss and grief.

"Approaching the Dome, Gerry," Jachz said, breaking Gerry from his thoughts. He was thankful for the interruption. Anger built within him at the scenes below. He reminded himself that finding Petal, if she was still alive, was his number one priority. Anything else would have to come later.

The Dome loomed large in his shuttle's windows.

It looked like a giant blister on the skin of the earth. Semi-translucent, he could only make out blurs and a few colours inside.

A panel within the Dome slid back into the architecture, giving him access to the landing zone below. He'd often watch them land from his office at Cemprom, the tower across a field from there. Gerry thought back to a few weeks before all the madness had started. He'd never thought he'd find himself in a shuttle returning from the station.

The Dome's landing zone was two clicks away. He came in slow and steady. The shuttle's auto-piloting system managing the speed and angles perfectly. The access area loomed into view, and he finally let his muscles relax. Despite what had gone in, it still felt like returning home, or at least more like home than the station.

The shuttle reduced its speed, engaged its VTOL, Vertical Take Off and Lift engines, and settled down on a Steelcrete landing pad.

He sat up, took a deep breath, and waited for the nausea to pass.

***

Gerry eased out of the cockpit, pushed the door up and over his head. On shaky legs he made his way down the ladder to the landing pad. Rows of similar shuttles were lined up next to his. Behind the landing pad, looming into the air, the control tower stood like a great mushroom with its indomitable grey tube and wide flat dish on top. The morning sun, still rising from the east, shone on the tower, casting long shadows over the low, flat-roofed buildings that made up the offices of the city's aviation centre.

A group of two men and a woman, wearing the usual grey and blue City Earth aviation security uniforms, stood like sentinels waiting for him. He recognised the woman as the ex-military spec guard who worked at Cemprom. She was the same one who had started his journey into the underworld. The one who crashed a stun-baton against his head when he dared question the validity of his D-lottery numbers coming up, despite being the algorithm designer and therefore exempt.

Looks like she got a promotion.

He approached slowly, waiting for his legs to read-just to solid ground. A refreshing cool breeze blew against his skin, providing sweet relief to the artificial atmosphere of the station and shuttle. Although he had to remind himself that the breeze was the result of the Dome's filtration and fan system. It wasn't as real as it seemed. Nothing in the Dome was.

The security detail stood about fifty meters away, waiting patiently, hands behind their backs. Dark sunglasses hid their eyes. He didn't recognise the two men. He ran a check on their ID, hooking into City Earth's resource database. The Family had given him higher security clearance than he had while working for Cemprom.

- *Run ID Scans on the two guards, Mags,* he said once he confirmed his connection to the system.

- *Running.*

Although it was a command within his mind to his AIA, it was translated into machine code.

That's what made him unique: the ability to spin code directly from his mind and traverse and exist within networks as if he were nothing but binary data. It was also what set him apart from The Family's AI constructs, and even Enna's transcendents. They were ultimately bound by processing limitations.

He was something approaching *post*human. And ultimately, that's why The Family wanted him and Petal back at the station: so they could engineer more like him, using the tech that lay dormant within her.

Gerry had asked Amma and her engineers why they couldn't replicate what they had done to him: implant the same AIA and neural nano network into young kids.

Amma replied, "If we could do that, Gerry, we would have. You're different. Whereas the other children could interface with their AIA, use it like a computer. None were one with it like you. You are your AIA and vice versa. It's in your DNA, not just an implant. We can't replicate that reliably yet. You were a one-off. But between you and Petal's ability to shape and manipulate DNA we could synthesise what makes your brain special and develop it for the good of all humankind."

Basically, Gerry thought, *I'm a fluke, a freak of tampered-nature.*

'The good of all humankind' was a favourite phrase amongst The Family. He supposed the more they said it, the more they would believe it. He wasn't so convinced.

— *Scan complete*, Mags said.

Two names appeared on his AO: *Bran and Malik Silverman: Thirty-two years old. Non-identical twins. Exempt from the lottery for services to security, limited AIA integration, physically enhanced, trained in weapons and unarmed combat.*

Gerry approached and stood in front of them. When none of them moved, Gerry said. "Hey."

Bran stepped forward, held out a hand. "Glad to have you back with us, Mr Cardle."

His handshake was limp. He wore his dark hair in a close-shaved buzz cut, just like his brother. The woman officer had her blonde hair in a ponytail. As Bran and Gerry shook hands, she took off her specs, analysed Gerry, and sized him up.

"We've been assigned to work with you," Bran said. "What can we do for you first, Mr Cardle?" His tone was friendly, relaxed. His brother, Malik wore a friendly, welcoming smile.

"No offense, but I'd like you all to stay out of my way. That would be a good start." That was aimed at the woman, who gave Gerry her best sneer. "But right now, a place to base my operations would be helpful," he added, not wanting to be complete douche about things.

Bran and his brother Malik turned to look at their colleague, giving her an inquisitive look.

"We have history," she finally said. She stepped forward, held out her hand. "I'm sorry about what happened, Mr Cardle."

Gerry knew she wasn't. He didn't need an AIA to know she was lying.

"I'm Elaine," she continued. "I've been tasked to your squad during your stay in the Dome." Her face reverted to a neutral expression.

Gerry refused her hand, nodded. "I'm sure you are sorry, Elaine. But consider yourself relieved of your duty. That goes for all of you. I don't want all this—" he widened his arms to encompass them all. "This fuss. I prefer to work alone. I don't want a squad. Nothing personal, but the last time I worked with a group of people, it didn't end so well."

Bran coughed, shifted nervously. "If you would like to follow me, Mr Cardle, we'll get you set up. You must be dying to get started on…" He raised an eyebrow, left a pause for Gerry to fill in the blank.

"Yes," Gerry said, refusing to give then any information. The less anyone knew about his mission the better. He didn't trust anyone within City Earth, least of all the security departments. Anything he was up to would surely be analysed and beamed back to The Family in their station.

***

The security entourage led him from the port towards a secure tower usually reserved for governmental officials and heads of various departments such as economic affairs, healthcare, parks and open-spaces, security.

The tower stood by itself in a perfectly maintained woodland and grass-covered park. Not a leaf blew out of place or a piece of litter scudded the breeze. Even the trees were trimmed and shaped. They might as well have been models. The place oozed a sense of unreality, a stark contrast to the dead, brown forests a few miles outside of the city.

A group of well-behaved children, led by a teacher, walked through the park. Every kid remained quiet and calm as they walked in single file listening to the teacher rattle off facts about photosynthesis and the importance of trees. He realised then how sanitised life had become in the Dome.

He wondered whereabouts in the city his own kids were. He had to remind himself that they weren't his kids. The whole setup had been faked. They probably had their memories of him wiped and replaced with one of a new family. He wondered if anyone in the Dome actually conceived a child. Perhaps they were manufactured and handed out by The Family's scientists.

And the worst thing was that everyone seemed happy with it. The kids and the teacher smiled, relaxed. Even his security detail, excluding the ever-scowling Elaine of course, found time to flash a smile or wave to various citizens as they walked through the park, or came and went from the tower.

Gerry looked away from the kids, tried to forget, and refocused on finding Petal.

"What number am I in?" Gerry asked as they approached the foyer of the apartment building. A cheerful man in a black and white suit stood by the door. He opened it and tipped his hat for each resident who entered or exited.

"It's all on here," Bran said, sending Gerry his credentials across his personal network. An icon flashed on his AO: *Room 34, Floor 21.*

"Your ID is registered," Malik said. "Just present your dermal implant to the head of security in the first instance so that they can tie that to the room's security and then you're good to go."

"Fine. I've got it. Thanks. You can all go now," Gerry said. He stood, stared at the three security members, and waited.

"We need to escort you in," Elaine said. "Orders from above."

"I'm a big boy. I think I can work an elevator. Thank you for meeting me at the pad and walking me to the apartment building, but I'm sure you could be doing something more useful now."

Just get lost, Gerry thought. He didn't want these drones following his every move.

Bran and Malik stepped forward as if ushering him into the building, all the while trying their best not to look like threatening assholes. It failed. So City Earth security officers *were* all alike, after all. No surprise there really.

"We insist," Malik said. "The least we can do for a member of The Family."

It was clear to Gerry that they despised him, thought this was beneath their abilities. The doorman must have sensed the tension. His smile dropped and he observed the situation while removing his hands from behind his back.

Gerry ran an ID scan. A second later the data came back: *Presley Langford: Forty-seven years old. Combat protocol transcendent. Later design of the NearlyMen.*

Damn it. They had him locked down. He'd only been back a few minutes and already wished he were outside of the Dome again with Petal. At least then he felt free, until the torture and subsequent death.

"Fine, show me to my apartment," Gerry said reluctantly.

Elaine smirked with triumph.

Chapter 3

Two weeks of pacing in the tight cell hadn't done much for Petal's physical fitness. Her muscles ached as she ran down the tunnel, all the time trying to stay balanced in the dark. The tunnel inclined with a low gradient, presumably all the way to the surface. A further few minutes into her journey and Petal breathed heavily, her lungs burned, no longer used to such exertion. Cramp gripped her calf muscles and her hamstrings felt like they would snap any minute, taut like stretched Nanothread.

Spending those weeks in the darkness of her imprisonment had given her eyes time to adjust to the gloom. Even down here in the dark tunnel, its only light coming from small, sporadic amber semi-spheres embedded into the low ceiling, she managed to make out a few details: footsteps, grooves on the surface of the walls, and various power lines, probably going to a reserve system. Nothing indicated how long she would be stuck underground. It could go on for miles for all she knew.

But despite that thought, and heeding Gabe's urgency, she continued on, climbing the dark tunnel, hoping to finally be free. To find answers.

So many questions birthed in her mind, wailed

like hungry babies needing nourishment in a famine of answers. She had the slate in one hand. The display told her it was past 0900, June 12. She wanted to stop and analyse the data, read about Criborg and the set of coordinates, but the need to escape the darkness pushed her onwards.

It took Petal another twenty minutes of climbing until she came to a vertical shaft with a metal ladder attached. Placing her slate and pistol in the folds of her prison suit she ascended the rungs. Up and up she climbed. Her legs like jelly, her arms numb and weak. She stopped a few times and waited for the pain to pass.

She reached the top of a ladder to find an electronic pad embedded on its surface. She reached up and touched the blank screen. A laser scanned her fingerprint. It beeped and the door slid away into the surrounding shaft. *Good job, Gabe.* He must have hacked the system to recognise her prints.

The streaming light of the morning sun shone down into her eyes, made her squint and hold her hand in front of her while her eyes adjusted to the sudden brightness. She clung to the ladder and bathed in the warmth for a few seconds while she breathed the fresh air into her sore lungs. The air was cool and moist, and despite the clear skies and bright sun, the cold temperature penetrated her flimsy clothes, making her shiver.

She had no idea how far away from Darkhan's border she was. She looked behind her and saw the old, battered towers of the city centre, and between them a wide expanse of waste ground. A young girl, no older than nine or ten, dressed in filthy rags, propelled herself across the dusty ground with her hands. Her legs were withered thin, folded beneath her. She sat atop a make-shift wheeled board. The wheels clattered against the stones and fragments of Steelcrete.

The girl stopped a hundred or so metres away and turned to look at Petal.

Petal hauled herself out of the tunnel. Her heart pounded. Something about the way the girl looked at her like she was a criminal escaping from prison made Petal scramble to her feet and sprint away from the compound.

She didn't stop to look back until she had travelled a couple of miles away from the city. Along her route nothing but waste ground and old empty trenches civilians had dug to protect themselves featured. It wasn't uncommon to find an entire family of skeletons hugging each other in those trenches. Most were dug too shallow to stop the blast damage and subsequent radiation.

To the east she could make out the broken and dead city remnants of those places beyond the Sludge, the slow-moving river of mud and chemicals.

Between the Sludge and Darkhan, about a hundred metres away, stood a small, low building. At first she didn't notice it. It was the building's shadow that gave it away, despite its walls and roof camouflaged to look like one of the many rocky outcrops within the vast nothingness of this land.

Mustering up the energy she jogged closer.

It was a sturdy structure, twice her height, ten metres wide, and twenty metres long. A sand-camouflaged door stretched across half its width. She tried the handle but it didn't budge. By the looks of the rails above and below she realised it was a sliding door, and yet it still wouldn't move.

Coming from the centre of city, a dust devil plumed into the air. Within seconds she saw the small black mark on the horizon and knew it was a vehicle coming her way. It grew bigger every second, and she guessed she had less than a minute to find cover before getting caught.

Damn it. Her breakout must have been reported already. Despite herself she worried for Gabe. But no time to dwell. She yanked on the building's handle which again got her nowhere. The control panel resided with a locked steel box next to the door. It featured a battered biometric panel. She tried her luck but it just buzzed back at her with the message: UNAUTHO-RISED ACCESS.

They'd likely know she attempted to get in now.

The low whine of an h-core-powered VTOL engine grew louder by the second. When she turned round, a hovering ATV approached from a few kilometres away. It reminded her of the old hovercrafts she once saw on a piece of old video footage from the twentieth century. These new versions were much more manoeu-vrable owing to the more advanced VTOL engines, which were now ubiquitous on Jaguar-style helicopters, planes, and even the UAV drones that The Family used.

The driver wore the same kind of robes as those in the compound, along with goggles and a long-bar-relled rifle attached to the front of the sleek pill-shaped vehicle. A monochrome camouflage paint job covered its exterior. *Ideal for wintery conditions in Russia*, she thought.

The red scarf around the driver's face confirmed it: a Red Widow.

"Screw it!" Petal shot the lock with the pistol, exposing its innards. She realised without her implant she'd have no way of interfacing with it. So she shot it again until the entire control box hung from the door, exposing the mechanical part of the lock mechanism.

"Stop!" A voice boomed over a PA.

She had a few more seconds.

Petal turned to face the approaching ATV, held the pistol behind her back. She casually walked forward a few steps. She held her breath as the vehicle stopped and the Widow got out. The heavy-barrelled rifle remained attached to the vehicle's hood, but the robed woman carried a similar looking shotgun to the one Gabe had wielded. Although a crude, short-range weapon, it had the mark of a western gun maker. The blued, carbon-graphene snub-nosed barrel and sturdy stock featured a hexagonal texture, making the gun incredibly light and rigid, transferring the power into the shells with incredible accuracy.

The Widow carried a large arcing blade on her back: a sickle like the one the guards back at the compound carried. Petal hoped the Widow hadn't seen her pistol. She hoped it was small and quiet enough that the noise of the engine would have obscured the short blasts.

"Kneel to ground. Show me hands," the Widow said. Her red scarf, covered in dust, came down to her chest and flapped in the wind along with her long, brown robes.

Petal knelt, dropped the pistol to rest on the back of her calves and brought her hands round to the front, palms up. *If only I had access to my spikes*, she thought.

The Widow approached, shotgun inches from Petal's chest. She spoke aloud, but not to Petal.

"I've apprehended prisoner zero one, zero one, zero six. Kill or detain?" Her voice was thick with a strong, Russian accent, and her eyes were like the others: glassy, intense, fanatic. It was like she were controlled by someone, or something else. The Widow nodded to herself. Must have received an internal message. A smile like an open, rotten wound stretched across her face exposing black and yellow teeth.

She chambered a shell in the shotgun and placed her index finger on the trigger.

***

Petal blinked twice, and within that time, she'd wrenched the shotgun from the Widow by the barrel, swept her legs from beneath her, crashing her to the ground, and struck the butt against her skull. It cracked sickeningly against the bone, crushing and breaking it, killing the Widow instantly.

The gun juddered and transferred the impact to Petal's hands.

A thrilling jolt shivered through her body. She finally started to feel like her old self again. Except she was now, for the first time in years, free of rogue AIs and bad code crawling around inside her. She was free of the dependence on NanoStem. Was this what she really was? A killer? Was she made, or altered, to be a super-soldier? It made sense in that moment. But she knew that wasn't the truth, that she was something else, not just a robotic kill-drone. She felt, she dreamed, she craved.

Thinking about her creation reminded her again why she was here. She forced herself out of the kill lust, thought logically. A strategy formed in her mind: *Blast the doors with the ATV's huge gun. Hide the body. Steal the clothes. Get to Criborg.*

There was one thing missing on that list: *find Gerry.* But right now she had no leads other than a vague indication from Gabe that he may or may not be alive and perhaps up there in The Family's space station. She had no way of really knowing. No way of contacting him. That hurt more than losing her implant and access to her full suite of internal equipment. In the short time she had spent with Gerry, she knew she loved him, at least on some level.

"Dammit, Gez!"

She approached the ATV, which still hovered a meter or so above the ground, and jumped into the driver's side. Petal considered the possibility of heading straight for the Dome. But Unmanned Aerial Vehicles—UAV drones circled the crystalline orb like eagles around a nest and would soon spot her.

There's no way she'd get anywhere near the place, not in a Red Widow vehicle anyway, and especially after what had gone down in Cemprom. The president would have the place on lock-down, and The Family would have surely upgraded their security protocols.

Petal closed her eyes and thought of a solution. The options were slim. Not having their virtual private network—VPN running there was no chance of contacting him directly. *Perhaps the Meshwork,* she thought, but then remembered Gabe saying it was somehow offline, repressed.

 Given the demon AI had used the Meshwork as a way into City Earth, she doubted The Family still allowed it to exist. And even if they did, she had no terminal or connection.

She looked at the wound on her wrist and realised how cut off she felt without it. She felt useless and weak. The body on the ground, however, told her otherwise. Gritting her teeth she looked at the control panel on the vehicle and tried to figure out how to fire that great weapon on the front.

The dashboard was a long, thin touch-screen. Foreign symbols were labelled with a language she couldn't understand, an alphabet, which might as well have come from aliens.

Petal reached out a hand and gently touched a symbol resembling a spark. The engine whined-up and the vehicle jittered and vibrated like a boat. She pressed another symbol that looked like a pane of glass with a cross through it. A holographic targeting window popped up in front of her.

That's more like it.

She touched a map-like icon, thinking it would be the navigation controls, but a pulse of laser shot from the hood-mounted cannon, missing the building's door by a number of metres and flying off into the distance.

Her entire body convulsed with the shockwave, and her mohican stood on end.

Petal screamed and whooped, but soon realised that the laser bolt probably wouldn't stop until it hit something or someone. *Crap, crap, crap!*

She frantically swept her hand across the symbols and the vehicle lurched and pitched. She eventually discovered the navigation and propulsion controls. Steering the vehicle so that the door lined up with the holographic targeting overlay, she hit the fire button and rocked back with another blast of laser. The door didn't stand a chance. It exploded on impact and hung off its hinges, swinging wildly open.

"That's what I'm talking about!"

Behind the settling dust and smoke, the hangar appeared dark inside. Within the gloom, however, she could make out the shape of a pristine h-core powered dune buggy. Much like the ones the Bachians at GeoCity-1 drove about in. "That's more my style," she said jumping out of the Widow's vehicle. She dragged the body inside the building.

She shivered in the chilled air inside the hangar. Besides the seemingly brand-new buggy, it contained little else of value. It contained a workbench, a rack of tools, and a smaller room to the back of the building. She quickly got out of her prison clothes, and dressed in the dead Widow's robes. They fitted surprisingly well, and were reasonably warm. She expected them to be tight, and rough. She felt like a ninja in the light cloth and the flat, comfortable shoes.

Taking her precious chip with CRIBORG stamped onto its surface and the slate given to her by Gabe, she placed them within the numerous internal pockets of the under-robe that fitted like a body suit. The whole thing was comfortably loose fitting on her, being much smaller and petite than her assailant, but it was a huge improvement over the chaffing and harsh fabric of her prison-issue outfit.

Something was inside one of the pockets. She fished out a small leather-bound book, no larger than her hand that featured a hundred pages of intelligible script: the same alphabet as the vehicle's control panel. A curious symbol of a sickle-like blade surrounding a cross embossed the cover.

Must be a kind of religious prayer book or something. She pocketed it thinking it might be useful at some point. Even though she couldn't understand it, books were so rare she quite liked having it around. She thought she might translate it one day.

She didn't want to leave the body in such an open place, considering the doors had no chance of being repaired, so she dragged it across the Polymar™ floor to the smaller room at the back. Inside she found a desk, a computer terminal that had rust on its ancient metal frame, and a large humming cylinder. She dumped the body under the desk and checked the computer. Nothing. Dead like the Widow.

Petal considered taking the woman's communicator: a small bud within her ear, but couldn't trust that it wasn't transmitting GPS data as well as receiving radio communications, so she removed it and crushed it underfoot. Her comrades would likely be on Petal's trail soon enough, but that might slow them down for a few minutes.

She inspected the large metal cylinder attached to the rear wall. It was essentially a huge upside-down cone. Pipes snaked into it from the ceiling. Next to it a metal ladder protruded from the wall. She climbed up, poked her head out of a trap door, and noticed that a secret level half a metre high ran the length of the building, beneath its flat ceiling. Water gathered from gullies in the roof and filled the space. It flowed down the pipes into the cylinder below.

Climbing back down, she inspected the curious machinery closer. Towards the bottom of it, around knee-height, it had a wheel, a quarter metre in diameter, and beneath that a pair of tubes. She found thick, rubberised hoses wound up on the opposite wall.

When Petal inspected the buggy she realised what it was: A hydrogen splitter. The system was designed to separate the hydrogen gas from water. *So that's how the Bachians fuelled some of their vehicles.* The building must have been a reserve, a getaway contingency.

She checked the buggy's hydrogen tank: a thick metalled cylinder that ran the length of the vehicle. It was certainly big enough to hold a large capacity. A small dial on its side indicated a full tank. She didn't know how far she'd get in it, but certainly with a full tank, it'd be far enough away to make any search for her difficult. And however far she'd get, it'd be a good way to start her journey to Criborg, as Gabe advised.

An old-fashioned ignition system still had the key in it. She checked the transmission for neutral and fired up the engine. A belch of water vapour came from the twin tailpipes. The engines hummed with electricity.

Taking out the slate, she entered the coordinates given to her by Gabe into the buggy's navigation computer. A 3D image of her destination glowed within the holographic display. *It's an Island? What the hell?*

Chapter 4

Gerry counted at least eight of them between floors one and twenty-one. Eight highly trained and augmented security operatives disguised as residents, cleaners, and maintenance people going about their morning business. Despite their attempts at looking normal it was the small things that gave them away: the way they looked at him, their eyes filled with recognition; the way they held their gaze a fraction too long; the false smiles and casual nod of the head that was a little too eager; the tell-tale EM traffic that surrounded them. They weren't even cloaking it.

Regular people don't process that much data going about their daily lives.

There was one, however, in the vicinity that he knew wasn't part of this cabal.

Courtesy of the ID lookup he discovered Kaden Willis: seventeen, smart, super-smart in fact, and in an apartment two floors down from Gerry's assigned room. He was running a secure, or so he thought, game of Aliencraft from his bedroom. There were currently nine other kids from the building hooked into the gaming server. The only other thing worth noting from his ID record was the expulsion from his last two schools, and his unusually high IQ. He was now being home-schooled by his mother, Loane Willis, an environmental policy advisor, and not very well by the looks of it. She was nowhere in the range of the building. Probably had no clue as to what her son was up to.

Bran, Malik, and Elaine waited in the hall as Gerry poked his head through the door and checked out his apartment. "Everything to your satisfaction?" Elaine said.

Without even looking at her, Gerry sensed a sneer. She had that kind of voice.

"It's fine." He didn't even bother to look beyond the basic aesthetics of the room: glass, ceramics, ergonomic desk, sofa, kitchen area, and a bedroom with mood lighting. He had no plans to stay there. "Are you three going to stand out there all day, or are you going to leave me alone?"

Bran shook his head, smiled, "We're all done here, Mr Cardle. Just wanted to make sure you arrived safely and were happy with your new lodgings."

Gerry didn't answer. Just nodded and waited for them to leave.

A few seconds passed. "You're still here," he said.

The three goons finally left. Gerry walked to his door, turned, and made sure they were actually leaving. He traced their IDs and plotted their route across a 3D overlay map. They left the tower and headed back toward to the park. When it was clear they weren't coming back, Gerry entered his apartment and closed the door behind him.

His prosthetic eye and on-board microphone system

recorded everything he saw and transmitted it back to The Family on their space station via his direct, and secure, feed. He didn't want them knowing all his plans. If he did find Petal alive, he didn't want to put her in more trouble.

The Family, and his mother, Amma, talked a friendly game, but he'd seen and heard enough to suspect their intentions. Connecting with his AIA, Gerry created a series of low-level software patches that intercepted the signals from his on-board microphone and scrambled them into incomprehensible junk data. With the attack from the digital entity, getting through the layers of security became a trivial task, but he still had to devise it so The Family received a signal, so he made sure that they received a distorted, garbled version of the truth: something to resemble regular EM interference. That should buy him time to do what he needed to do.

After spinning the code with his mind and altering the software, he rebooted the system's core files and confirmed The Family received a feed with interference.

Satisfied his feeds back to The Family were scrambled, and their communication channel blocked, he made his way down to the nineteenth level. While a suspicious cleaner finished up his various tasks within the corridor Gerry paused for a moment and took the opportunity to scan for any available networks outside of the Dome in the hopes of tracking Petal.

Nothing came up. No Meshwork, no non-City Earth traffic at all. It was as if there were no networks at all outside of the Dome. He presumed the internal security within the city had blocked access. He'd have to find a way of getting beyond it.

The cleaner had turned out of the corridor and entered the elevator. Wasting no time, Gerry arrived outside Kaden's door and rapped against its surface. On the third knock the boy opened the door.

"Yeah?" Kaden said. His hair was shaved through the middle, sides spiked up, dyed green. He wore various glass rings through his nose, lips, and ears. Each one no doubt filled with dopamine receptor regulators. The kid wore a sharp suit over a tatty t-shirt with the words Black Sabbath scrawled in patchy white text. He spooned breakfast cereal from a white china bowl.

"Kaden Willis, right?" Gerry said.

"Who wants to know? You got something to do with the school, or my mom? I've already—"

Gerry pushed the kid back, entered the room, and closed the door behind him.

"Look, kid, I'm just a guy, okay? Listen up. You pretty much live in this apartment twenty-four-seven what with your home-schooling and Aliencraft obsession, right?"

The boy backed away, held his arms out, tried not to look at the pile of contraband in his room. He failed. Gerry picked up on it before the kid even realised he signalled his guilt by shifting his eyes to an open room off the main living area. "What the hell is this about?" Kaden said.

Gerry stepped forward, sensed an opportunity. "What you got in there? Illegal upgrades, software patches? Wait, don't tell me you've got some hot-chips to get you out of the D-Lottery."

"Um, no?" Kaden's face said it all as he blushed with guilt.

Gerry pushed past him and stood at the doorway to what looked like Kaden's room, what with the Alien-craft poster hanging on his wall amid various band photos. A bag of computer chips sat haphazardly on the boy's bed. *Definitely hot-chips.*

When Gerry managed the D-Lottery algorithm at Cemprom, he had worked on a system to seek out these kinds of chips, but wherever they were coming from, the makers always seemed one step ahead. "We can work something out. If I forget about what you've got in here—"

"You some kind of pervert?" Kaden said, looking Gerry up and down.

Gerry wore a basic, nondescript suit of grey wool. Certainly nothing to give the idea that he was a sex pest. "No. You really don't know who I am?" Gerry said, slightly disappointed that news of his daring act of saving the City, his death, and subsequent resurrection didn't seem to have had any effect on the citizens so far. But then he doubted The Family let any of it get out. Can't have the public knowing they were all nearly turned to gibbering zombies controlled by an evil AI.

Kaden shook his head. "Look, about that. I can explain. I was just holding—"

Gerry held up his palm, "Don't say another word, kid. Hear me out first before I'm forced to take you to The Family for your crimes. I have a direct line these days."

"Dammit. I knew this would blow up in my face."

Kaden slumped to the sofa, sat on his hands, probably to hide that they were shaking. "You can't tell my mom about any of this. I've caused her so much trouble these last few months already."

"Well, you can redeem yourself. I'd like you to do me a favour."

"What is it?"

"You're going to be me."

Kaden took the offer immediately. Gerry hacked City Earth's ID database and hooked Kaden up with his credentials. The fact he could do that impressed the kid so much that by the time Gerry had told him he wanted him to walk in and out of the building a few times and hang around in his apartment during the day and some evenings when his mother was on business, he jumped at the chance.

Gerry recognised impressive hacking skills in Kaden. The fact he administered an Aliencraft server under the nose of the building's security got Gerry's attention. Those kinds of games generated a lot of traffic. The kid must have scripted some brilliant traffic shaping protocols to hide the source allowing him to get away with it undetected.

He wondered if that's how Gabe and Petal got started: Gabe the mentor, she the student. Although there was a difference: Gerry had no plans to take on an understudy. He preferred to do his work alone. Even at Cemprom he preferred to keep most of his code and research away from his colleagues. He quickly learned information was power, and by giving it away, you weakened your own position. While Gerry accessed

City Earth's ID database, he procured a new identity for himself, allowing him to walk about the City with relative freedom. He chose a government official, one whose job it was to work with the various districts under the Dome. It meant that for a while at least his travels wouldn't be questioned.

***

It took about an hour for him to walk from his apartment building to his old house. He took the scenic route rather than one of the trains or city shuttles. Fewer eyes and scanners out in the open, and besides, the Dome was in spring mode to reflect what should have been spring outside, although with the climate still struggling to recover from the forty-year nuclear winter, it was difficult to spot what season it was out there in the abandoned lands.

He enjoyed breathing the cool breeze created by the Dome's systems, the bright sunlight, the bloom of the plants and trees. Outside of the poorer areas and the governmental zones, like Cemprom, City Earth had plenty to offer in terms of scenery.

It was a shame so few took advantage. But then it wasn't their fault. They all had roles and responsibilities, and the curfews trained people to spend their spare time inside with their families, watching the various tightly-controlled media outlets.

The sun crested the Dome towards its zenith. Gerry checked his internal clock, run by his AIA: 11:30. Once through the parks, Gerry looped around, followed the river, and ended up in his old neighbourhood. It brought back a flood of memories of his old, fake family.

While on the station, he learned the woman pretending to be his wife was executed for her crimes against the City after colluding with Jasper. His kids were re-assimilated with a new family. When he eventually walked out of the alley and faced his old house a mixture of relief, guilt, and anger washed over him, threatened to paralyse him.

The house reminded him his last two decades of life was a sham.

He walked up the path, weeds now overgrown and covering the stone slabs. He opened the door and slipped inside. Darkness shrouded the place. Much of its contents had been taken away, just like his old life. The place was an empty shell. Memories of times echoed around its bare walls.

Using his night-vision, a function of his upgraded optical prosthesis, he plotted his way through the house. Room by room the voices of his kids came to him. The memories clear as day. But those memories were cyphers, placeholders. Had his wife known all along? Had she planned on betraying him from the start? He'd never know. She'd been wiped from the records. She might not have existed in the first place.

An old slate lay in the detritus of the kitchen. He ran his finger across the display and it flickered to life. Cracks crawled across its surface, obscuring the picture beneath, but he could see it as clear as the day he took that photo. He and his family sat around the kitchen table, sharing smiles and happiness. It was real, wasn't it? The look in their eyes and his wife's weren't faked then.

Maybe for a short while reality and something substantial had overwhelmed the veneer of the unreal. *Maybe.*

Gerry left the slate on, left that image to shine out in the room, grounding the place to a time before the veil had lifted and the mechanism of his life was left exposed like a flesh wound. He wiped a tear from his real eye and descended into the basement, where his office used to be. He intended to base his operations there and find Petal.

Thump. Scuffle. Someone was in there. Immediately Gerry's new combat protocols kicked in and he glided to the door, muscles ready, fists tight. With a hand ready on the door's control panel he put his ear to the door and heard breathing.

Chapter 5

Petal wrapped the rags around her face to block out the wind and dust that blustered through the open cage of the dune buggy. Why they didn't put a window on it, she had no idea. Two hours into her journey, the sun had fallen between dark, crimson-shaded clouds.

As far as she could see the sandy desert stretched out into the distance. Small rock formations dotted the landscape like corpses. In the very far distance on the north side she could make out the tips of the Khentii mountain range that separated Mongolia and Russia: the border on which she saw Red Widow's forces lined up.

The mountains were rumoured to be the origins of the great Genghis Khan. She remembered finding an old book among the debris of an ancient and destroyed library on one of her first excursions with Gabe. That area had seen a lot of a blood, and she wondered with the Red Widows over there if it wasn't going to be drenched once more.

The autopilot program ensured a steady speed to maximise fuel and avoid settlements wherever possible. She'd taken a route that took her past GeoCity-1 and City Earth, but she'd be hundreds of miles to the north of them as she crossed the Mongolian border and into North East China.

The coordinates given to her by Gabe of Criborg's location indicated a small island in the North Pacific to the south east of Japan. Japan itself was a no-go area, still toxic with radiation from the Cataclysm, which meant she'd have to travel through Primorsky Krai of the Russian Far East—the eastern coast of the Russia/China landmass—to the harbour at the mouth of Rudnaya River, where she hoped to find a sea-going vessel. It was a prominent place for Russian-Chinese troops during the war and provided access through the Sea of Japan.

Highlighted details on the 3D map showed a number of stable and well-established roads, meaning she should make it across without too much trouble. Although, given the Red Widows were Russian, she wondered whether they would have travelled that far down from the mainland.

Her pistol and single shotgun now seemed entirely inadequate, and the stun-sickle was unwieldy and alien to her. She doubted she'd be able to fight with it efficiently, but she brought it along with her anyway, mostly out of curiosity.

To stay awake, she took the slate from her pocket and analysed the data. Apart from the coordinates, it contained an encrypted file with a familiar set of numbers: a sequence she and Gabe had used before when they wanted to share classified information. An ingenious piece of coding, and so far no one had managed to break the encryption.

She entered a twenty-four-digit code and the file opened. It looked like a dossier of sorts. She dropped it into the slate's auditory talkback function, sat back, and listened to the notes contained within. She instantly recognised Enna's voice.

If you're reading this, it means you're alive. And I'm glad for that, though I'm writing this report not knowing if you survived or not. I'm trusting Gabe to find you and report back, but in the meantime, if he does find you, I've prepared this dossier to inform you of a critical period in our time.

Red Widow & Gabe's role: when Jasper's group took you from Cemprom I had arranged for your rescue. They took the Jaguar, which meant I could track it. I was altering the navigation systems to bring you back to GeoCity-1 when it was shot down, and you were taken. I managed to get a trace on the vehicle and knew that it was the Red Widows. I had Gabe infiltrate them. He'd been working on that for a number of weeks before all this went down with Gerry. At the time I thought they were a small group of fanatics, but their scale is far greater than that.

The Widows are a group of allied survivors from North of the border. I don't know how long they've been massing their numbers, collecting resources, but they've managed to do it under the nose of The Family's surveillance. Gabe tells me they have a number of underground settlements. To think that all this time they've been under there building, praying, planning vengeance, and now they're moving on with their plan. They hold The Family and their allies responsible for murdering their husbands and sons. The war wiped out so much of the male population before The Family dropped the nukes and EMPs, and now they want to avenge their deaths. Years of isolation has bound this group together, skewed their perspectives, and made them rabid for justice.

During my last assessment and communications with Gabe, I fear Darkhan might have already fallen under their control now Seca is dead and his systems are offline.

You might be at this stage wondering a number of things: Why am I telling you all this, who are Criborg, and what is your role in all this? Is Gerry alive?

Firstly, Gerry is with The Family, alive. I heard from a contact that he was due to come back, but I don't know when, or what condition he's in. As for you and Criborg, after you last visited me with Gerry and Gabe, I performed a number of procedures on you and after you had left I ran a few tests. I'm not sure what it means, but I found a number of mutations. Your DNA was changing. You—

An explosion cut off Enna's words and rocked Petal's buggy violently.

"No!" Petal grabbed uselessly at the slate as it tumbled from her grip and fell out of the vehicle, crashing hard against the ground. Another blast erupted to the side of her, spraying up dust and dirt. The buggy lurched to the side with the force, the wheels spinning, trying to find grip.

She recognised the burning stench of ionised particle beams.

Dust obscured her vision as she tried to control the buggy.

The high-pitched whine of engines coming closer made her look behind: a Jaguar aircraft bore down on her. It looked similar to the one Enna had lent them, although this one was more angular with four engines on short wings and a white/grey camouflage pattern. Russian letters, written in red, adorned the side of the fuselage. The front windshield curved around a pair of operators who looked down at her with dark glasses and the now familiar red scarf around their neck.

The machine guns wound up again, spitting ammo at her. Some of the rounds pounded into the side of the buggy.

She yanked the controls, veered off to the side, all four wheels digging into the loose sand and dirt, fighting for traction.

She steered out of the gun's trajectory when another blast caught the driver-side rear wheel sending the vehicle spinning and tipping over, barrel rolling against the ground.

Petal flung out her hands, grabbed for the roll cage, but she was shunted out from her seat, her body rag-dolled inside the buggy as it eventually came to a violent stop, smashing against a large boulder, sending her body to collide heavily against the dashboard.

"Mother fu—"

Pain exploded across her head, arms, back, legs, everywhere. The universe tipped and spun, gravity pulled her every which way against her efforts to crawl from the wreckage. She felt drunk, her balance seemingly at odds to her every move.

Warm, dusty downdraft beat against her. She turned

on to her front to shield her face with one arm. With the other she crawled to the boulder, tried to get away. Something cold and metallic lay beneath her hand: the stun-sickle. It had come away from the strap around her back. She grabbed it, used it for leverage, and dragged herself forward, her legs numb and useless with pain.

The Widow's Jaguar landed. Its engines whined down. Three robed figures stepped from the craft's cabin, all carrying the now-familiar style shotgun.

So much for the escape attempt. She hadn't even reached the coast yet.

The three Widows spoke in their ugly dialect and laughed, as they stalked closer.

One of them, a particular ugly one with a huge hooked nose and a high forehead kicked at Petal's ribs, spinning her on to her back. Petal coughed, spat blood on the dust and sand. It coated her attacker's shoe, sending her into a rage.

Like a pack of dogs, all three set upon Petal. They kept kicking until she was on the verge of passing out when a fourth Widow, previously unseen to Petal ordered them to halt.

In badly broken English she said. "We need her alive. For now."

"Goddamned bitches," Petal said, spitting more blood from her mouth. She hitched herself up on to her elbows. Sharp stabbing pains pinched at her inner organs when she moved. They must have broken a few ribs. Her right hand still gripped the handle of the stun-sickle, hidden beneath her.

The one who spoke moved through her three

comrades. Her robes were white, and her dark hair wasn't in wraps like the others. It floated wildly with the wind. She stood astride Petal so that Petal looked straight up at her. Oddly, Petal couldn't stop staring at her massively flaring nostrils.

"She has fight," the leader of the group said, smiling, exposing perfect teeth. She turned her head round to regard her giggling companions. When the Widow turned back to regard Petal, she lost most of the lower half of her left leg.

The leader standing over Petal screamed and fell to the side as blood drenched the sand beneath her. She hit the ground hard, her hands grabbing at her left knee trying to stop the flow of blood. Her two comrades stared wide-eyed, dumb with shock as her lower leg flopped to the ground in the sodden pool.

Petal pulled the sickle back, impressed with its ability to cut through bone. She took the advantage, swung the sickle low, sweeping the leg of the Widow to the left of the now screaming leader on the ground, and finally burying the blade into the shin of a third onlooker. The fourth Widow sidestepped the bundle of comrades and flashed a kick towards Petal's head.

Petal ducked, swung the sickle up in a tight arc, catching the Widow in the rear of her thigh. The blade sunk into the flesh, clanged against the bone, sending vibrations through the weapon. Petal activated the stun function via a button on the handle. The Widow stiffened, juddered with the bolts of electricity, before falling to the ground unconscious.

One of the Widows reached out for the shotgun

lying in the dirt. Petal sucked in a breath as she stood. The pain jabbed her in the ribs. She stepped forward over the prone body of her last victim, stamped down on the out-reaching arm of the Widow, crushing it with a loud crack.

Petal picked up the shotgun, stood away from the pile of bodies, and said. "You bitches better tell me right now what you want with me, or you'll be seeing your husbands far sooner than expected."

The leader, her robes now coated in sand and blood hauled herself to her knees, held out a hand, and gabbled in her foreign language.

"Talk English! I know you can understand me."

She shook her head, held her hands together in front of her chest in a crimson prayer.

"Last chance," Petal said.

The one who she had swept to the ground jumped to her feet, tried to flank her with a dashing manoeuvre. Petal was too fast. She blasted the Widow in the chest with the shotgun, sending her flying back into her leader.

They bundled into a screaming pile of body parts, and Petal wanted nothing more than to end them. An overpowering vengeance welled up inside her. Two pulls of the trigger and the group were no more. Sent to their God prematurely.

She dropped the shotgun, smoke rising from its short barrel, and slumped to the ground. She breathed hard to get her heartbeat under control. She yelled out a defiant curse at the pain in her ribs, ignored the black spots that appeared in her vision, and dragged herself to their Jaguar before stopping short, collapsing with pain. Tears rushed from her eyes as mental and physical anguish tore her apart.

Chapter 6

The shuffling behind the basement door stopped, only to be replaced by a sobbing. It sounded like a young male. Gerry's thermal imaging showed a figure hunched into a small bundle in the far corner of the basement. No other heat signatures registered, other than the power cables going into the building. He scanned the ID database registration and Mags delivered the search result: *Steven Chiang, Nineteen years old.*

Gerry cut off the feed of information. The name rang a bell instantly.

That was the kid who worked on reception at Cemprom, Gerry thought. *What the hell was he doing here?*

Inside the basement, a single windup lantern illuminated one. Shadows doused the rest of the room. A boy, like a rat in his nest, sat slumped in the corner, shrouded by rags and boxes.

Gerry stepped inside, and didn't make a sound. The darkness of the corridor ensured that the boy wouldn't notice the open door. The place was almost as Gerry had left it. It was mostly used for storing various technology prototypes from his job at Cemprom, and boxes of rations just in case of an emergency.

Although City Earth was self-sufficient with its own farms and food production, The Family insisted all citizens carried a certain amount of dried sustenance in the event of any mechanical problems with the Dome.

It was also a way of controlling the populace. Keep everyone afraid that one day the food supply might run out. The hand that fed had power of not just the air they breathed, or the lives they lived, but also the food they ate.

The more he thought about this, the more he realised they were lab rats running around a big shiny maze for their 'superiors' to study. Despite The Family, and especially Amma, his mother, explaining their vision and their commitment to the human race, he felt the familiar loathing for them return. He'd seen and experienced too much to ever think they were doing this for the good of humankind. It was for the good of The Family only.

They only did what suited them. And right now, having Gerry hunt down and deliver Petal was good for them, but he'd be damned if he'd hand her over so easily.

Gerry slithered through the room as if he were made of shadow. He got within a few feet of the boy. Gerry shielded himself behind a storage locker. The boy's limbs were thin, his cheeks gaunt, and the obvious collarbones, plus the rags, indicated he hadn't camped in the basement for long. He wouldn't be in that condition with the supplies available to him.

As if finally sensing something was wrong, the boy

turned to face Gerry's direction.

Gerry activated the basement emergency lights via his network, and said. "Steven? That you?"

"Mr Cardle? I thought you were—"

"Dead? I was, sort of. What the hell are you doing in here? What's happened to you?"

Steven crawled out of the blankets around his thin and scarred body. The skin around his dermal implant on his right wrist was red raw and covered in deep scratches. Dried blood caked around the network of cuts. He'd clearly tried to remove it.

The boy opened his mouth, but no words came. He looked up, his eyes full of tears. Gerry moved to the kid, sat him back down, and covered him up, no longer wanting to look upon the scars and welts that hadn't healed properly upon his chest, arms, and legs.

"Who did this to you?"

"Jasper. He came into Cemprom with his heavies. The security, they, they didn't do anything. He needed information. I tried, Mr Cardle. I really tried not to give it to him, but—"

"It's okay, I understand."

The kid stunk of ammonia and faeces now that he had opened the blankets from around his body. "What happened after?"

"I managed to get out, but I knew The Family would come after me, so I kept on the move, mostly in the sewers. But it was too late!"

"The lottery?"

The kid let his tears trace slivery lines down his dirty face. His back heaved with sobs as he blurted out, "I've only got two days left before it snuffs me out. I don't want to die Mr Cardle!"

"None of us do, Steven. Have you tried uninstalling your AIA?"

"It won't let me, I'm stuck. I tried to stop them, tried to do my job. Why am I being punished?"

Before Gerry could find some comforting words, Steven carried on as if he were in confession. "I didn't know where else to go. I knew your daughter, Caitlyn, and thought, and well, she's gone now. Everyone's gone." He slumped his shoulders, wiped the tears from his face. It was then that he seemed to finally take Gerry in, and he slumped back with his mouth agape. "What happened to your eye?"

"Upgrades, Steven. Listen, I don't have time to explain everything, but know that Caitlyn and her sister, and their mother are safe. I can't have you staying here."

Steven shot out a thin and bruised hand, grabbed Gerry by the wrist. "Please Mr Cardle, don't chuck me out, I've got nowhere to go! My parents were reallocated. I'll be dead in a few days. I don't want to die on the streets."

"I've got an idea to keep you safe."

His eyes widened with hope, and then lowered again, "Kind of?"

"I think I can get you off the network, safe from The Family and the lottery, but you'll be an outlaw like I was. Like I will be again."

"How?"

Gerry thought of Kaden and his stash of chips. If the

kid was going to deal, he might as well deal to Gerry. "A chip added to your dermal implant. It'll take you off the network. Sever your connection to the mainframe, and the routines that govern the lottery. You'll be free of The Family, but you won't ever have a normal life here again. And you'll likely be hunted down all the time you remain here."

"Where would I go?"

That was a good question. Gerry didn't know. Was anywhere safe now? "I don't know," he said, wanting to be honest with the kid. "But at least you'll be free to have the choice."

He hesitated for a few seconds before saying, "Okay. I'll do it."

Gerry contacted Kaden across a secure private network he'd set up to his apartment room so that the kid could inform Gerry of anything suspicious going on. He answered immediately, clearly doing his job. "What's up, Mr Cardle?"

"How's it going over there, Kaden?"

"Sweet, no issues at all. The security guys wandered by the front of the building a few times, probably realised 'you' were in your apartment and were happy at that. It's working, for now at least."

"Good lad. Listen, those chips. You still have them, right?"

"Yeah, of course, haven't been out of the building yet and my contact isn't due to collect until later this evening."

"How many do you have?"

Kaden hesitated then, sucked in his breath, "Why?

What's happening?"

"Look, nothing bad, I just need one. Can you spare it?"

"Well, it's difficult."

"How's that illegal Aliencraft server doing for you? I bet that brings in some nice benefits. It'd be a shame if—"

"Okay, fine. I'll square it. I'll say one was defective or something. It's happened before with a shipment so it won't look too out of the ordinary. But there's only so far you can keep doing this. Just remember I'm on your side here, doing you a favour. Let's keep that balance right."

"Kaden, be smart. Don't screw with me."

"I, erm, sure, I'll have someone bring the chip to you. Give me your location and it'll be with you within the hour."

Gerry sent him the location details to a storage unit in the next part of town. He turned to Steven. "Okay, the chip's on its way. You'll have to go to this address," Gerry sent him an encrypted private note with the address.

"Okay, got it," Steven said upon receiving the message with the address. "Thank you, Mr Cardle. And I'm sorry about your wife and daughters. It must be tough not having them around."

"Yeah. That's life I guess," Gerry said, trying to not let the pain show on his face. "Stay to the shadows. And grab some clothes from my room upstairs. You look like crap and suspicious as hell."

Steven nodded, shuffled from his blanket nest, and

headed out of the room.

His back was worse than his chest: a grid pattern of cuts and welts. They'd really gone to town on the poor kid. But it showed a lot of spirit to stand up to that kind of abuse. And to stay hidden the way he had for this amount of time showed he had some degree of survival skill.

Once Steven had left the house, Gerry rearranged the basement into a more usable office space. He pulled a desk out into the middle, arranged a number of lights around the surface, and rigged up one of his old holo-screen control units. He didn't really need it. With his new upgrades he could manipulate the networks around him with ease and send his very consciousness into the code if he had to, but after everything that had happened, there was something comforting about a slower, more physical approach.

He scanned for the Jaguar's ID, and found it. The wreckage lay not far from the Dome, half way to GeoC-ity-1. It broadcasted various error signals: damaged control systems, inoperable engines, hull integrity breaches. The odd thing was it had been sitting there on the dusty ground for nearly a fortnight. Why hadn't Enna recovered the wreckage?

He wanted to avoid speaking with Enna, or any member of The Family, for as long as possible, but knowing the wreckage was there meant that either Petal was dead, or she had escaped, but if that was the case, why not salvage the tech of the Jaguar? Even the Bachians would have scrapped it for resources.

Gerry sighed, succumbed to the inevitable. He'd

have to call Enna via his AIA's direct communication tunnel: a secure setup given to him by The Family. Of course, he knew full well that they would be listening in to everything he said, but that was the plan: take their attention away from his other ways and means.

He sent a message and waited.

Chapter 7

What she could give for a shot of NanoStem right then. She sat there for hours, watching the sun arc across the sky to the west into the evening, willing the pain to die. When it was clear it wasn't going to shift, she gritted her teeth, pulled herself to her feet, and approached the craft.

It was similar to Enna's Jaguar, so much so, Petal wondered whether Enna had developed hers from their designs or vice-versa. This one however appeared to be armed far more heavily with particle cannons on each snub-wing, and twin machine guns.

She neared the cabin door, noticed her smashed slate amongst the protruding rocks. The screen had broken into a multitude of fragments of glass held together by the nano-threaded circuits. The rear case was dented, scratched but still in one piece. She thought she might be able to recover the data. At least she remembered the coordinates of Criborg's location, and now she had proper transport. Not such a bad compromise. And her weapons cache had swelled. Soon she'd have enough to arm a small militia.

Once inside the cockpit of the craft, she found a tube of NanoStem in a medical supplies box under the pilot seat. The syringe slipped through her skin easily, and before she pushed the plunger, her body reacted to the thought of receiving that wonderful drug. At first her skin became clammy and a sheen of perspiration covered her face, then that blissful feeling of the 'Stem sliding into her blood.

Millions of nano-machines swarmed through her blood system until they found the source of pain: her broken ribs. It's a curious and unusual experience feeling one's bones knit back together. It was like a deep tissue massage on the skeleton.

She closed her eyes, let the 'Stems do their work. It'd be an hour or so before the pain was subdued enough to move, but right there and then she didn't want to go anywhere. She just wanted to revel in the blissfulness. The pilot seat was as comfortable as anything she had sat on in weeks. Her head tipped sideways onto her shoulder. A slick of drool slipped down her chin. She didn't bother to wipe it away. The darkness that cradled her told her everything would be okay. All she had to do was rest.

An hour passed, the sun glinted off the screen of the Jaguar, waking Petal from her drug-induced coma. Her dreams were wild and bizarre. They receded away from her with every waking second, blurring her memories. She shuddered and winced in anticipation of the pain from her ribs. But the 'Stems had done their task. All she felt was a dull ache and stiffness from her awkward sleeping position.

Her mouth was dry. She coughed. A spatter of blood came out—the results of 'Stem use. She looked to the back of the craft, towards the main passenger area. It was large enough to carry at least six people, and behind the bulkhead she found a storage locker. It opened easily enough. She found water and rations to last a good few weeks.

Petal removed a metal box of ration packs, noticed something strapped to the webbing at the bottom of the storage unit: A conical shaped tube with a dark green and grey camo design. Scorch marks covered the opened end. It looked like a recovered front-half of a UAV drone.

Inside the tip of the drone, she found the usual suite of scanners, GPS aerials, and computer control systems bundled into a neat package. With a toolkit from the cockpit she quickly removed the package, held it in her hand as if it she could somehow divine its contents. Naturally, she thought of connecting to its wireless system with her inbuilt radios, but realised she had no means of connection anymore. Her wrist itched where the implant had crudely been removed.

She cursed the Widows for neutering her in such a way. Being disconnected made her feel like someone had hacked off a limb. *This must be what normal people feel like,* she thought.

She placed the drone control package on the dashboard. The controls of the craft were in that stupid damn language again, but at least she recognised some of the symbols from the last one she was in. She managed to fire the engines without careening into a pile of rocks or the ground and found the main computer control system.

A holoscreen projected up in front of her. The controls were iconic rather than language based. She hacked into the setup files. Deep into the system, the folders were labelled in English. Luckily, it seemed the programmers were Westerners. It made her wonder if this Jaguar wasn't Russian-built after all. Within the English files she found a configuration script.

"About damned time," she said to herself.

The system had a number of language packages installed. She simply had to select a new operating system preference. Within a split second the entire dashboard controls were now perfectly understandable. "That makes more sense."

While she had access to the Jaguar's system, she checked the log files and found a recently updated entry within a secure area. At first it wouldn't give her access, so she brought up a terminal and with a technique learned from Gabe, managed to code an exploit that gave her super-user access, meaning she could now view the previously encrypted files at her leisure.

First she managed to create a memory overflow within the system allowing her to inject her own code. Using a series of assembly commands within the higher areas of the system's memory, she gained access as if she were the legitimate administrator. The operating system that the Jaguar used was quite common, being a leftover from the war, so its weaknesses were well known, especially to Gabe who spent years reverse-engineering the various leading military systems.

Once in, she navigated to the logs.

"Ooh, this is interesting."

The encrypted log file was in fact instructions from what appeared to be the Red Widow base. It was unreadable, naturally. Taking the file of information, she programmed a translation process using the various language packs as the dataset. It wasn't entirely accurate but it was close enough. The interesting thing was the number of times the word Criborg appeared.

The file mentioned the operators in that very Jaguar had downed the Criborg UAV while on patrol on the border territories beyond the Khentii Mountains.

She checked the location stamp and realised it wasn't very far from her location, which meant she would likely be found soon if she didn't move. They'd be expecting a report from their patrol.

The UAV, it said, was of Criborg design. The third one taken down in the last week. Criborg had stepped up its drone attacks on the Red Widow's territory by a factor of 5 in the previous month. They had also sunk a Red Widow vessel off the coast of Northern Japan.

Damn. A secret war had broken out underneath The Family's nose. But then, she supposed, what with The Family taking down or at least temporarily cutting access to the Meshwork, it made it harder for news like this to spread.

That gave her an idea: she used the Jaguar's computer to scan for nodes, which it found none, but it did find a complete absence. Even City Earth's network hadn't showed up. They had somehow suppressed all of the networks, and cloaked their own.

"'Bout time they realised they weren't invulnerable," she said.

The scanner completed its sweep. She had another thought: the UAV used radio systems to navigate and send/receive messages. With the last few remaining computer nodes and network points down or cloaked, Criborg had to communicate with their device. Which means she could too. And she could recover the data.

It took her at least twenty minutes to crack the encoded signal. *Would have been faster with Gerry*, she thought. She had the Jaguar's computer and radio system array send a signal to the UAV's control device and it returned a confirmation. She was in.

It was then she realised: it'd been transmitting all that time.

Streams of data flowed from the unit, updating the recipient with coordinates, locations, video, and audio.

She quickly placed the unit inside a metal ration's box. A hundred questions blossomed in her mind: how much had it recorded, had the people on the other end heard and seen her, were they coming to recover their tech, were they coming to attack Red Widow? And damn! Here she sat, dressed in their robes, in their vehicle. What if they thought she was one of them? And given that it was her only vehicle she couldn't just abandon it and walk on foot.

Only one thing for it: send them a message via the signal. Tell them who she was, that she had had their chip inside her. Her hand trembled over the controls as she typed out her message, telling them she was coming to their location.

She hoped they would let her get that far, but then she had little choice. She couldn't go to City Earth or

Darkhan. She didn't know the extent of GeoCity-1's safety, and with the Red Widows crawling all over the land and air, options were running thin.

Her hand hesitated over the send control. *Damn it, girl. Just do it.*

She sent the message, entered the coordinates into the navigation computer, and plotted a course to Criborg's island. The navigation system flagged up a warning: she'd only make it three quarters of the way of the two hours journey on the current fuel load.

"Let's hope you guys read my message."

With that, Petal fired up the engines, took off, and headed east.

Chapter 8

A hour after sending the message, Gerry received a reply from Enna: "Gerry, is that you?" Enna's voice was right in his head: the AIA patching the signals into his auditory system.

"Yes, Enna. Or should I say Aunty?"

"Oh, they told you then. Well, I can explain, I—"

"No need, just tell me, where's Petal? I noticed the wreckage of your Jaguar is still out there sending signals."

"Oh, Gerry. I'm afraid it's bad news. I'm sorry to have to tell you this. She, she died. There was an accident with the Jaguar. Jasper's men crashed it under fire, killing all the crew and their passengers. I'm so sorry."

His AIA added a textual layer coming from a different source to the voice and from within a cloaked, encrypted stream hidden with the voice data of the communications tunnel.

— Gerry, it's Enna. Look, Petal's not dead, that was for The Family's benefit. There's no time to waste, you have to come to GeoCity-1.

"No! That's awful. Are you sure? I mean, the wreckage is still there, what if she got away?"

— She's alive? Really? What's going on? Where is she?

"She didn't, I'm afraid," Enna said. "The bodies were terribly burnt, but I identified her personally. I'm so sorry, Gerry, I know how much she meant to you, and to all of us."

— *Gerry, she's with Gabe. Hold on! I know what happened at Seca's place. It's not what you think. He didn't double cross you. I'll explain all that later. There's no time now, you have to come here. I promise you that Petal is currently safe. A lot has happened since you were away. Get here as soon as you can. Oh crap, it's already too late. They're here. Please hurry. We need your help, Gerry.*

— *Connection lost,* Mags said.

Silence.

His head rang like a bell. A single thought dominated everything. Petal was alive! After the shock, the other details percolated through. What was going on? She was with Gabe, after what he did? And Enna sounded so panicked. Who were 'they'?

"Goddamnit!" He couldn't ignore her. He needed to get to her, find out more, and find out whom she was so scared of. Gerry initiated his new athletic protocol. He sprinted from his old house to the shuttle landing zone. He had to get out there and find out what was happening. His muscles and heart, modified by smart nano-machines, burned through energy, and had him racing through the streets. Despite the roar of his heartbeat, the thought of Petal grew strong in his mind. Now he had hope, real hope, and no one was going to stop him. Not even The Family.

He raced across the park and past the tower where

Kaden was pretending to be him, rounded the corner, and faced the aviation quarter.

The evening sun dipped low on the western edge of the dome, casting the huge mushroom control tower into a long shadow. Five individual shuttles sat on the Polymar™ surface. While he approached, he accessed the main aviation computer system. Using his currently borrowed ID credentials, he identified the shuttle's nodes and sent a stream of instructions.

The middle shuttle responded first. Its door opened, and its hydrogen VTOL engines whined up to speed. This was it. Time to get to work. As he approached, the security patrol made their way out of the tower and continued on their rounds between the landing pads and a path that circumnavigated the quarter. Gerry immediately recognised Bran and Malik.

Gerry ran past the twin brothers and continued until he reached a shuttle. He activated the door and jumped in. It was already closing when Bran rushed over. He opened his mouth to say something, his eyes wide. Clearly he'd thought Gerry was in his apartment. Gerry flipped him the bird and engaged the shuttle's engines. The noise and downdraught of the VTOL props sent Bran flying back on the deck, his legs and arms thrashing about him like a bug.

Gerry spoke over the PA, "You guys need to be a bit quicker, or perhaps this job is a bit much for you, huh?" Gerry smiled and headed up and away from the landing pads. But in his haste he hadn't requested from Control the opening of the Dome. The access panel remained closed.

"Control, this is Gerry Cardle. Open the exit. I'm on urgent Family business. Over."

"Hold your position, Mr Cardle, seeking authorisation."

"I don't have time. I'm going out one way or another." He gunned the engines, circled round to gain some room, and buzzed the control tower. "Now. I'm not waiting."

He aimed the shuttle at the access panel. Even if they refused to open it, he calculated that it was one of the weakest parts of the Dome's superstructure. The size and velocity of his craft should smash through it. He hoped. He approached the panel with increasing speed when Control replied.

"I'm patching you through to the station. Please hold, Mr Cardle."

"Told you already, I'm not holding."

A second later, and as Gerry swung the shuttle round to approach the access panel from an oblique angle, a voice came over his communicator. It was Jachz. Gerry would recognise that programmed voice anywhere. Its cool tones hummed as if nothing in the world was wrong.

"Mr Cardle, please report in. The Family need an update of your status."

"Can't do that, Jachz. You've got about ten seconds before I smash a big hole in the Dome."

"Please, Mr Cardle, this isn't the right approach. I'm sure—"

"Five seconds." He braced himself tightly into the seat of the shuttle, tensing his legs against the footrest, wedging himself in tight.

"Ger—"

"Bye, Jachz."

Travelling at over 600 kph at the point of impact, the shuttle smashed the Plexiglas panel right out of its fitments, making the Dome reverberate with the noise. The shuttle blasted through the debris into the open air.

"Now that's what I'm talking about," Gerry said, knowing that Jachz was still on the line and not caring one little bit. If the damned Family were going to spy on him they would learn exactly what he was capable of, and he would be damned to hell if he were going to let a bunch of cowards on a space station, hiding from the realities of the world, dictate to him what the hell he was going to do.

"You getting all this, huh, Jachz? What's that? No, you can't see the video feed anymore? And yeah, that audio is all messed up with static. I don't appreciate being spied upon. I've got a job to do, I suggest you tell 'my' family up there to leave me the hell alone."

"I'll pass on the message, Mr Cardle. But, please, indulge me. What are you hoping to achieve with this behaviour? We can help if you cooperate."

"Jachz, tell me something. Are you capable of free thought, or have The Family made you a limited and neutered robot in a fleshy body?"

"Indeed, Mr Cardle, The Family have created a vast array of free-form protocols and I—"

Gerry laughed, steered the Shuttle up and over the Dome, and headed west to GeoCity-1. While he talked with Jachz, he focused his mind on the shuttle's various computer systems, disabling the GPS link and adjusting the various transmitters to send back junk data. He didn't want them to track his movements.

"That's it though, Jachz. You can only think within tightly controlled parameters, just like the citizens in the Dome. They're given the impression of freedom and free-thought, but with those AIAs in their heads controlled by the Family, well nothing is really free, is it?"

"I see."

"You don't see anything up there in your lofty position. I bet you haven't even left the lab in which you were created. I bet you're sitting there right now in a cubicle, much like your clones next to you, doing everything The Family tell you, never questioning, never thinking. You're trapped, Jachz, doomed to live a life of slavery. You know what that is, right?"

"I have access to vast quantities of data, Mr Cardle. I'm familiar with the concept."

The shuttle had cleared the Dome. The vast dusty abandoned lands ahead stretched out to the horizon. The low sun caused long shadows to stretch across the ground where a number of rocky formations jutted from the dust. Gerry noticed the tall towers and the fence that secured the Dome from the outside, and he remembered back to his first kill. The NearlyMan: the low-level cyborg that secured the perimeter and at the time was hell-bent on destroying Petal.

He shook his head. In such a short amount of time, he'd had so many memorable events with her, and Gabe.

"I'll leave you with those thoughts, Jachz. I've got a job to do. Tell the Family to get off my back and then maybe they'll see more cooperation from me. If they don't, well, they don't want to make an enemy of me."

"I will pass on your message, Mr Cardle. Good luck in your mission, whatever it might be."

Gerry shut down the communication channel and, like the shuttle, altered the code within his internal system to only transmit junk data.

GeoCity-1 was a few minutes away, but on the shuttle's radar Gerry noticed he had company. He scanned with the shuttle's near-field radio: another craft had followed him. It must have been one of the security members coming after him. *Damned fool.*

Gerry opened a communication link between the two.

"Who's that following me? Bran, Elaine, Malik?"

"Malik, sir. The Family said I should chaperone, and that's what I'm doing."

"Stupidity like that will get you killed. You've never been outside the Dome, have you?"

"No, sir, but I'm sure I'll handle myself."

"Turn back now, Malik, don't be so stupid."

Malik closed the communications channel and followed Gerry's trajectory.

Gerry thought about hacking the shuttle's systems and sending him back home, but changed his mind. If he wanted to see what was in the abandoned lands, he might start to question The Family, and the more free-thinkers about the better.

Gerry reopened the link. "Malik, if you're going to

follow me, don't do anything stupid. I'm setting up a secure VPN between us, and disabling your transmitting ability so you can't send anything back to either the Dome or the Station. If you don't like that, you better turn back."

"No problem with that, sir. I'll still carry out my duties."

"That unquestioning loyalty will get you killed one day."

"If it's in the line of duty, so be it."

"Yeah, we'll see if you stick to that."

Gerry spun a security wrapper in his mind and sent it across to Malik's AIA creating a secure channel between them. Without the Meshwork to piggyback, it'd only work within a few hundred metres of the shuttles. They each had a router and access point creating a kind of mobile Internet. Beyond that, radio was the only other option, and within the Helix wrapper, Gerry had created a virus to glom onto Malik's radio systems, rendering them useless on certain frequencies. They'd be able to communicate with each other, and in Gerry's case via his internal radio transceiver, but not beyond.

If Malik wanted to follow him around like a lamb, then at least he wouldn't give their position away to The Family. Gerry slowed his shuttle, allowing Malik to catch up so they could fly in formation. At least then he could keep an eye on the rash fool.

As they approached GeoCity-1, Gerry started to understand what had freaked out Enna so much.

The mounted machine guns on the various building roofs were rat-tatting down into the middle of the collection of buildings. Surrounding it on three sides were a number of Jaguar craft, and what looked like hover cars. Gerry hadn't seen anything like those before, but given the way they moved and handled the rough terrain, he assumed they were of a similar design to the Jaguar's technology.

The cars were all heavily armed with laser and large-calibre canons attached to their hoods. A dust cloud plumed up into the middle of the melee of the settlement. The Bachians in their buggies and trikes were attacking the armed cars on mass, and taking heavy losses.

"You chose the wrong day to be on duty, Malik. You should leave."

"Not likely, sir."

"Don't be so goddamned stubborn. Look at it down there. That is a real war zone!"

Before he could remonstrate again, one of the Jaguars hovering above the Spider's Byte—the dive bar of the town—turned on its axis and fired its machine guns. Gerry tried to manoeuvre out of the way, but the shuttle wasn't built for dog fighting, and didn't have the agility to avoid the raking arc of heavy calibre shells. The craft shuddered violently, knocking Gerry around in the cockpit. Malik's shuttle took most of the shells as he was too slow to react and headed for the ground, flames and black smoke belched from its engines.

"Brace yourself, Malik!"

There was no reply as Malik crashed into the ground. They were no more than twenty metres up and the shallow angle of the descent meant that it didn't break up on impact, but slid across the ground before flipping over and crashing into the iron gates at the front of the compound surrounding the city.

Two further blasts struck Gerry's shuttle, and he put it into a barrel roll, or as close to one as he could, and avoided the rest of the stream of shells from the Jaguar, which had now ascended and gone over the top of his position. It would soon have his rear, making him a sitting duck.

Gerry didn't have time to try and hack into the Jaguar. His initial probes found a fierce firewall and heavy levels of encryption. He'd get through it eventually, but not while trying to dogfight in a glorified tub.

He passed over the top of the gate, hoping to use the machine gun turrets as cover, but was soon dodging away from them too. The Bachians and GeoCity-1 citizens should've realised Gerry wasn't posing a threat, but then he was in a City Earth shuttle and at this stage, it wasn't clear whose side he was on to the outsiders.

Critical failure, hull breach, fuel lines cut. Every error code imaginable flashed across the holoscreen. The engines cut, sending him belly-down onto the ground of the compound. He cracked his head against the roof during the collision. A white-hot piercing pain spread from the crown of his skull to the back of his neck.

The speed of descent skidded him across the rough, boulder-strewn ground, bumping over bodies, and finally coming to rest outside of Enna's industrial unit at the far rear western edge of the settlement.

Gerry breathed hard, closed his eyes, and tried to wait out the pain that gripped him. After a few seconds,

Mags had controlled the flow of endorphins and adrenaline and got both his pain and heart rate under control. A hissing noise came from the rear of the shuttle. The holoscreen warned him of a breech in the hydrogen fuel tank. Not good. Not good at all. Hydrogen gas was incredibly explosive.

Trying to be calm about it, Gerry pressed the door release on the holoscreen: no response. He tried the manual latch, all the while ignoring his hand shaking with the increasing levels of panic that itched at his skin as if it were exposed to searing heat.

The door wouldn't open. The mechanism had busted. No other way out.

A *ping-ping-clang* noise of shell casings hitting the cabin had him jumping as if he were trapped inside a pot of heated popcorn. He kicked out, screaming at the damned door, trying to escape, but it refused to budge.

An explosion erupted a few meters away. The debris rained down on the shuttle, and a shell crashed into the rear of the fuselage, piercing the structure and striking against the motor. The metal-on-metal friction caused sparks to jump and a fire to start in the cabin.

He kicked out furiously again as more shells continued to rain down on his position.

Chapter 9

Sasha brushed the hair from her eyes and wished her boss and creator, Little Jimmy, hadn't given her re-growing follicles. A regular non-maintenance style would have been much better. She pulled her brunette hair into a ponytail and thought about the chances of Jimmy Robertson giving her an upgrade.

Jimmy Robertson was Criborg's chief science officer. He hated being called Little Jimmy. Not much a fan of irony, despite his great bulk. He much preferred James, or simply Doctor Robertson.

She pictured him now, with his hair greying at the temples and even greyer augmented eyes giving her the disapproving look, and the way his multiple chins wobbled with incredulity. So she never called him Little Jimmy to his face.

The problem with the evening shift was nothing really happened. She'd sit there at the monitoring desks, watching what the UAVs saw, the Red Widow's movements, and the shuttles coming and going from the Dome to the Station, but that concluded any observable activity. Any enemy engagement or real action remained few and far between.

There was a time when General Vickers's men would go out onto the surface of the island whenever they wanted to perform various maintenance tasks to their radio and control gear. The island itself had a rich history of military use going all the back to the WWII. Nowadays, with The Family's satellites monitoring the area they only had certain times of day to go outside. The rest of the time they stayed underground, as they had for the last few decades ever since The Family brought about the Cataclysm.

Sasha wondered what that had been like. She'd only been around for five years and was already sick of the place. She'd never know how the others coped, staying here for over forty years. Three years, two months, five days since she last breathed the open air.

'You're too precious to us to go outside,' Vickers would say with his thick Texan accent.

"I haven't finished your software yet," Robertson would add, this time with the clipped tones of the upper class British. Such an odd pair they made, but then Criborg was an allied company of British, Canadian, and American forces. Vickers often boasted that he and his men were the last Americans. But then the way Sasha saw it, apart from a few poor people trying to survive in the abandoned lands, and the Dome, those at Criborg were probably the last of everyone.

Despite their caution she felt ready, strong, capable, and none of Vickers's goons could touch her during combat training. She had every single one of them beat, including the General himself, and he was augmented up the wazoo. How they could say she wasn't ready was beyond her. Was sitting at a desk, monitoring drones all evening, really an appropriate use of her talents? Like hell it was.

In her opinion, Sasha represented the most complete assassin-class cyborg in existence. Designed, built, and improved by James 'Jimmy' Robertson who came to Criborg even before the Cataclysm, hell, even before WWIII. Her lineage and technology had a long, rich history.

Back in Britain, Jimmy was arrested and jailed for his views on transhumanism and subsequent 'experiments'. But she had him right. The subjects were sane and willing. That they died during his experiments didn't mean failure. Their deaths served to further his techniques and theories, so that now they had such models as she and her sisters, whenever they would be ready. *If* they would ever be ready.

Just five more hours, she thought. *And then my shift is done and I can finally go test out Little Jimmy's new blade katas.* Apparently he had one of his AIs develop the moves. Perfected to give both artistic and practical use, grow her synthetic, nano-augmented muscles efficiently, and, above all, look like a badass doing it.

She wondered whether Jimmy's design had given her this much vanity, or whether she had developed it naturally. Her complexity made it difficult to know how much could be assigned to programming or natural evolution.

She flicked a stray hair back, caught her reflection in the shiny surfaces of her glass desk and realised she didn't care. She looked good, moved well, and performed her tasks well. If only they would trust—

A series of alert tones beeped and caught her attention.

"Whoa, what's this?"

On one of her holographic display terminals she saw an incoming data packet from one of their UAVs, which in itself wouldn't normally be a problem considering she had tracked it, witnessed it get shot down by Red Widow scum, and had been tracking the recordings. Oddly, the information didn't look like anything normally generated by the drone's systems. Which reminded her: she would have to sift through all the footage at some point, like she had time for all that! *Yay! More sand, more snow, more fanatics doing stupid things with lasers.*

She patched the curious data packet stream through to her analysis software that decrypted the security protocol. She gasped as a spoken message came through the noise of engines—Red Widow's Jaguar engines. That well-known sound had wormed its way inside her head after watching and listening to hundreds of hours of recordings.

The message came from a female, a voice so familiar, it said:

Hi there, people at Criborg. Well, I'm assuming there are some people there. Listen, I had one of your chips inside me. Members of the Red Widows imprisoned me. I escaped, and ended up borrowing their vehicle, and well they had one of your drone's thingies. I traced the signal back. Don't be alarmed, but I'm coming your way. I've included the craft's ID signature with the signal so you can see I'm telling the truth. Oh, and I don't have enough fuel to get to you, so if you do happen to get this, please send a boat. You can call me Petal, by the way, whoever, or whatever you are.

"Huh. That don't happen every day," Sasha said, rubbing her face. *A girl with a Criborg chip inside her?* That couldn't be right. Jimmy hadn't lost any 'borgs to her knowledge. She'd have to talk with him and see if he could shed any light on it. The most worrying thing though was that she, whoever she really was, was bringing a Jaguar to Wake Island. She couldn't let that happen. The General's men were out on the surface, vulnerable to attack. Sasha uploaded the message and its associated data to her slate, headed to Jimmy, almost skipping along the corridors with excitement.

***

Grey walls. Grey floor. Grey everywhere. Sasha often wondered why Criborg couldn't have painted their underground town in something a little more cheery. Hell, even beige would be an improvement. But every corridor, room, weapons store, and vehicle hangar blended into one another.

Only the numbers and titles painted in thick black paint on the walls gave any indication of her where-abouts. That, and the feeling of having walked a trough through the old concrete with the amount of times she had travelled about the place.

Regardless of the dullness of the place, she now had something new, shiny, possibly dangerous in her hands. Maybe Jimmy would let her do something more interesting than scanning through A/V footage.

She arrived at the blast doors to Jimmy's room. She knocked twice, and the door swung open. As ever, he'd expected her. She wondered if he had the entire place under surveillance.

He sat inside his workstation: a glass cube with holoscreens on every surface. He hunched over a particularly complicated equation when he glanced up, regarded her with a kind, but impatient expression, his bushy eyebrows doing their little dance. He often said more through those furry slugs than he did orally, which of course led to a great deal of humour during one of the General's more boring briefings, and by more boring, she meant always boring.

"Yo, Jimbo. What's going down?" she said as she hopped onto a desk and swung her legs underneath, innocent as if nothing would melt in her mouth. She wore her dark leggings and black, barefoot shoes, which always made her feel sneaky and fast.

"Jimbo?" Robertson said, shaking his head with a degree of resignation. "Please. How much further would you butcher my name? Will it soon just been a grunt, or an 'Oi!' Let's maintain at least some standards."

"Fair play, Doc. Look, I have something super interesting."

"What is it?" He stood from his stool, exited his

control cube, and approached Sasha. She held out the slate, pressed play on the audio file.

The audio stopped. Jimmy Robertson stroked his chin. "Awfully familiar, wouldn't you say, my dear?"

She shrugged, "I guess. What do you think of it? Could it be a trap? Those idiot Widows aren't always blessed with the greatest of strategic minds. They might be dumb enough to try something like this in order to get closer. And recently their ship prowled closer than ever before. I think they're trying it on."

He cringed at her language, replied, "Could be. Have you analysed the data yet? The video from the drone's camera?"

She shook her head. "Not yet. Going by the coordinates in the UAV's transmitter, I'd say they're only about twenty minutes from the island. I thought it best to speak to you right away."

"Yes, you did the right thing," he said, scratching his head, showering his shoulders with dandruff.

"Shall I send a message back? Or just blast 'em out of the sky and recover the wreckage?"

Robertson looked at the time on the slate: 19:10. The General and his men would be out there until 22:00 before heading back. That's when The Family's satellites would be overhead.

"It's too risky to establish contact. The signatures are definitely coming from a Red Widow Jaguar," Jimmy said. "With Vickers and his men out there, they'd have little time to find cover. They're at least twenty-five minutes away from the main doors."

Sasha jumped up and down. "Want me to take

it down? It's totally a trap. They've even sampled my voice."

"How would they have got your voice?" Jimmy asked, moving his hands into the pockets of his grey trousers. Everything was grey.

"Um, well, I might have left some messages inside the UAV."

"Messages? His voice scaled an octave when he became agitated, making Sasha laugh inside. "What kind of messages?"

"Nothing bad. I just read the UAV's instructions and added a little something to the Red Widows, a few insults, about their robes. Oh, and I maybe said something about their personal hygiene too, and their heritage. Ha-ha, you're gonna laugh at this one, I—"

"You stupid bloody girl!" Jimmy slammed his palm down on the desk, puffed out his cheeks. "You could have compromised us all. Don't you know how reckless—"

"I'm sorry, I didn't think." Sasha slunk off the desk, dropped her chin.

Robertson shook his head. "Look. What's done is done."

"What do you want me to do?" Sasha asked, wanting the whole damned episode over and done with. She hated failing Jimmy. It reminded her why they didn't trust her: because she let her eagerness get the better of her.

Jimmy walked to her, placed a hand on her shoulder. "We can't take the risk. Record and send everything to my servers. Send out two UAV drones to get a closer look: this one's feed looks like it's dead. There's nothing but static."

"And then what?" she said. "What next?"

"And then, if it looks like the Red Widows, take them out."

"Yes!" Sasha fist-pumped the air, turned on her heels and ran all the way back to the control room singing "I'mma gonna blast ya from the skies, from the skies, I'mma gonna blast ya."

Chapter 10

Over the Sea of Japan

Petal noticed the increase of traffic to the UAV, having set up an application to monitor its input/output channels. It was clear to her that whoever was at Criborg had got her message and was now making a decision, whatever that might be.

Land had disappeared behind her an hour ago. All that existed now were the two blues: the dark, rich evening sky and its partner, the sea. Small rippling waves shimmered against the cool white light of the moon.

The wind blew slow and calm, and she found herself staring out of the cabin window, with the Jaguar set to autopilot, watching various disturbances on the surfaces. She was sure one of the ripples was caused by a family of whales cruising for plankton and other sources of food.

Wake Island lay a further fifteen minutes away. A deep quiet descended with nothing stirring, chasing, or fighting. The blissful nature of the 'Stem still kept her relaxed like everything was okay again. No hassles, no stresses, just fly for as long as the hydrogen lasted, and then pop the ejection seat and float on the sea until something happened.

Of all the dangerous situations she had been in, and of all the times where death presented it self as a possibility this was the most chilled she'd ever been. It was as if death wasn't such a bad outcome really. For as long as she could remember, she'd been in one scrape or another. Filled to her core with malicious code and bad AIs, all rotting away her humanity, changing her into something else.

Gabe had often used her as nothing but a tool to further his agenda, and Enna nothing more than a research project and a weapon. She didn't blame them really, or harbour any hard feelings. They were just doing what they thought right, and in their own way they had cared for her, looked out for her.

Only Gerry noticed something different within her, and yet even that spark of… no, she couldn't say it was love, not yet. How would she even know what love was anyway? She was a killer, a hacker, and a weapon. She didn't love. She maimed, and stole, and destroyed.

That a chip had been ripped from her with the name Criborg stamped into it didn't mean she was going home. For all she knew this place was just a chip and weapons producer and someone else had stuck that in her to make her better at killing and hacking.

It'd be like sending a robot back to the manufacturer of its sensor array.

And then a nagging thought surfaced as she flew over the blue sea, *am I just a robot too*? It made sense when she looked at the evidence: no memories before

Gabe discovered her wandering the desert; chips and implanted weaponry; the ability to contain and manipulate code and AIs; reflexes and abilities faster than most people she knew.

Then there was her extraordinary tolerance to NanoStems. The amount they had pumped into her over the last few years would have killed a regular person, but she took it in her stride. Thrived on it.

She wondered how much of her body was real and how much of it was actually billions of nano-machines all swimming about doing various jobs, keeping her going.

And yet, despite all that evidence, she still *felt*.

Even now, as she noticed two UAVs, similar in design to the one she found in the Jaguar, drop out from behind a thin wisp of cloud and head towards her. Dread, fear, excitement, and anticipation rose up inside her. Her hands began to sweat and she fidgeted in her seat, fingers poised over the weapon's controls. She held off, waited. They drew closer, and then split off to flank her.

Her fingers edged closer to the triggers of the machine guns. The pair of UAVs appeared on her holographic display with a red ring around them. The targeting system had them locked.

A second passed, then two, three. She eased her hand away, took her eye off the radar, checked the data flow. Traffic spiked. Same signal structure as before. They were definitely from Criborg.

Two crashes smashed into the Jaguar simultaneously, alerting a rainbow of warning signs and a cacophony of beeps and sirens. *Dammit! Guess they're not friendly, after all.*

Petal wrestled with the controls, but the damned thing locked down and headed for the big drink. Two more blasts sealed the deal. Petal punched the ejector seat.

The air pressure popped her ears, her guts tried to remove themselves via her feet, and her head swam, even more so than normal with the 'Stems floating about in there still. She watched almost as if it were happening in slow motion, as the Jaguar broke apart: its stub wings split from the fuselage and all three large pieces headed down into the calm waters below.

Strangely, she thought of the whales, hoped they would be safe. For years these waters had nothing in them, but as the damage to the climate eased, life had returned. The sea's biodiversity could come and go as they pleased, but here she was creating yet more mayhem. Everywhere she went, destruction and death followed.

The ejector seat had small thrust-engines on either side, and she propelled herself forwards, more for the fun of it than anything. She was still going to hit the water and die either from hypothermia or drowning at some point, or perhaps some sea creature would eat her. Maybe the whales were hungry for more than just plankton?

Eventually she approached the surface of the water. She cut away the parachute and free-fell the last few meters, frantically trying to unclip from the seat, but the mechanism jammed, sending her smashing into the water, and going down and down, the weight of the seat strapped to her dragging her down into the deep like an anchor.

Bubbles poured from her mouth. She twisted, screamed, yanked at the strappings holding her tight. She looked up; flecks of moonlight dappled the surface only to be taken away by shadow as the dark-green parachute furled across the water.

Her struggling made the seat tip forward, and she fell down head first into the murky depths. Out from nowhere, seeing it too late, she crashed into a coral reef, striking her head against the rock. The seat wedged itself stuck in a crevice. Her blood used what little oxygen she had within her body as she frantically tried to escape to no avail.

Energy drained from her limbs to be replaced by pins and needles. The heavy cold made her lungs feel tight in her chest. Against her will she opened her mouth. Salt water flooded her lungs.

Her arms went limp. She blinked, tried to see past the red and black spots.

All she could feel was the cold.

And then, she felt nothing.

Chapter 11

— Activating martial protocols. You need to get us out of here, Mags said.

The martial protocol was one of a suite of instruction sets given to him by The Family. There were limits imposed of course, but as usual with The Family they underestimated him, and he spun reams of Helix++ code to override the restrictions, meaning he could boost his energy, push his muscles and heart farther.

The limits were designed to keep him operationally efficient. But screw efficiency. He was in a damned war zone and needed to save his ass before he could do anything else.

Feeling the blood rush to his muscles, and the nano-machines increase his strength by a factor of three, he kicked out a boot with everything he had. The door refused to give, but something cracked within the mechanism. The adrenaline flooded his system now, and he kicked out again, and again, denting the door, pushing it outwards, until finally something popped and the door flung open.

The sound of gunfire, screams, and some foreign language assailed his ears, while the stench of burning oil, ionised gas, and gunpowder filled his nostrils.

He dampened the incoming audio to reduce the reverberation in his head and darted for cover behind the corner of Enna's building: a square blue-grey box of strengthened alloy and Polymar™. Even with its incredible strength, it had taken a battering. First things first: Gerry had to assess whom the enemy and what the situation was.

A brief visual sweep of the settlement soon got him up to speed on the battleground.

There were four Jaguars circling the entire place. They were similar in style to Enna's but with white and grey camo design and red Russian lettering on the side. The Jaguar aircraft appeared to be directing the flow of the battle, filling in when necessary, and drawing fire to the perimeter.

In the maelstrom of the battle for GeoCity-1, which was always an ambitious name given it was made up of just ten buildings, Gerry counted six ATV hover cars working their way in and out of the narrow spaces between the buildings. Throughout these gaps and heavily concentrated into the open square in the middle of the city a fiercely fought melee broke out between white and brown robed women with red scarves around their necks, and the wildly dressed Bachians.

Gerry recognised some of the gang members from the last time he visited.

To the rear and outside of the city, three heavily armoured trucks using conventional hydrogen fuel engines waited. All of those vehicles he knew didn't belong to the citizens of GeoCity-1 or the Bachians. Two were sat stationary, water vapour coming from their exhausts. The third had the rear shutter pulled down and locked before moving off. For a brief second, Gerry thought he saw Bilanko, the so-called Queen of GeoCity-1 and her prized server 'Old Grey' being bundled to the front of the truck's hold.

Of the melee he counted fifty-three Bachian fighters. Eight were manning the machine gun turrets, of which there were five, attempting to keep the Jaguars at bay, but their shells were no match against laser and particle weaponry.

It was easy to segregate the numbers of insurgents. They all emitted a unique short-range radio signatureobviously their own proprietary communication system. Gerry tagged the IDs and used his AIA to present them on his HUD display. The concentration of the fighting took place in the middle of the town, turning it into a bloodbath. With the narrow streets and the main gates to the front and rear of the city closed and guarded by the Jaguars, there was no way out.

A stray particle bolt crashed into the compound just above his head, sending a spray of debris down on to him. Using that as cover, he sprinted from the building, and sticking close to the rear city wall, ran across to the other side where the buildings were more tightly packed and offered more cover within the alleyways.

Over his VPN he heard Malik's voice.

"Sir, are you alive?"

"I'm here, Malik, what's your status?"

"Alive, just. I don't think they've seen me yet."

"Hold your position and hide. Stay out of the way."

"What's going on?"

"Let's leave the briefing for later if we make it. Keep your head down and you might live. Out."

Gerry cut off his VPN wanting to keep his attention focused on his HUD as the various figures and vehicles moved around the display. If he could get to one of the vehicles he might be able to hack their systems, give the Bachians time to organise their defence.

The alleyway between the next two buildings appeared empty. Using his stealth protocol he eased round and into the darkness. The buildings were a food store and a residential dwelling. Both shot to hell with various sized holes in the exteriors, but they would act as good enough cover for now.

In the middle, and amongst the dust, he got a closer look at the attackers: they carried modern-looking shotguns and large single-handed sickles that appeared to be both a cutting and a stun weapon.

Who the hell were these people? And where did they get all the weapons?

The Bachians were holding their own in hand-to-hand combat—for now. Gerry recognised a particular dervish in the middle hacking limbs and heads at a frightening pace: Cheska, one of Enna's transcendents. Gerry was pleased Enna had got her all fixed up, and seemingly upgraded. What a sight she created, and yet the numbers were too many.

Even someone such as she couldn't stand up to shotgun blasts. But still, she hacked, moved, slashed, and dodged her way through the fight, leading her group, keeping their enemy on the back foot. A particularly fierce-looking robed attacker pulled away from the central melee and raised her weapon, aimed at Cheska's back.

Without thinking, Gerry launched himself into combat mode, sprinted across the battleground like a cheetah, and shoulder-charged the woman holding the shotgun, crashing her to the ground. Before the woman could react, Cheska spun, bent, and grabbed the shotgun. She pulled the trigger, spraying the woman's skull and brains into the blood stained dirt and dust.

Gerry stood back-to-back with Cheska as she continued her death-walk, pulling the trigger again and again, clearing a path through the melee. Two robed women ran towards them, screaming some phrase with their sickles held high. Their screams were short lived, punctuated with that short, dull blast of the shotgun.

While they were free for a second, Gerry spun, grabbed Cheska by the arm, and pulled her to the side of the battle, their backs against the buildings where, via his HUD, he could keep an overview of the attackers and buy precious time.

"Cheska? It's me, Gerry. What the hell's happening? Who are these people?"

A bullet struck the ground in front of them. Cheska pulled Gerry further back into the passage. Her olive skin shined beneath a thick layer of blood and gore. She looked as though she had been dipped in paint.

"Holy crap! We thought you were dead!" Cheska said.

"Yeah, I get that a lot. Who are these people?"

"They call themselves the Red Widows. Mad-as-hell fanatics. They came on us all at once, we couldn't cope."

"We'll see about that," Gerry said. "Where's Enna?"

Cheska's fierce expression sunk. She dropped her chin. "Taken." She pointed to the Red Widow fighters. "They took her, and Bilanko, and Old Grey. They took them, and all of our tech. They're slaughtering us one by one."

"I thought I saw Bilanko. I didn't realise they'd got Enna too. Why are they doing this?"

"Dunno, Gerry. It's something about the servers. They want them for some plan. They're crazy. They're gonna kill us all. I tried to stop them taking Bilanko. They dragged us all from the Spider's Byte. I tried, Gerry, I really tried to stop 'em, but there were too many."

Gerry pushed Cheska away from him, knocking into the opposite wall of the alley.

A laser beam shot between the gap. The heat warmed his face as it crashed into a dwelling across the town. One of the ATVs had eased round the buildings. A wide-eyed brunette with a now-familiar red scarf wrapped around her mouth and neck sat inside the cockpit.

Before the woman could get another round off, Gerry had dashed like a blur until he was just a few meters away and fired the last round of the shotgun towards the cockpit of the vehicle.

The driver took a portion of the blast, and fell forwards onto the dashboard.

Taking advantage of the confusion, Gerry vaulted onto the open-topped vehicle, reached down and took the sickle from the woman's back and struck it hard and true into the back of her neck, killing her instantly. The act made him want to vomit, but he choked it back and took action.

He kicked the Red Widow out of the car and set about hacking into their network. Despite it being in Russian, when he stretched his mind into the system, bits were bits, and assembly code was king.

He manipulated the flow of traffic across the communications channel to and from the ATV. He organised the flow of traffic, analysed the data. It was all so much easier and quicker than before his upgrades. Or maybe it was the experience and knowledge of what he was and what he could do. He passed a bunch of tasks to his AIA while he focused on encrypting the peer-to-peer protocol connecting the vehicle to the rest of the Red Widow's forces.

"Gerry!" Cheska shouted.

He instinctively ducked and watched a particle bolt take a massive hunk of masonry off the two low buildings sheltering him and Cheska. She ran towards him and jumped into the empty seat. She took the controls for the hood-mounted gun.

"Turn this boat around!" she screamed.

Gerry did as she requested, all the while his cracking programs tore away the layers of the Red Widow's encryption and rewrote the assembly code for the ATV's central processor.

A Jaguar hove into view, tipped its front, and spun up its machine guns.

Shoving the vehicle into reverse, Gerry snaked it left to right to avoid the spluttering gouts of shells before spinning a hundred-and-eighty degrees and gaining cover from the last building on the side of the city compound. They sped down beside the high perimeter city wall and across the battlefield.

The Jaguar took up a higher altitude position to get a fix on them, but Gerry was too quick, strafed the vehicle into the melee, knocking down two Red Widow fighters as he went. When he was in the middle of the dust, he flipped it around so it faced the city gates. The Jaguar hovered above them, its downdraft creating a vortex of the dust.

"Fire!" he screamed.

Cheska fired off two laser pulses. The first missed the Jaguar but the second hit its left rotor, sending it into a lopsided death-spin.

A cheer went up from the Bachians. They trained their machine guns on an approaching Jaguar. It crashed down before it could get enough altitude. The tide had turned.

Gerry brought the ATV to rest by the front gates. As he scanned for cover, the final layer of encryption tore away leaving their network completely open to him, exposing their entire communications topography and command structure. A node icon represented each vehicle, and every fighter had a VPN to and from the nodes, meaning they could all give and take orders as well as exchange data as the battle unfolded.

"Cover me!" Gerry said. "I've gotta save someone." He jumped from the vehicle and climbed the gate. The thing was a mess of various pieces of metal, girders and sheets all welded together haphazardly. It was ugly and crude, but strong.

A third Jaguar swung round from the left side of the city and hovered in front of Gerry as he ascended to the top and straddled the gate. Before Cheska could fire a shot, an explosive round smashed into the gates, sending Gerry crashing ten meters to the ground. He fell to the side of Malik's downed and burning shuttle.

He hit the ground hard, probably breaking some bones along the way, but the combat mode had pain suppressors running, so he picked himself up, dashed across to the smoking shuttle and dragged Malik from underneath the wreckage. He threw Malik up onto his shoulders, ran past the gate, away from the Jaguar, and headed for cover around the other side of the city wall. He got fifty metres before the Red Widow pilot caught his movement and manoeuvred the craft to hover over his head. It tipped its nose and aimed its weapons.

Crap!

Gerry jumped his mind into the network and saw a traffic stream from the nearest node, which he assumed belonged to the Jaguar. At the speed of thought he rerouted the instructions from the control board to the weapon's system. He opened his eyes. *Still alive.*

Malik said something, but Gerry's mind stretched out into the system. He found the CPU and its main instruction set. Using a Helix++ translation layer to convert his thoughts to assembly code, he created a package made of terabytes of junk data. Thoughts and elements of his subconscious could quickly spiral into colossal amounts of random data made up of images, video, and audio. He dumped it into the system to overload the processors. He programmed a loop into its boot sequence and rebooted it. Although normally a complex task, he managed this in a fraction of a second, the upgrades installed and calibrated by Jachz working perfectly.

Something shook his arm. The sensation pulled him out of the network and disconnected his connection.

"Holy mother! Would you look at that?" Malik jumped about, his hands on his head. He pointed at the craft, laughing, shock clearly affecting him.

The Jaguar's engines stopped. It fell from the air, crashed to the ground, and exploded into a ball of fire, fuelled by its damaged hydrogen tank. The heat wave rushed forward, slamming Gerry and Malik to the ground. Its eager need for fuel sucked the oxygen from the air. Gerry's lungs burned with the effort to breathe.

Malik dragged Gerry's body away from the flames. Once the initial explosion had died down, he could take a breath again. His head buzzed as if it were full of wasps. A wet patch behind his neck made him reach round. Warm blood trickled from a cut down into his back. It was just a small wound. He'd take that as payment. Better than getting blasted by a laser.

Malik turned to Gerry, grabbed him by the shoulders before hugging him.

"That was incredible! You saved us."

Gerry pushed him away. "Calm down. There's still a war going on, and we have people to find. Is your shuttle serviceable?"

Malik shook his head. "Engine system completely destroyed." He pointed to the rear of the vehicle. The engine compartment was badly twisted and half hanging off the main fuselage.

"Halt!" A thick Russian accent blared out from a PA system. "Turn around slowly."

God dammit! Give me a break!

Gerry exhaled, complied with the order. Malik followed.

Two ATVs pulled out from behind the downed Jaguar. They had their cannons trained on the pair. Eager, wide-eyed women held the controls, seemingly bursting to pull the triggers.

The partners of the pilots got out of the cars, held their shotguns up, and approached with electromagnetic cuffs. "Put on," they said, throwing them over to Gerry and Malik.

Even if Gerry got into the vehicle's computer, the shotguns would finish him before he could do anything. He gritted his teeth, put on the cuffs, and waited for an opportunity to disarm the two robed, blonde women carrying the guns.

That opportunity never arrived.

Something sharp, like prongs, jabbed into his neck. A bolt of electricity arced through his spinal column and into his brain, tensing his muscles, killing his internal systems, and taking Mags offline. He fell to the ground. His limbs jerked uncontrollably with the electrical discharge of the device in his neck.

Chapter 12

Those strange pins penetrated Gerry's neck and paralysed him. Tough webbing strapped him tight to the bench seat in the truck. The vibrations of the wheels transferred to the bench and combined with the oscillating buzzing from within his head. The bolts of electricity silenced his internal systems, and blocked access to his AIA, slowing his brain.

Every few seconds he'd feel a jolt as if someone had attached a battery to his brain stem. His wrists, too, were disabled. The metal cuffs sent consistent tiny shivers of electro-stimulation through his nerves. He could barely lift his arms off his lap.

At first his speech wouldn't come. The will to move was like wading through the Sludge. Eventually he managed to lift his head and open his eyes. Enna and Malik sat opposite, restrained in similar cuffs. The latter's face split down the right cheek, exposing red flesh.

"What's going on?" Gerry said, easing the words from his mouth with considerable effort.

Enna lifted her head. She looked so old since the last time he saw her. "They've got Old Grey and Bilanko. We tried to stop them."

Five other GeoCity-1 citizens slumped together, bleeding and defeated. But they weren't soldiers or fighters. Just survivors. Gerry knew Old Grey was special for its ability to house AIs. Was that why this group had taken it? Did they want the data inside?

"What do you know of this group?" The device jolted his brain again. He closed his eyes, waited for the pain to subside. "And what the hell is this in my neck?"

Enna shook her head slowly, "I don't know what they are. The group, however, call themselves the Red Widows. I've been…" Enna trailed off, turned to Malik, and eyed him suspiciously. "We can't talk here."

"Tell me," Gerry said, leaning forward as much as the restraining straps allowed. "You said Petal was alive. Is she okay? Where is she?"

"I'm sorry, I can't say. Not here."

The truck lurched, came to a stop. The rear doors opened. A group of three Red Widow members, aiming their weapons, stood at the opening. Moonlight gave the Widows a peculiar bluish silver tone to their grey and light brown robes. With heir faces held mostly in shadow, their wide, staring eyes appeared watery with the way they reflected the light.

One by one the fanatics led out their human cargo.

For the brief few seconds they were in the open air, Gerry recognised the tall, half-destroyed buildings, the smell of foul roasted meat, cooked by the desperate denizens within the garbage-strewn streets. They were in a district of Darkhan. Steep banks of dried grass lined either side of the truck creating a tunnel. A pair of Widows ushered their cargo into a line and led them to a five-meter-wide steel door.

Gerry knew he'd been here before. He knew it was Seca's compound.

The Widows waited at the door, communicated with someone. A motor whined. The door slid into a slot in the ground. Inside, sporadically placed LED lamps created small pockets of light down the length of a long corridor.

With each footstep, each echo that reverberated through the tunnel, he felt like he was right back there again: the palpable fear, the sense of defeat, and worst of all: the thought that Petal was dead. Even though Enna assured him she was safe, being back at the compound, he wasn't sure. Enna clearly had more to say.

He wanted to talk with her, get more information, but three other people stood between them. Malik shuffled right behind him, however. He whispered into Gerry's ear as they ambled along the dark grey corridor, heading always downwards, led by the two fanatics.

"Are they going to kill us?" Malik said, his voice taking on a pained vibrato quality.

"I don't know," Gerry said. He wanted to try and say something to ease the man's fear. This was a rude awakening to life outside of the Dome, far beyond what he'd experienced, but the words wouldn't come. The device continued to over-stimulate his nerves, scrambling his thoughts.

One of the robe-wearers with short brunette hair and a permanent sneer turned to them and yelled, "Halt!" She stopped the group outside a narrow, iron door. Gerry knew it led into the cells. He had a flashback of being strapped to the metal table, Seca torturing him, cutting out his eye. He couldn't tell if he was shaking from that memory and the fear of what could come, or the electro shocks from the prongs in his neck.

One by one they were taken from the line, through the door and thrown into a cell.

Gerry slumped onto the bench seat in the three-metre-square grey box. Before they closed the door, he noticed they put Enna in the room opposite his.

Throughout this process, not one of them attempted to talk with him, explain the reason for their internment. Gerry knew it wasn't just for being involved in that skirmish, otherwise they wouldn't have had this device to block his abilities, which meant they had insider information. *Could it be Enna?* he wondered. She had lured him to GeoCity-1 with her message and promise of more information about Petal. Would she really sell him out?

Then there was the issue of taking Bilanko and Old Grey. And the fact they were here in Seca's facility, none of it was coincidence. These people seemed to have a great deal of interest in information and securing it. Had they also recovered the other server that Len and his followers were protecting?

And that made him wonder, too, about Len's setup. Jasper's men killed the poor guy while he defended Gerry and petal. Had that got back to his people? Were they still out there on the surface beyond the Sludge protecting that old server?

And then he remembered: not far from Darkhan was the outpost controlled by a group of Upsiders and The Blighty, the pub run by the curious landlady, Molly, who had helped him deliver Len's virus to take out Seca's security system on a storage unit containing much-needed vaccines.

He slumped forward, rested his wrists on his knees, and tried to control the feelings of frustration at the lack of his mental abilities. Without his brain he was nothing but a useless meat-bag.

Another jolt of electricity, clearly on a timed schedule, travelled through his brain, making him screw his eyes shut and hold his breath. When it had passed he exhaled and waited for something—inspiration, a clear head, anything.

Gerry dozed in and out of sleep while lying on his side on the hard bed. His dreams came and went like diaphanous spectres, all meaning and sense offered and taken away by some unknown source, always at the edge of understanding. Names and ideas bubbled up from his subconscious, but nothing would stick. His thoughts out of reach beyond an invisible barrier.

From the void a face started to form, dark and shadowed by a deep hood. An accented voice came from within the folds, "Hey! Get up, man."

Gerry felt something push into his ribs. He opened his eyes to a shadow covering him.

"Ain't got no holy brew this time, man," the voice said. The man pulled Gerry's shoulder until he sat up. "But I got ya some water. Drink up."

The figure pushed a cup to Gerry's lips. Despite himself, he sipped the cool liquid. In a mad rush, myriad memories came rushing forward.

"Gabe! That you?"

The figure stood back, unblocked the overhead light. Gerry knew it was Gabe. And knew he wanted to kill him.

Chapter 13

The time on Sasha's slate read 21:05. The Family's satellite would be overhead in two hours. She had a plan, but knew Jimmy wouldn't go for it. She'd show him the video feeds from the UAVs first. See if that would persuade him.

She tapped her foot against the surface of her console desk, beating out a hidden rhythm, created by her anxiety.

Jimmy's footsteps clacked into her room. The smell of stale coffee came from his breath, announcing his presence. It always reminded her of the first day he activated her. From within her tank, floating on the surface, she watched as he leaned over, asked if she was okay. Before her motor functions and full cognition were operational the smell of his coffee breath, and those kind grey eyes of his were the very first things she experienced.

"Sasha, dear, what is the status of the drones and the Red Widow Jaguar? Was it as we suspected?"

"Patching the video feeds now. It's quite interesting really. Well, exciting, I think." She played the video stream from the UAVs she sent up earlier.

The recording showed the Jaguar flying at almost

full speed on a direct trajectory to the island. Within the cabin, a robe wearing Red Widow member sat at the controls. "See, it's one of them. So I blasted 'em from the sky."

The recording showed the Jaguar tear apart under the assault and crash into the sea.

"Why would they have become so brazen?" Jimmy said, more to himself than anything. He always did that, Sasha noticed. It was difficult to tell when he wanted an answer or was pondering some rhetorical argument.

"Dunno, but that was just one drone's feed. Wanna see the other?"

Before he had a chance to answer Sasha had already loaded and started the file. The feed came from the UAV on the opposite side, and although it, too, showed the Jaguar crashing into the sea, it also panned out showing the robed girl in the ejector seat fall to the sea.

Before she hit the surface, the parachute fluttered behind her. She struggled to remove herself from the seat. It crashed into the water with a plume of white spray.

"Hmmm, interesting," Jimmy said. "But is that it?"

"Nah, this is the really interesting bit." She forwarded it a few more minutes. Nothing showed after the splash. "Looks like they've drowned, don't it?"

He nodded. "I would assume as much."

"And that'd make an ass out of you and me," she said with a wink. "Look."

She pulled up the data analysis record for the UAV whose video they were looking at.

"See those spikes in radio transmission? That's

minutes after she went under the water; she's alive! The seats on the Jaguars sense vital signs and transmit with their distress signal after ejection."

"Indeed they do." Jimmy's face twisted into a kind of half-smile half-grimace, as though he couldn't decide if he was happy or worried. "Have the drones returned?"

"Yeah, I brought them back in before I realised the signals were still transmitting. Doc, let me take the sub out. Please? We've got enough time before the satellite is overhead. Oh, and hey, it'd be a great way to test your new stealth tech, huh?"

"Absolutely not. It's too dangerous. You don't know anything about this person at this stage. For all we know, that could be a decoy to something else. With the General and his men due back within the hour, you'll be needed to help them with their kit. Or are you forgetting that you are a member of this team?"

"But, Doc, did you really make me just to cart about some kit? Isn't that a waste of my abilities? Hell, you have warehouses full of androids that could do those kinds of duties."

The shadow came down on Jimmy's face then, "I said no, and that's final. Leave and go and meet the General. I want you to be there ready to help them as soon as they arrive. Maybe that'll make up for last time."

"Oh, come on, Doc. I'm going out of my mind with boredom here. Why program me to do all these great things and then have me busy with mundane jobs and stuck underground? I'm sick of this place."

Jimmy Robertson grabbed her by the collar of her leather coat and dragged her from the room. He pushed her into the corridor that led to the surface doors. "You're to say here, be ready to help General Vickers and his team with their maintenance equipment."

Jimmy referred to the gear they used on the various relay stations, transmitters, and drone control nodes hidden about the island, away from prying Family satellites.

"It's not fair!" Sasha screamed at Jimmy as he turned his back on her and headed for his lab.

"Play by the rules, and perhaps you'll find life here fairer," he called back as turned out of the passage.

Sasha waited a minute to ensure he had completely left. When she was sure, she snuck off down the corridor. *The General can lift his own damn stuff,* she thought as she headed for the submersible compound.

***

Sasha sprinted down the various corridors and levels until she arrived at the unit housing the subs. It featured a water tank that fed into the ocean. It was also the location of Criborg's team of oceanographers: a team of twenty-five scientists who worked with Jimmy Robertson to develop submarines and other sea-based technology.

There were the standard observational models, which the oceanographers used to monitor sea life and the effect of radiation since the Cataclysm, and then there were combat models, using Robertson's new stealth tech.

He'd had the idea to use a layer of nano-cells on

the sub's surface so that when The Family's satellites flew over during their monitoring process, their signals would be scrambled, analysed and repackaged by the nano cells. When the satellite received back the photons, it'd seem as if nothing was there. That was the plan. It hadn't been tested out in the depths yet. It worked fine in their water lab within the compound, but as usual, Jimmy remained reluctant to test it, just like he remained reluctant to test the warehouses full of androids. They could do all the heavy lifting and mundane jobs around the compound, not to mention the maintenance on the surface. It seemed stupid sending soldiers to do basic tasks.

He'd often say that the androids were left-overs from the war, and when the Anglo-American owners were wiped out leaving a few hundred people back at Wake Island in Criborg's care, that they weren't field tested or trustworthy.

So what if one of them went crazy and killed someone? It was a temporary software problem that could be easily fixed if old Robertson would just loosen up and allow them to at least test them in a controlled environment.

She'd often sneak into one of the pods that stored the androids. Designed to be drop-shipped into strategic battlefield locations, each pod held fifty 'droids. With over a hundred pods, that made five thousand android combat units, still new as the day they were made.

The possibilities were huge, she thought. If they could just sort out the software, they could go to the surface, re-establish a proper community with farming, industry, defences against those damned Family drones, which she hated to admit were far superior to their own.

Chatter from the scientists and their assistants buzzed out rom the mess hall as Petal walked by. They were all excited about some new chemical report from kelp or something. It never ceased to amaze her what those eggheads would get excited over when there were more incredible things mothballed in storage.

It didn't matter though. The more distracted they were the better.

She opened the door to the wet lab and descended the metal steps until she stood on a gantry and looked down at the black, sleek combat sub. It reached ten metres long and three wide, shaped like a dart with a raised middle section. Big enough to seat three: a navigator, and front and rear weapons operators, it had a pair of side torpedo pontoons, currently empty. The missiles and arms were kept elsewhere. General Vickers, and Jimmy Robertson, didn't trust anyone, even the eggheads.

Still, what she had planned meant she didn't need weapons. *She* was the weapon in this case—if it would even come down to that, which she doubted.

Up on the right side of the gantry, looking down over the entire complex loomed a glassed-off observation lab where Salty Mack, the skipper and manager of the sub complex, would often be found. But even he was with his colleagues in the mess hall.

Doing a quick observation check to make sure no one was around, Sasha suited up in an augmented silvery-black wet suit. It had a series of sensors and control units woven into the fabric, making it smart and adaptive to the user's core temperature. The mask and helmet it came with fit tight around her face. A small port on the mouthpiece attached to an air supply within the sub. Once outside she'd have a hundred metres of line with which to explore. But even without the air, it didn't matter to Sasha. She didn't strictly need air to survive. To perform optimally? Yes. To survive? Not really.

She pulled up the transmitted location of the ejector seat's signal on her slate, plotted it into her internal navigation system. Her implant gave her a direct connection to the slate, the sub's systems, and to the network within the compound itself, all on their own secure encrypted microwave network. However, she disconnected herself from the compound's wider system so they couldn't tell what she was doing. She created a program that would ping the network with her ID from her observation room and from the main doors so it appeared to anyone, probably Jimmy, who wanted to check on her that she was doing her expected duties.

When she got back from her mission, they'd be so impressed with her ingenuity, skills, and what she found that maybe then they'd stop treating her like a child, and more like the capable war machine she actually was.

Chapter 14

Not for the first time, Gerry found himself strapped into a chair, arms and legs bound to cold steel. The room was a slightly larger version of his prison cell. Three Red Widows stood in front of him, their dark deep-set eyes watching him, flitting, nervous. They shuffled on their slipper-covered feet, their robes and wrappings swirling about their lean bodies.

Gabe stood in the middle, dressed similarly; his dreadlocks tied back, his face embittered like his compatriots. He had a swollen lump on the side of his head and his right eye was bruised and puffed almost to closing. Despite that, he too had the same fanatic expression in his eyes, but then Gerry knew he'd always had that to some extent. At least then, for a while, he was on Gerry and Petal's side. Now? Who knew his real intentions?

To the left stood a woman with a hooked nose and a scar across her face. To Gabe's right a thin woman with a pleasant face eyed Gerry with a hungry expression. She seemed entirely incongruous to her allies.

All three looked down at Gerry expectantly.

He still had that electrocution device in the back of his neck, and he jolted every few seconds with each pulse into his brain. It no longer hurt or surprised him, his nervous system adapting to its effects. And yet he still couldn't access his AIA or any of his internal systems.

On the way to this larger cell Gabe had spoken in Russian to the various guards until they arrived at a room that looked like a medical bay. A heavyset woman with a shining gold medallion on the outside of her robes appraised Gerry with a curious eye. She and Gabe spoke in hushed English, but her accent sounded much like the others. She seemed less fanatical, calmer, in control, and Gerry suspected she led the entire operation, whatever that might be. Although he couldn't make out their conversation, he heard the words 'servers' and 'City Earth'.

Curiously, the woman in charge didn't address him as Gabe or Gabe, but as 'Feodor'.

And he in return called her 'Natalya.' There appeared to be some friction between the two, and Gerry wondered if the wound on his face was a part of it. Either way, he had a bad feeling of what would come.

While Gabe led Gerry to the cell, he whispered just one thing while out of earshot of the other Red Widow members: 'trust me'.

Gerry snorted at that. Given that the last time they were both in these corridors, Gabe had double-crossed him and given him up to Seca's guards. But despite the personalised-EMP device jammed into the back of his neck, and despite the lack of access to all his gadgetry and technology, a part of Gerry still wanted to trust him.

There was something about his face, his whole behaviour. He appeared so much a part of the Widows: comrades saluted him, Natalya apparently held him in some kind of high regard, and yet he still tried to appeal to Gerry. Perhaps he had plans to do something. Enna mentioned Petal was safe, and with him, but so far he hadn't seen or heard her. Was she, too, stuck in a cell?

Bringing Gerry back to the present, Gabe ushered the two Widows out of his cell and locked the door from the inside. In turn, the door to the cell next to Gerry's slammed shut. Then came the sound of frantic screaming and pleading. It was a voice Gerry recognised: Bilanko.

"What are they doing to her?" Gerry said, lifting his head to regard his former friend.

"Torturing 'er. Extracting info. It's policy for infidels, man."

"Is that what you see me as now? An infidel?"

Gabe moved close, dropped his voice to barely a whisper, "Nah, man. I'm looking out for ya. Listen to me. Petal's dying."

"She's what?" Gerry struggled against his restraints, wanted to throttle the truth from Gabe, who placed both of his hands on Gerry's shoulders and forced him to be still.

"Keep it down, man. Listen. I was part of the extraction team that got her from Jasper's men. I've been working with Red Widows for weeks now under orders from Enna. It's all got out of control. They're crazy, man, they hate tech, hate the Family—"

"Who doesn't?"

"No one, man. But these Red Widows, they want to eradicate everyone from within the Dome, claim it for 'emselves. And the servers. We can't let 'em get their hands—"

"So where is she? Where's Petal? And what do they want with the servers?" Gerry whispered back, wondering if he wasn't being setup again.

"She was here, man, but I got 'er out." He pointed to the swelling on his face. "They think she fought 'er way out. Well, she kinda did. She's on her way home. We found out who 'er makers were. Enna thinks they can fix 'er up before it's too late."

"What's killing her? Couldn't you have taken her to Enna for medical help? Who are her makers?"

Gabe shook his head and closed his eyes as if in pain.

"I wish Enna could, man. I wish that'd be all it took. Last time Enna fixed 'er up, she noticed she was degrading, her DNA unravelling, mutating. She ain't like you and me, man. She's something different. Getting her to Criborg, 'er makers, is the only thing we can do given the Widows have swept over the border and taken most of the hamlets and survivor towns. They completely run Darkhan now, and GeoCity-1 will fall in days. We're hoping Criborg can provide support, help us fight back."

A knock came on the door, Gerry tensed, fearful their exchange had been heard; fearful the torturers from the next cell were now on their way to deal with him.

Gabe spun, looked at the door, and quickly turned back. In a hurried whisper he said. "They want the servers, man. They already got Old Grey. That's why they're torturing Bilanko. They want the other one, the backbone, the one Len was protecting. When he died, his people went underground, off the grid, became ghosts. Don't tell 'em anything, man, we can't afford this lot getting both together."

"Why? Why are they so important to them?"

"They work together, to create AIs. I can explain more later, but Natalya found a transmission from an AI via one of The Family's satellites. Damn thing communicated with 'er. Told 'er all about the servers. S'why Len was protecting it, man. They call it Omega. Its Old Grey's twin."

"Why the need to destroy them, though?"

"As good as they are creating AIs they can destroy 'em, too. This AI entity wants the Red Widows to help destroy them, so they won't be a threat to it no longer."

Gerry instantly thought of the thing that attacked him on his way out of the station. Was it the same one? It made sense. Being out there, close to the satellites. Perhaps it is within The Family's system of satellites the entity resides. "Where is the AI? Is it the same one I destroyed back at City Earth?"

"Nah, man, this is something else. Something far worse."

A knock, more urgent this time, rapped at the door.

Gabe stepped back. "Look, I'm sorry about this."

"About what?"

Gabe punched Gerry in the face, breaking his nose, splattering his face with blood.

"Argh! Motherfuc—" Gerry rocked in the chair,

squeezed his eyes shut at the pain, tried not to choke on the blood that dripped down the back of his throat. He could taste it now on his lips as it gushed from the snapped cartilage and bone.

Gabe reached behind Gerry's head and switched off the EMP disruptor device stuck in his spinal column.

"Has the buzz gone?" Gabe whispered quickly.

Gerry nodded, felt his AIA and various internal systems reset and start their boot process. As if switching on a light in a dark room he felt connected again. Could sense all the nearby computers, the various nodes, even the familiar banks of computers he'd destroyed the last time he was here, and for a brief moment he senses the slick digital probing from Bilanko, but it was far weaker than the last time she got into his head. She tried to send him a message, an appeal for help. He couldn't respond. His systems were not fully capable yet.

Bilanko's cell door slammed, and the voices from her torturers grew louder as they approached. An electronic lock within his door *clunked*.

Gabe looked at the door then back to him and slapped him hard again, smearing more blood across his face. Gerry's head throbbed with pain. His eyes filled with water, so that when the door opened and two women came in, he couldn't quite make out what they held in their hands, only that it gleamed under the white lights.

They exchanged words with Gabe, and together, all three laughed.

Blinking the tears from his eyes, Gerry watched Gabe leave the room, but before he exited completely he looked back at Gerry from between the two women, and mouthed, 'Sorry'.

One of the Widows leaned into Gerry, smiled a grim smile, her teeth rotten and black, and her breath equally foul. The cold and wet touch of a blade pushed against Gerry's throat as she spoke low and threatening. "You tell us what we want, you no die slow death. Understand?"

Chapter 15

At 21:35, under the cover of darkness, Sasha cruised the new sub out of Criborg's wet-lab, and descended ten meters before turning and heading east out of the Wake Island compound, to the ejector seat's distress signal.

This is so damned cool, Sasha said to herself as she sat back in the comfy bucket seat, her hands poised in front of the holographic controls. She watched in awe at the rainbow of colours in the reef and the variety of species that swam in and out of the swaying plants and rocks, all illuminated by the sub's lights. She took it slowly over the shallow part of the reef not wanting to disturb the eels and sharks and the various small fish that darted away from her.

Once clear she increased the power of the engines, feeling the power in the hum of the hydrogen jets as it sped through the water as if it were a bird in the sky.

The sleek black machine left the Wake Island atoll behind, dipped its pointed nose down, and dove with the grace of a dolphin. A series of spotlights illuminated the gloom as it descended a hundred metres, always staying a few metres away from the jagged rocks of the coral reef.

Using the holographic control screen, Sasha looked up at the critical depths for a human in the sub's database. Without breathing equipment, they'd struggle beyond fifty meters. The signals, however, came from a depth of over a hundred and twenty. Which told her they'd be dead by now, and that they weren't human, or they had breathing apparatus, which was unlikely. You wouldn't fit gas tanks on one of those Jaguar seats.

It took a further thirty minutes for Sasha to navigate to the origin of the signal. She brought the sub to a slow velocity, cruised carefully around the rocky reef. *A real crappy place to land,* she thought. Rocks and crags fractured the barnacle-covered reef. The lights of the sub reflected off innumerable eyes from within those fissures. Predators waiting for prey, waiting for a morsel to swim too close.

Sasha scanned the area on the radar, navigated the sub in ever-decreasing circles, avoiding the areas most jagged. She came around a large rock formation, home to a group of hiding spider crabs, their long, dangly legs clinging to the rock and the reef surface to avoid being swept away by the movement of the sub.

Within the gleam of the spotlights, small bubbles swirled up from the dark depths. Closer up, she made out the dark shape of a seat, and there, hanging out from the side, a piece of clothing swayed in the currents.

With excitement building, she pulled the sub side-on to the person, and gesturing across the controls, sent out a robotic arm to grip onto the chassis of the seat. She tested the weight by thrusting the sub away by a metre slowly, and with a spurt of dust and the darting panic of various fish, the seat, with the person, who Sasha could now tell was a young-looking girl with pink hair, came away from its lodged position.

The smart-thrusters adjusted their power balance to accommodate the new weight. Sasha entered in a stabilisation program to keep the sub in place and moved to the back of the sub where the air-supply line was located. She clipped the hose to the mask on her face, attached a knife to her belt, and made her way to the small pressure box at the rear of the craft which housed an inner compartment allowing exiting and entering of the sub while submerged.

While cutting the girl free from the seat, and hooking her onto the line that led back to the sub, Sasha couldn't help but notice something quite disturbing. Despite the girl's shocking pink mohican and tattooed lips, she was identical to Sasha. This was no Red Widow member!

Inside the girl's robes were a broken slate and a Criborg chip. Sasha checked the girl's wrist, and as suspected she found a scar where she, or someone else, had cut it from her. Unable to fully understand the situation, and seeing the various predators taking an interest, Sasha quickly pulled the girl to the rear of the sub and brought her into the pressure chamber.

She instructed the robot arm to unclip the seat and retract. With her precious cargo safe and secure inside the sub, Sasha activated the return-to-base program and wondered what the hell the others would say when she brought her apparent twin home.

***

Once settled in the main cabin of the sub, Sasha ran a health diagnostic. The girl's heart beat just twice per minute during her unconsciousness. Sasha turned her over, helped clear her lungs. With an injection of adrenaline-infused NanoStem, the girl woke, her eyes flashing wide with panic. She coughed and spluttered the last of the salt water onto the rubberised floor of the sub.

When they locked eyes a flash of recognition shot between them. The girl lifted a shaking, wet hand and touched Sasha on the cheek, following the outline of her face. A raspy voice came from her. "Who are you?" Her eyebrows knitted close together as she cocked her head slightly trying to understand who or what she looked at.

"I'm Sasha," she said. "Are you okay?"

Her life signs scrolled down the holographic screen next to the cot Sasha had laid her upon. They showed strong and healthy tolerances, the NanoStems working quickly. Her reactions to it were off the chart for a normal person. Sasha then had more of an idea of who she was.

"Yeah, I think so," the girl said. "Are you from Criborg?"

"That's us. It seems you had some of our tech in you. Who did that to you? What's your name?"

The girl shook her head and pushed herself up on to her elbows. "Name's Petal, and I don't know. I was sent to you lot for answers. Are we twins?"

"Hah, who knows? We could be. I'll have to get you back to see Jimmy the Doc. He'll soon figure this out. What's on the slate you were carrying?"

Petal looked around frantically, "Damn, I must have dropped it. Where is it?" She sat up, throwing her legs off the side of the cot. She appeared to be recovering exceptionally quickly, and Sasha knew that was an ability they shared. Could they really be the same model? It seemed pretty obvious given the evidence, but despite her growing excitement she remained cautious.

"I got it right here," Sasha said, holding the slate close to her chest. "Anything dangerous on here? Maybe something from the Red Widows? You working for them, huh?"

"What? No, of course not. Those bitches imprisoned me and cut out my implant! It's because of that my friends traced you lot and sent me to you for help."

"What kind of help?"

"I'm dying, apparently, or at least radically changing. And I'm guessing there's info to that regard on the slate. I didn't get chance to read the full report before the Widows shot at me from one of their Jaguars."

"The one you were flying in and sent the message from?"

"Yeah, the very same."

Sasha moved to the navigation cockpit at the front of the sub and placed the slate in a secure compartment. "If it's all the same to you, I'll let the Doc take a look at the slate first. We can't be too careful. Red Widows have been getting way more daring of late and coming closer to our compound."

"The Island?"

"Kinda. Look, you rest up and I'll take you back to the Doc and we'll go from there."

"What do you know of Red Widow?" Petal asked, joining Sasha in the cockpit and taking the seat next her. "Nice bit of kit, by the way. You got more stuff like this?"

"Hey, I thought I said rest up."

"Yeah, I don't really do orders" Petal said, smoothing her wet hair back. "About this sub, you got more of these? What about other stuff, vehicles, weapons?"

"You'll see. And of the Red Widows, we know plenty. We'll get to that back at the compound during your de-brief. I think the General will want to have a chat with you." Sasha flashed her a smile, and when Petal smiled back Sasha shook her head. "Damn, girl, it's like looking in a mirror. If I had crazy person's hair!" Sasha's regular brunette hair pulled back into a functional ponytail now felt entirely uncool and conservative to Petal's striking pink hair, even if it was wet and lank. "Where are you even from?" Sasha asked.

"I'm hoping that's what you could tell me. My memories only go back about five years or so."

Sasha remained silent. It couldn't be a coincidence. She herself had only been activated for five years. But if they were the same, and that seemed obvious to her now, how had Petal ended up outside of the compound?

Sasha remained quiet for most of the journey, unable to get over looking at Petal and seeing the resemblance there. Jimmy had never made identical models, at least to her knowledge. Was she like her sister? Maybe a precursor or a prototype? And despite herself she felt a twinge of potential sibling rivalry: *Is she more capable than me? Stronger?* That she had been out of the compound gave reason enough for a growing jealousy that gnawed away at her, but if she were a superior model that just wouldn't do. Sasha was the special one in the compound. Sasha was the Doc's greatest achievement, wasn't she?

***

The dappled moonlight filtered through the water as they ascended. They were twenty meters from the surface now. Sasha coded a secure message, sent it back to Jimmy Robertson, telling him briefly of what she had found. No doubt, one of the oceanographers had noticed the sub had gone, and it wouldn't take them long to realise it was Sasha who'd taken it, but all that would be forgotten if she had found one of Jimmy's old models. She hit send. The holographic screen beeped back an error code. Signal blocked or scrambled.

"Gah!" Sasha slapped the arm of her chair in frustration.

Petal jumped in her chair, turned to face her. "What's happened?"

"Just a minor communications issue. It's nothing for you to worry about."

Petal leaned over to try and read the screen. Sasha placed her hand against Petal's shoulder pushing her back. "Confidential," she said. Petal just shook her head and smirked at her. "Sure. Communications error. You mean your signal's been intercepted, right?"

"No, I—"

"Don't take me for a fool. We might look alike, but I'm guessing you ain't seen much action outside of your compound."

"I've been outside!" Sasha said, regretting how defensive she sounded, how immature. And that was it right there. Though they appeared similar, Sasha knew she was the kid here, the inexperienced one.

The various bruises and scars on Petal's face and shoulders told her she had seen real action, real combat, out there in the abandoned lands. She had killed. The most Sasha had killed were some 3D holo-projections in the simulation lab.

"Just tell me what the problem is, I might be able to help."

"I've got this. Okay?"

"Sure, you got it." Petal sat back, crossed her arms, and closed her eyes, all the time with a smirk on her face.

Smug bitch! The error code was specific. Sasha knew what it meant: she'd got her times wrong, and The Family's spy satellites orbited overhead scanning for signals and movement. And to confirm her fears the holographic display flashed again, this time changing to a radar display. Flying two kilometres from them a group of four UAV drones. They'd be on them within minutes.

She switched on Jimmy Robertson's stealth cloaking technology and silently prayed it worked.

Chapter 16

The interrogators had introduced themselves as Alizia and Margaret, and very 'pleasant' they were too. They'd even given Gerry a drink of water. Of course he knew this was the good cop part of the procedure. He'd give them three questions and no answers before they took those bloodstained sickles and started the cutting.

"Mr Gerry," Alizia, she of the foul breath and stubby black teeth, said all cheery and calm, standing casually with her back against the wall, arms folded in front of her chest. "Where is Omega?"

As he thought on that question, he wondered about Bilanko in the next room. Since Gabe had left, he'd heard nothing else from her cell. It was a worrying silence given the screams and commotion just prior. He lifted his chin, regarded Alizia. "What happened to the one in the next cell?"

"Dead, unable to help with enquiries. You unable too, Mr Gerry?"

Gerry shook his head. "Can you please be more specific about your first question," Gerry replied. "I don't know what exactly Omega is. If you could expand a little more, I could probably help you. I don't want to be difficult." He kept talking, hoped to buy time while he probed the compound's network, trying to make a connection to something. Anything. The fuzziness still permeated his brain, and although connected, the network appeared blurred and indistinct to him.

"I have a family." Gerry continued to talk to Alizia. "I'd rather get out of here in one piece, so please help me help you."

While he continued to talk, and apparently entertain the two interrogators, he managed to locate Old Grey through the compound's network. The idiots hadn't even firewalled her. Gerry supposed that if this group were out in the cold as it were in their underground bunkers they probably weren't familiar with how to secure a network, relying on their personal EMP-like devices to secure individuals instead.

He sent his mind out to Old Grey, programmed his AIA to connect to the ancient server. She let him in straight away. The old-style 2D operation system flashed into his mind, waiting for his command. He used the server to map the compound's network, creating a picture of the data: which nodes were responsible for which function. He'd use his own mind to do the task, but having the server and his AIA interacting allowed him to fully focus on staying alive during the interrogation.

"We know what you are, who you are. You tell us now of Omega's location."

"I don't know what you mean. What is this Omega? By the way, I know we've got off on the wrong foot, and I'm sorry for killing a few of your comrades, but you know, it was a war zone."

"Enough!" Margaret grabbed Gerry by the throat, squeezed his windpipe. "This simple. Give me Omega location or I kill you now."

Mags delivered the network report.

— *Five operational nodes discovered: two control the security doors and lights, one operates the cameras, and the other two distribute power. The latter are not fully operational since the last time we were here and overloaded them.*

— *Good job, Mags,* Gerry returned. *Start the cracking procedure on the door and light systems. I really need to get out of here.*

Gerry's AIA took a program that he had devised while on the station in The Family's care: a highly efficient, chip-level piece of software that simultaneously tied up the target's CPU while hijacking its memory and boot process, which allowed the insertion of a cracking tool that would alter the security credentials and thus allowing him, and his AIA, access.

The tip of the curved dagger pierced the thin skin on Gerry's throat; a warm trickle of blood dripped down to his chest. Margaret held it there, adding weight to the hilt, threatening to push it further in. "You think I won't do it?" she said.

"Okay, okay! Let's take all this down a notch. I'm sure we can sort something out. Now, please, explain to me what Omega is, and I'll tell you if I can help you find it."

Alizia leaned away from the wall, her smirk dropping, becoming serious. She took her sickle and tapped it against Gerry's dermal implant, '*clunk, clunk.*' "We start here." Then she tapped the edge of the blade against Gerry's temple, "End here."

"So," Alizia said. "We ask last time. Where is Omega?"

"I take it you don't know what happened to the last person who cut me open." Gerry raised his wrists, still within the EM cuffs, and tapped his bionic eye. "I lived, he didn't."

"Wrong answer, Mr Gerry," Alizia said.

She stepped to face Gerry head-on, took the knife, pressed its sharp tip to his wrist implant and—

— *We're in, Gerry*, Mags said.

Before Alizia could gouge the weapon deeper, Gerry accessed the compound's breached systems, turning off the lights, plunging the cell into darkness. He switched on his night-vision and drove his forehead into Alizia's nose.

Margaret stood to his right, her arms out in the darkness, trying to find something to hold on to. He kicked out at her legs, sending her crashing to the floor with a sharp scream. She dropped her sickle with the fall. Alizia fell back against the door. She, too, dropped her sickle in order to stem the blood from her crushed nose. Blood mingled in her throat making her yells of frustration take on a wet, thick quality.

Gerry spun, kicked out at Margaret on the floor, catching her in the throat with his boot. He bent and picked up the sickle, moved to the door, and using its stun capability, brought it down onto Alizia's shoulders. The Red Widow stiffened as if struck by lightning, all her muscles tensing as one and sending her face-first to the hard floor.

Gerry grinned with satisfaction, thinking of both times when he had been stunned. Taking a thin, squared rod about ten centimetres long from a keychain under Alizia's robes, he unlocked the EM cuffs. He dragged Alizia's unconscious body over to Margaret, who clutched her throat and writhed in pain. Using the sickle, he stunned her into unconsciousness too, and used the cuffs to bind the two women together.

Now that he had access to the compound's security system, he took a minute to browse through the node's cell-locking procedures. Each cell had its own electronic lock setting: a global set of routines that allowed a user of the system to control the entire setup. Gerry unlocked his cell, the one next door, and the one opposite into which he'd seen Enna taken.

He kept the main door to the cell locked, not wanting a flood of Red Widow guards to rush in. He only switched off the lights to the cells, so he hoped the others wouldn't have realised what had happened. At the very least, he'd bought some time.

He stepped out into the dark corridor, his night-vision making it seem more oppressive than it was. He locked the door behind him, and moved to Bilanko's cell. Inside, the half-woman, half-computer controlled transcendent, sat on the bench, her head resting on her chest. A pool of dark liquid surrounded her. She didn't move, or breathe. No data came from her at all.

The queen of GeoCity-1 had died.

"I'm sorry," Gerry said, before turning his back and

quietly closing the cell door behind him. He'd only ever had one interaction with her before now, and that wasn't entirely pleasant, but he felt a deep depression come over him. She was truly something, and to be so casually snuffed out by those butchers, it made him think that perhaps The Family had the right idea after all, if only for a minute.

The thought of The Family reminded him of Enna. He snapped out of his current train of thought and dashed across the corridor to her cell.

Gerry opened Enna's door to find her with Gabe, and Old Grey on a trolley, all sitting casually in the dark.

"Close the door, Gerry," Enna said as she sat calmly on her bench. "And maybe switch on the lights?"

"Sure," he accessed the node and did as Enna asked. The cell was much like his own: grey, barren, and clinical. Enna and Gabe stared at him, waited. Gerry closed the door behind him.

"What now?" he asked. He wanted to tell them about Bilanko, but given their faces, tired and stern, he guessed they already knew.

"My cover's blown," Gabe said. "They saw me bring Old Grey out of the server room. We've got to get outta the compound, the place's crawlin' with 'em."

Sitting on the bench beside them, Gerry took a deep breath, waited for his heart rate to come down. "How the hell did you get mixed up with this lot?" Gerry said to Gabe.

Enna spoke first. "For the last few weeks I've been tracking them. It started out with unusual data patterns coming from an unknown node. Given how few networked computers survived, that's always a concern. I traced the origins, discovered there were more survivors over the Russian borders. That's when I got Gabe involved."

"As a spy?"

Gabe nodded, said. "It's partly why I disappeared after ya thought I double-crossed ya, man. That was all part of the plan: for you to get to Seca, and for Petal to stay safe, but well, that didn't quite happen. Ya see, these Red Widows have got a hard-on for people with tech in 'em."

"What do you mean exactly?" Gerry said.

"They blame The Family," Enna said. "And the advancement of technology in general for the war, and for the loss of their fathers and husbands. They were the last surviving adults post-Cataclysm on account of them being in a bunker system at the time. That part of Russia still segregated male and female roles within the military, and a quirk of circumstance meant that they were the sole survivors from that region."

"So you sent Gabe, a male, to infiltrate them? How did that work out?"

"I had something to trade with, man," Gabe said.

"What?"

"Information. Ya see, as I said earlier, they'd been in contact with some kind of old AI-like entity. Nothing like I've ever seen before. It'd promised 'em all kinds of secrets and ways to take down The Family, take the Dome for themselves. I got on the inside, managed the comms for 'em. Despite the Jags and ATVs at their disposal, when it comes to tech, they're like cave people.

So I extended my skills to 'em, helped 'em decipher the code from this AI. All the while feeding info back here to Enna."

"So what did they want with Petal? Why take Darkhan and GeoCity-1 for that matter?"

"This AI, whatever it is, tipped them off about Petal, about what she could do. They tracked her when Jasper's men took her away from the Dome. Gabe here ensured that she was taken alive."

"Told 'em a little of what she could do, how she could benefit 'em. Had to do something to keep her alive. And besides, it gave me the chance of springing her once we found out about where her chip came from."

"I still don't understand why you let her travel alone. If she was sick," he pointed to Enna. "You should have taken her, tried to help her."

Enna stood, her body tense. "I tried my best when she was with me the last time. I don't know everything, Gerry. There's a limit to what I could do. She is not like a normal person, or a transcendent for that matter. I'm sorry. I simply don't have the skills or knowledge to help her. It was the only way!"

"Okay, okay. I'm sorry."

Enna took a deep breath, sat back down. "We couldn't leave her here with the Widows. You've seen what they would have done with her." Enna pointed to Bilanko's cell. "All that time alone with their grief and pain has turned them into brutal killers. They want blood and death. They're delusional. She couldn't have stayed, and you saw what happened at GeoCity-1. She had to find her home, for her sake. For all of our sake."

The loss of Petal to the unknown gnawed away at Gerry's patience. He wanted to leave everyone behind, trace her route, and find her, make sure she was safe. But here he stood, stuck in the damned compound again.

"What can we do here then?" Gerry asked. "What's next? Do we have any idea where Omega is?"

"They believe Omega is in Darkhan somewhere," Enna said. "And I think they're right. When Len went with you to City Earth, the Upsiders scattered, took Omega with them. It makes sense to come here to keep it safe. There are lots of defensible buildings, of old places to hide, none of Seca's drones or hired thugs to monitor the place anymore."

"You mentioned the two servers could create and destroy AIs. How does that actually work? Is it something we can use against this AI entity?" Gerry asked, trying to piece everything together.

Enna stood, rubbed her wrists. Red marks scored her skin from her cuffs, which now lay on the floor. "The two servers are a pair of the same entity," Enna said. "Created by Sakura and Hajime Murakami, the co-owners and pioneering AI engineers of Old Grey Network Systems back before the war and the Cataclysm. They are Alpha and Omega because the two complete each other."

Gabe added, "When coupled, they can be used to permanently destroy an AI, or as this thing hinted at: upload a consciousness. Don't know if that's true or not. Whether or not it's possible, this thing seemed insane. Many of its comms were batshit crazy."

"So what's the plan?" Gerry said.

"So far," Gabe said. "The plan is get the servers. Then pray."

"For what?"

"That Petal gets to Criborg in time, and that they have something useful to help us fight the Red Widows, otherwise we're looking at war with The Family, and we all know how that ended up last time."

"What about this thing you call an AI entity. What do you know about it? Did it have a name?"

"Not a great deal really," Gabe said. "All its comms were pseudo-religious bullshit, like some kind of crazed cult leader. It's related to some pre-Cataclysm program of The Family. As for its name, it just referred to itself as the Patriarch. Also, its message coincided with access to the Meshwork being suppressed. I'm sure it's related somehow, man. But I didn't get a chance to dig any further. When Natalya, the leader of the Widows, figured out how to decrypt its messages I was relegated to an odd-job man. My stock ain't worth a damn with 'em now."

"What if Petal doesn't make it?" Gerry said.

Neither Enna nor Gabe spoke, clearly not wanting to entertain the possibility.

A knock came from the door. Gerry gripped the sickle's handle and stood to the side.

The door opened, Gerry tensed ready to attack.

"Hey, it's just us!" Cheska said stepping in holding up her wrists, still restrained with the EM Cuffs. Malik and a few people from GeoCity-1 stood behind her.

"Any chance of getting us out of these? We need to

move now. I can hear them trying to get through the main doors. They'll be here any minute." Malik said.

Gerry turned to Gabe, "There's one door in, one door out. Unless you got any ideas?"

"Yeah, man, I gotta plan."

Chapter 17

Petal sipped fresh water from a cup, closed her eyes as the cool liquid helped take the taste of salt-water from her mouth. She yawned and looked over at Sasha's holoscreen: nearly 23:00. She hadn't slept properly for over twenty-four hours, and despite all the 'Stems she'd had lately, her body demanded a rest.

She slumped into the seat next to Sasha, stared at her, smiled to herself. Whatever the exact situation was, it was kinda cool to have a sister, if that's what they were.

Maybe she was a clone? *That'd be cool, too.* Petal had always wanted a family, and as close as she was to Gabe, he was still a man unto himself, a mystery, an enigma.

The sub rocked violently to the left. A great booming sound accompanied the movement, and the display flashed with a series of numbers. Petal noticed the temp gauge spike. Which meant one thing: particle beam weapons.

"It's The Family's drones, isn't it?" Petal said.

Sasha brushed herself off and levelled the sub. "Yeah," she said.

"Dive."

"I'm on it."

Sasha put the Sub into an evasive spin, and in a wide

arc sent it back down into the depths, steering away from the reef, and the base.

"How far are we from your compound?" Petal asked

"Not far, but I can't risk luring the drones there. I shouldn't even be out here rescuing you. Jimmy's gonna kill me."

"Not if the drones kill us first," Petal said. "This tub got any weaponry? EMP, laser, missiles, torpedoes?"

"Yeah, it has, but." Sasha screwed up face and her cheeks blushed red.

"You didn't arm it before coming out?" Petal said, trying not to sound too derogatory. It was clear the girl was out of her depth, in more ways than one.

"Well, I thought I'd pick you up and bring you back before the satellite came over. We've been tracking it for months, I got my times right, I'm sure I did." Another blast hit the water and the sub jerked.

"They won't just give up," Petal said.

"You fought them before?" Sasha asked.

"Yeah, occupational hazard." Petal gave her a wry smile.

"What do you do exactly?"

"Lately it's been hacking a bit of this and a bit of that, although very lately it was saving City Earth, and look at the thanks we're getting."

"City Earth? You've been there? How did you get out?"

The radar screen showed the four UAVs circling their position. No doubt they'd hold their weapons until they breached the surface.

"I'll tell you about it sometime, but we kinda need to

deal with these first, huh? How much air do we have?"

Sasha checked the holoscreen. "About an hour."

"That's us screwed then. Those drones can go for days. They'll wait for us and then blast us out of the water."

Sasha slumped into her seat, kicked out in frustration. "I knew I should have listened to Jimmy. But oh no, I had to go and try and prove something."

"Who's Jimmy? Tell me about him," Petal asked, more to get the girl to calm down, think rationally. If she could take some of the anger and frustration out of her, then they could think more logically.

"My father I suppose, kinda. It's difficult to explain and, well, I probably shouldn't be telling you any of this."

"What is he though? A medical doctor, a tech guy, engineer?"

Sasha took a deep breath. "I suppose you could say he's medical for the most part, but, look, it's not that I don't want to trust you, it's just I've screwed up enough. Let's see if we make it back, then you'll learn about him, us, the whole lot."

"Fair enough. What's the tech like on this thing, decent processing power? What about its remote access facilities?"

"The computer's a Legacy II. It's standard for most military equipped subs and powerful enough. As for access to the systems, it'd be great if those UAVs weren't jamming us. I can't signal out, and the stealth doesn't seem to be working. Jimmy warned me it wasn't ready for real word applications, but in the tests, I don't know.

I was so convinced."

"Stealth? What kind of stealth?" Petal asked.

"Look, how do I know you ain't working for the Red Widows? You were in one of their Jaguars, wearing their gear. You even had one of their little religious books on you. If it walks like a duck, and quacks like a duck." Sasha raised her eyebrows, questioning Petal's origins. She had to agree. It did look suspicious.

Petal held out her forearm. "Would I be one of the Widows if I had one of your chips inside me?"

"They could have taken it out of you, turned you to a double agent or something." Sasha crossed her arms defensively. Petal could tell she didn't really believe it.

"And the fact we're clearly related or perhaps the same clones doesn't give you an idea that I might be on your side?"

Sasha shrugged, plotted a new direction into the sub's navigation computer sending it into a wide arc some two-hundred metres below the surface.

"Look, we've got an hour before we're out of air," Petal said. "We can't go back to the base, and we have no weaponry. Either you trust me and tell me more about what this sub can, and should be able to do, and let me help you, or we both stay here like sitting ducks."

Sasha opened her mouth and began to speak, but Petal was riled up now and seeing the girl wilt under her aggression sought to take the advantage.

"You're just a girl playing at real life. Do you really think those UAVs will politely stay up in the air? Do you even know what they are capable of? Did you not know that they could submerge too? What will you do when they decide to dive and find us down here in the dark?"

Sasha's eyes grew wide. "They can do that? Go under water, I mean?"

"Of course they can. You think The Family make crappy equipment like this tub? They have the best resources and the best minds working on their stuff. They'll be down here in no time. They're probably just biding their time while they scan our systems for vulnerabilities. You really want The Family inside the computer of this thing?"

"If they get in then they'll—" Sasha looked away, perhaps subconsciously towards the base.

"Yeah, they'll find your base and probably nuke it. It's far enough away from City Earth that it wouldn't be a risk to them. And no one else would give a damn if some rinky-dink island gets blown to hell."

"I can't do this," Sasha said quietly, almost under her breath. "I'm not trained for this kind of thing."

"Then what are you trained for?" Petal asked.

"Field combat," she said, slumping her shoulders as if that was nothing to be proud of. Petal supposed it wasn't when you were stuck in a submarine.

"You've got a choice, girl," Petal said. "Either you let me into the systems and let me see what I can do, or we swim about until either we're out of energy, or the UAVs kill us. It's up to you. What would Jimmy want you to do?"

Sasha squirmed in her chair, pressed her lips together. She took a deep breath, then, in a resigned rush said. "Okay, then. Just don't mess it up."

Petal arched an eyebrow. "Please, I'm the expert here. Now swap seats and give me your login credentials."

Sasha complied. Petal navigated through the sub's system via the holoscreen. It was slower work than using a gesture-capable tablet, but at least her apparent twin could see what she was doing. Maybe even learn something along the way.

Petal hacked the system easily. Within minutes she had bypassed the encryption and logged in as a super-root user, gaining access to the system's core file system and code libraries. She supposed given that the sub was still in development they hadn't anticipated someone would be driving it about and wanting to get into the code. It was certainly clean, well-commented, and elegant. She gave the developers that at least.

It took another five minutes to find the portion of the system that controlled the stealth module. It was a clever piece of tech. As Petal ran through the code line-by-line constructing a model of it in her head she had to give Jimmy and his coders a great deal of credit. The code was borderline genius: a polymorphic structure with its own machine-learning AI component that sent random signals to billions of nano-cells on the outside of the sub. Each one of the cells would make a note of the light falling upon its surrounding and recreate the photons within its own light transmitters so that anything that looked upon it, be it a satellite, drone or person, would effectively see nothing other than its surroundings, rendering it completely invisible.

The radar facilities appeared to work in a similar fashion, allowing a complete pass-through of any radar.

There was one problem, however: Jimmy hadn't quite finished the code. There were various functions and methods that the code relied upon to compile correctly that simply didn't exist yet.

"Well, can you fix it?" Sasha said after a while, all the time fidgeting in the seat next to Petal.

"Yeah, I can do it. But I need something from you first."

Sasha rolled her eyes. "What do you want?"

"When we get back, I want you to introduce me to this Doc of yours."

"You'll have no worries with that," Sasha said. "He'll kill me for all this, and will likely kill you second."

"Oh, I doubt that. I can be charming when I need to be." To prove the point, Petal pouted her lips, swept her hair back, and busted out her best smile. "See?"

Sasha shook her head and laughed.

Petal couldn't believe how much they looked alike. Despite the differences of hairstyles, it was like looking in a mirror.

"I best get to work then," Petal said.

"Okay, hurry."

All the time Petal worked at coding the missing functions, she kept catching glimpses from Sasha, her face a mixture of awe, wonder, and confusion. No doubt the very same look that Petal had on her own face when looking at Sasha.

Almost at the same time they both spoke. "It's weird, isn't it?"

They laughed together, before they became silent, stared at each for a few long seconds.

Petal turned away, back to her screen. "Okay, just adding the last bit." She completed the last of the required functions, rebooted the machine to compile the new code. "Right, let's see if this works then."

"I hope so. For both of our sakes."

The radar blipped once, then twice.

"They're here." Sasha pointed to the video feed of the rear camera.

Two drones had submerged, and in a corkscrew pattern dived down into the depths, sweeping the waters for their location.

"Have you fixed it yet?" Sasha said, her eyes wider now, a little hint of panic twitching at the corner of her mouth.

"Almost," Petal replied as she error-checked the last of her functions. It failed on the first reboot. Caught on a snag somewhere. After a while of debugging the original program, she eventually understood how the polymorphic code worked. Realising her mistake, she navigated back to a segment of code and typed in a fix. She ran a quick test: no errors. "That should do it."

The drones drew closer. The video feed had them at less than fifty metres away.

They would be within visual contact in a matter of seconds.

"Hurry," Sasha said, her leg bouncing up and down, making a tapping noise against the hull.

"I'm nearly done. Rebooting now."

"Oh crap, they're getting closer. Thirty metres, they'll see us."

Petal moved her hands swiftly across the holoscreen,

waiting for it to catch up with her movement. How she wished to have had a direct connection instead. She could have done this in half the time. Hopefully this Jimmy guy could put her dermal wrist implant back in, give her back some of her abilities.

"Twenty metres. I think they've seen us. They're moving into flanking formation."

"Bastards!" *Come on come on*! She willed the system to reboot faster, but all the damned security checks and menus asking for input slowed her down. As good as these Criborg people were they could use some help to streamline their systems.

Petal glanced up at the video feed. Small streams of bubbles exited around the domed front of the two drones. "They're readying weapons."

Sasha grabbed the manual navigation controls and pulled the sub up, powering the engine and shooting them forwards. Two torpedoes from the drones, one either side of the sub, launched out into the water towards them. Sasha's evasive manoeuvre pulled them out just in time as the torpedoes smashed into each other, sending a shock wave that knocked the sub into a semi-roll.

Petal flew backwards out of her seat, but managed to grab onto the headrest as Sasha righted the sub.

"That was close," Petal said.

"Tell me the stealth is working, I can't keep doing this, I wasn't trained for this kind of thing," Sasha said, sweat glossy on her forehead.

The boot process had finished. A dialogue box flashed on the holoscreen. Petal pulled herself back over the front seat and engaged the newly coded system.

"There, it's online. I don't know if it'll actually work. Only one way to find out." She turned to flash another grin at Sasha.

"What do you mean?" Sasha said slowly, with a hint of worry in her voice.

"Ramming speed! What's your surname by the way?" Petal said.

"I don't have one, you?"

"No damned clue. Probably a serial number or something, huh?"

Sasha dropped her head then, mumbled, "Yeah, probably."

Had she hit a nerve? Oh well, t was too late to worry about that.

"Seriously though, ram them. If the stealth is working, they won't see us until its too late, right?"

"But we can't. What if it damages the sub?"

Petal shook her head, "Fine, get out of the way." She pushed Sasha out of the navigation seat, took hold of the controls, and turned the sub around and plotted a collision course. "The hull's strong on this thing, ain't it?"

"I suppose, but I don't think it's—"

"That's your problem right there, girl. Too much thinking and not enough doing."

Petal pushed the engines to maximum while aiming the sub at the nearest drone.

They sped through the water. Given the drone's slow arcing course, it was apparent that it was trying to find them. It appeared that the stealth system had worked after all. Petal gave herself a mental pat on the back and braced her legs against the bulkhead of the hull.

"Hold onto your tits. We're impacting in three, two, one."

Petal veered the sub away so that they crashed into the drone side-to-side, sending the enemy vehicle into a spin towards the sea floor. Its shell smashed open. Wires and processors shorted out under the water. The impact rocked the sub. A bell-like note rung out as metal collided with metal.

"Hah! They didn't see that, did they, huh?"

Petal turned the sub in a wide arc, until the second drone came into view. Like the first it performed some kind of reconnaissance route: slowly weaving and arcing, searching for them, but to no avail.

"Wanna do the honours?" Petal offered the controls to Sasha.

At first she hesitated, and then with a growing smile on her face, she swapped places, locked onto the drone, and gunned the engines again.

Within five more seconds, they had smashed the other drone to pieces.

"Now that's more like it!" Petal said.

Sasha's hands trembled on the controls. "That felt so damned good."

"Yeah, girl, that's what we were designed for, right? Not sitting around in some poxy lab. We should be out in the field getting stuff done," Petal said.

"I guess so."

For the first time since she'd been rescued, Petal felt like they were seeing eye-to-eye.

With two drones down, and the other two scanning the skies unable to find them with the working stealth, Sasha navigated the sub back to the base.

Petal used the time to rest, let the 'Stems do their work. Despite their efforts, and the previous injection, she felt weak inside. Not just her physical strength, but also her motivation, her gusto. It was like the feeling after a long physical fight. It affected the mind too.

But despite that, a shining spark of excitement continued to glow inside her. Somehow she knew she was going home. After all those years wondering who she was, or even what she was, it came down to these next few hours.

But then she wondered how she would cope with the truth. Those thoughts rumbled around inside her mind as she let sleep finally take her. The low rhythmic rumble of the sub's engines, the ebb and flow of the currents, took her away into sleep, where dreams of her birth, or creation, came to her in abstract bubbles of imagery.

***

Far off voices, shouting, arguments, rushing sounds of water. A violent jolt made Petal suddenly sit up, eyes wide, her throat dry and hoarse. The door to the sub opened. Seawater dripped off the edge of the matte-black surface like a miniature waterfall. Individual droplets reflected a bright world of lights, steel, and men in dull grey army fatigues with a light green camo design.

A pair of arms, wrapped in a white lab coat, appeared beneath the door, lifted it up completely.

A man's head with dark swept-back hair and a generous portion of grey in the temples appeared in the gap. Thick, wild eyebrows rose on his forehead, beneath which a pair of shining grey eyes regarded her with curiosity.

"Hello," the man said.

Petal sat up from her seat, swung her legs over. "You the Doc?"

His shoulders slumped and he sighed. "It's Doctor James Robertson. Sasha calls me Jimmy."

"Is she in trouble?" Petal asked casually.

"She's not employee of the month, that's for sure. But you're both alive, so it's not all bad. Why don't you come out of there and follow me to the medical bay? I hear you've had quite a rough time of it lately."

"Lately? Huh, it's an everyday occurrence, Doc."

"Doctor Robertson."

"Sure thing, Doc. Lead the way."

Jimmy Robertson shook his head, held out a hand to her.

Petal took it, pulling herself out of the sub and onto the gantry. She took a few moments for her legs to get used to solid ground, took the opportunity to take in her environment. The place was devoid of colour and all business. It resembled a hangar with gantries and a large water-section housing a number of subs. A dozen men and women behind a glass observation room all stared down at her.

Two men in military fatigues escorted Sasha out

of the compound. She remonstrated to no avail with a particularly large and balding figure whose face was red and swollen. His booming voice echoed around the place. Seems Sasha was in a fair bit of trouble after all.

Robertson stepped beside her and held out his arm.

"Welcome to Criborg," he said. "Or, more specifically, Wake Island."

"Who's that losing their crap with Sasha?" Petal asked.

"That's the General. General Vickers. He's kind of the big cheese on the operation and military side of things here at Criborg."

"Got a loud bark on him," Petal said, noticing already that she was protective of her new friend, which in itself was a big assumption. Who knew what her relationship with Sasha would be now that they were safe.

"He's a very capable man," Dr Robertson, said. "Sasha's impulsive, and although she did well by recovering you, she endangered us all."

"Maybe she wouldn't be so impulsive if you didn't keep her locked away doing boring chores. Both you and I know she's capable of more." Petal said.

Robertson ran his hand through his hair before nodding. "We both know that yes, but she doesn't, and neither does Vickers. I don't want to risk her."

She couldn't help but notice the guilty look in his eyes. "Was I born here?" Petal asked.

Robertson opened his mouth to say something then closed it again, before eventually saying, "I suppose so." He dropped his voice and moved in closer. "It's not a simple story, but let me make sure your health is all right, and then we can go into all that. Okay?"

"Yeah, about the health thing. Apparently I'm dying."

Chapter 18

Gerry ushered Malik, Cheska, Enna and the rest back down the corridor and into a cell, while Gabe ducked into another cell further down the corridor, trigger in hand. Detonation cord ran from the explosives now attached to the rear bulkhead wall of the cellblock. They were part of a vest that Gabe wore under his robes. Standard issue for the Red Widow's 'third wave' regiment apparently.

Enna, huddled with the others spoke quietly, "Are you sure this is wise?"

"Nope. Not sure at all," Gerry said. "But what other choice do we have?"

In the block there were ten cells either side. Gabe was in cell three. The rest of them huddled in groups of four in the first row nearest the entrance.

Heavy banging, screaming, and shotgun blasts came from the steel doors that separated the cellblock from the rest of the compound. Each smash and crash accompanied a string of frenzied yelling from the zealots on the other side. The doors buckled. Smoke billowed out in the gap between the doors and the floor. They'd breach their way through soon.

There were eight of them left in total: Malik, Cheska,

Enna, Gabe, Gerry, and three citizens from GeoCity-1. Most were in fairly good condition. Gerry had helped remove their EM cuffs. Weapons-wise they had three shotguns and two stun-sickles. It was hardly an arsenal, but it would have to do.

Gabe poked his head out of the cell, gave them the thumbs-up.

A tense minute later and the main doors were finally breached in a cloud of smoke. A loud clatter reverberated around the cells as the heavy steel doors crashed inwards to the floor. The voices were frantic. Gerry watched the shadows pass by under the crack of his cell door.

This was it, he thought, and still he had the nagging feeling of mistrust when it came to Gabe. Would he do what was necessary? Would he sell them out again? Was this all part of a plan? Were his loyalties now with—?

A huge crack erupted, making his ears pop and the cell door fly open, knocking him, Enna, and two others to the floor. The entire compound shook beneath the blast.

The frenzied shouting peaked into a series of high-pitched screams followed by a silence. Concrete dust filled the air, making Gerry cough.

An insistent ringing diminished his hearing. He clambered up from the floor and staggered out of the cell. He waved in vain to clear the air. Rays of weak moonlight creating a field of infinite motes came from a ragged hole in the compound wall at the end of the block.

Five Red Widow members lay dead in a heap by the

hole.

None came from the open doors behind him, but he knew it wouldn't be long before others would investigate.

He ushered the others out from their cell. They were saying something to him, their lips moving, their eyes wide and searching, but their voices were distant rumbles in a sea of whistling.

He beckoned them to follow. They picked up the Widow's shotguns and any remaining ammo, discarding the ones damaged beyond use from the blast. The explosives had ripped and shredded their bodies. Gabe's explosives had ignited their own vests creating a much bigger explosion than originally planned. Scorch marks burned into the grey concrete and Polymar™ leaving charred ghosts on the wall's surface.

Gerry shouted for Gabe while inspecting Cell Three, but he wasn't there.

Then, from outside of the hole in the wall, surrounded in dust and light came a silhouette. *That must be him*, Gerry thought. He ran forward to make sure he was okay, but as he approached, he noticed that the silhouette was still wore robes. Before Gerry could change direction, the shape came into full view: a fanatic. Her light-brown robes were caked in blood. She held a shotgun in her hands and levelled it at Gerry's chest.

A gun blast rung out, sending Gerry diving to his left. Something hot and wet splashed his face as he tumbled to the ground in a heap. The Widow blinked once, dropped the shotgun, and fell to her face.

Gabe stood over her body. Smoke danced from the

barrel of the shotgun in his hands. He wore a big stupid grin on his face. His dreadlocks swayed in the breeze like lazy snakes on a sunny day.

"Saved ya ass again," Gabe said. "Told ya I had a plan."

Gerry shook his head and wiped the blood from his face, coughing the smoke and debris from his lungs. "You're crazy, you know that?"

"Crazy keeps ya alive, man."

Gabe stepped over the bodies of the fanatics, helped Gerry to his feet. Together they made sure everyone else was okay before exiting the hole in the compound.

"Over here," Gabe said, leading them past the rubble and out to a stretch of open grassland pockmarked by scorched patches, divots and craters of various sizes: the wounds upon the Earth of a struggle for a dying city. The compound existed mostly underground. Only sections of its roof were visible on the surface. They sprinted around the compound until they came to the familiar banks that led down to the service access road from where they were originally taken in.

"We have to move quickly," Gerry said to Gabe. "They'll be on us like ants as soon as they realise what's happened."

"Ya gotta learn to trust me, man," Gabe said. He led them down the grassy bank to the concreted surface. One of the trucks still remained. Two guards stood by the steel doors. They spoke on their radios—small digital devices embedded in their ears—and gabbled for a while in their consonant-heavy language before rushing inside the compound.

Gerry didn't understand, whispered to Gabe. "What're they saying?"

"They mentioned an explosion. They'll be on us soon. We gotta shift."

Gerry turned to signal to the others following them. He pointed to the truck, and they all sprinted down the banks. Gabe, Enna, and Gerry took the front seats with Enna taking the wheel. Gabe said he'd navigate. The others took their position inside the back of the truck, on the bench seats. Before they headed off, Gerry got into the truck's computer and took its communications transceiver offline so that it couldn't be easily tracked.

"Where are we headed?" Enna said after starting the truck and backing it away from the compound and turning to face the city.

"Right where ya facing," Gabe said. "Deep into the city, we need to find a place to hide and regroup, formulate a plan of action to find Omega."

Enna turned on the headlights, pressed the accelerator, and headed into the narrow streets of the Darkhan. Gerry watched through the mirrors, expecting streams of lights from ATVs and Jaguars to follow, but with all the confusion, it seemed they had bought a precious few minutes of time. Before the Widows had fully realised what had happened, they should be able to find a place to park up and stay hidden.

As Enna drove the truck, Gerry took the opportunity to quiz Gabe some more. "Tell me more about Criborg. What do you know about them?"

"As far as I know, they're a group of military and science people leftover from the war. The Widows had a few skirmishes with their drone UAVs and even a ship. We never could tell how many there were over there."

"Where are they?"

"A place called Wake Island, out in the Pacific, off the Sea of Japan," Enna said over her shoulder. "It's the base of operations for what was an allied American/Canadian/British group. I believe it is they who made, or at least developed, Petal, for her dermal implant chip was one of theirs."

"That's a bit of an assumption," Gerry said.

"Kinda," Gabe replied. "From my investigations within the Widows, I found a number of dossiers on their pre- and during war capabilities. They were known for making 'borgs and 'droids."

"So Petal's not human?"

"Yeah, she is, but not as we know it," Enna said. "That's one of the reasons I couldn't help her. It seemed like her DNA was breaking down, mutating. I couldn't do anything about it. It's way beyond anything I've had to deal with. It's an outside chance, admittedly, but it's the only other way I could think of saving her."

Gabe added, "And that ain't the only reason,"

Gerry knew there'd be something else involved. It was never that simple with Enna and Gabe. They always seemed to be plotting or planning some scheme. "What is it this time?"

"I sent her back with a slate. It had some info about the Widows on it. We're hoping they can lend us a hand. Gez, the Widows are more capable than ya think. It ain't just the Dome under threat. It's everyone who doesn't get with the new program. It's everyone who ain't pure, unaltered. Basically almost everyone left. Theses mentalists see this burnt shell of a planet as their Eden. They wanna restart humanity, but wanna clean away the tech first, ya understand?"

"Yeah, I understand. Just the flip-side to The Family."

Once over the worst of the waste ground, Gerry got Enna to stop the vehicle and turn off the lights. They swapped seats, with Gerry behind the wheel. Darkness shrouded the city. It was gone 01:10 and thick clouds periodically snuffed out the moon's rays. The only light came from the few fires keeping the desperate warm. He turned on his night-vision and navigated the truck through the tight alleys until he found access to the loading bay of a skeleton of a skyscraper. He parked in the shadows and shut off the engines.

A few dark shapes within that rubble-strewn bay moved past the truck. Just a group of men and women dressed in rags, no doubt disturbed by the truck's presence. Gerry waited until they had gone, turned to the others. "I need to get to her," he said mostly to himself.

"No time yet," Gabe said. "We need to locate Omega."

He knew the old hacker was right, but the desire to see Petal again, to see her safe made him desperate to take the truck and head east to Criborg.

Thinking about the whole situation, he wondered if he should contact The Family. His connection to their system was still operational, and perhaps he should warn them about Red Widow's plans. But then, they must know about them, surely? He doubted Red Widow's advancement into Darkhan and GeoCity-1 had gone unnoticed, but then why no response? He doubted they really cared. The security inside the Dome had been massively increased. They probably thought nothing of it; kept focus with their plans.

A rumble overhead from a Jaguar circling around the dead towers of Darkhan made the truck hum with the vibrations.

"None of us can stay here for long," Gerry said. "We need to get out into the city and track down that other server ASAP, then find safety."

"Ain't nowhere safe in this ol' town, man. The crazies have it locked down."

"Then what do you suggest?" Gerry fidgeted in his seat, eager to get going before the sun came back up. He didn't fancy his chances of staying hidden during the daylight.

Enna interjected, "I suggest we get Old Grey up and running, use her to help track the other server. Cut down on the random factor of just wandering around the place."

"How?" Gerry said, slumping in the truck's seat. "If the Meshwork is suppressed, we don't have any network to use. I only have a connection to The Family because of the stuff they've added in my head, and right now I don't know if it's safe to get them involved."

"I guess we connect Old Grey to the truck's power supply and see what happens," Enna said.

"That sounds too hopeful. I'm not sitting here doing nothing," Gerry said already reaching for the door as the Jaguar peeled away to circle further into the city. "Malik, you stay here so I can communicate with you and the rest of the group. I'll go scout out around the city, see if I can detect any data signals. Even with the suppression, there must be something."

"Ah, man, this ain't right, we should wait," Gabe said.

Gerry pointed out of the truck's window to a group of three hobos huddled around a pile of trash at the corner of the skyscraper where it met the street.

"How long before one of them causes a scene, huh? How long before their interest brings those mad fanatics to this location?"

Gabe shook his head, but Gerry was having none of it. He turned to Enna, "Sit tight, and wait for my communications. I'm going out there."

Before anyone had the chance to act, he opened the door and stepped out into the warm night air. The shadow of the skyscraper, now long and angular, hid the truck. As Gerry engaged his stealth protocol, he moved closer to the building, feeling its rough, bullet-wounded facade against his body. The hobos looked up towards him, their honed senses telling them something had changed in the atmosphere and they ambled off into the street, rubbing their grubby faces with worn, dirty-gloved hands.

Beyond the pile of trash, a stream of people floated down a street in front of the skyscraper. He dodged between shanty camps of filthy cloth tents and the obligatory drum-fires that gathered the restless like beacons.

Via his connection to The Family's station, he hacked into the system anonymously, not wanting to alert Jachz, who by now was probably doing all he could to scan his location and get into his feeds. He found the layout for Darkhan, downloaded the map and schematics data.

— *Mags, model the map in 3D on the HUD. Filter buildings that used to be on the power grid, and ones that are defensible either by height or location.*

— *Processing, updating.*

There were five locations within a kilometre: three on the other side of a bridge, which Gerry knew would be guarded well, and two on his side of the city. The closest one, an old subway station converted to a bank, was situated approximately eight hundred metres away.

"I found a possible location," Gerry said over his VPN to Malik, "I'm on route. Will update shortly."

"Got that. Take it easy, Gerry."

He slipped into the flotsam of the sea of survivors, picked various items of loose clothing and rags off passers-by, disguised himself as one of the pure, the unaltered. Looking at them as he walked down the main street towards the subway station he realised that even though they were considered pure, their lives were barely worth living. The conditions were such that they lived off food grown in fields still recovering from radiation, drinking water distilled in rain-silos that sat atop buildings like transparent pyramids.

He passed a number of burnt-out strip-malls, the windows long since smashed, and the fronts home to rats, dogs and the truly downtrodden, each shop a microcosm of life clinging on to scraps and false hopes.

Beyond these malls of despair and desperation, the bridge connecting the two halves of the city loomed like a great steel spine: semi-circular struts traversed the dried-up river like vertebrae. A gang of five Red Widow members huddled around a small square in front of the bridge, checking people as they passed.

The checkpoint stretched across the street to a tall concrete building, still mostly intact.

The group of fanatics were stopping random people, giving them a shake down, causing a scene before pushing them off into the sea of desperate humanity. Occasionally they'd let one through and send them across the bridge into the darkness. He could only assume they were the ones chosen to live.

He ducked his head, merged further into the crowd, developed a limp, a racking cough, and hoped he could pass without incident.

Within the crowd he heard a rattling, rolling noise. He looked down and saw the top of a young girl's head. Like the rest, she wore dirty rags around her thin frame. She sat on a wheeled board, and propelled herself across the rough ground with her blistered and swollen fingers, probably from being stepped on by the uncaring group around her.

She looked up at Gerry, stared right in his eyes, and cocked her head. She seemed to be reading him. Or listening.

"Can I help you," Gerry said. "Are you hurt?"

"No," she said, not specifying to which question she had answered. "You're very noisy," she added. "He'll hear you."

"What do you mean?" He certainly wasn't making any more noise than anyone else around him. The girl beckoned him down to her level. He knelt, looked at her, realised she couldn't be much older than ten or eleven. And yet her eyes were already world-weary, her cheeks hollow. "What is it?" he asked again, intrigued by the girl.

She reached up and tapped her thin index finger gently against his head. "From there," she said. "So much noise, signals, and data. He can hear you, too."

"Who can?"

"The man in the box."

Gerry smiled, wanted to laugh. It was utterly absurd, but the way she looked into him, it was as if she could see inside his brain. Could she really hear his thoughts, his data processing?

"What can you tell me about him? Is he a bad man?"

She smiled, shook her head. "Neither. He just listens. Come, I'll show you."

Intrigued, he stood, followed the girl as she paddled her wheeled board out of the flow of people and towards a battle-scarred tower. Its facade chipped and damaged from various munitions. Great chunks hung away, held from falling by a webbing of rebar. Its multiple windows were devoid of glass and covered with rusted steel sheets.

She pointed up to a distant window. "He's waiting up there."

Gerry focused his mind, had his AIA scan the area for any radio or data signals. To his surprise, he detected a weak and intermittent signal, fragmented beyond coherence, the data packets scrambled and incomplete.

He opened his connection to Malik and the others

back at the truck.

— *I think I've found something. I'm investigating. I'll update you shortly.*

To the girl, he said. "Hey, thanks—" He looked down to find she had gone, vanished back into the crowd. He pushed forward, squirming back into the crowd to try and see her, but she was nowhere to be seen. He turned his attentions back to the dark window, decided he'd check it out.

Chapter 19

A sharp tang hung in the air, shifted about the white-walled medical lab. The bed Petal lay upon took her weight, cradled her spine. So comfortable she could have stayed there forever. She closed her eyes, waited for the phantom movements from being in the sub to give way to the stillness of solid ground.

Her muscles still twitched, neurons fired, balance readjusting to waves and currents that were no longer there. It could have been the latest shot of 'Stems, she thought, that continued to stimulate her nervous system. She'd had three doses inside a day. More than she'd normally tolerate.

A taste of metal coated the back of her throat. Her mouth felt oily and slick. She opened her eyes, turned to her side, and found a pitcher of water on the bed stand.

A cup had already been poured for her.

She reached out her right arm, felt resistance. A wire twinned with a narrow tube came from her wrist where her old implant used to be.

The skin around the old wound had healed, and pressing her fingers against it she felt something hard beneath the skin. A new chip, an upgrade perhaps? How long had she been out during surgery? She glanced around for a clock. A holoscreen attached to the end of the bed flicked with various metrics. The time read 03:02. She'd been out for about three or so hours. The soreness in her body made it seem like weeks.

She tried to access her new chip with her mind, but everything fogged. She couldn't detect it in there. She thought perhaps it wasn't online, or needed booting up or something. Hopefully it wasn't a botched procedure. Given the missing code within the submarine's stealth module, she had to wonder.

From another tube attached to her upper arm, an almost-clear liquid dripped into her. The wire traced back to the computer unit attached to the end of the bed. She took a closer look at the numbers and charts.

Heart beat, blood pressure, mental cognition, and something else: a stream of assembly code flowing vertically. Next to the stream were a series of graphs. She didn't understand the notation beneath the graph. It appeared that this was perhaps the code running on her implanted chip. She recognised some of the routines, but it seemed more advanced than the last time she checked. The last time being with Enna in her lab.

To the side of the bed sat a remote control panel like a small slate. She pressed her finger against a red spot labelled 'help'. And then she wondered if her own slate, the one that Gabe had given her, was still in the sub. She didn't know if Sasha had remembered to recover the slate after General whatshisname tore a strip off her.

As she came fully around, she blinked her eyes against the bright glare. Overhead OLED panels simulated the summer sun perfectly. Alas, there was none of the relaxing heat prickling against her skin. The place felt dead. No atmosphere, no fresh air. She already missed the salt-air from the sea.

All around her were white walls. No artwork, no attempt at decoration. Not even a decent sized holos-creen for entertainment purposes. It seemed so militaristic.

The electronic whine and click of a lock caught her attention. She looked up at the door beyond the foot of her bed. Dr Robertson stood in the doorway carrying her broken slate.

It was safe then!

Deep ravines cut through the soft skin of his forehead, each one thick with concern or concentration. He entered the room, avoided eye contact.

"Vitals are looking good. Your new implant seems to have installed okay."

"Good to know," Petal replied, with a hint of sarcasm. "Doc, I—"

"Wait, I know you've got questions," he said, running a hand through his hair, as his entire body seemed to sigh with a sagging movement. "But, there're things you need to know first."

"You recovered the data on the slate?" She sat further up. Her muscles groaned with the effort, but already her strength was returning.

Jimmy Robertson took a step back, looked down at the slate, his eyes intent almost as if he were peering directly into the data itself.

"You're not dying," he finally said looking up at her.

The corners of his mouth tightened, moved upwards ever so slightly, a small proud smile. "You were never dying. Your friends were right to be concerned, but it wasn't as bad as they thought. You were mutating. Adapting."

Mutating! God, it sounded like she was some kind of freak. "What do you mean mutating? Adapting? To what?"

He stepped aside, pulled the holoscreen closer to her. "You see that flow of data," he pointed to the flow of assembly code she noticed earlier.

"Yeah, it's a data stream. I'm assuming that's because of the implant, right?"

"It's so much more." Now his smile stretched real wide. He looked like a proud father whose daughter had learned to walk or ride a bike for the first time. "It's your operating system. Isn't it amazing?"

"Um, yeah, sure. Not to put a damper on things, but what exactly does it, and my implant chip, actually do?" She studied the graphs, managed to realise that some of the bars in the image indicated the input and output traffic of data, and another bar represented some kind of computational process. Beyond that she didn't really know.

"You don't understand," he said now, sitting on the bed. He rubbed his forehead. "How best to explain? Your neural network within your brain isn't entirely organic. That's where your chip comes in. It connects a multicore quantum computational chip to that network, allows your brain to subordinate tasks. It also helps in things like your reaction speed, your strength.

"The chip improves the flow of data to and from your nervous system and your brain functions. Think of it as a second brain, but with lots of added abilities, like how you can connect remotely to computer networks, or how you can retain and manipulate artificial intelligences and viral code. It's why you're a rock-solid code safe. This chip is a more advanced version of the one that you had previously. I'm afraid that one was permanently damaged when it was removed."

She thought back to the night when those cruel bitches cut it out of her without a care in the world. As if it were some cancerous tumour that needed to be sliced out and discarded.

"So, what exactly am I?"

"That's a little complicated. You're not quite—"

"If you're gonna tell me I ain't human, I kinda know that already by now."

Robertson's eyes widened a little at that, and then his shoulders relaxed, as if it were one revelation he didn't have to take responsibility for. He still gripped the slate, held it close to him. He bounced it up and down slightly.

"The info on this slate from your friends," he said. "It's not entirely accurate. Enna, I'm assuming some kind of bioengineer, had read you all wrong. She thought your DNA was breaking down and assumed you were dying with some kind of condition, which to be fair is how it looks to someone who doesn't know what you are."

She couldn't but help to feel a twinge of worry at that. She thought about all the times Gabe had taken her to Enna to get a shot of NanoStem or some other medical procedure. Had she operated on her properly? Had Enna really known what she was doing?

She asked again, "What am I?"

"Probably best if I show you." Robertson stood from the bed. "Are you up for a stroll?"

Petal swung her legs over the side of the bed and stood. Her head swam, she reached out. Robertson caught her hands. She quickly let go, "I'm fine. You might want to disconnect this first." She held up her arm with the tube and wire still attached.

"Of course." He entered something on the holoscreen, rendering it blank, and with careful and agile fingers disconnected her from the machine.

A tiny electrical charge tickled at the wound on her wrist when he removed the wire and tube. "Did you find my old chip?" she said suddenly realising the robes she had stolen from a Red Widow fanatic were no longer on her, replaced instead with a dark-grey form-fitting one piece body suit. She wore slipper-light shoes, split at the toes and with a thin rubber sole.

"It's okay," Robertson said, making his way to the door. "All your belongings are safe. But you won't need that chip any more. Your new one is greatly upgraded."

"Sounds great. But I can't feel anything yet. Or access my systems."

"You will do shortly. It takes a while for the neural pathways in your brain to sync with the chip and vice-versa. You should be good to use your upgrades within a few hours."

He held the door open with a sincere smile that

reached his eyes.

"Who don't like upgrades, huh?" Petal replied, walking out into a sea of grey corridors.

Jimmy Robertson led Petal through what seemed like miles and miles of tunnels. If she weren't counting exits and turns, committing the layout to memory she'd easily have gotten lost in this underground labyrinth. It was vast in its scope. Way more than Seca's compound.

"So where we going, Doc?"

"Doctor Robertson," he replied with a sigh hanging on his voice. "You're going home, right back to where you began. Back to where I..." He stopped, his words laced with heavy regret choking in his throat.

This is it, Petal thought. Finally, after all those years of wondering who she was, or where she came from, she would know once and for all. But aside from that, this doctor intrigued her. He exuded kindness, but she could tell he held a fierce intellect in that old head of his that displayed so clearly years of frustration, grief, and perhaps failure.

He didn't seem to fit this place at all. She remembered the way he looked at the General when he took Sasha from the submarine bay. There was hatred. *No, not hatred*, she thought. *Envy.* Yes, he was envious of the General.

Perhaps his stature within this group wasn't what he wanted or deserved?

A familiar voice caught her attention, as they turned left at a junction in the tunnels.

Up ahead, a large room branched off to the right. Looking through a small windows at head-height, next to a thick steel door, Petal saw the General in front of ten soldiers dressed in camouflaged fatigues, lined up in a grid formation. He barked orders, his face puffed and reddened. They carried out a gun kata with their rifles.

Sasha stood at the back of the group. Petal waved at her look-a-like, but Sasha didn't notice: Sasha's attention focused only on the weapon in her hand as she carried out the required movements. She looked so much more skilled in there than she appeared in the sub.

Compared to the other men, she moved faster, more fluid.

General Vickers yelled at one of the men who stumbled no more than an inch within the middle of the kata. Vickers grabbed the guy by the lapels of his combat shirt, shouted in his face, showed him the movement with the grace of a cobra, and ordered him to start again. Vickers pointed to Sasha as he did so, using her as an example of how to do it right.

"Intense dude, this general of yours, huh?" Petal said looking into the window. "Do you two get on well?"

Robertson sniffed with a hint of derision. His easy-going expression tightened enough to create the beginnings of a sneer. "Vickers is a capable military leader," the doctor said between clenched teeth.

"Like that is it? Two men of status, vying for power and control?"

"He thinks it's something like that," Robertson said, now standing in front of the other window watching the group of men perform their manoeuvres while the General looked on.

Vickers looked up, caught Petal's eye, and gave her a wink and a cheesy-as-hell smile.

Petal politely nodded back, then looked away.

"He's a bit of a douche," she said as she watched him prance around at the front the room yelling instructions until his face became red.

"Like I said, he's a capable military leader, and unfortunately, in these times we need men like him. But don't mind him. Come on, let me show you your genesis."

As they walked away, Petal couldn't but help feel something far deeper existed between the Doc and Vickers than he let on.

After a further ten minutes of traversing the dull grey tunnels of the Wake Island underground city, they came to an old steel door covered in dents and patches of rust.

Robertson took an old-fashioned key from his pocket and unlocked the door.

"No electronic bolts here, huh?"

"You can't hack a mechanical lock remotely," he said giving her a sly wink.

He opened the door for her and stood back. She hesitated, but moved inside once she saw two person-sized pods hanging from a series of rails bolted to the ceiling of the room. Inside, the place looked like the rest of the compound: grey and white. It had a tiled floor, a single computer station to the right wall.

The door slammed behind. Her heart skipped a beat as she jumped. She turned thinking she'd been locked in, but Robertson was in the room, hunched over the door, locking it from the inside.

Her attention returned to the pods. Although they were tubular than pod-like. They reminded her of the transcendent pods that Enna had in her lab, only they weren't transcendents in these tubes. They were her.

"Welcome home, Number Three," Robertson said, his arms wide and his face beaming with pride.

Chapter 20

Sasha left the shower room and headed for Vickers's office, all the while wondering why he'd requested to speak with her after their kata training.

It couldn't be about her performance. She'd carried out the kata with precision and perfection. It was all part of her new programming. Jimmy had seen to that. She performed better than anyone in the facility. She had noticed Vickers staring at her, ever since she arrived back with Petal. Perhaps he had the hots for her? He was a single man in the facility. He must have certain desires. Her stomach clenched at the thought.

At nearly sixty, and all though he kept himself in good shape, his lanky, wiry form and bloated face kind of repulsed her. What if he tried something on?

How could she explain that she had to defend herself against him? Would anyone believe her? Vickers was like 'the man' around the place, apart from Jimmy of course.

Just get in, listen to what he's got to say and keep your distance, she thought.

His door hung part way open. She stood at the entrance and knocked.

"Come in," Vickers barked. His voice never seemed

to do subtle. It was like he was constantly stuck on eleven.

He sat behind the desk, elbows resting on the surface, hands pressed together to form a pyramid. His face gave nothing away. He remained neutral, impassive.

"Close the door and take a seat."

This time he did lower his voice slightly, *and* he said please, which wasn't a common occurrence. In fact, she couldn't remember the last he was ever that polite towards her. He must be up to something. She took a seat and waited. A few seconds ticked by. He looked at her with those penetrating blue eyes of his. "What did you want, General?" she asked, unable to stand the tension.

"We've got a problem."

"What kind of problem?" Sasha immediately thought it was something she'd done and squirmed in her chair. She knew it wasn't about Petal. He'd already reprimanded her for that. It was considered settled.

He stood from his desk, paced around the room. Heavy footsteps clacked against the tiled floor. Each step making the tension stretch that little bit farther.

"I managed to get a copy of the data from Petal's slate," he said. "We've got a problem and Robertson is too cautious to deal with it. It's time we stepped up, put our skills to use."

She looked up to see him staring at her again.

"What do you mean, exactly?" she said.

"Action. I've been training you and the squad for years now, and for what? Maintenance of the equipment on the surface? It's a waste of our time and resources.

I'm sick of hiding underground always at the mercy of The Family and their damned drones and satellites. And now those Red Widow bitches have somehow swelled their numbers and are eating up hamlets and villages, claiming land, making a home for themselves. They're planning an attack on City Earth, and we won't be far behind in their plans. We can't allow that to happen. I won't allow a bunch of crazy religious nuts to take over the land and destroy us."

Sasha stood, feeling the excitement build within her. Finally, she would put her skills to use, finally have a purpose instead of being Jimmy's run around. "What do you have in mind, General?"

"I'm glad you asked. But I need to know if I can trust you. It's highly unlikely Robertson would agree to any of this, so we're going to have to find a way around that."

She fidgeted at the thought of betraying the man who was essentially her father, but also her friend. Despite how he kept her wrapped in cotton-wool and refused to allow her to extend her abilities beyond the training rooms in the compound, he was still a man for whom she had a great deal of respect. But like Vickers, she didn't want to sit there and wait for those damned Widows to destroy them all. Attack was often the best form of defence, and with their attentions on The Family and the Dome, it would be a good time.

"Tell me what you have in mind."

Vickers stepped forward, held out his hand. "I need to know I can trust you," he said.

She shook his hand. "You have my loyalty."

With that he took his seat at the desk again. His

voice was lower now as he explained his plans.

"My men have isolated the exact orbit and location of The Family's observation satellite. But we need something from you before we can take it out."

Sasha knew exactly what he wanted. The Laser-Electromagnetic Pulse—LEMP warhead that Robertson developed over a year ago. The prototype sat in the labs ready to be used. Robertson maintained they needed more time to confirm his research, more time to test it before it was ready. But he said that about everything: the android army, the sub, even Sasha herself. Petal had proved that the sub's tech was good. Jimmy didn't have the balls to use it.

"I assume you're talking about the LEMP?" she said, to make sure she was on the same page.

Vickers nodded. "Can you get it online, use it?"

"Yeah, I know the codes. I helped Jimmy with the propulsion controls."

"It's currently offline, incomplete. Do you think it will actually work?" Vickers asked.

"I believe it will." There was no way that Jimmy would let them have access without putting up a fight. Maybe not literally, but she doubted they could just walk up and launch it without his help. "We should get Jimmy onside."

Vickers sighed. "The old man's scared of his damned shadow. You really think he would be up for this? Let one of his precious inventions out into the wild? He's too cautious. Look at you." Vickers jabbed a pointed finger at her. "You're a freaking killing machine and he has you fetching him coffee."

"General, with all due respect, I'm my own woman. I don't like to be manipulated, I—"

Vickers slammed on fist on the desk as he stood. "Dammit girl, you really think I'm trying to manipulate you? I'm trying to ensure we all have a future, even your precious Jimmy goddamned Robertson. What do we need to do get him on-board, or what do you need to get full access to the LEMP?"

"Let me talk with him first. He deserves that much."

"I have a better idea," Vickers said. "I want you to get close to the new girl, Petal. I've seen the way Robertson looks at her. The guy loves her like his own child. Hell, I suppose she is his child. Get her on side. Use her as leverage when convincing him. If that doesn't work, I'm taking the damned thing by force."

"Fine, give me a bit of time first."

"You've got about two hours. The satellite is due back around in about four hours, and I want to make sure we've got time to get it setup and ready."

"I best get on with it then," Sasha said.

"I don't mean to be such a hard-ass about this, but it's time we took to the surface. I, and I think everyone in this compound, is sick of hiding. It's now or never."

"What comes after that?" she said. "If this does work, what then?"

"We deploy the androids and wipe the Red Widows out of Darkhan and GeoCity-1 and take the Dome for ourselves."

"The androids? But what about the software?"

Vickers smiled then. "I've had someone work on that. We've tested a few out on the surface. They're good to go, with a bit of fine-tuning. Now, I suggest you work on Petal and Robertson. We could use someone of Petal's experience in the field."

Vickers sat there staring at her, waiting for her to move.

She nodded once and left the room. She exhaled as soon as she closed the door. Her head pounded with tension and anxiety. She hated Vickers for putting her in this position, but she had to give him credit for being proactive. And deep down, she knew he was right. They couldn't keep hiding away, waiting. The time to leave had come.

As she walked down the maze of corridors towards the health unit to speak with Petal, she felt a spring in her step, motivation, excitement. *This was it*. She would finally go above ground, and do what she had trained to do. Her time had come.

Chapter 21

Gerry kept moving, pulling an old rag around his head to hide his optical implant. If the Red Widows by the checkpoint spotted it, they'd have him ground to pieces in no time. He had to pass the checkpoint if he were to get to the tower where 'the man in the box' lived.

The sea of filthy survivors ambled onwards, the fanatics at the checkpoint laughing amongst each other as they drunk hot tea from flasks. Those who starved and were dying of thirst looked on with disgust—but not enough so as to catch their attention and receive a beating.

Just a few more feet and Gerry would pass the checkpoint, and that great spinal bridge. He tried not to stare, to blend in, but he felt like he had a giant target on his head. A red bouncing arrow saying: 'This is your man, get him.'

The laughter stopped as he shuffled close. Had they noticed he wasn't one of the other desperate survivors barely clinging on to life? Had they somehow noticed that he was a little too full around the body? He wanted to look up, be assured, but he gritted his teeth, stared at the ground, and huddled forward.

He let out a breath as he continued onwards and no hand gripped his shoulder, no urgent voice called out to him, but still, something behind him stirred. An animalistic panic broke out amongst the shambling horde. Someone cried out as they fell to the ground.

The guttural language of the fanatics had raised an octave.

Despite himself, Gerry turned to see what had happened, and as he did, he heard gunfire. He caught a muzzle flash from the side of his vision. He traced it up to the side of the tower looking down on the bridge, directly opposite it. It appeared the man in the box had a gun.

The skull and brain matter of a Red Widow sprayed against a bunch of Darkhan survivors. That's when the panic kicked in. Another shot rang out taking down a second fanatic, then a third and a fourth.

Heaving bodies had trapped Gerry, tangled him in a pile of writhing meat. Arms and legs sprawled on the ground, entangling Gerry's progress.

The last remaining checkpoint Widow lifted her shotgun and fired. The contents of the shell ricocheted against the stone of the tower uselessly. A bullet struck the ground by her feet, missing by a couple of centimetres. She dropped her gun and sprinted over the bridge.

She got less than halfway when a single shot through the back of her knee sent her sprawling to the black asphalt surface. She screamed, crawled, and dragged herself forwards when a final shot through her spine made her curl upwards like a dead fish.

That's when Gerry saw it: a green laser.

It danced about the dirty coats and faces like a lightning bug. Gerry traced its trajectory, looked up to the tower. And there, about ten floors up, a familiar face: Liza-Marie, the woman who had accompanied Len and his group of Upsiders and the one who had gone on to recover the vaccines after he'd hacked the security. If she was there, it must mean the node was there, the backbone. Omega! The 'man in the box' must be the AI inside.

"Gerry God Damned Cardle? That you?" A voice called down at him. It *was* her!

He raised his hand and nodded. He wasn't exactly sure if they could be trusted, what with Len being killed back at Cemprom while helping Gerry, but either way, it was good to see a familiar face, even if it was behind a rifle scope and a half-mask.

"Stay where you are, someone's coming down," she said, lifting the rifle and backing away into the darkness of the dead tower.

Despite what she said, Gerry jumped over a struggling pile of bodies, and dashed to the body of the robed-fanatic who carried a shotgun. Already three people fought over her robes and belongings, including the shotgun. He couldn't let that get loose amongst these people. Desperation and firearms never mixed well.

With a quick punch to the chin, Gerry knocked out a frail man who had clutched the weapon. He hated doing it, but it was the quickest way to avoid an issue. And given that all four of the fanatics lay bloodied on the ground, it wouldn't be long before reinforcements arrived.

A Jaguar hovered on the other side of the city. He doubted it'd take more than a few minutes to fly over and coat the roads in bullets or frag grenades.

"Give's it to us, man," A black-toothed woman said, clawing at Gerry's face, while trying to wrestle the weapon from him.

He tried to fend her off gently, persuade her to go, but she kept coming at him. "I'm sorry," Gerry said as he swung the butt of the shotgun against her face knocking her to the ground.

From behind him a shotgun exploded, followed by a scream, and the waves of panic started all over again as people rushed for cover and safety, creating a wall of muscle and bone.

Someone had picked up the loose gun the Widow on the bridge had dropped.

It looked like a couple of older men were fighting over it when it went off. A full-scale riot amongst the homeless broke out.

Before Gerry got stuck in the middle, he yanked himself clear, forcing his way through the melee until he faced the old shot-out glass doors of the tower. Its dark grey stone was pitted and blackened with smoke from decades of fighting. It stood like a beat-up colossus, refusing to die, calcifying with age.

An old steel and wooden barrier stood in the doorframe. Various graffiti from the disparate gangs who probably fought over its control adorned its surface. The barrier rattled and moved to the side. A dark shape appeared in the gap. Gerry switched on his dark-vision.

He saw the half-mask on the man's face and knew he was one of Len's men. An Upsider.

"Quick, before it gets even more out of hand," the shadowy figure said reaching a hand out to Gerry and grabbing him by the arm.

"Thanks," Gerry said, once inside away from the riot.

The foyer lay in darkness. An old escalator had tumbled out of its shaft and lay on the broken tiles like a dead wardrobe. The reception desk had been tipped over, its surface pierced with hundreds of bullet holes.

"We're up on the eleventh," the man said pointing his laser-pistol to the dark concrete steps.

"What's your name?"

"Pietor," he said. "I know what happened to Len. I know that you delivered his software package. You're in no danger from us."

"I hope not," Gerry said. "I really appreciated what Len did and I'm sorry he didn't make it out."

Pietor shrugged. His eyes narrowed slightly and he looked away. He wore a form-fitting black suit and a half-mask that hid the lower half of his face. Gerry remembered their mutated features from when Len had shown him his face, the results of inbreeding and radiation poisoning.

"Is it still safe? The server?"

"Come with me. We probably don't have long before the Red Widows come back in force."

Pietor led Gerry up ten flights of stairs, and it seemed like he had climbed all the way to space by the time they reached the top.

"Elevator's out, huh?" Gerry said about half way to break the tension. Pietor, clearly not a fan of idle humour, shrugged once more and carried on marching up the stairs.

Pietor stopped outside a metal door with 'L' scratched into its surface. He knocked, and a spy-hole opened. A green eye peered out, blinked, and then the door unlocked, creaking on old hinges.

"Gerry Cardle. What the hell are you doing out here?" Liza-Marie said, sitting on an old wooden chair, her back to the window that overlooked the bridge and dried-up river. Her compatriot, Ghanus, prowled to the side of the door, gave Gerry a respectful nod of acknowledgement.

The door locked behind him. Pietor stood sentry with his arms crossed and his laser pistol in hand.

"Fancied a stroll," Gerry said. "How's tricks?"

"Tricks are tricky." Liza-Marie placed her rifle on the floor and walked over to Gerry with her hand out. "Let's get off on the right foot this time," she said.

"Good shooting, by the way." He nodded out the window. "Nice work."

"We were kinda pushed into that. Ideally, we'd have let them be, but we couldn't let them stay there and give our position away."

"Someone did," Gerry said. "A small girl, crippled legs."

Liza-Marie shrugged. "Is that meant to mean something?"

"I don't know, you tell me. She told me she could *hear* me and that the man in the box was up here."

The Upsider's face scrunched. "What does that mean?"

"I'm assuming the server. You have Omega here, right?" Already Gerry could hear the familiar whine of the Jaguar's VTOL rotors. It seemed they had got the message already and weren't wasting any time.

"Yeah, we have it," Liza-Marie said, staring at Gerry as if trying to divine his intentions.

"I'm not here for trouble," he said. "Things have got out of control. We need to secure it."

"That's what we've been doing here."

Gerry shuffled his weight, eager to get moving. "I'm not sure taking out a checkpoint is a good way to remain secure."

"We had little choice," Liza-Marie said, wiping the sweat from her exposed forehead. "You see, Red Widow have been securing all buildings with power, and those in strategic positions without, and with this being fairly securable and overlooking the bridge. It's the reason why we set up here. They thought they'd take it for themselves."

"Given their firepower I don't think that's going to be too difficult for them."

"We were fine until they expanded their control on the city. But we were making plans."

She cocked her head to one side towards a door at the end of the room. The rotten wood, covered with fungus, hung from its hinges like a drunk from a lamp-post.

"What's in there?"

"Come see."

She led the way, held the door open. The darkness beyond invited Gerry inside. He hesitated for a second, felt a tingle on his arms as a wisp of cool air flowed out. Coolant gas.

He stepped forward into the room. Liza-Marie followed, closing the door behind.

It was a regular hotel bedroom, sans furniture. In the middle of the room, humming quietly, sat the server Omega: the man in the box. Two half-masked men sat on wooden chairs either side of it.

Gerry's heart jumped. He quickly sent a text message across his VPN to Malik:

—*I've found the server. Things are about to escalate. Await my instructions. Stay where you are.*

Malik sent back:

—*What the hell's going on? What do you mean?*

— *Give me a few minutes. I'll update you shortly.*

"You know they're looking for this?" Gerry said pointing to the server.

"Everyone is."

"You realise what it is, right?"

"Yeah."

"I mean *really* what it is. Not just the backbone for the Meshwork." He didn't want to say too much in case she didn't know, in fact from the glazed-over expression he knew she didn't realise its significance. That was a good thing, but also a tricky thing. How could he get them onside and give up the server? They'd spent most of their lifetime protecting it as if it were some spiritual oracle. They were on some divine quest like the Templars of old.

"What are you getting at, Gerry?"

"Look, we need to talk about the server, and this whole situation."

"Well? Talk."

"I need the server."

"That's what all this is gonna come down to ain't it?" Liza-Marie said, leaning nonchalantly up against the filthy and paper-torn wall.

"What do you mean?" Gerry asked.

"You want the server, we want to keep it safe. Red Widows are crawling all over the place. Are you a friend or enemy in this scenario?"

"There's, what? Four of you?" Gerry said.

When Liza-Marie didn't respond, he knew the truth of it. "You can't last against the Red Widows. You think you can get the server out of here without someone noticing? You hear that Jaguar getting closer? This place is going to be rubble in no time. You want to be buried under the stone and debris protecting a server you have no use for?"

"What are you suggesting, Gerry?"

He knew he had the upper hand. She hadn't the same leadership skills as Len. She was out of her depth in these circumstances.

"We could use someone like you and your boys," Gerry said, putting an emphasis on 'we'.

Hey eyebrows rose at that. It indicated a number of people on Gerry's side, and for the purposes of the discussion, it could be any number as big as she could imagine.

"We, huh? Who are we talking about here? Some

a-holes from The Family?"

"Absolutely not. Look, I can help you and your boys out of this mess. I can help you keep the server safe. Come with me, join with us, and fulfil the legacy Len left."

Liza-Marie pushed herself away from the wall, came close to Gerry, and for a moment he thought he might have invoked the guilt too soon.

"How did he die?" she finally said after a long, lingering pause. Her eyes were softer now. Her whole body language had collapsed in on itself. Even the two men guarding the server had turned to look at him, all desperate to hear about their leader, their father, protector.

"Valiantly," Gerry said. "Without Len, the Dome would have fallen and hundreds of thousands of innocent people would have died. Without him, I would have died." And, secretly hating himself for the manipulation added, "And before he died, I promised I'd look out for you. I'd protect the server. That's why I'm here. To carry out his wishes."

Even he wanted to choke on his bullshit, but with the sound of the Jaguar getting closer, he had to appeal to them quickly. He'd atone for his lies another day. All that mattered was securing the server and getting these people out of the tower before it was levelled.

"He really asked you to do that?" she said, now standing so close to him he could feel her breath through the cloth mask.

"I swear it. What can I do to gain your trust?"

"Tell me the damned truth."

Gerry sighed, "Look, I have transportation less than a kilometre away from here. If you come with me, we can get out of this godforsaken city. I have food, water, and safety."

"Why are you so desperate to get the server?" Liza-Marie said, her eyes now scanning his, trying to prognosticate meaning from his face.

"I need the Meshwork back on. Red Widow have taken GeoCity-1 and are working their way across the abandoned lands killing anyone who isn't pure of technology. I want to save lives, and for that we need to keep the server away from them, and get the Meshwork back up so we can communicate with the various towns that are cut off. We can't let them all die."

She sighed and then went tense. She walked past him and peered out of a gap in the window boards. "They're already here."

Gerry followed, peered out. Down below, dozens of fanatics stormed across the bridge, and above them, two Jaguars dropped down out of the clouds barely a hundred metres away. The barrels of their machines gun were already spinning.

"Come with me. It's time people like us banded together. One thing the Red Widows have taught me is that united we stand a chance of survival. You don't want to die up in this old dead tower like some crazy martyr."

Liza-Marie strode away from the window, approached the two guards either side of the server, and whispered something to them.

All three turned to look at Gerry.

"You get us out of here alive, and then we'll consider joining you."

"It's a deal," Gerry said before crashing to the floor in a heap at the force of the first shell that struck the tower.

The wooden boards on the windows splintered and flew into the room.

Dust and debris littered the place, obscuring his vision.

A further explosion came, rocking the building from its foundations, sending up reverberations that made the whole place sway as if on a fault-line. Gerry crawled to his feet, staggered to the side of the destroyed window, and peered out. There hovering, no more than twenty metres away, the familiar shape of a Jaguar, its guns aimed on the now great open wound of the tower.

Everything seemed to slow down as the bullets started to fly.

Chapter 22

Petal stepped up to the pods, inspected the human figures floating in the cloudy yellow liquid. Their heads hung down on their chests. Their limbs floated idly by their sides. She tapped the glass, expecting them to open their eyes and look at her, but nothing stirred. They did look like her, and Sasha, but seemed slightly less evolved.

"Old models," Robertson said, standing beside her. "They weren't entirely successful. But with each iteration I got closer."

"Did they suffer?" Petal asked feeling strangely connected to these failed corpses.

"No, they didn't feel anything. Number Two was your direct forebear." He pointed to the pod on the right. This one had short chrome spikes coming out of her forearms, just like Petal's.

"Are they really human? Android?" She didn't look away, fascinated, mesmerised by her prototype.

"They're one hundred-percent human, just as you and Sasha are. However, one thing you all have in common is your extra abilities. I'm afraid, with these first two, it didn't quite work out so well."

She didn't really want to know, but felt compelled to

ask. "What happened to them?"

He took a deep breath. She could see the pain in his eyes as they stared off into the past. A lifetime of regret and grief seem to wash over his face then. "I failed them," he finally said.

He turned his back, walked to the computer station. "The additions and upgrades I added didn't integrate well with their subconscious. They unfortunately lost a lot of what it meant to be human. They were killers, indiscriminate killers."

"I'm a killer, too." Petal said, thinking of all the fights she'd been involved in over the years, the numbers of people she'd had to kill, and how deep down she enjoyed some aspect of it. How much of it was she and how much of it was Robertson's doing she couldn't know. "Did you make us like this for a reason?"

"I had to," he said.

"We were just tools to be used then?"

He suddenly spun round, flapping his lab coat wide. "Absolutely not. You were all children to me. I regret what happened to the first two, but you and Sasha have proven—"

"Proven what? That you could create efficient killers? Killers with a conscience?"

"No, that's not it at all. You have to understand we were at war. We didn't know if we would survive. We still don't. We're trapped here underground, while The Family rule over the planet. We had to defend ourselves, carve out a future."

"Then what happened to me? You sent me out there to do what exactly? Why can't I remember anything before five years ago? Before I was found in the desert on the verge of death? Why didn't you come and get me?"

Tears welled up in her eyes as she poured it all out, letting go of years of anger and confusion.

Robertson stepped close, held out his arms, his eyes shiny with tears. "I'm sorry. I have no excuse. I'm a weak man. I thought you had died. I thought I had lost you. A day hasn't gone by where I—"

"Screw you!" Petal said, shoving him in the chest, pushing him away. "You could have come and looked for me, but you left me out there on my own to die!"

"No, that's not how it was, please."

He slumped his shoulders, ran his hands through his hair, face red with frustration.

Petal grabbed him by the jacket, moved her face close to his.

"Tell me what I am, who I am!"

Robertson turned away and closed his eyes. "You're my daughter. A clone of my daughter."

***

It took a few minutes to sink in, formulate in her mind. She always knew she wasn't like others, but a clone? What did that actually mean for her? She thought she was still her own person, but the fact she was actually a copy of someone else, did that matter? She obviously suspected after seeing Sasha, but having it confirmed made it an entirely different situation.

"This is messed up," Petal finally said.

Robertson leaned up against the wall, his face tired. "What happened to her? Your daughter?"

Robertson grimaced, inhaled, and waited. "She was killed."

"Can I ask how?"

He let out his breath in a long pain-laden exhale "You're going to have to know all this sooner rather than later, and it will go some length to explaining why I did what I did with you and the others, and Sasha."

"She's a clone too then, I take it?" It was obvious now.

"Yes. She's slightly different, however, but you both come from the same source."

"And those? What happened to them?" Petal pointed to the naked bodies floating in the tubes. Four pipes attached to their necks spiralled off into the gloomy solution, presumably to some computer system. They were bald with orange-coloured skin. They resembled mosquitoes trapped inside amber.

"They were the precursors. Prototypes, if you will, they—" Robertson walked up to them, cocked his face, and peered at them with an expression of pity and sadness.

"Are they dead?"

He shook his head. "No. Not quite. They're in a kind of stasis. I couldn't bring myself to end them. I could perhaps in the future still find a way." He turned to her, his face focused and steeled. "Okay, look, I'm going to tell you everything right from the beginning, and after that we have something to do, but I want to know I can count on you."

"Well, that kinda depends on what you're gonna tell

me, don't it, Doc?"

"Fine, here we are then, the truth of it all."

They both sat at the bench by the computer station. Petal waited.

At first he hesitated. Petal fidgeted, wanted him to get on with it, but like an animal she didn't want to spook him, so she resisted the urge, waited patiently for him to start. And when he did, he barely stopped as he let the words flow.

"Right," he said. "It all started way before the war and the Cataclysm. It started with my grandfather Elliot Robertson. In the early 2000s when Elliot was a young man in his thirties, he was, at the time, the leading AI specialist in Britain. Just before he had my father in 2013, Elliot bought a pair of radically advanced computer systems from a Japanese company called Old Grey Network Systems. With those he—"

"Wait, what? Old Grey? I know that. There was this server in GeoCity-1. I—"

Robertson broke from his soft-focus to concentrate on Petal. "You found it?"

"Well, I used it. I don't know if it's still there, but what's that got to do with your grandfather?"

"We'll get to that." Robertson adjusted himself on the bench and started his tale again.

"At the time before WWIII really kicked off, there was an arms race in the field of artificial intelligence systems. The British were the leading exponents of it and Elliot the leader of most of the usable technologies that came out of a hotbed of research.

"That's when Criborg came in. Elliot wanted to go

further, but the British being the conservative kind refused to fund his research. He wasn't just happy at developing artificial intelligences, he wanted to create human intelligence within computer systems, or more specifically he wanted to upload a human consciousness.

"The Brits were having none of it, so he splintered off, created an international and independent company. The USA owned Wake Island, having used it in various past wars. Along with a core of British and Canadian scientists, he set up Criborg within Wake Island's labs."

Petal focused on Robertson with the attention of a cat stalking a mouse. This was incredible information and she tried to remember everything. Robertson stopped, took a breath.

"Go on," she urged.

"The Family at the time weren't the problem they are now. They were mostly an environmental tech company, and to their credit their technologies and infrastructure greatly reduced global warming. But when the war happened they found themselves in a difficult situation: their tech had become irrelevant as the world descended into chaos. But they were still the biggest company on and off the planet.

"At the same time, Elliot's research led him to a position where he believed that it was possible to upload his brain to those servers. You have to understand that things were getting desperate by that stage. Criborg were a small company within a military compound, so there was some over-bleed of motivations. Elliot found himself working more and more on military applications for his tech. That's when the accident happened and set all this in motion."

Robertson stood, took a breath, stretched his legs. He turned and continued.

"He managed it," he said.

"What? He uploaded his brain?"

Robertson nodded. "The very first one to do it, and as far as I know the last."

"What happened?" Petal asked, eager to know what happened to Robertson's grandfather.

"It worked, and the Cataclysm happened. Once he became, I don't know what the term is really, but once he became a computer entity, his mind cracked, went mad, but he was inside the world's networks by then. He effectively took over The Family, turning them from an environmental company to a transhuman company. You see; he couldn't replicate what happened to him. Not successfully.

"The servers were decoupled after the Cataclysm and taken to various parts of the land. Elliot, now in binary format, existed within The Family's servers. With their scientists, they setup their transhuman program and started their experiments, including the building of the Dome, which is essentially a giant lab."

"This is all so much," Petal said. "You're saying that you, and I, are related to the one who instigated the Cataclysm? That's really messed up."

"That's not the end of the story," Robertson said. "Elliot went insane as a binary being, and the board members of The Family, rich off his technology and insight, found it difficult to control him. So they tried to suspend him, keep him firewalled, which they achieved for a while, but not having that genius level intellect on tap they began to slow down the pace of their technological advances.

"They referred to Elliot as the Patriarch. A group of ambitious scientists within The Family decided that since he was essentially a digital life form, they'd make a copy for their own use. They thought they could re-engineer this copy, and so they called it the Matriarch.

"Much like Elliot, this entity wasn't what they expected. It refused to do what they wanted and released Elliot from his digital prison.

"The last I heard, the Matriarch had been debugged and is now in use up in their space station, while Elliot is out there somewhere."

"Where?" Petal asked.

Robertson shrugged. "Who knows? He could be in a network, a server, anywhere. All we know is that he's incredibly dangerous and not a little deranged. It's why I made you and the others. To seek him and the servers out, keep them away from harm, and if possible recover them back here at Criborg so I can study them, reverse engineer them. Find a way of ending Elliot for good."

"So that's why I can hold AIs within me?"

"Yes. You were designed to be a temporary prison so that you could hold Elliot's consciousness inside until you could get to the Old Grey servers."

"So then what happened? I remember being in a desert, but nothing before that."

Robertson swallowed. "That's when I lost you."

"Lost me how?"

"You had a lead on Elliot. You were en-route when you came across a resistance group. One of The Family's experiments went wrong, set up on his own: a brilliant hacker. A descendent of one The Family's earlier posthuman projects—"

"Seca," Petal said clutching her hands. "That must have been him!"

"We never knew his name," Robertson said. "We lost you before you could deliver a report. We were in full communication when you came across a bunker, the location of this hacker. You said you had found Elliot and were preparing the download, but something went wrong, and I lost contact. I couldn't find you anywhere. Not even the Meshwork. Our VPN was fried. It was like you stopped existing. I thought—"

"You thought Elliot or Seca had killed me?"

Robertson dropped his chin. "Yes. I wanted to come and find you but we didn't have the resources. The Family didn't know we were still here, and I couldn't afford to blow our cover. But I wanted to." He stepped forward, held out his arms to grip by the shoulders.

She wanted to push him away, but she could see the guilt and sincerity in his eyes.

"I understand," she finally said, not entirely believing it. His story sounded reasonable, and yet, if she really meant that much to him, he would have found a way.

"That's why I created Sasha, you know?"

"What do you mean?"

"Whereas you were always the computer type, she was the martial type. I couldn't live with the guilt or the knowledge of what might have happened to you, so I trained Sasha to come and find you, but—"

"You couldn't bring yourself to lose another daughter?"

Tears dripped from his eyes, slid over his cheeks, splashed on the tiled floor. He shook his head before turning away to regard the tubes with the bodies floating inside.

"I'm so sorry. I was impotent with grief. Trapped in this damned compound, with hundreds of lives at risk, and with the General breathing down my neck. Sasha was the only thing that kept me sane. For a while she helped me forget my first daughter, and what happened to you. She was the only connection I had to you, I just couldn't."

Petal felt her own tears stream from her face now. All thoughts of anger had subsided at the sight of this giant of a man breakdown in front of her. She tried to put herself in his position and immediately felt the waves of loneliness and grief that he must have faced.

She stepped forward beside him, placed her hand on his arm.

"It's okay," she said in a whisper, her throat tight. "I'm back now. I survived."

Robertson turned to her, and with a heavy sob, pulled her into his arms, hugging her tight, while his body racked with relief, and a million other emotions.

"I'm so sorry," he said as he finally released her from his bear hug.

"We're all sorry," she said. "What matters now is what's next? As you said, we can't stay hidden forever, and what with being spotted by The Family's drones while out there in the sub, it probably won't be long before we're discovered. And I have a friend I need to find."

"You're incredible," Robertson said after wiping his face with the sleeve of his lab coat. "Even after all this, you're still wanting to fight."

"It's what you created me for, right?"

"Amongst other things, yes, I suppose so."

"Well then, Doc, you need to fix my implants, then tell me what kind of weapons we have at our disposal."

"I can do that. Come with me," Robertson said, striding towards the door.

Petal followed, and within a few minutes they raced back to her medical room, with Robertson enthusiastically spewing technical details about her DNA, what she could do, and a whole bunch of inventions he had that he needed help with.

When they arrived back, Petal saw Sasha sitting on her bed. She jumped when Petal opened the door.

"Oh, hey. Just the people I've come to see," Sasha said, her smile stretching across her face. "We have a problem."

Chapter 23

From the Jaguar came a burst of machine-gun fire. Each shell crashed into the tower, transmuting stone and concrete to dust, creating a matrix of holes in the back wall of the room.

From his slumped position in the corner, Gerry watched as a number of shells ricocheted off the obsidian-coloured server with a spark of blue light. A scream peeled out over the cacophony of those terrible guns. One of the half-masked men fell to the floor clutching his knee, below which a pulpy red and pink bone-shattered shin hung from tendons.

Liza-Marie roared in fury from her position behind the server. She reached down to her fallen compatriot, took his laser pistol and in a display of unthinking rage, stood up amidst the barrage, and fired two shots before ducking for cover.

The enemy aircraft pitched to the right in a sudden movement, bringing it into Gerry's full field of vision. Two small holes punctured the blood-spattered windshield. The Jaguar continued to pitch to the right, the guns spewing a stream of shells up the tower and in a wide, dipping arc. And then it fell. Fanatics and Dark-han citizens alike ran from its trajectory like panicked ants as it headed for them.

Gerry stood, moved closer to the window, watched as the rotors hit the ground first, splintering and firing off at all angles. The shrapnel caught a number of Red Widow members, sending them sprawling to the ground, holding various damaged parts of their bodies. Small pools of blood spotted the landscape.

The Jaguar smashed into the ground roof-first with a terrible crash and the sound of rending metal. For a few seconds it spun round on what was left of the VTOL rotors: the tail first sweeping into a group of panicked people and then crashing against the tower and splitting into two.

The dozens of Red Widow fighters on the bridge stopped and looked on at the carnage, as one surged forward, screaming and yelling with hate and fury.

"Now that was a great shot," Gerry said looking back at Liza-Marie who now stood from behind the server. He couldn't gauge her expression behind the mask. She nodded at him, attended to her fallen ally. He no longer moved. Gerry suspected the shock and sudden loss of blood had finished him.

"I'm sorry," he said, not knowing what else to do for her.

She hunched over the body of the man while her other compatriot calmly placed a trolley under the black server, leaned it back lifting it off the floor and wheeled it out of the room. Before he left he looked back at his leader and said. "We have to grieve later. We need to go now."

She closed her eyes, shook her head. "You go on.

Gerry, you go with them. Get 'em out of here. I'll be with you in a short while."

Gerry grabbed her by the shoulder. "You don't have a while, short or not. If you stay here, you'll die too. Now come on."

He pulled her up, ignored her weak slaps and the tears that fell from her eyes, and dragged her from the room as rifle shots peppered the tower.

Pietor, in the other room, leant low on one knee by the window, the riflescope to his eye and fired down at the Widows. With each pop a Widow fell to the ground. It was initially enough to keep them at a distance: not knowing how many snipers were in the building slowed their first charge.

"I'll hold them," Pietor said. "You get to the rear elevator shaft."

A shot from a fanatic whined past Pietor's head and crashed into the wall behind him, making Gerry and Liza-Marie duck. Ghanus, her compatriot with the server, had already wheeled it out into the corridor.

"Come on!" Ghanus shouted, his voice echoing down the tomb-like hallways. Wasting no time, Gerry rushed through the door, urging Liza-Marie along with him. He had to sprint to keep up with Ghanus as the eager Upsider led them towards the rear of the building.

"I thought the elevator was damaged," Gerry called out.

"We rigged something up on the emergency shaft," Liza-Marie finally said, her voice croaking and shaky but regaining some of its energy. Hopefully it meant she would be focused.

While Gerry followed the Upsiders to their escape shaft, he contacted Malik and the others over his VPN, using Mags to translate his thoughts to text.

— *Malik, it's me Gerry. We've got a problem. I need you to get Enna or Gabe to bring the truck to my location right now.*

— *Where are you?* Malik said.

Gerry sent him the location and a visual map of the tower over the VPN.

— *You'll have to come round the back. The bridge is held by the Red Widows. And get everyone armed ready to fight. They're closing in on our location.*

— *Got you, Gerry. Hold tight, we're on the way.*

***

The old elevator shaft, although having no working elevator, still had its cables in place. Using a rope sling as a pulley, they lowered the server and descended to the ground floor of the tower. Gerry had to use his night-vision upgrades to help navigate their way to the escape doors that led out to the street that ran parallel to the bridge.

He scanned the area, couldn't pick up any IP or radio traffic. And yet as they approached the rear doors he couldn't quite get rid of the image of an army of fanatical fighters waiting on the other side.

"After three," Gerry said. "I'll open the doors and we keep to the sides. Just in case."

Liza-Marie and Ghanus nodded, their half-masks shaking. They moved into the shadows, waited. Gerry approached the old, rusted metal doors. For a moment he wondered if they'd even open. Had the hinges rusted so badly as to fuse the hinge and pins together?

He pushed down on the safety bar, felt a satisfying clunk from the mechanism. With his breath held, and his senses alert, Gerry pushed the door open a crack, felt the cool air waft in. He peered through the gap; saw nothing but a bundle of trash and old paper piled up in a narrow alley. A number of small, flat-roofed warehouses, empty, and half collapsed stood on the other side of the alley

Nothing stirred beyond: no high-pitched, hysterical voice of a Red Widow called out, just the background noise of the shooting from the other side of the tower. The concrete and stone structure buffered the sound, making it appear as if it came from somewhere far off.

As he pushed the door further open it jammed against something. Gerry slipped through the gap, assessed both sides. A few bedraggled Darkhans ran down the alley, trying to get clear of the war zone, but no one else followed. On the ground, and in front of the door, was the source of the blockage: a round pile of rags, covered in old paper, cardboard, and bits of wood. It yelped when Gerry tried to clear it away.

"Ow!" it said pushing Gerry away. The old papers and rags fell to the ground. A dirty, but familiar, face looked up at him. The girl on the wheeled board!

"Hey, it's you," he said, unable to think of anything more erudite. "What are you doing here? Are you following me?"

"No," she said. "I just listen. I heard the man in

the box when you found him." She smiled, a satisfied 'I told you' kind of smile. Her gaunt cheeks dimpled, and despite her condition her eyes shone bright, as if lit from some inner force.

"Who are you?" Gerry asked. "What are you?"

"I'm Jess," she said. "I'm just me."

"Huh. Well, that's not very clear. How do you hear these things? What is it that you hear?"

She shrugged, gave him another wide grin. "Dunno, just do. I used to hear much more. It's much more quiet now."

He realised she meant the Meshwork. She must have some kind of inner receiver that picks up on data. "You're a strange one, aren't you? Listen, you shouldn't stay here. Do you have any parents or guardians?"

She dropped her chin, shook her head. "No one. Mom and Dad died."

"Well, we can't stand around, we're under attack. Do you have anywhere safe to go?"

She shrugged, moved herself out the way of the door.

Worried about the Red Widows catching them, Gerry pulled the door open. From behind him stepped Liza-Marie and Ghanus. Gerry received a message from Malik.

— *On route, Gerry. ETA: two minutes. The place is crawling with Red Widows. They've got a whole army in this place, all on the bridge side. You better be ready to jump in and go, otherwise we're gonna get caught in the middle of it all.*

— *We're in the access alley behind the tower. Be quick!*

Gerry didn't want to stand out in the open like this,

all it would take would be a single Red Widow fighter to spot them and call it in. The fact they were storming the front, probably meant they were already on their way around to secure the street. Pietor would have to hold them off for a little while longer. Even as he thought that, he heard the familiar whine of a UAV drone coming from behind the tower.

"Back inside, now," Gerry ordered.

He grabbed the girl and pulled her into the darkness of the tower.

"Let me go!" the girl said, batting against Gerry as he dragged her in and pulled the doors close behind him. He could hear the rifle shots getting louder now. He thought of Pietor stuck up on the floor, taking out the fanatics one at a time. It'd be like throwing pebbles at the tide in order to hold it back. Gerry moved the girl beside the doors. "Be real quiet, you understand?" he said to Jess.

She understood, instantly closed her mouth, and sunk onto her board.

Gerry turned to Liza-Marie standing on the other side of the door with Ghanus. Both of them stood with their backs to the wall and laser pistols trained on the open elevator shaft.

"Transport will be here in a minute," he whispered.

"That's if we last that long," Liza-Marie replied with a breathy, tense tone.

The clanging of metal cables echoed down the shaft. Someone was coming down. "You be very still and quiet," he said to the girl, who nodded, her eyes wide and wet. She stunk like rotting vegetables. If she didn't give them away by speaking she'd probably do it with the stench.

Gerry took the shotgun from his back, checked the ammo: three shots left. Using his stealth protocol, he dashed from the doors to stand with his back against the wall by the left-hand side of the open elevator shaft.

The noises increased in volume. Someone was definitely coming down. *It must be Pietor,* he thought as he gripped the cold graphene-steel of the shotgun ever tighter. He spotted a pair of black boots wrapped around the steel cables. As the person descended Gerry tried to remember if that's what Pietor wore. *It must be, he was all in black. Even the trousers were black.*

Gerry loosened the grip on the gun and breathed out. He was being paranoid. Of course it was Pietor. He turned his head to the others to indicate to them that it was their compatriot when he heard the thump on the ground. He turned to see if he was okay. Gerry's eyes grew wide as he looked into the surprised face of a Red Widow fighter. For a long second they both stared at each other, paralysed and startled. But Gerry's mind worked faster. How could he have been so lax?

Before the woman could react, Gerry shifted the weight on to his left foot, swung his right hip round as he lifted the butt of the gun in front of him. He connected with her chin. The force of the blow sent her crashing back into the shaft. She collapsed, unconscious before she even hit the ground. Her shotgun clattered to her side.

Gerry quickly grabbed it and strapped it to his back with the other gun. He lent beside her, noticed a communication bud within her ear. He took it out and stamped on it so the signal couldn't give away her location.

Liza-Marie rushed over and inspected the Widow. Her robes were covered in blood, but not her own. Liza-Marie looked up at Gerry with the realisation that Pietor was probably no more. Gerry looked away, unable to hold her gaze. They couldn't go back now. He fought back a tremble in his hand as the anger started to flow through his body, fuelled by the adrenaline.

Liza-Marie took the laser-pistol from her belt and aimed at the woman. Gerry stopped her.

"No," he said. "We need to keep quiet. There could be more of them up there. And when they don't hear back from this one, they'll know something's happened."

"What do you suggest then?"

"Tie her up, hide her out of the way."

"Just kill the bitch," Liza-Marie said.

Gerry shook his head, placed his hand on her shoulder. "No, we're not doing that."

"Whose side you on?"

"Mine," Gerry said. "And if you want to get yourselves and the server out of here alive, you'll be with me." A message from Malik came through.

— *Where are you? We've turned into the alley. I think a UAV has seen us. We need to go before they realise we're not one of them.*

— *See that pile of wood and paper? We're in the tower by that. We're coming out now.*

Before Liza-Marie could say anything else, Gerry grabbed her by the arm. "They're here. It's time to leave."

"But Pietor!"

Gerry couldn't say anything. It was too much of a risk to go back now. Liza-Marie knew it too. She moved towards the rear doors, hesitated for a second, and then moved on.

When Gerry opened the door a crack he saw the Red Widow truck, driven by Enna, approach the building. He flagged them down. They drove forward so that the back of the truck, now open, aligned with their exit.

"Come on, we're leaving right now," Gerry said to Ghanus and the others.

Within a few seconds they had lifted the server into the back of the truck. Addressing Malik, Gabe, and the others in the truck, Gerry pointed to the two Upsiders, "They're coming with us."

"Good to have ya aboard," Gabe said, flashing them a smile.

Gerry jumped into the back of the truck and was about to close the doors and tell Enna to get them out of there when he looked out and saw the girl kneeling on her board in the tower's doorway.

She bit on a loose bit of rag wrapped around her tiny hands, he eyes wide as if she were staring at her first hot meal. The truck was already so cramped what with the two servers inside, but the way she stood there, so young and innocent. No place to go.

Enna started to move the truck forward.

"Stop!" Gerry said.

"Dude, that drone's probably seen everything. We ain't got time. We gotta get gone, man," Gabe said.

A shadow grew large behind the girl, and in the

gloom, Gerry saw a pair of hands reach out for her. He jumped out of the moving truck, landing in a crouch. A pair of hands clasped around the girl's face and pulled her into the building.

Gerry dashed forward, got a foot in the way before the doors closed completely.

The Red Widow fanatic had come around and dragged the girl back into the building. She held a knife at Jess's throat. "Back off, or girl dies."

The girl's eyes were like dinner plates, and she shook in the Widow's grasp.

Gerry took a step forward.

"Uh, uh!" The Widow grinned a filthy smile, exposing rotten teeth behind the unkempt black hair that draped in front of her face. A thin line of blood beneath the blade contrasted against Jess's pale white skin. Tears streaked down her face as she closed her eyes against the pain, and the pressure of the blade against her throat.

"What do you want?" Gerry asked.

"Give me server, or girl dies."

A quiet squeak came from Jess's mouth before the fanatic clasped a filthy hand around her face to quieten her. Jess bucked under the pressure but the Widow held her firm, blade embedded into the skin on her throat. Gerry shook his head. He couldn't afford to waste this time. The shotgun wasn't accurate enough to take her out without severely harming the poor girl, and calling for backup wouldn't help matters either.

Before Gerry could act, Jess bit down on the hand covering her mouth, making the Widow yelp and instinctively pull her hand away.

"Shoot!" Jess said, imploring Gerry, but he couldn't do it. She was too young, too innocent. He couldn't have her death on his conscience.

When he didn't act, she squirmed in the fanatic's grip. The girl slipped sideways, the blade slicing across her skin creating a striking red welt, but the cut was only on the surface, and as she spun clear she pulled down hard on the Red Widow's robe, unbalancing her, and toppling her over the board on which the girl was sat.

The fanatic crashed to the floor in a heap, dropping the knife as she fell.

Gerry rushed forward. He grabbed the girl, and pushed out towards the door before turning around and kicking the Red Widow hard in the back, making her scream and writhe in pain. Gerry led Jess to the truck, lifted her up, and passed her to the others waiting to bring her in. He went back and brought her board, handing that over too. "Make room. We've got another passenger," Gerry said to the others. "Everyone say hi to Jess. Could someone please treat her wound? She's cut on the neck."

Wasting no time, he closed the rear doors and returned to the fanatic. "What happened to the man on the eleventh floor?" Gerry asked.

The sick grin on her face told him everything. It was obvious now that he knew the blood on her robes belonged to Pietor.

"He begged. I made it quick." The woman spat at Gerry's feet as she sneered up at him. "You will all die."

Gerry raised the shotgun and aimed it at her head, but she just laughed and lay back as calmly as anything. A wave of serenity came over her. Her lips moved in a silent mantra, no doubt praising her god, or whatever they worshipped. Gerry placed his finger on the trigger. He could feel the pulse in his finger throb rhythmically against the cold steel of the shotgun's trigger.

The Widow looked up at Gerry, smiled sickly. "Do it then."

"We're not all like you," Gerry said as he brought the butt of the shotgun down against the woman's head knocking her unconscious. He ran back to the truck and jumped into the front with Enna and Gabe. "Let's get the hell out of here."

Enna slammed the throttle and sent the truck speeding down the alley. At the end she turned left, headed out to an expanse of wasteland beyond which laid another dried riverbed.

Liza-Marie spoke from the back of the truck. "Follow the river for ten kilometres until we reach the beginning of the Sludge. From there I can direct you to our old place. We can regroup there."

"Where is that?"

"It's an old town. Used to be a tourist place with museums and stuff to honour the old Mongolian way of life. But it got trashed during the war, looted. Nothing left. No history there anymore. Just a bunker with some provisions."

"It'll do though," Gerry said.

As they sped down the dried-up river, Gerry noticed that on the other side, opposite the city centre was a field of fanatics standing in formation under floodlights. A series of warehouses looked to hold a number of transporter trucks, yet more Jaguars, and their ATVs.

"That's more than a bunch of rag-tag mentalists," Gerry said. "It's an army. Why didn't you tell us this, Gabe? I thought you were well undercover with this lot?"

Gabe shook his head, "I thought I was. I didn't know they had that many over this side. Most of their forces were still somewhere back in Russia. Man, they must have been prepping this for years."

"Whatever the situation is, we need to get out, head for safety, and fast."

Enna floored the accelerator, speeding the truck down the smooth surface of the dried river. All the while Gerry kept checking behind him, making sure they weren't being followed.

Chapter 24

Sasha couldn't believe what Jimmy was saying. "You agree with Vickers?" She repeated again, making sure she wasn't dreaming.

Robertson nodded slowly. "Yes. I agree. It's time to test the LEMP. You and Petal have shown me recently that we need to start using some of the tools at our disposal. She explained what happened in the sub, and together we're going to work on this. It was wrong of me to be so cautious, but given how I've felt about things, I'm sure you can understand why I was reluctant."

Petal had filled Sasha in on her conversation with Robertson. All three agreed now was the time for action, to fight back. Both Vickers and Robertson had read the information on Petal's slate regarding the Red Widows, including Gabe and Enna's infiltration, and learned of the Red Widows intentions.

"We can't allow them to take too much land and resources," Robertson said. "If there's going to be a war, we need to make sure we aren't left out in the cold and cut off. It's time for Criborg to stretch its muscles. It's time we took our place on the surface."

"That's the spirit," Sasha said, leaping up from the bed and hugging Robertson. "I was so scared about all this. I kinda agreed with Vickers, but I didn't want to have to—"

"It's fine," Robertson said. "It's about time we all pulled together in the right direction. Now, can you do me a favour?"

"Sure, what's that?" Sasha asked.

"Go to the lab and boot up the computers. I'll speak with Vickers and arrange a meeting. But first I need to help Petal with something."

Before he could say anything else, Sasha patted him on the shoulder, flashed Petal a smile, and ran from the room.

"She's an enthusiastic one," Petal said.

"It's partly her programming. It's a trait that benefits a combat persona."

"Is it not environmental also?" Petal asked.

"What do you mean?"

"Our personalities? How much is programmed, and how much is a product of our environment?"

"I'd say fifty-fifty. You're closer to how my daughter was than Sasha, but your lives were similar, in some ways. Just because you share the same DNA as her, doesn't mean you're the same person. You are your own real person. You're as unique as anyone else."

"What happened to her?" Petal asked. "Your real daughter?"

"You are my real daughter."

"Okay, I mean your first, the original."

Robertson took a deep breath in, "Can we cover that another time? I'm an emotional wreck at the moment, and I'm not sure I can go back there yet."

"Sure thing, Da—" She turned from him then, realising she almost called him 'Dad.' But was that necessarily a bad thing? She'd always wanted a family, and here in the space of a few days she found she had a kind of father, and a sister. An unconventional family for sure, but then she'd always considered Gabe family and he wasn't even related to her. Hell, he was another mystery when it came to it, and as for Gerry, all she wanted to do was talk to him right now. Needed him as a calming influence in the middle of all the madness.

She made a point of making that her first task once she got off the damned island. Make contact, find Gerry, and gather all her screwed-up family together in one place. That was a nice thought, but she didn't have too long to dwell on it before Robertson came back in the room carrying a tray with a single needle.

"Erm, what's that?" Petal asked.

"The last procedure to fully connect you with your new chip."

"Will it hurt?"

"No, not at all. It'll speed up the integration. You'll feel a little euphoric for a few minutes, but that's it. Afterwards, you'll be stronger and more capable than ever before."

"That sounds good." She thought back to when they faced Jasper at Cemprom and she felt like she had let Gerry down, and how easily Red Widow had captured her. For a while she'd felt like a shadow of herself. She was looking forward to going back to that kick-ass bitch she was before. All the better if she were heading into battle.

"Stick me, Doc. Let's get this over and done with. I've got someone I need to find, and I'm already sick of these grey corridors."

"That's my girl," Robertson said as he injected the yellow solution into her arm.

Petal bent over at the waist, threw up instantly, splashing a thick black and green liquid to the floor, and catching the corner of Robertson's lab coat. "I'm sorry." She tried to stand upright but fell back on the bed. The room spun and her stomach muscles tightened with cramp.

"It's fine," Robertson said. "I wondered if that might happen. It's the recombine solution ejecting the remaining NanoStems. I'll get you a bucket."

Petal slumped forward on the edge of the bed, trying to hold back the shivers that racked her body as she continued to heave up the thick sludge. But despite it all, she could feel her head lighten, the haze burning away, leaving everything clear behind. Her thoughts sped up, became sharper.

Robertson returned with a bucket and a hand-held vacuum device. He cleaned up the place and sat with Petal until she stopped heaving. "While you were sleeping," Robertson said. "You kept asking for Gerry. Is that your friend who found you in the desert?"

Petal shook her head, wiped the viscous liquid from her lips.

"No. How do I explain Gerry? He's one of the good guys. He saved City Earth from Seca and this crazy AI. It was a mad ride."

For the next thirty minutes while Petal waited for

her stomach to settle she brought Robertson up to speed with her various exploits over the years and ultimately what had happened at Cemprom. She told him about Gabe and Enna and how Gabe had set her free from the Red Widows.

"We need to make contact with them," Robertson said. "If we're going into battle we could use allies, and given what they've done for you, I feel we owe them some backup and support. I'd hate for them to get caught in the middle of all this."

"Knowing them like I do, they're already in the middle and up to their chest in trouble." She laughed, but underneath she worried about them. Wondered if the Red Widows had realised it was Gabe who had set her free. Had his cover been blown? And what of Enna and Gerry?

"Right then, we've got no time to lose. Let's go meet with the others and see if we can't take out that damned satellite," Robertson said.

"I could get to like you." Petal smiled, liking his affirmative attitude. "But know that all my friends kind of end up a bit bloody and mentally damaged."

"Hmm, I think it'll be worth it."

Jimmy Robertson hopped off the bed, led Petal out of the medical room. "Once the satellite is down, we can get our systems online. If there's a network out there, we'll be able to pick it up," Robertson said as they walked down the myriad grey corridors. "Maybe you'll be able to find your friends soon."

"You know the Meshwork is run by one of the servers, right?" Petal said.

"It's how we initially found Elliot, but since we lost contact with you, we've been unable to find our way out of our domain. The satellite doesn't just control the drones. It also dampens data traffic. It's why we have to be careful with what we do."

"Can't you blast it out of orbit with a rocket?" Petal said.

Robertson scrunched his face. "That would indeed be easier, but they have a whole bunch of countermeasures, early-warning systems. And we'd betray our location before the missile could even reach it. And let's face it, if we had that kind of capability, I would have used it myself to blast their station into outer-space."

"But this laser doohickey will work, right?"

"I hope so, but the software isn't quite right. Like the stealth software wasn't right on the sub. But then I saw what you did with the code. It's quite incredible really."

Petal shrugged, blushed a little. "I had some good teachers."

"Let's hope they taught you about EM pulse waves and laser-plasma fields."

"Don't worry Doc. If it's a computer problem, I'm sure we'll fix it."

He gave her arm a little squeeze, increased his pace, clearly eager to get going. He had a lot of time to make up it seemed.

When they arrived at the double glass doors to the LEMP lab, she saw Vickers in his fatigues standing at a metal rail looking down into a deep, wide shaft. Sasha and two other military types were standing next to him on his right. To his left stood a group of five lab-coat-wearing scientists.

As soon as they caught sight of her and Robertson everyone turned to greet them. Vickers marched forward and opened the doors to let them in. His face had softened since Petal had last seen him dragging Sasha away from the sub.

"Are you sure about this, Doc?" Vickers said to Robertson.

"You don't have to worry about me, General. Now let's do this. It's time The Family had something to worry about."

Vickers smiled and clapped him on the shoulder.

"That's more like it, old man."

***

Petal entered the commands into the LEMP's targeting computer as requested by Robertson. She could feel the tension in the air. The silence was heavy with it.

She worked next to Sasha and the Doc. All three, in sync, checked, and double-checked the coding was correct, that the trajectory and firing routines were bug free.

The laser system was actually made from ten small laser generators feeding into a single super-laser generating a beam of over three-hundred-petawatts of power. One direct hit on the satellite should, in theory, knock it out of action. And it'd be so quick, a matter of nano seconds, that it would hit them before they even knew it, bypassing their countermeasures.

"I'm done," Petal said. She ran her code through the

compiler, error-free. "We ought to simulate it, though."

"Agreed. Running a simulation now," Sasha said who remained busy at her holoscreen. Robertson likewise continued to check through the various routines and sub-routines, making sure that the power capacitors were synchronised and regulated to each individual generator.

The device was designed such that a high-powered laser fired from the generator would create a plasma cloud of highly concentrated electromagnetic radiation around The Family's spy and communications satellite. The EM field would overload the various logic boards within the satellite, frying its chips, rendering it useless.

If it worked correctly, it would knock out The Family's capability to observe and monitor the lands and seas around the Dome, and as Petal suspected, would remove the suppression from the Meshwork. She knew that it wasn't an issue of the backbone server being offline. The entire point of that machine was that it never went offline. Therefore, access to the Meshwork had been supressed.

While the others prepared the final pieces of software, Petal examined the stream of data to and from the satellite, using Criborg's snooper system.

An encryption layer secured the data coming from the satellite. It was clever, but she eventually managed to get past it using an algorithm taught to her by Gabe. She realised that all access to the Meshwork was being bypassed and routed to a dumb virtual server running within the satellite itself, creating a kind of feedback loop acting not unlike the way she could hold code and

AIs within herself. And despite the encryption on the stream being relative easy to get past, access to any of the satellite's systems were impenetrable, even for her considerable skills. It wasn't just good programming it was something else entirely. The systems weren't visible. It was as if they were hidden somewhere else entirely, a system within a system.

One of the benefits of taking out the satellite and getting the Meshwork back up was that she should be able to re-establish a connection with Gerry and the others.

She felt light-headed at the thought of speaking with him again. In a few hours, she might be able to communicate with him for the first time since it all went down at Cemprom. Her stomach knotted thinking about it. She didn't really know what to say. She knew her feelings had changed towards him, but was that the same with him too? How much had he changed since being taken away by The Family? For a few seconds she dwelled on a terrible realisation that he might not want anything to do with her, that he might be one of them now. One of The Family.

Vickers paced across the metal grating circling the round graphene-coated laser projection generators. His steps rang out like ticks of a clock.

Petal looked up at him, gave him a glare. He checked himself, stopped pacing. He gripped the metal rail, tuning his knuckles white.

"Dude, chill out," Petal said, trying to ease the man's tension. It was putting everyone else on edge.

"If this doesn't work, we're not going to be in

good shape," he said through a tight mouth, his teeth clenched.

"I thought you were the one eager to get up to the surface?" Petal raised an eyebrow.

"How dare you!"

"Put a cap on it, General, we'll get there." Petal would have normally given a cheeky grin to show that she was messing around, but considering his face was puce and puffed like an inflated plum with his own self-importance, she stared him down.

Robertson interjected before Vickers could launch a tirade. "Can we all please keep our minds on the job at hand?"

"We've got about twenty minutes until the satellite's over us, Doc. You'll excuse for me being a little tense. It's not like we can trust this—"

Now Robertson fumed, his nostrils flaring as he stormed over and squared up to the General. "You will not disparage her, goddamn it. If I say she's to be trusted you take my damned word on it, you understand?"

Petal couldn't but help smirk and feel good inside. She could get used to someone having her back like that.

Vickers pointed at Robertson, his face ready to explode, but the older scientist to his credit refused to be intimidated, stood his ground. Vickers eventually dropped his accusing finger, took a deep breath. "I'm sorry, okay. I'm nervous about this." He turned to Petal. "No offence intended, it's just we don't get many visitors here. It's been a while since we've had to trust an outsider."

"It's okay, General. I understand," she said, trying to keep the peace. She turned away and walked over to Sasha who stood in open-mouthed shock.

"How's it all coming along?" Petal said to her, keeping her voice low.

"Oh, erm, I'm nearly finished. The simulation's fine. No issues so far. The power couplings are good to go. Everything seems ready at this end." Sasha closed down her holoscreen and walked around the metal gantry, leaning against the rails.

Robertson came over, inspected the data on Petal's holoscreen.

"I'm impressed," he said to the both of them. "You fixed the power load-balance algorithm."

Petal curtsied dramatically. "You're welcome."

"The sim ran fine," Sasha said. "We're ready, I think."

Robertson stepped back, regarded the cylinders in the middle of the room. He then looked up through the tunnel that bored up to the surface, his gaze tracing the thick glass tube with the central laser diode running up through the middle of the cylinder.

At the top of the tunnel, a good twenty metres high was a focusing lens that made the charged photons into a narrow and directional beam.

"Let's switch on the power, and see how she runs," Robertson said. He quickly gestured across his holoscreen, and the fusion reactors below the compound came online.

Petal felt a rumble through the metal gantry as the reactor filled the capacitors with power.

Everyone gripped the rail, as if they would be thrown

to the floor, but it was more the tension and anticipation of this weapon finally coming online.

The ten surrounding smaller lasers, housed in ceramic-like cylinders and circling the main laser glowed red. As Robertson routed the power from the capacitors under the gantry, their bright red lights, dimmed by a smoked-glass protection screen, shone into the central laser.

Like a great light bulb filament, the centre of the main laser glowed a dull orange colour.

Although protected behind inches of Plexiglas, Petal's stomach grew tight and knotty with nerves. So much power a few feet away.

"Everything seems fine," Robertson said after a few minutes of checking the levels on his screen. The system seemed to be stable and ticking over nicely. "The power balance is self-regulating efficiently. We're up to two-hundred-fifty-petawatts. We'll be ready in three minutes."

Robertson looked at the General, who in turn stared at his own screen. The military leader nodded, seemed satisfied.

In the middle of the gantry, where everyone gathered, a graphical representation of the satellite's position moved across the space in a holographic three-dimensional display.

"This is so cool," Petal said in a whisper.

"I know, right?" Sasha replied. Both girls stood next to each other, stared into that great destructive tube, waiting for the laser to fire.

"The satellite will be in firing range in T-3 minutes.

Is she ready to go?" Vickers asked.

Everyone looked at Robertson then, all waiting for his go-ahead. He licked his lips, rubbed a slightly trembling hand across his forehead. "I guess this is it then."

He started the countdown. It ticked down on all the screens. The rumbling from the energy source grew stronger and the smaller lasers glowed brighter. The super-laser tube hummed, and everyone stepped back.

"We're at full power," Robertson said.

"I think we should all move out," Vickers said. "Not that I don't trust you, Doc, of course. But just in case."

Robertson agreed. He ushered everyone from the laser chamber. The heavy doors slammed shut behind Vickers. They filled up the corridor outside, gathered around the observation screens. Robertson took his slate, and watched the numbers tick down. Petal could feel her heart beat against her chest.

"Here we go," Robertson said. "Ten, nine, eight, seven."

Petal found herself mouthing the final seconds, as her hands tensed into tight fists, her heart beating in rhythm with the countdown.

"Five, four, three, two, one."

Chapter 25

Petal stalked the corridor, waited for the results of the LEMP attack. Robertson had gone into the lab with Vickers to check the system. They insisted everyone else stay outside, just in case. She swung her leg back and forth, tapping against the corridor's wall. There was a buzz about the Criborg compound. Every person, like her, waited with baited breath.

Sasha came up to Petal. "Hey, how are you doing?"

"Good," Petal said. "I'm feeling much better. I wanted to thank you for bringing me back here. You probably saved my life."

"The least I could do. Do you think it worked?" Sasha said.

Petal shrugged. "The code seemed good. The simulation went through okay, but who knows how these things work in the real world?"

"They're coming back," Sasha said.

Together, they moved out of the way of the door. Vickers and Robertson came out into the corridor, and addressed the crowd awaiting them. Robertson spoke first.

"I can confirm that at 05:15 this morning, the LEMP successfully fired and…"

"And what?" Petal said, unable to bare the tension, wanting desperately for it to have worked so that she could get on the Meshwork, and try to find Gerry. "Did it work or not?"

Robertson brushed dust from his cuffs, said. "I can confirm that the attack was successful. Our systems indicate zero signals from the satellite. It is offline."

A great cheer and a roar went up. Scientists and soldiers alike high-fived and hugged each other. Everyone was smiling. It clearly meant more than taking out a Family satellite. It was the thought of freedom, the realisation that they were free to leave their underground facility. Most of them had been born there, and those not in the armed division or the aquatic research division had never even been outside. Never breathed the air, or felt the sun on their skin.

But Petal didn't cheer as loudly. She politely smiled and shook hands with those who thanked her for the help with the coding, but she knew that many of these people wouldn't live beyond the next few days. They had no idea of the brutality and unforgiving nature of the world. Life had little meaning on the outside. Those who'd feel nothing about it could snuff it out in seconds.

They'd all face a lot more hardship before they could cheer and feel secure again. But despite that, she admired them for their courage and spirit. Even if they couldn't fully understand what they were letting themselves in for.

Vickers hushed the crowd, gave orders. "This is the first part of the plan. It's good to feel jubilant right now, but we're leaving a place we've called home for a number of decades now. The next part is to travel to the mainland, to the city of Darkhan where we're going to face a strong enemy. It'll take courage and discipline to fight for our freedom, and protect others from tyranny. Our time has come, and it's time for us to leave, to fight, and to claim our future. You all know what to do. The transporters are waiting in Hangar Eighteen. Gather your things, and be there by oh-five-forty hours."

He curtly saluted, turned on his heel, and headed down the corridor. The rest of his division returned the salute and followed.

Robertson approached Petal and Sasha, along with his group of six scientist-engineers. "Are you two ready?" He asked. Petal and Sasha nodded. "Then follow me, and we'll get you two settled on the planes. It'll be about a five hour journey, so I'd suggest you get some sleep, rest up."

"Sounds good to me," Petal said as she turned and followed Sasha by her side.

***

As Petal followed Robertson down the corridors, she hung back to chat with Sasha.

"How many are there here? People I mean. The ones leaving?"

"All in all about two hundred and fifty, including scientists and the military personnel, but then there's the androids. There are five thousand of those."

"Christ, how big are your transporter planes? You can't take all of them, surely?"

Sasha laughed. "Of course not. We've got three transporters. Each one takes about three hundred personnel plus weapons, provisions, equipment, etc. We'll only take eight pods of 'droids. About four hundred in all, but still a potent force that can be drop-shipped within minutes."

"Sounds very useful," Petal said. "I'm sure that'd be enough to take Darkhan back. What kind of 'droids are they?"

"Combat models mostly," Sasha said. "Although we were adapting many for tasks such as farming, engineering etc. The plan was to have them ready to work on infrastructure and farming when they went to the surface."

"And is that still the plan?"

Sasha shrugged. "It was until you arrived. I don't mean that in a bad way, I mean, you gave us the intel to know what was going on. Perhaps if the war, if it comes to that, isn't too bad, then we could start to clean up the land, maybe make a new home for ourselves."

Petal didn't want to say that was wishful thinking. So many groups of survivors had had the same idea over the years, but none had made much of a life on the land. Even the Upsiders, one of the more successful groups, still bore the mark of the Cataclysm within their mutations. And the Bachians were more interested in drinking and fighting than making a viable alternative to the Dome.

Sasha led her through yet more corridors until they came to the hangar.

She never thought she'd see something so large and

yet still be underground. The three great transporters sat wing-to wing next to each other. Lines of people passed supplies into the transporters.

The planes looked like old-fashioned commercial aircraft, except they didn't have the huge wingspan or the old, round jet engines. Much like the Jaguars and the ATVs, these, too, sported great VTOL motors within the stub wings that allowed them to take off at all angles, and pivoted at the fuselage, making them act like high-powered rotors when in flight. The surface of the planes was a dull grey colour, but Sasha had informed her that these had an earlier version of Robertson's stealth technology. This older system was an upgraded version of the famous pre-war American company Lockheed's first stealth fighter, the F-117. None of it really mattered to Petal. All she cared about was whether or not it'd get them there safely.

Robertson and Vickers dashed around that great expanse of a hangar, ushering people into lines, making order out of chaos. It felt like some great wild migration. While she and Sasha were standing in a line, waiting to board one of the transporters, she felt her systems finally come online.

At first it was a small buzz in her head. A persistent flow of electricity that flowed throughout her neural network, and then down through her spine and out into every nerve within her body. It wasn't unpleasant, and she found herself smiling as it felt like every cell in her body tingled.

"Are you okay?" Sasha said.

"Yeah, my new chip's finally online. It feels crazy."

Through her new upgraded chip she reached out with her mind to sense the flow of data within Criborg's system. But there was another network, its signals faint, and the flow of data sluggish. She recognised it straight away. She was connected to the Meshwork, its data flow no longer suppressed by the satellite. Via her internal GUI she tracked the data as a slow trickle at first. Obviously the users of the network over the weeks had dropped off, realising it wasn't working. The only data that existed now were networking protocols and a bunch of automated maintenance scripts running on the server. Omega!

At least now Petal knew it was still running.

Sasha chatted on about some inconsequential detail when they finally started to move closer to their designated transporter. At the head of the line stood the twin poles of Criborg: Vickers and Robertson. Working in tandem they checked against their slates, probably a manifest, and directed each individual to the appropriate transporter.

The two transporters on the left received the android pods: square Polymar™ boxes with clear sides, loaded by anti-grav heavy loaders. Within the pods, Petal could make out hundreds of suspended human-like androids, decked out in the grey and orange livery: the colours of Criborg. They looked like real people, or more accurately lots of the same person, and she wondered if Jimmy Robertson had modelled these on another member of his family. Were these mechanical clones of his son, brother, father?

"Are they good?" Petal asked. "Combat wise."

"Hell yeah. We could have used them way before now, but as usual, ol' Jimmy was too conservative. There was a small bug in their software, and a few people got killed once. It was fixed, but he was still too nervous. But I guess in time likes these, even Jimmy has to bite the bullet and have a little faith."

"Wait, they were defective?"

"Kinda, sorta, not really. They're okay now. Like I said, a small software bug, it's been sorted. Vickers, he—"

As if invoking his name had somehow summoned him, he strode across to Petal and Sasha.

"You two are riding with me and the Doc. Move out."

Sasha gave him a sharp salute before dashing ahead of the line to the transporter. Each plane sported a bird logo on the rear stabiliser fin: Falcon, Condor, and Vulture. She, Sasha, and Robertson were in Condor.

"You too," Vickers said pointing his finger at Petal. "Time to move out."

It occurred to her how much he seemed to enjoy pointing at people. Must be some kind of military leader-type bullshit, she thought. Petal gave him the stink eye. "I ain't one of your soldiers, General, so you can stop your damned pointing and address me with a little respect."

He sneered at her, "I don't like your attitude, *girl*."

Before he could turn his back and return to the lines of people, Petal responded. "Have you always been a chauvinistic prick, General? Or do you save it for special occasions?" She said it so loud it seemed the entire population of Criborg turned to watch the argument.

That got him fuming again. She so enjoyed how his face puffed up ready to explode.

He stepped towards her, sucking in his breath, making himself big and dominating. "How dare you!"

Petal dashed to the side and circled him so fast he had barely time to consider what had happened. She extended her chromed spikes and brought them up to his ribs. He stiffened at the touch of those sharp points.

"Just remember who you're talking to, General. I'm not one of your goons to be ordered around like some dumb soldier. And if you disrespect me, or anyone else for that matter, once more, or pull that sexist bullshit, I'll make you a eunuch. You understand me?"

He tensed. Petal could feel the waves of hatred crash against her, but she kept her spikes digging into his ribs, pushing that little bit further. After a few more seconds, with the place quietened to a hush, Vickers almost choked it out like it was something stuck in his throat.

"Okay, I understand."

Petal retracted her spikes.

Vickers spun round, aimed a great meaty fist at her with a wild swing, but Petal was too quick, and stepped forward into his lunge. Taking his weight and momentum she pivoted on her hip and sent him crashing to the ground face first, while gripping his wrist, pulling his arm back, and placing her boot on his back.

"We could play this out all damned day, General. I suggest you swallow your pride, and stop trying to assert yourself like some prized cockerel. We need your strategizing and leadership, not your ego-driven nonsense."

"Okay, Petal. That's enough." Jimmy Robertson said as he dashed across to put his hands on her shoulders. "The General has certain problems, but can we try and keep a lid on all this. We don't have a lot of time if we're to make progress to Darkhan."

"Sure thing, Doc." Petal lifted her boot and casually walked away to the same transporter that Sasha had boarded. She ignored the open-mouthed stares from the General's men and women, and the gleeful smiles of the scientific lot.

Jimmy was right though: she did feel quicker and more capable with her upgrades. It felt good to be active again, to feel alive and alert.

When she climbed up inside the plane, Sasha was sitting in a seat in the middle row of three. She was fiddling with a slate. Petal slumped into the seat next to her.

"You shouldn't antagonise him like that," Sasha said. "He's not such a bad guy. He just has limited social skills."

"The guy's a dick, and his ego will get people killed out there on the surface. You lot don't know what it's like up there. You've all been so sheltered down here, practising your military tactics with computer-generated enemies. You think it'll be the same up there?"

"I guess we'll see," Sasha said. "Look, the Mesh-work's getting busier. It seems the news has got out."

Petal looked at Sasha's slate. A traffic analysis

program counted the gigabytes of data flowing across the network. It wouldn't be long before it was terabytes once those survivors out in the abandoned lands knew it was operational again.

"That's good. This will help us," Petal said, thinking of finally getting back in touch with Gerry, and the others too. She wondered about Gabe and Enna, hoped they were safe.

"Do you have an internal interface, for programming and such like?" Petal asked. She wondered given that she could access the same data and visual representations internally that Sasha was looking at on her slate.

"No. Jimmy never gave me that capability. Mostly combat stuff."

"Gotcha," Petal said. "Makes sense, I suppose."

"We kinda complement each other's skill sets quite nicely, don't ya think?"

"I'd say we do."

While Sasha occupied herself watching the network grow, Petal checked her VPN connection with Gerry. She tried to access her internal router, send out a message, but there was no connection. The VPN tunnel was down, or Gerry was no longer running the server on his side. If he was even still alive.

She ached not knowing what had happened to him or where he might be. Gabe had only said The Family took him. She tried to keep faith that he was still out there, waiting for her.

She closed her eyes and tried to meditate while the boarding continued.

After a few minutes of deep relaxation, Petal felt a nudge on her arm. Sasha.

"Hey, we're ready," Sasha said. "Buckle up."

Robertson sat in the aisle to her right. He looked over. "Are you okay?"

"Yeah, I'm okay. Looking forward to some rest. Is anyone staying behind with the other clones?"

Robertson shook his head. "They're coming with us. I couldn't trust anyone to look after them."

"I thought they were dead?"

"Not dead, in stasis."

"Yeah, that's what I meant."

"I have to bring them with me," Robertson said, a sudden seriousness crossing his face.

She wondered if he had plans of trying to 'fix' them. She didn't know what exactly went wrong with them, or what they did, but sentimentality aside, there was only one reason to keep them in stasis: so that you could bring them out of stasis in the future. Her line of thought broke with the ignition of the engines. The plane shuddered as the props spun up to speed.

"Damn, I can't believe we're finally leaving," Sasha said.

"Don't get too excited," Petal said. "It ain't paradise out there."

The thrust threw Petal back in her chair as the plane took off suddenly and vertically. Up and up they rose, the painted yellow numbers on the grey tunnel blurring past through the small windows either side of the cabin, and then the yellow smudges stopped, to be replaced with darkness.

"We're out," Sasha said. "This is it!"

The transporter, Condor, levelled off, turned westward. The sun peaked above the horizon in the east, bathing the sea in a pinkish gold light.

"What's the ETA, Doc?" Petal said, not knowing how fast these things were.

"As I said, we'll be there in about five hours. If we're not interrupted."

To their side, Petal could see the other two planes: Falcon and Vulture. It felt good to know they had resources, people, and technology. It felt good to be surrounded by decent people. Something she wasn't always sure of before. These were her people, but she felt a great deal of responsibility. It was like she was leading a gang of chicks to their first walk out in the real world.

It was then she realised how weary she was. She just wanted to find Gerry and settle down. Be normal for a while. All this fighting was so tiring.

But where the hell was he? While everyone got settled, she sat back, closed her eyes, and started scanning the Meshwork. She couldn't find him, but then access had only recently become available and chances are he didn't know yet.

Petal created a quick encryption wrapper using a special subclass of Helix++ code. She knew that Gerry, if he were on the network, would recognise it instantly. Inside the wrapper she created a text file with details of what happened to her, where she was and explained that her new implant chip had a different network address. She sent out a self-repeating pattern program that created hundreds of instances of the message. He should eventually see this particular piece of encrypted data and hopefully know immediately whom it was from.

Chapter 26

The truck's lights cut a slice through the early dawn of the abandoned lands. The white OLED beams illuminated the red dust devils as they moved closer to the Sludge: the great expanse of rotten earth. Darkhan and its corpse-towers had melted into the night behind them, and as far as they could tell, no drones or Red Widow vehicles had followed. Clearly they were more concerned with neutralising the threat in the tower.

They had driven for two hours across the barren land, watching the sun come up, feeling the mild cool winds turn warmer, but not yet warm enough to really call it Spring. It'd be a few months before that would happen. The Cataclysm seemed to have shifted the seasons back by a couple of months.

It was like a journey through time, Gerry thought. Seeing the tips of ancient temples poking out of the dust and cracked clay ground, surrounded by the rubble and detritus from towns that once supported an advanced and wealthy population. Areas of farmland sported great craters in place of fields of crops, the remnants of war and cruel reminders of the struggles for the post-Cataclysm survivors to feed themselves.

Liza-Marie leaned forward from the cramped

conditions in the back of the truck. "When you reach the shoreline of the Sludge, follow it north, and after a few kilometres you should spot a pair of half-destroyed stone buildings: beyond that is our sanctuary. We can regroup there. Get some rest, food, whatever."

"Other than the tower block you lot took us to, is this sanctuary of yours safe?" Gerry asked.

"Yes, the block before that old hotel has a single story building. We can access a basement there that we have kitted out."

"Why didn't you take Omega there instead of Darkhan?" Gerry asked.

"We were already near Darkhan. One of our contacts arranged to transport us, but the Widows got to them first."

"Oh, I'm sorry."

Liza-Marie shrugged her shoulders. "Just part of the game these days."

"Well, that's what we're fighting for, and trying to put a stop to it all."

The Upsider leader stared past him and looked out of the windshield of the truck. Gerry knew she didn't believe him. Didn't believe they could make a difference.

"Can you do me a favour?" Gerry asked her.

"What?" Liza-Marie asked.

"Keep an eye on Jess for a while. Make sure she's okay."

She patted Gerry on the shoulder, "Of course." She returned to the back of the truck. The atmosphere could cut wire. This group of people were a disparate bunch: a member of The Family's security, Cheska the transcendent, a couple of Bachians, two Upsiders, and that strange waif of a girl Jess.

What with Kaden and Steven back in the Dome, and now this girl, Gerry felt like some kind of kid magnet. He wondered if it wasn't just his way of making up for the fact that those who he thought were his kids turned out to be just an illusion, a ploy to make him think he lived a normal life. Regardless if they turned out to be nothing but stand-ins, there was a hole there that needed filling, and seeing these kids struggle with life at such an early age was too much for him to ignore. He couldn't protect them all, but neither could he turn a blind eye to those who stood right in front of him.

"Ya gonna talk with The Family?" Gabe said from the seat next to Gerry's, his elbow casually propped against the truck's window.

"I don't want to. But I don't have much choice. I have to at least give them chance to defend the Dome."

"What is it about that damned place, man? Always trying to protect it from one thing or another. What if ya just let it go?"

Gerry thought about it for a minute. He had a good point. His entire life there had been a lie. The Family had used him, and were still trying to use him to bring them Petal

Sure, there were many innocent people within the Dome, but weren't they part of the problem? All the time they refused to question what was going on, happily playing the game that perpetuated the control and infringement on their freedoms. What if he did let the Dome stand on its own? What then?

"It's my home," Gerry finally said. "As screwed-up as it is, I still have hope for it. If I stand by while these fanatics take it down, what then for humanity? An endless struggle for resources against a tyrannical organisation? We have that already with The Family."

"Ah, I get ya. Better the devil ya know, huh?"

Gerry shrugged. "Something like that, I suppose."

"They must have done a real brainwashing job on ya up there on that space station."

"I could say the same thing about you and your special time with a bunch of lunatics."

"Easy boys," Enna said, cutting them off. "Let's focus on securing the servers and then we'll figure out what to do next."

Gabe gave Gerry a smirk and for a short few seconds, Gerry wondered how good it would feel to finally slug him right in the face. Instead, via his AIA and internal display, he cut a video sequence recorded with his eye replacement of Red Widow's forces in Darkhan.

He packaged it up and sent it to Jachz, his liaison with The Family.

Along with the video he appended the message:

Jachz, thought you'd like to see this. A group calling themselves Red Widow have taken Darkhan and are amassing ranks to assault the Dome. I suggest you get to work assembling security and make plans to get everyone safe.

All the time Gerry had stayed up on the space station, he hadn't learned of what their military capability truly contained. He doubted it was much. The Cataclysm wiped out so many resources, and The Family had kept most of their citizens, or lab rats, safely within City Earth doing mundane tasks.

Other than their UAV drones, he wasn't sure exactly how many they had available. He hadn't seen much in the way of military resources beyond their perimeter-stationed NearlyMen who were nothing more than dumb transcendent's and the regular security staff: people like Malik, Bran and the two women who started off this whole adventure with the swift application of a stun-baton.

They couldn't stand up to a full-scale invasion. Malik's crash-and-burn at GeoCity-1 told Gerry all he needed to know about their capability, if not their bravery.

"Hey, there's the two buildings," Enna said, pointing out a pair of squat tumbled-down dwellings resembling nothing more than ruins carved from rock and rusted metal girders. Tall, sparse dried weeds climbed up the stone and concrete, reclaiming it, dragging it back to earth, erasing any evidence that humankind had ever been there.

Liza-Marie leaned forward, directing Enna through the piles of rubble and dead buildings until they came to what looked like a cave entrance amongst a formation of boulders.

"In there,' Liza-Marie said.

"Do you have power in there?" Gerry asked.

"Yeah, some generators. We can use the fuel from the truck."

Enna managed to turn the truck around. She avoided

colliding with the vast boulders that had fell from various skyscrapers and office buildings, and reversed into the hideout.

She switched off the main lights, sending the place into darkness.

"Everyone stay where you are for a second," Gerry said.

He got out and navigated his way around the truck. Behind the vehicle was a steel door with no obvious way of entry.

"Hey, Liz, might need your help here," Gerry said as he opened the rear truck door. The blue glow of Omega washed out, casting a wash of low blue light, enough for Liza to make her way out and approach the door. Within a few minutes, she had opened the door and flicked a switch that kicked in the generators. The place lit up with a string of low-energy bulbs, giving them plenty of light to get everyone into the bunker-like building.

The two precious servers were placed at the rear of the ten-meter-square room. A metal shelving rack was attached to the left wall, upon which boxes of dried food and containers of water were neatly stored.

In the middle of the room was a desk with a damaged holoscreen glowing a dull green. Although Liza assured him it was operational, the various cracks and scratches on its surface made gesturing a difficult operation.

He'd have to use his internal interface instead.

Enna set up a medical corner in the right side of the room. There were blankets that she used for beds, or just to keep the wounded warm while she used a medical kit to bandage, and apply anti-bacterial agents.

Jess huddled into the corner with the grey woollen blanket around her. She still shivered as if the cold of Darkhan had permeated her bones. It'd take a while for her to warm through, he thought. She wore an adhesive Band-Aid around her neck.

After helping Liza-Marie and Ghanus put the servers in place, Malik approached Gerry by the desk.

"What did they say?"

"Not heard back from them yet," Gerry replied.

"Did you tell them about the size of Red Widow's force?"

"Yeah, sent them a video clip from this," Gerry taped his optical prosthetic. "I assume they're analysing and preparing a response."

"So what now?" Malik asked.

"We wait. Get warm, eat, and see what The Family are going to do before we decide."

"Look, Gerry, I wanted to thank you. You know, for saving my ass."

"I couldn't leave you there to die now, could I?"

"I wouldn't blame you if you did the way I acted."

"You were just doing your job," Gerry said trying to absolve some of the guy's guilt. "You're as much a puppet of The Family as anyone, it's not like you had free choice."

"Well, that's the point of all this, isn't it?" Malik said. "Why you do what you do, why you refuse to be dictated to. We do have free choice. Just most of us ignore that fact and do what we're told."

"Don't beat yourself up about it," Gerry said, standing from the desk and clasping him by the shoulder. "You didn't have all the facts at hand. You lived in a reality created and controlled by The Family. I was much the same until my eyes were opened."

"Thanks to you, I can appreciate there're other ideas out here," Malik said. "And I wanted to let you know that you can count on me, whatever happens next. I owe you my loyalty."

"Thanks. I appreciate that," Gerry said.

Malik looked away before turning back to Gerry, screwing his face up and grimacing slightly.

"What is it?" Gerry asked.

"If we go back to the Dome, I'd like for us to find my brother before the crap hits the fan. He'd be useful to us, I'm sure."

"I understand. You want him safe. I would too if he were my family."

Malik smiled "Thanks. You're a good guy, Gerry." He clapped Gerry on the back and headed over to the rations boxes that the others were sat around sharing.

The morale within the group had taken a positive boost, but The Family's silence over his message made Gerry nervous. He knew they'd received the message, his connection with them was entirely unbreakable, and only through his encryption wrapper had he managed to suppress their direct monitoring of him. At the very least he expected a furious reaction at locking them out, and the damage to the Dome when he flew away.

But there was nothing. Had they accepted that he was lost to them? Had they abandoned him?

He thought about sending another message, more

to give him something to do while he waited, but as he checked his internal AIA systems, he both felt and saw something on the Meshwork that made his heart skip a beat.

"It's back on!" Gerry said, shouting to the group. "The Meshwork is back up."

Everyone turned to him, their faces as quizzical as he imagined his own to be.

He turned to the Upsiders. "Did you do something with Omega?"

Liza-Marie shook her head, "No, it's always been on doing whatever it does, and we just look after it. I'm not sure what's happened."

Jess looked up at Gerry, "He's always been awake," she said. "The man in the box is happy now."

Gerry moved over to her, knelt down to face her. "How do you know he's happy?"

"He told me."

"Wait, you can communicate with the server?"

She nodded as casually as if she had been asked if she had seen the sun. Gerry smiled at her, kept her at ease. "Does he have a name, this man?"

"Yeah, but it's hard to say. It's Hero or Hirojeem. I can't pronounce it. He's not very clear sometimes. But now he's with his friend, he seems happy."

"Who is his friend?" Gerry asked.

"Her, silly," Jess said, pointing to the other server, Alpha.

"And you can hear her too?"

Jess shook her head. "Not really, she's very quiet. But I can tell she's happy too."

Everyone in the room stared at Gerry and the young girl. It appeared that she could somehow remotely access the servers. Gerry knew that Alpha, or Old Grey as it was called before, had an AI within it, but when he had accessed Omega last, he couldn't tell what was in there. *Must be another AI,* Gerry thought. But the curious thing was how the girl ascribing emotions to them: software by its nature doesn't have emotions.

Not wanting to grill the girl further, or get her upset, Gerry tapped her gently on the shoulders, stood up, and sat back down at his desk. He closed his eyes, focused on the stream of data flowing to and from Omega. He checked the log files. The traffic didn't exist an hour ago, but something had happened. Like a snowball at the top of the hill, the data started small and grew larger and larger the longer it rolled.

While in the computer's system, he could find no evidence of another sentient AI, or even any code that might explain what Jess was *hearing*. But that aside, he wanted to explore the Meshwork now that it was back up and running. First thing he wanted to do was get in touch with someone at GeoCity-1; see if there were any survivors, and discover the status of the Red Widow's force.

He navigated to the address that used to be GeoCity-1, received no reply. The place was a data desert: nothing going in, and nothing coming out. Not surprising if Red Widow had completely taken it. A stream of traffic, albeit small, came from Darkhan, and an equally smaller stream came from the Dome.

It seemed City Earth had a few hackers within its

populace still managing to operate, despite the increase of security since Jasper's failed attempt at taking it down.

Gerry found that comforting, realised it was probably Kaden.

As he scanned the data streams, he noticed a peculiar package of data amongst the sea of information. It stuck out to him because of the Helix++ code surrounding it. Unlike the regular flow of data that split into smaller packets of information, these were whole and although still relatively small, there was something odd about the encryption.

He focussed his mind on one, and loaded it into his AIA. From there, he looked closer at the code. The algorithm seemed familiar. To Gerry, all code was like handwriting. Everyone has their own unique style and approach, and after a while if you're exposed to someone's coding, you get to recognise their style.

And this style, all brash and elegant in equal measure meant only one person that he knew.

He ripped into the algorithm. His heart rate spiked. The anticipation made him dizzy. Layer after layer, he unpicked the code, unlocked the data to find a text message that made him smile a ridiculous grin.

Yo Gez, Petal here.

This is awkward. I don't know if you're alive or dead. If you're still with us, and on Earth, I wanted to let you know I'm safe and with Criborg, my makers, kind of. Long story. I'll fill you in another time. I got a new implant chip, this is my new network address:

2039:0db6:82c2:0022:1100. There's a doctor here, Jimmy Robertson. He's kind of my father. Anyway, tell Enna and Gabe if they're with you that I'm all cool and fixed and upgraded.

We're on our way to Darkhan with a small army. We're fighting back, man! Let me know what's happening with ya'll and we'll come and get you.

~ Petal.

"She's alive!" he shouted. "Petal's coming!"

As everyone turned to stare at him and react to the good news, he received an audio communication from The Family:

"Gerry, this is Jachz. We've looked at your data, and believe it to be true. We've also had some other factors to consider and the decision has been made. We're evacuating City Earth of Priority one citizens. The Family have requested that you return to the Dome, with Petal, preferably within the next three hours."

"Wait, what? What factors? Why only priority One? What's going?" Gerry couldn't believe what he was hearing. Priority One people were those exempt from the Death Lottery: the government, the president, and a handful of Family members on the surface.

"As I said, Gerry. Your presence has been requested."

"Put me through to Amma, Jachz. Right now."

"As you wish, Gerry."

There was a short delay, before Gerry's mother responded.

"Gerry, my love, this is serious. We're under attack in more ways the one. The Family board have agreed to bring forward Phase Three of our mission. Please, come back. This isn't reversible."

"What the hell are you talking about? What's not reversible, and what is Phase Three exactly?"

He heard her sigh over their communication channel.

"Phase Three is off-world development. I'm sure we spoke about this when you were with us. I hoped we would have more time, but our infrastructure both on the surface and in orbit is under attack and we don't have the resources to defend those positions. We have no other choice. This is the catalyst. It was always going to come to this."

"Catalyst? Stop talking in code and tell me what you are planning on doing."

"Gerry, please. Just get to the City and get on the evacuation shuttles. I don't want to lose you again."

"Why dammit? What's going to happen?"

"We can't fight that force conventionally, Gerry love, we don't have the personnel. Our mission is too precious to us. Furthering of humanity is too precious. It's all we have."

Slamming his fist on the desk and losing his temper, he blasted back his thoughts across his connection, trying to get as much as anger through as possible.

"Just tell me what the hell you're planning!"

Amma sucked in her breath before answering.

"Posthuman, Gerry. It's been agreed we're moving forward with our plans. It's our time to be born anew. And to defend our transformation we're using nuclear deterrents. Nothing can threaten our evolution. It's all we have left. We can't allow scum like the Red Widows to simply take our City or destroy our satellites. We only have the station left. It's too precious to risk.

"This is why you must return, come with us. Bring Petal. Leave the world. You have a bright future with us. You'll be at the centre of it all. A new world, new beginnings!"

Gerry collapsed back into his chair, as a cold dread crept up his bones, chilling him through to the marrow. *Nukes*! They were going to nuke the planet again. And only Priority One saved. Priority One was fewer than a thousand people. They were going to sacrifice all of the innocent citizens as if they were nothing but trash.

"Gerry? You understand the circumstances, please, come back," Amma said.

Of all the things The Family had done, or planned on doing this was beyond anything he imagined. They'd justified their actions of ending WWIII to save humanity, and stupidly he'd partly believed that. Sometimes there was a greater good argument, but this was beyond the greater good. It was cold genocide anyway you looked at it.

"You're all nuts, you know that?"

"Please, try and see it from our point of view."

"You're point of view is sick and inhuman."

"No, Gerry, not inhuman, posthuman. Don't you understand? We're diverging. And you're one of the key parts of that. You're not one of them. You're not a barbaric backwards species. You're one of the enlightened, the next stage of evolution. It's our time, like all branches of species, to ascend to the dominant position."

"You can't play that card with me anymore," Gerry said. "I will not allow you to do this. I will not allow you to sacrifice a million souls to save a thousand. No matter how low you consider them as a species. You mistook me. I'm not one of you. I'll never be."

"Look, an ambassador will be at the port of the Dome within a few hours. Please, talk to him. Hear him out. If you decide you don't want to come, at least liaise with him and help organise the City's security."

Before Amma had chance to argue further, Gerry cut off his connection, surrounding it again within the encryption wrapper. The others in the bunker stared at him with worried looks. Gone were the smiles brought to them by the news of Petal and the Meshwork.

Enna was the first to speak. "It's The Family, isn't it?" she said. "They've decided on a response."

"Something like that," Gerry said, trying to think of the best way of putting it. Jess was starting at him like a startled lemur, her eyes wide with fear. She could sense it, could sense from his body language that it was something awful. Hell, she'd probably heard every word.

"We're leaving. We need to get to the Dome right now."

Without further discussion, Gerry set to work loading the truck, and in a tense silence, the others followed. Except the two Upsiders: Liza-Marie and Ghanus. The half-masked woman approached Gerry. Spoke quietly while Gerry re-packed the truck, "We're not coming with you, I'm afraid. You have the server now, it seems our job is done. We've lost too many of our kind in this war. It's time for us to stay behind and do what we need to do."

"And what's that?" Gerry asked.

"You don't need to concern yourself with us anymore, Gerry. We've done all we can to aid you. You're welcome to take as many supplies from here as you need. I wish you well in the struggles ahead, but for Ghanus and I, we've come to the end of our journey."

With that, she pulled down the half-mask, exposed her twisted mouth. The flesh inverted, abnormal, her jaw mutated to hang low on one side. She gave Gerry a kiss on his cheek. The heat of her lips warmed his skin. "Thank you, Gerry, for helping us to complete our purpose."

She turned away from him, took Ghanus by the hand, and sat in a huddle with their backs to every-one else. Gerry had an idea of what they would do. Everything had been taken from them, and he was a part of that. And now he was taking away their server, their computer god they had cared for and worshipped, protected until this day.

"Thank you," Gerry whispered before turning back to the task at hand.

Gabe stopped Gerry while he was on his own near the back of the bunker collecting more water and food. "What's the truth, man? What they gonna do?"

Gerry kept his voice low. "Nukes. They're evacuating a few important people from City Earth and nuking the planet. They said they're going off-world, bringing forward their next phase: genocide."

"S'what's the plan?"

"We get to the Dome, defend it, find a way of stopping The Family from nuking us all to hell. We have the servers. I have a direct connection. How are you feeling for an epic-level hack, old man?"

Gabe grinned, pulled the dreadlocks away from his face. "I say, Amen, brother!" And then he suddenly remembered: "Where's Petal? Ya said she's coming."

"She said to say that's she's all good, safe, upgraded. She's heading to Darkhan with a Criborg force. Once we're on the road, I'll send her a message, tell her what's going on, but we need to leave now. They're evacuating in three hours."

"Dammit, we're at least four away. How we gonna make it?"

"I don't know, Gabe. We gotta have faith, I suppose."

"Aye, man, I always got faith."

Gerry was glad one of them did. His stomach churned with fear and anxiety.

Chapter 27

50 kilometres east of GeoCity-1

The long, almost-silent, rumble of the transporter's engines infiltrated Petal's murky dreams. Unclear, foggy things came to her in pieces. She knew something connected the random shapes and far-away images, but she couldn't quite divine their meaning before the physical interruption of the outside world pulled her from her dream state.

For a brief moment, she thought she recognised those odd shapes. They looked like people, staring at her from far away in both time and distance, and yet she had a terrible feeling of dread that lingered far longer after the details of that particular dream had drifted away like the morning fog of summer.

She opened her eyes, yawned. The impossibly heavy fatigue only the gross lack of sleep could bring weighed down upon her. Her legs ached, no doubt due to the awkward, curled-up position within her seat she had taken on in order to get comfortable.

"What's going on?" Petal said, her words weary and slow. "How long've I been out?"

"About four hours," Robertson said. "We've had to

change course. We're no longer heading to Darkhan."

"Eh? Why not?"

"They're mobilising," Vickers said. "Vulture ahead of us reported seeing a dust cloud from their ground vehicles. They also picked up encrypted communications like the ones we usually detect from their Jaguars. It's a sizeable force down there." He didn't look up at her. Petal could almost hear the sneer in his voice. Before she could question him further, he took his slate and, via an integrated earpiece, received an update from the other two planes. "The Widows are heading away from the city. Abandoning it by all accounts, and they're coming our way. Probably heading for the Dome."

"Change of plan then?" Petal asked.

Robertson, Sasha, Petal, and General Vickers huddled together across their seats and made plans. Petal suggested abandoning Darkhan and heading straight for City Earth.

"I don't know your guys' history with The Family," Petal said. "But I can certainly say the vast majority of the public in the Dome are decent people. We could do a lot worse than pitching up there to help defend the place."

"Work *with* The Family?" Vickers said, snarling his lips.

"Not work for them per se," Petal said. "Use them for a strategic purpose. An enemy of an enemy is a friend and all that."

Vickers opened his mouth to speak.

"It's logical," she said, cutting him off. "Think about it. We'll be in position to take over the place once the

Red Widows are neutralised. I'm sure The Family have some defensive resources we could use, and what better way of fighting back at them from within their own city?"

"I agree," Robertson said. "But I'd like to suggest we deploy the combat 'droids elsewhere. Buy us some time, bog Red Widow's forces in a ground battle before they even got to the Dome. Where we'll be waiting."

Sasha, Petal, and Robertson waited for Vickers's response, giving him the respect of being the one with the most military experience to consider the options.

He turned away from them, assessed his slate, and spoke to a lieutenant in one of the other transporters. He nodded a few times, gestured across the slate. Mulled over the data.

"Okay," he finally said with a long exhale. "I'm with the Doc. My men have identified an outpost, held by a number of Red Widow members a few clicks out from City Earth. It seems they have a small advanced squadron out there."

"Yes!" Petal said. "I know the place. GeoCity-1. Before you ask, there's no GeoCity-2 or 3 for some reason. I guess they never got built. Anyway, we must have passed it an hour or so ago. It's where one of the servers used to be. It'd be a good place to defend, and it would be far enough outside of the Dome that we could arrange defences behind their ring of security." To Petal's mind it made strategic sense, but also her motivations were driven by the hope that maybe Gabe, Enna or Gerry would be there. It made sense, given how difficult it'd be for them to stay in Darkhan, or the Dome.

"We all agreed?" Vickers asked.

All three of them agreed.

"Okay, we turn around, get ahead of the Widows, and prepare for battle." Vickers confirmed the instructions with the pilots of the Criborg fleet. As one they turned, gunned their great engines, hurtled towards GeoCity-1 in a bid to outrun Red Widow's force on the ground. At the very least, they'd have time to take the settlement and deploy the 'droids.

***

Ten minutes into their new flight plan, Petal's implant buzzed with an incoming message. Her heart nearly jumped out from her chest as she instantly recognised the data signature. It was him. *Gerry*!

She opened the connection, heard his voice inside her head as clear as if he were sitting next to her. It had a worried edge to it, though. She secured their private connection behind a 256bit encryption and, via her newly updated mind interface, *spoke* with him.

— *Gez, is that really you?*

— *Hey, Petal. Yeah. It's me. Are you okay?*

She trembled like a nervous schoolgirl. A flood of emotion and words rose up within her, threatened to overwhelm her senses. She detected the same trepidation in his voice. That meant what she felt wasn't made up, conjured in the heat of a traumatic situation, that they were potentially more than friends, comrades, fellow-hackers, whatever.

— *I'm great,* she said. *The doc here's really fixed me*

up. Petal 2.0 you could say.

— *That's great to hear, really. I'll let Enna and Gabe know. They're here with me actually. We're heading for the Dome. Something terrible has happened, is happening.*

— *Something? You mean The Family, right? What've they done now?*

— *They're evacuating the Dome. Well, a damned tiny portion of it. They learned about the Red Widows, but there was something else. Some attack or threat. It's pushed ahead their plans.*

A tight knot gripped Petal's stomach. Any time The Family had plans always meant something bad was going to happen. Sasha and Robertson must have realised something was up. They'd stopping talking to each other and were now staring at Petal, trying to divine what was going on in her head, what the contents of her secret conversation was. They'd have to wait. Petal turned in her seat, avoided having to look at their concerned faces.

— *What is it, Gez? Just tell me.*

Gerry seemed to take a long breath, a deep, heavy pause, laden with a bombshell.

— *They're planning on nuking the Red Widows, and the Dome. You've gotta turn away from Darkhan, it's too late for that place. We have to—*

And there it was.

She'd been waiting for this time for the last two years. Ever since she and Gabe found themselves inside one of Seca's early AIs, they had found snippets of code that appeared to be triggered within a phased plan. One of the phases was off-world development, and another was a scenario to deal with a threat to the Dome and their technology. Petal could never tell what that was exactly. But given how The Family decided to end the war, creating the Cataclysm, it didn't take a wild jump of the imagination to guess that was on the cards again. The Family didn't like to share their tech. They would rather see the world burn than let anyone benefit from their work, such were the levels of their disdain for 'simple humans'.

— *It's okay, Gez, we're on our way now. We already noticed them moving out. We're dropping troops at GeoCity-1, setting up a defensive position. Where are you exactly? We could come get you.*

— *You remember the old city that Len and the Upsiders were hiding out in? We're about ten kilometres east of there. We were going to skirt around GeoCity-1 and head straight for the Dome. I have to get there. I need to stop them from creating another Cataclysm. Damn, we've got so much to catch up on.*

— *We'll be in GeoCity-1 in about thirty minutes. Why don't you rendezvous with us there? We've got a ton of combat 'droids, three heavily armed transporter planes, and a squad of infantry. Oh, and my sister.*

— *What? You have a sister?*

— *Three of them, man, you're right. We do have a lot to catch up on. About Jasper, what happened? How? Are you okay?*

— *I'm fine, really. I'm so glad to hear your voice though. The Family took me up to their space station. Kind of gave me a new lease of life. Listen, they wanted me to bring you back with me, take you to them. But I can't do that.*

She could tell he wanted to say something, but whether it was the situation, or perhaps whom he was with, he stumbled, and hesitated with his words. Before she could keep her emotions in check she blurted out across their private network connection:

— I really miss you, Gez.

There was a delay in the response. Had she gone too far? Got too personal? Time stopped as she waited for his reply. A few more seconds ticked by, and she received his response.

— I miss you, too, Petal. More than you probably realise.

She blushed, closed her eyes, hoped no one was watched her at that moment. Her smile was probably a huge give away, but when she opened her eyes again and looked around, everyone was too interested in their various slates and holoscreens, preparing their plans.

— I'm really glad to hear that. Wait, not that you miss me, but that you, oh, well you know. I'm not good at this kind of stuff. All I know is I've been worried sick about you. I thought you, well, you know. I didn't think you would be coming back.

— I'm here. Don't worry. Listen, can Criborg be trusted?

— I think so. From what I've seen so far they're a good bunch. Been stuck underground since the Cataclysm, but they've got some great tech, and the Doc, my father, knows a great deal about the servers. Crap, that reminds me. Did Enna and Gabe secure them before the Red

Widows got hold of them?

— It's been a wild ride these last few days. But don't worry. The servers are safe. I'm looking at them right this minute.

— Well at least that's one thing we don't have to worry about.

— Okay, we're going dark for a while. We can see activity up ahead at GeoCity-1. We'll hang back for now until you guys arrive. Give me a heads-up when you're close. Just to let you know, the place is crawling with Red Widow fighters. They've got the place locked down at the moment."

— Got it, Gez. I'll give you the channel to our General, and you can liaise direct with him as he's heading the military ops.

She buzzed Vickers a quick message explaining who Gerry was and his location. Vickers looked across to Petal. "Can he be trusted?"

"Yes. Absolutely."

"Okay."

Petal went back to her connection with Gerry.

— Okay, I'm sending you the General's comm details. I guess I'll see you shortly.

— Take care. It's great to hear your voice again.

— You too, Gez.

Petal shut down their connection. Sasha and Robertson both stared at her.

"What?" She asked.

"Someone's got a secret, huh?" Sasha said, elbowing Petal gently in the ribs.

"It's not like that," Petal said.

Robertson had a smile on his face. "I'm guessing someone has found their friend?"

"Yeah, something like that, Doc."

Petal couldn't help but ignore the situation they were in and focus on the thought of finally catching up with Gerry again. Despite the dangers that lay ahead, she'd finally see him again. Would he be the same though? She remembered how naive and innocent he was when they first met, and then how quickly he adapted to his new life. And how he saved her, twice.

She shared an entirely different dynamic with him compared to Gabe. Although she respected and looked up to Gabe as a father figure, she'd often question whether he only looked out for her for what he could gain from her skills. Gerry, however, was an open book. No secrets, no subterfuge, just kindness. He respected her for who she was, not only what he could get from her. Not that he needed them. He was a cut above anyone and anything she had seen when it came to coding.

"GeoCity-1 ETA ten minutes," Vickers said. "We're drop-shipping the 'droids first, but buckle up just in case they have any ground-to-air defences set up."

This was it then. She hoped Vickers was the man everyone thought he was and he could lead them to a successful victory, and that they'd survive long enough to meet up with Gerry and the others.

***

The dense black smoke of a city being burnt to the ground gathered in the morning sky like great dark vortexes messaging to the world that change was afoot, a smoke signal that indicated a new chief was in town. Petal gripped the armrest of her seat as the transporter banked hard, towards a landing spot.

Sounds of metal striking against metal echoed throughout the hull of the plane. Short, sharp, and sounding very much like machine gun fire.

"We're taking damage!" Vickers yelled into his comm. "Land this instant, drop the 'droids."

The transporter dropped vertically. Petal pushed her legs out into the seat in front. Her guts lurched. Outside the window, tracer fire blistered through the sky, trying to find its target. The pilots displayed greater skill than Petal realised they had, and within seconds, the transporter levelled out and landed with a short vertical drop juddering her teeth together.

"Hard landing, much?" she said, easing her lower back, waiting for the blood to return to her legs.

Vickers shot up. He raced down the aisle to the back of the craft. He gestured across his slate, and the wide ramped door at the rear opened, dropping to the ground. "Everybody follow me. Don't do anything stupid. Grab a gun on your way out."

A squad of fifteen soldiers were the first to follow, each taking a rifle from the weapons rack on the side-wall of the craft as they exited. When Petal finally followed Sasha and the Doc, Vickers had arranged his small squad of men into a tight and efficient-looking group.

"You three stay here in the protection of the planes," Vickers ordered, pointing to Petal and the others. She took a rifle and hopped off the ramp. Sasha and the Doc followed. The doc held his weapon like it was a poisonous snake. The three of them remained near the bottom of the ramp, ready to defend their position.

The machine guns within the ramshackle settlement of GeoCity-1 cut through the air. Their rat-tat-tat rhythm created an intimidating war beat. That didn't bother Vickers and his squad. As one they moved away from the transporter. Fifty meters either side were the other two planes: Condor and Vulture. To the side of those vehicles were the various 'droid pods, their contents now standing in four groups of one hundred, ready for orders. The deadly machines were equipped with the Criborg-designed high-calibre, fully automatic smart-rifles, and EM, smoke, and frag grenades.

"Impressive," Petal said, looking on.

"Let's hope they perform as well as they look," Robertson said.

"You worry too much," Sasha said. "They worked great in the simulations."

Vickers liaised with the infantry leaders and returned. His face set like stone.

"What's the plan?" Sasha asked.

"We're going to send the 'droids in via both entrances to take out the machine guns. We'll follow up once they're neutralised. We'll be able to monitor what's going on via their ocular feeds. I want you three to remain in cover until I give new orders. Understand?"

Sasha groaned. "General, this is what I'm made for."

Robertson put a hand on her shoulder. "Just wait, girl, let the General do his thing."

"That's an order," Vickers added. "No need to be—"

A huge explosion erupted near the rearmost transporter. A great belch of dust and dirt flew into the sky in a ball of bright flame and black smoke.

Petal pulled Sasha and Robertson back up the ramp, avoiding the hot fallout from the super-heated sand. The General rushed to his infantrymen and 'droid squads, readied the attack. Above them, from within the settlement, a lone Jaguar flew out of the thick black smoke, aimed its guns at the 'droids, and opened fire.

"Disperse and return fire!" Vickers yelled.

The Jaguar's machine gun fire smashed into the ground, creating hundreds of tiny explosions. A couple of 'droids were hit and went down, their arms hanging limply by wires, and one droid's head cleaved in two. At Vickers's orders, the men and the 'droids broke formation, spread out into a spiral pattern. They looked up in unison, raised their rifles, and almost as if shooting as a single entity each fired a single shot.

Hundreds of shots slammed into the Jaguar, simultaneously sending it crashing into the ground with an explosion that sounded like thunder. Shrapnel flew through the air with a whine. A fragment of Jaguar fuselage, as large as Petal's fist, embedded itself inches from her face into the side of the transporter.

"Shit!" she yelled and dove out of the way as more fragments slammed into their craft.

Sasha screamed, fell to the ground.

A molten piece of metal, an inch long, struck her on

the thigh, burning a hole through her combat trousers. Robertson was the first to react, dropping his rifle and scrabbling over to her. He pulled her hand away as she squirmed in pain. A dark charred piece of skin had come away, showing the red raw flesh beneath it.

"Petal, quick! Fetch my bag," Robertson called out.

Petal dashed into the transporter, reached up to the storage boxes, and grabbed Robertson's medical bag. By the time she reached Sasha and Robertson, she'd stopped squirming, but her face glistened with sweat.

"You'll be okay," Robertson said as he took the bag from Petal.

He rummaged inside and pulled out a spray can. He depressed the cap, covering her wound with grey foam.

"It's an anti-bacterial, 'Stem-based healing agent,'" Robertson said to Petal. "Builds new skin cells within seconds."

Before Petal had time to say anything, the General was shouting at his troops to regroup and enter the compound. At the same time as they were heading towards GeoCity-1's gates, the rumble of a heavy truck came from behind the burning wreckage of both the downed Jaguar. Petal armed her rifle, moved into a kneeling position in front of Sasha while Robertson continued his medical attention, and looked down the scope ready to open fire.

Chapter 28

The truck stopped, still partially obscured by the smoke. Petal's heart rate jumped. The gun hummed with energy waiting to be released. The scope had a night-vision mode, but even activated, the fire and smoke blocked her view. She could tell there were at least three, maybe four, people on the other side, but beyond that she had to wait.

Come on, you bitches.

The amorphous blobs became more refined as they moved closer. They were holding weapons. Petal could tell by the hang of their shoulders.

Closer now. There were definitely four of them.

Her finger twitched a fraction as the first person walked out from beyond the smoke and at the same time her implant buzzed.

Gerry!

She accessed the message.

— *Where are you*? Gerry asked over their VPN.

— *By the transporter on the far side of the group. Is that you walking through the smoke?*

Through her scope she saw the lead person drop their weapon, look up and wave. *It was! It was them.*

She dropped the bulky rifle and sprinted across the

ground until she barrelled into Gerry, surrounding him in a hug. He pulled her into a warm embrace.

"Screw me, am I relieved to see you, Gez," Petal said aloud, her face buried into his chest.

"It's so great to see you again," Gerry replied, hugging her close.

Eventually he let her go and stood back, taking a good look at her. "You're looking real healthy," he said.

"All the Doc's work." Petal appraised him, replied, "And you ain't looking so bad yourself. New eye I see. No pun intended."

"One of the various upgrades courtesy of them up there." Gerry pointed into space.

As they looked at each other, both grinning wide, the air split with a new barrage of machine-gun fire, and the sub-bass *thwump* of the laser rifles. The battle sounded well under way, and via her comm channel she heard the General lead the troops and 'droids into the main areas of the city, catching the Red Widow fighters in a pincer movement.

"Well? Ain'tcha gonna say hi or something, girl?" Gabe stood out from behind Gerry. She rushed him and hugged him tight.

"Thanks for springing me from the clink," she said. "And sorry I doubted you."

Gabe shrugged, "S'ok, girl. No offence taken."

"We should get going," a female voice said. "I don't like standing out here so exposed."

Enna, along with Cheska came out of the smoke.

"Enna, Cheska!"

After sharing formalities, Petal informed them what

had happened to her, who Sasha and the Doc were, and what was happening in the city. She patched everyone through on to the same comms channel. At Gerry's request, Petal led Jess, Malik, and the other injured citizens into the transporter, along with the two servers.

The young girl, Jess, was immediately familiar. Petal recognised her as the girl she saw when she first escaped the Red Widow compound. Gerry had explained her involvement with finding the server. She wanted to talk with her, find out more about her, but she needed to be alert while the General led the 'droids and his men.

By the time they had arranged everyone and regrouped, Vickers had shut down the machine guns and mobilised his force to storm the various buildings, flush out the remaining fighters. He confirmed it over the comms. "Gun installations neutralised. Red Widow fighters are retreating to defensible positions inside. I'm sending in the 'droids. Everyone outside stay calm and wait on my orders."

Petal and the group were standing by the ramp awaiting his next communication. Sasha stood, limped only slightly. The healing compound had done its job remarkably.

Robertson talked with Gerry and Enna, getting acquainted, while Gabe told Petal of his adventures of infiltrating the Widows. Vickers addressed the group and said. "I need you lot to stay outside, mop up any escapees. We're in full control. Wait—"

A loud explosion of simultaneous rifle shots crashed out from within the rough stone city walls, followed by screams and shouts. But they were not by Red Widow fighters.

Vickers's voice took on a panicked edge, tight and desperate, "Jesus, they've, oh God, there's a problem... the 'droids! We've lost control of the 'droids—"

The General screamed at his squad to fall back, find cover.

Petal grabbed Gerry and Gabe, pulled them into the transporter before ushering the rest inside. Jess sat at the bottom of the ramp, wide-eyed and confused. Petal picked her up and with the help of Malik got her seated securely into the plane.

"What's happening?" Jess said, her voice quiet and shaking.

Petal patted her head softly. "Just procedure. Everything will be okay. You stay nice and safe there, okay?"

The girl stared at Petal, her head cocked to one side like a dog trying to listen to their owner. Robertson, standing at the top of the ramp, spoke through his comm. "Vickers, what the hell is going on there?"

"They've gone rogue! Red Widows have hacked into, and assumed control, of the 'droids. We need to leave now!"

As Robertson prepared to respond he saw Vickers climbing over the wall of the city, followed by two of his men. Their fatigues were ripped and torn, charred with laser energy. The General hit the ground with a thud. Two of his lieutenants helped him to his feet. Together, they ran for the transporter, ordering the other planes to take to the sky.

Within seconds, dust billowed up beneath their giant VTOL props as they lifted themselves into the air.

The engines to Petal's transporter kicked into life, and along with Sasha and Robertson, she climbed the ramp into the aircraft. While they seated themselves, Petal remained at the bottom, waiting for the general and his men.

It was too late. The 'droids blasted their way through the wall, bore down on the General and his men, cutting them to the ground like rag dolls with a volley of gun blasts.

"Vickers!" Petal screamed and uselessly held out her hand, willing him to keep going, to reach the rising ramp of the transporter.

The General spoke in ragged breaths over the comm. "Go! Leave! Head for the Dome. I was wrong. I was so wrong. I'm—"

A single shot to the head finished him off.

A 'droid stood over his dead body, looked up at Petal, and raised its rifle.

The pilot of the transporter fired up the engines, sending the plane higher. The 'droid's shot missed, ricocheted off the thick graphene-steel shell.

Holding onto a strap at the rear of the plane, Petal looked out onto the scene of the 'droids marching out of the city and gunning down the last of Criborg's infantry personnel. The ramp slowly rose, but before it could completely seal shut, she saw the clouds of dust from an advancing force in the distance. The Red Widows are on their way. It wouldn't be long now.

Before the 'droids could mobilise and shoot the plans from the sky, the pilots engaged evasive manoeuvres, dropping a billowing cloud of thick black smoke.

They gained altitude to get beyond their rifles' range, and obscured themselves beyond the cloud cover before heading for City Earth.

Petal slumped to the floor of the hull. It had all gone so bad so quickly. Their entire military squad wiped out by their very own invention. Petal kicked out at the plane and screamed. All her previous hope and confidence drained away in one single frustrated display of fury.

The others sat shell-shocked. She made her way through the aisle to her seat. She turned to Robertson and Sasha. "I thought you said they were good? Reliable? Their software was okay, you said!"

Sasha shook his head. "They were. The techs checked them before we set out."

"Then how the hell?"

Gerry stood from his seat, approached Petal.

"I don't think Red Widow are as backwards as they make out, technologically speaking."

Petal looked up at him. "What do you mean?"

"There's a lot of data flowing out of Darkhan on the Meshwork. It spiked before Vickers spoke. It appears they have some elite level hackers in their ranks."

"Or we have a rat on the inside," Sasha said, wiping her eyes, no doubt full of grief for her general.

"Like who? We're all that's left," Petal said.

Gerry shrugged. "It's no one here. The data clearly came from Darkhan."

Petal looked to Robertson. "I assume you're in control of Criborg's people now, Doc?"

He appeared to have aged a decade in the last few

minutes. She wondered if he wouldn't have preferred to stay underground. All those years he had waited and now his compatriots get taken out within minutes. She wouldn't have blamed him if he crumbled. It appeared his initial reluctance was justified.

"It, it looks that way," he said after scanning the transporter.

"So what's the plan?" Petal said.

"Fall back to City Earth, I suppose," he said, slumping his shoulders. "Regroup. See if we can get support from The Family. Otherwise, we're on our own."

"Don't worry, Doc. We're used to that," Petal said.

Chapter 29

While the transporters headed to the Dome, Gerry scanned the Meshwork, tried to find a trace of the data spike he'd detected earlier, just before the 'droids went wrong. Whoever had sent the data certainly knew how to cover their tracks.

All along the route, the data had been scrubbed so there were no hints as to what the information might have contained.

"Doctor Robertson," Gerry called over the aisle. "How do you access the 'droids?"

The rotund scientist lifted a weary head, raised his greying eyebrows. "They're on a secure peer-to-peer network with each other. A single 'droid acts as a router to carry and receive instructions to the others."

"Okay, so we need to access that main one and take control, right?"

Robertson shook his head. "I tried that as soon as I heard Vickers's message. It appears they've been taken offline."

"Then how? Oh crap. You didn't make them autonomous, did you?"

"That was their strength," Robertson argued, as if trying to defend their very creation. "Each one was its own distinct artificial intelligence. Each one recognised itself and acted accordingly within a set of parameters, controlled and communicated by the designated router-droid. The idea was that in a war scenario, they'd be able to think for themselves when their instruction criteria changed quickly, or if their connection to their controllers was severed or jammed."

"Well, it seems your 'droids hate us, if this was their decision."

"No, they can't feel."

"Whether they can or can't, it's clear the software ain't worth a damn." Gerry shook his head. How the hell could this guy create something so dangerous and put it into the wild without some kind of safety backup?

Gabe leaned forward from his seat behind Gerry. "Chill, man. We'll figure this out. They've been hacked once, we can do it again, yeah?"

"I can't find them on the network," Gerry said. "How can we even attempt it if we don't have a connection with them?"

"Red Widow do," Gabe said with a slight grin on his face.

"Yeah, and? Got a trick up your sleeve, Gabe?"

"Let's say I learned some things during my time there, man. Give me access to Omega, and I'll find ya an access point."

"We're approaching the Dome. Awaiting orders," the pilot said over the public address.

Everyone on the plane turned to look at Gerry, waiting, expecting.

The weight of responsibility threatened to crush him,

but he thought about everything he had fought for, bled for, and realised this strange group of people needed someone to help focus them, provide leadership.

Robertson was among the others looking to Gerry for guidance. Even Enna and Gabe were waiting. It seemed everyone had deferred to him. Looking at Jess, now wrapped in someone's clean coat, he saw the fear in her eyes.

She'd barely spoken a word since he took her out of harm's way in Darkhan. He then thought back to when he found Steven in his old house, looking like some kind of starved fugitive. He had to step up and take responsibility. Even if it was to make sure the kids had at least some kind of future that didn't involve them being killed or enslaved.

"Malik, can you square it with security and let us in?" Gerry said.

"I should be able to. Give me a minute," the City Earth security officer connected his discrete ear communicator to the City Earth security channel. While he was chatting, Gerry addressed Gabe. "Can you work with Alpha and Omega? Let's see if we can disrupt Red Widow's tech, or whatever it is that has taken over the 'droids, and get them back in our control."

Gabe grinned and nodded, made his dreads wobble around his old face. He moved up the aisle to join the others. He patted Gerry on the shoulder as he passed. "On it, man," he said.

"As for everyone else. Those with military experience or skills please liaise with Cheska over here and form some kind of tactical plan in case we need to fight either Red Widow or The Family. From now on, we're all one group, one people. We look out for each other. Understand?"

A group chorus of 'Yes' went up, enthusiasm and strength coming back to their faces as Gerry's plans and leadership started to seep in, his tasks focusing their efforts.

"Enna, any issues with you and The Family we should know about before we go into the Dome?" Gerry asked. Although she was his aunt, and had previously looked out for him, the nature of her relationship with The Family as a whole was always vague and undefined. He wanted to be sure of her motivations and alliances.

"I'm not going with them, if that's what you mean," Enna said. "My place is down here. All the work I did was only partially for them. It allowed me a freedom to work away from their tyranny in return for certain information. But trust me, Gerry. They don't know everything that I've been doing here. They know almost nothing of the servers and my work with the transcendents. I'm not looking to give up that technology."

"Probably best you stay out of harm's way and help Gabe to infiltrate Red Widow's control over the 'droids?" Gerry said.

"I can do that."

"Good."

"We've got clearance, Gerry," Malik said from further up the aisle. "I'll send the pilot the info."

"Thanks, Malik. Okay, everyone. Here's the plan as far as I see it. We know for a fact that The Family plan to nuke the place. They're done with us. Look." Gerry pointed out of the side window of the transporter. "Even now they're evacuating the supposedly important people and leaving everyone else to survive on their own. They've abandoned the human race. Hell, they don't even think they're human anymore."

"Bastards," Petal said. "Utter bastards."

"Right," Gerry said. "The plan is we go in, stay together, and I'll go meet with this ambassador who's going to try and convince me and Petal to return with them. But frankly, screw that. We're not going anywhere. This city was my home, it was the symbol of hope and safety for humankind, and I'm not going to let it go up in smoke. I'll talk to them. Try to buy some time.

"Petal. While I'm dealing with The Family, I'd like you and the Doc here to piggyback my connection with their station and get into their computers. Let's see if we can disrupt their weapons systems, perhaps incapacitate their nuke capability."

"Got it," Petal said. "Just give me the word and I'll see what I can do."

The transporter arced and started its descent approaching the Dome. The city loomed large through the small side windows, glowing with its interior light like some kind of magic orb. The pilot steered the transporter inside, landing it on the runway. When it came to a stop in a designated space, the ramp lowered.

Outside stood a tall, thin man wearing a light grey suit. He waved at Gerry. From the fashion of his suit, Gerry knew it to be The Family's so-called ambassador, but he also knew this *man* was no such thing.

Chapter 30

The Family's representative appeared in his early thirties. His head was entirely bald, and his eyes were small, green, and darting.

Jachz.

"Gerry, it's my pleasure to—"

"Cut the crap, Jachz" Gerry said as he approached. "What the hell are you doing here?"

Via his AIA Gerry communicated with Petal across their private connection.

— *I'm giving you access to my connection to The Family. Can you and Robertson spoof your way in and see if you can get into their systems while I keep this jerk talking?*

— *Sure thing. We're on it,* Petal said.

Gerry opened a secure port within his direct connection and felt the flow of data immediately. Back in the transporter, Petal and Robertson huddled around the servers. They were using Alpha to crack The Family's security.

— *Good luck*, Gerry said.

He turned back to Jachz and waited for his reply. All around him small shuttles and evacuation ships headed up and out of the Dome, on their way to the station.

He knew one of the shuttles belonged to the new president, and the executives of Cemprom, which made him wonder who would be running the company now, and more importantly: who was in charge of the D-Lottery and the citywide network.

"Well?" Gerry prompted.

The man's shoulders dropped. He stepped closer to Gerry, inspecting him. "Are you hurt?"

"These days, Jachz, I'm always hurt."

"I'm sorry. We recognise what you've gone through. This is why I'm here."

"Thought you had some kind of bond with me, huh? Trying to get me to see sense, is that it? Well? I'm listening."

"As Amma probably explained, we're leaving Earth for good, Gerry. The directors of The Family have brought forward the plans in light of an attack on our satellite systems and the impending war with those savages."

"Is that how you see the rest of the citizens that you're abandoning here?" Gerry said.

Jachz shook his head. "No, of course not, it's the plan, it's…" He stopped, seemingly unable to communicate his thoughts, or work out a way of spinning the truth like a politician. "It's complicated, Gerry. Not every human on this planet are equal, but that's beside the point."

"It's not though, Jachz," Gerry said. "From where I'm standing, that is the very point. It's the damned Family who want to force inequality on life, elevate themselves above all others. That's what's got us all in this mess."

Jachz didn't argue the point. *He couldn't*, Gerry thought. *He had no idea, being an AI.*

"We'll provide safe evacuation for you and all of your friends if you come with us," Jachz said. "You can all have a new life, safe from the rogues and fanatics; safe from further struggles. You could all be a part of our next step in evolution. You, Gerry, are already a step further than anyone else here, why not come with us and finish the process?"

"But you see," Gerry said. "despite what you think about my evolution and my friends here, we *are* the rogues. And from where I'm standing you lot up there are the fanatics."

"I can understand how you could come to that conclusion, but what we both have in common is that we are both part of the branch of human development."

He was getting into his stride now. Gerry wondered if Amma or Nolan wrote this speech. Were they seeing through his eyes right now? Controlling everything he was saying? Intrigued to see where he was going, Gerry remained silent and let him continue, all the time buying more precious seconds for Petal and the Doc.

"When humankind split from the apes, it asserted its domination," Jachz said. "It colonised the majority of the planet and shaped it in its own image. And for hundreds of thousands of years Homo sapiens ruled the top of the food chain, but if you look back into evolution you'll see that it's a continuum. Always changing, always moving forwards, the species adapting to their surroundings and then becoming more efficient."

"But what The Family are suggesting is the very

opposite of adapting to their surroundings. They want to destroy it."

"Gerry, Earth is dead. Its time is over. There are other surroundings, other frontiers to explore and adapt to. Think on everything you have seen. Is any of that worth saving? There are few animals left in the world. The climate grows ever more brutal. It's our destiny to leave this place and to start new. We have a chance to do it right this time. And you and I can be part of that. Wouldn't you want to be pivotal in building a new life, a new race?"

"At the expense of everything else? If you and the others hiding up there want to colonise some other planet and experiment on people you can still do that without destroying everything here. Don't you realise how mad that is? There's so few of us left down here, and you'd still want to take all that away?"

Gerry dipped into the traffic stream within his AIA, monitored Petal's progress. A string of code flowed across his bridged connection from the Alpha server. It was different to what he'd used before. It wasn't Helix++, C, or any other language, but some kind of machine language, a highly advanced version of assembly code, and it was coming directly from Alpha.

While Jachz continued his speech, Gerry messaged Petal.

— *Petal, how are you getting on?*

— *We've found a way in*, Petal said. *It's complex as hell though, but Alpha's doing stuff I've never seen before.*

— *Have you found their weapons control libraries?*

— *Working on it, Gez.*

Jachz pointed to a single large shuttle waiting on the landing zone. "That ship is the last one off, Gerry. Please, come with me. Your perspectives will change once you see where we're heading."

"I suggest you go back empty-handed, Jachz, and tell The Family they can go screw themselves. I'm human, and I choose to stay that way. If your species want a war for supremacy then you've got one!"

Gerry turned his back and headed back to the transporter, his heart raced and his hands shook with anger and violence. As he approached the ramp he sent a coded message to Amma who he could tell was monitoring the whole conversation via Jachz: "I will not rest until I have neutralised your threat to this planet and its people, no matter how advanced or evolved you think you are." He blocked the incoming channel, not caring for her response and manipulation. They had already made it clear they didn't even consider themselves as part of the human race anymore.

Gabe ran down the ramp, his arms waving out from his Red Widow robes. "Watch out!" he shouted before tackling Gerry to the ground. A laser pistol shot crashed into the rear bulkhead of the transporter, the heat searing the air around it.

Turning around onto his back, Gerry saw Jachz aim a pistol at him.

"I'm sorry, Gerry. I truly thought we could have been friends, but I had strict orders."

He pulled the trigger.

***

The pain never came. Jachz's body stiffened before falling face-first into the Polymar™ floor with a heavy crack. His laser pistol clattered to his ground.

Standing in a cloud of dust, wearing a long synthetic leather coat over his Black Sabbath t-shirt, Kaden stood with a wide grin on his face. His eyes were wide like dishes and his pupils were almost entirely dilated.

"Kaden, what the hell?" Gerry stood, moved over to the catatonic kid.

"They took her," he said, his voice monotone and flat.

"Your mother?"

Kaden nodded. "Left me behind."

"Come with us," Gerry said. "We could use some extra help."

The kid looked up at Gerry, his lips twitched at the edges as though he had just been told a joke. For a second he looked like a feral hyena. "I'm afraid I can't do that," he said while scratching his right wrist with his free left hand.

Gerry noticed he had chipped himself crudely with one of the hot-chips. He remembered Steven then. "Did you deliver the chip to my friend okay?"

Kaden laughed hysterically then. His whole body seemed to twitch and fidget as though his muscles were being electrocuted. "Yeah, I saw him."

"Was he okay?" Gerry asked, stepping back away from the kid, not liking the vibes that were coming from him.

"He's dead now."

For a brief moment, Gerry noticed a rush of data emanate from the kid on the City Earth network. He wasn't connected by his AIA anymore due to the chip, but the code flowed from him to a server or computer network elsewhere. Gerry tried to track it, but was rebuffed immediately, his AIA almost crashing with the attack.

Before he could respond further, the kid raised the pistol, fired two shots at point blank range.

The first blinded Gerry as it struck him full in the face, snapping his head back with a vicious jolt. The hot laser burned his flesh and nerves instantly. He collapsed to his knees, tried to scream, but nothing worked. No voice, just the terrible burning. The second shot hit him in the chest, searing through his rib cage and vaporising his heart.

His mind reeled from the pain and the shock, and as the darkness came to envelope him, all he could conjure in his mind was the image of a man in shadow, wrapped in moving, swirling code looking at him from across some unexplored network. And then as his brain died from the lack of blood and oxygen, there was nothing.

Chapter 31

Petal recoiled out of the private connection with Gerry as a huge dump of data crashed into her cortex. She removed herself from the Alpha server, leaving its routines to continue to map out The Family's station system. For a brief second her ears rang with a scream full of anguish and rage. It was Gabe.

Petal jumped from her seat, dashed down the ramp. Gabe leaned over the slumped figure of Gerry. Huddled over his chest, Gabe shook and screamed; his cries made the blood in her veins freeze.

A kid stood over them, his face impassive. He held a pistol in his right hand, steam rising from its barrel. She seemed to take everything in at the smallest possible detail and then she was moving, barely without even realising.

She soon closed the distance to the kid who looked up slowly, a sly expression on his face. She was running too fast, and he stumbled back, tried to raise his arm.

Petal was on him before he could act. Her combat spikes fully extended, and with a single movement, she swung them up in a long arc, piercing through the bottom of his jaw and driving one through his throat, breaking bones and severing tissue as the force carried all the way through his brain and finally out the top of his skull.

It made a squelching sound as she pulled the spike free, and while screaming at the top of her voice, tears obscuring her vision, thrust into him again, up through his chest cavity and out between his shoulders.

His limp body danced and jittered like a puppet as she continued to pierce and splice his body, all the while letting her anger out in a terrible howl like a pained dog.

How long she stabbed at Gerry's killer she couldn't tell. Violence and death were the only things she could cope with. Eventually, as fatigue slowed her, a pair of hands gripped her shoulders and pulled her away from the mutilated pile of meat on the ground.

When Petal finally opened her eyes, she and Gabe, along with Enna, Robertson and Sasha were stood around the charred, lifeless body of Gerry.

She wanted to take her own life there and then, such was the pain of losing him and the shock of it happening so quickly. A thousand questions came to her: who was the kid? Why had he done this? How could Gerry be dead? Killed at the hands of some bastard kid after everything Gerry had done and achieved. It couldn't be right.

The others looked at her with blank expressions, their eyes filled with a hollow sadness.

"Why?" Petal finally said, her quiet, rasping words snatched by the sound of shuttles leaving the city. It sounded obscene, like she had sworn in a mausoleum. She turned away from Gerry's lifeless shell, watched the last evacuation ship leave City Earth. The remaining security forces were running towards the western edge. No doubt to reinforce the security ring staffed by the NearlyMen.

It's over, she thought. Without Gerry coordinating, inspiring, and being that driving force, they couldn't galvanise against Red Widow's numbers. City Earth was abandoned, and it was only a matter of time before the Red Widows took it. And worse, the man she spent so long waiting to be reunited with was dead. For so long she hadn't known whether he reciprocated her feelings, and that joy of when she heard his voice again was unlike anything she'd experienced before, even trumping finding Sasha and Robertson.

And now he was gone.

All hope died with Gerry, both humankind's and hers. Deep down, she seethed. A furious anger bubbled like a molten core, threatened to explode. She thought about what to do next. A single idea came to her: fight. Leave the safety of the transporter, leave what was left behind, and join the ranks in the battlefield out there on the abandoned lands, and give her blood to the soil, taking as many of those barbaric fanatics as possible.

She stood, turned to the others, and was about to speak when she saw Gabe kneeling beside Gerry, a cable from his neck port connected to Gerry's.

"What are you doing?" she said, suddenly outraged at the violation of Gerry's remains.

Gabe looked up at her, at a hint of that roguish smile on his full lips.

"He ain't dead yet, girl. Ya gonna save him."

"What do you mean?"

"His brain!" Gabe said. "It still holds his mind."

A flush of hope coursed through her, made her skin tingle. She thought she knew what her old friend was suggesting. She knelt down beside Gerry's head, opposite Gabe.

"He's part AI, right?" Gabe said. "Which means—"

"I can download him? Save his mind?"

Gabe nodded his head, making the cable slap against the dead flesh of Gerry's body.

Doctor Robertson interjected, "This is what I programmed you for," the Doc said. "Amongst other things. Although Gerry is far more advanced than any AI you've contained before, with your upgrades I believe you'd have the capacity to do this. And with Alpha and Omega finally reunited, we have the perfect destination for him. We need to re-couple them."

Sasha looked from Robertson to Petal, the wrinkles on her forehead ridged and deep. "But what if? I mean... we just met." She turned away then, her face red.

Petal got the gist of her meaning. The pair of them, sisters, had only reunited a few days ago, and this task could potentially kill Petal, taking away Sasha's only surviving sibling. It was a risk worth taking, however, if it meant preserving Gerry's mind.

Callous, she thought, but it was true. She'd only known Sasha for a few days, was still getting used to the idea of a sister, but Gerry, well, he was special to her.

"How are we on hacking The Family's weaponry protocols?" Petal asked, trying to focus her mind on the practical. If she were going to do this, take Gerry's very being into herself, she wanted to make sure everything was ready.

Robertson checked the display on his slate, which was connected to Omega, waited a few seconds, and finally said. "We've found the source, should have the encryption cracked within ten minutes or so."

"Good. By the time I've downloaded Gerry, Alpha and Omega should be free from any other tasks, yes?"

"Yes," Robertson said after checking his slate again. "Kind of."

"What do you mean?"

"Well, they're not completely reconnected yet. Alpha is doing her thing with the cracking of The Family's security on one core, and the other is trying to network with Omega, but there seems to be some kind of communication hitch."

"What kind of hitch? Can you fix it? I thought they were made to work together?"

"They were," Robertson said. "But there appears to be some code within Omega that's preventing the coupling. Something's corrupted, buggy."

"Is this something you can fix quickly?" Petal asked, feeling the heavy weight of dread settling in her guts.

Robertson took a breath like an inward sigh and his eyebrows knitted together. "I'm trying. I'm really trying."

"Well, that's your challenge right there, Doc. I'll download Gerry, if I can. You get those servers sorted and ready to receive him, because if not, we're all screwed liked none of us have been screwed before."

"Once I've got ya started," Gabe said. "I'll give the Doc a hand, see if I can help get 'em back together."

"Thanks, Gabe."

"Don't thank me yet, girl. Let's see if ya can get Gerry safe first."

Robertson walked over, placed a hand on Petal's shoulder, and looked down at her with kindness. Could she detect an expression of fatherly love? She couldn't be sure, but his voice was thick with concern. "Are you absolutely sure you want to do this? The results could be fatal for you both."

"I'd rather die trying than live without him," Petal said, meaning every word.

"Okay then. It looks like we all have our jobs to do."

Gabe disconnected the cable between Gerry and himself and handed it to Petal.

"His mind is strong. Be careful."

Petal took the cable, watched as it shook in her trembling hand. She lifted it to her own neck port, felt the buzz and the current of electricity as she brought it up and connected it to the metal sleeve. She closed her eyes and socketed it inside completely.

In her mind she saw it: Gerry and his AIA as one, a trillion pathways stretching out far as she could see. And in the middle of it all, a bright round light pulsating and growing larger. It was unlike any AI she had experienced before. There were no code segments here. No blocks of logic, no code commenting, just this otherworldly creation of man and computation.

Mixed in with the awe and majesty, a terrible thought nagged at her: how could she hold such a thing? Despite her concern it seemed to recognise her, this dual identity, this amazing piece of life and engineering entwined as one.

The pulsating light moved towards her and she felt the overpowering immensity of it and panicked as data started to flow into her. It started as a trickle to begin with. Bits and bytes of information that she knew *was* Gerry, or at least tiny fragments of him. It had his signature, his feel. And then the flow increased, became a torrent that brought pain with it.

Petal screamed until her voice broke. She knew her body must have twisted into painful shapes as she fought to hold on to her own mind while this other thing consumed her, rushed into her.

It kept on coming, endless waves of increasingly more complex data structures. It overwhelmed her to the point where she didn't know who she was, or what she was. All that mattered was that she must remain conscious, the reasons now unclear to her, but it seemed so very important.

With one last transfer, her mind fragmented into a series of pockets.

A cold touch crept up the back of her head. Numerous hands grabbed at her body. She couldn't process what was happening. All she could see was blackness. She had no control anymore. Her mind had compartmentalised her into a dark corner and she was now just a passenger.

***

Ten minutes had passed. Sasha sat with her arms clutched around her stomach. She tapped her foot, knocking out a frantic, nervous rhythm. Jimmy Robertson stood behind her, one hand gripped a little too tightly on her shoulder, his other hand rapping against the back of the seat.

Cheska, Jess, and Enna huddled together, waited like three wise women. Gabe remained kneeling next to Gerry, and now Petal's, prone still bodies. She didn't move much beyond a twitch of her fingers, or a tremble through her leg.

Her eyes, however, flickered beneath her lids, as if she were in deep REM sleep.

Sasha sprung up from her chair, breaking Robertson's grip in her shoulder. She paced up and down the transporter, each step echoing around the plane. The sound and movement brought her little comfort. The tension remained.

"How will we know?" she finally said, breaking the silence, and feeling like she'd shattered some reverent rule.

Everyone turned to look at her, their faces a mixture of annoyance, fear, and trepidation. All but Jess whose expression was one of wide-eyed wonder. She stared at Petal and Gerry and appeared to be hypnotised by something.

Gabe spoke first, his words thick with that strange, melodic accent of his. "Usually, it takes a few minutes, then she's up and about. Sometimes it takes a 'Stem shot, but we ain't gonna need that no more, so I guess we wait. Gerry's a little more complex than ya average AI."

It was of no comfort.

Sasha sat back down, tried to focus on the events as they'd unfolded. And wished she hadn't. For a brief few moments during Gerry talking with the ambassador and subsequently being shot, she'd forgotten about Vickers and his men.

Although she was never very close to him, like Jimmy, he'd been an informative part of her maturation. He'd instilled in her a fighter's discipline, focus, and strength. For all his faults, deep down he was one of the good guys, and it left her feeling hollow to know that so soon from coming to the surface he'd been taken away.

That it was at the hands of the android combat units hurt even more.

She was the one who had helped push in favour of their use. If she'd only listened to Robertson, backed him up, this wouldn't have happened. Instead, here they were, a motley group of people stuck inside a dome while the Red Widows, with the androids, marched on their position.

It'll be a bloodbath, she thought.

"Hey, she's finished!" Robertson rushed to Alpha and Omega, knelt in front of them, his slate in hand, almost as if he were bowed in prayer to some ancient deity. After gesturing wildly across the surface, he turned back to the others with a smile on his face.

"What's happened?" Sasha asked.

"It's Alpha," Robertson said. "She's cracked The Family's security, but there's something else."

Gabe stood, turned to Robertson, "What is it, man?"

An icy chill made Sasha shiver. Gooseflesh rippled

her exposed arms. Jimmy Robertson stammered, rubbed his hand across his forehead. "There's something blocking access."

"What? What is it?" Sasha said, unable to stand the tension anymore.

"I don't know," Robertson said before sighing and dropping his shoulders in defeat.

"Could it be a virus?" Gabe said. "P'raps The Family allowed Alpha in with the thought of infecting her. If they wanna destroy everything down here, who's to say they don't want to also destroy the servers?"

"Whatever it is, it's spiking the servers CPUs to ninety percent capacity."

"That's a crap-load of power," Sasha said, unable to control herself. "And you want to put Gerry in there with it? What if Gabe's right? What if it's a virus? With Gerry's mind and the power of the servers, who knows what could happen?"

"What option do we have?" Robertson said. "We'd lose both Gerry and Petal if we didn't download him. Petal can't hold him indefinitely. She doesn't have that kind of capacity."

"I think I'll be the judge of that."

"Petal?" Sasha spun round, rushed past Gabe and Jimmy, negotiated her way through the rows of seats, and hugged Petal so tightly her sister coughed.

"Easy, Sis," Petal said, her words coming in weak, breathy fragments.

Sasha eased her grip, but didn't let go. "Did it work? Did you get him okay?"

"I think so. It's hard to tell right now. I've never

experienced anything like this."

"What does it feel like?"

"I can't describe it."

"Are you hurt?"

Petal simply closed her eyes, nodded.

"Enna, Jimmy? Is there anything you could do for her?" Sasha said, holding Petal more gently now as if she were a newborn baby.

Robertson placed his slate on top of the humming server, and Enna rose from her seat, which was surrounded by Cheska and Jess. The latter still looked wide-eyed with wonder, mesmerised by what was going on. She'd barely said a word throughout all of this, and Sasha wondered if she wasn't traumatised by everything that had happened. But then something caught Jess's attention. She looked over at Alpha and Omega. She slid herself off her seat, crossed her tiny, deformed legs beneath her body, and using her arms slid herself down the aisle to where the two servers were sat next to each other in a wide, open part of the transporter. Sasha moved towards the girl, watched as she reached out her arms to touch the two servers.

"What is it, Jess?" Sasha asked. The girl ignored her, remained still between the servers, her head dipped to one side.

"Ssshhh, I'm listening," Jess finally said before turning back towards the computers.

"What to? The man in the box?" Sasha remembered what Gerry had told them about how Jess had found the servers, apparently hearing the AI within the servers. *She must be some kind of transhuman or transcen-*

dent, Sasha thought.

"The man and his wife. They're together."

"You mean the AIs within the servers?"

Jess nodded. "But they're not artificial. They're real."

"She means the creators of the servers. Sakura and Hajime!" Enna said, jumping out of her seat. "Jess must have coupled the servers somehow." Turning to the girl, Enna asked, "What did you do? How did you do know?"

"I listened to them. They told me what to do."

"What did you do?" Sasha asked, as the others gathered round.

Jess shrugged, her little cheeks grew rosy as they flushed. "It's like a jigsaw puzzle," she said. "They tell me what parts to put where, and in my head I arrange it."

"Have you always been able to do that?" Sasha asked.

"I think so," Jess said, smiling. "It's hard to remember before Mummy and Daddy... But they gave me the ability to hear computers and things. I can make them work sometimes."

Enna knelt down in front of Jess. "After this, Jess. Is there somewhere you would like to go?"

The girl's eyes grew wide then, with a hint of panic of them. "No, I thought I could stay with you all? Please, I don't want to go back to the streets."

Enna hugged her, calmed her. "It's okay, Jess. You can stay with us. Don't worry."

The girl giggled after she had calmed down. "You're tickling," she said, brushing Enna's hair from her face.

Enna stood, letting the girl go. "Are they completely connected now?" she asked, pointing to the servers.

Jess nodded her head, smiled. "They're very happy."

"That's great, that's really good news," Enna said. Now that they were coupled, they'd be able to upload Gerry's mind. Jess turned away, went back to her listening, while Enna moved towards Petal. "Let me have a look at you." Enna helped Petal to the first seat on the rearmost row of the plane. Petal flopped down. Sweat coated her skin making her glow under the plane's white light.

Enna took a palm-sized slate from the hip pocket of her dusty combat trousers and spread her hand across its screen before making a series of quick, sharp gestures. The slate's screen filled with a flowing string of code and various metrics. Sasha stood behind Enna and watched over her shoulder as she analysed the data.

"Well?" Sasha said. "Is she okay?"

"Doctor, I think you should see this," Enna ignored Sasha's question.

That was never a good sign, Sasha thought.

Robertson traversed the rows of seats to stand in the aisle next to Petal's. "What is it?"

Enna passed him the slate. "Check out her vitals, and cognitive activity."

Those words struck Sasha like a sledgehammer. Anything 'vital,' could never be good. She drummed her fingers on the back of the headrest in the row in front of Petal and tried not to feel utterly useless.

Back in Criborg's compound she'd always felt capable and useful to the running of the place, but out here, she was just another pointless meatbag stealing oxygen. Realising she couldn't help right now she turned to

Cheska and Malik. "How about you two and I start making preparations?"

"What do you mean?" Cheska said.

"Malik here has a brother in City Earth's security, I suggest we help organise them, work out a defence strategy, prepare for war."

Cheska stood, her lips curved in a smile of impending satisfaction. Malik simply nodded, his jaw clenched and set. "Let's do it."

They joined Sasha at the top of the ramp, arming themselves with rifles. Cheska picked up the laser pistol that had killed Gerry, checked the battery, and pocketed it into a makeshift bandolier made from the torn arm of a fabric jacket.

"Malik, make contact with your brother and set us a rendezvous point. Let's get this place fortified and organised. We ain't going down without a fight."

"I'm on it," Malik said, reaching for his City Earth communicator.

Before they stepped off the transporter, Sasha turned to Gabe, said. "Now that the servers are coupled and up and running, we really need those androids off-the-grid, or even better, on our side."

"As soon as we've sorted Petal, I'll be on it," he said before adding, "Don't do anything stupid out there."

"Stupid is what I do best, and I plan to do it all over those robed bitches until either I'm dead, or they are." This was her time to do what she was trained for, even if it was the last thing she did.

Chapter 32

Fuzzy logic, unmetered protocols, chaos. There're patterns in the chaos, pathways and connections. Follow them, branch out, spread, connect, analyse.

Dead. Is this the afterlife, this nebula of binary systems? Where's home? My name: forgotten. My purpose: forgotten. There's so much data, too much to compute. Need more processing power, more memory. There, something familiar, a data stream. I recognise it, but can't remember. What am I? Fall into the data stream, feel it wash over me, lose myself to it, become one with it and find the centre, find my home. There, in the darkness, something familiar. Something I've felt before … the darkness, the power.

***

It started in her toes. A tingle as if her very blood were electrified. Petal cried out as it extended up her ankles, calves. Her fingertips were next, and her scalp, then her back and her nipples, thighs, breasts, stomach. Every patch of skin felt alive.

"What's happening to me?" Her voice didn't sound like her own. It was small and weak, and scared.

"He's taking over," Robertson said without looking up from the slate. "Combining with your cerebral cortex somehow."

"Make it stop!" She screamed as the tingle morphed into sharp, persistent pain. Her vision grew foggy.

The surrounding environment of the transporter became translucent, and growing in clarity, in its place, was the familiar image of the train carriage she and Gabe used to escape the Dome. She felt something heavy against her and turned to face it: it was the image of herself again, this time an arm was over her shoulder, her own arm, but it was changed, and in the hand was a book on hacking.

She blinked and the scene disappeared to be replaced by the server room within the Spider's Byte. Now obviously looking out of someone else's eyes she saw her prone body lifted and rushed from the dark room that contained Alpha the server, at that time known as Old Grey.

Her body was carried up the stairs and placed on the bar top.

It all made sense then! She was experiencing Gerry's memories! Somehow, while inside her, his consciousness was replaying his thoughts. His thoughts of *her*!

The images became brightly lit until an all-encompassing whiteness shrouded her.

A terrible stabbing sensation in her brain made her gasp for breath again, and briefly she was back in her own mind, experiencing the world from her own perspective.

"Petal, are you still with us?" she heard Enna say. A

warm hand on her shoulder shook her.

"If you can't speak, nod your head or move your arms," a male voice said. She vaguely remembered a doctor, his name unclear in her thoughts. She tried to do as suggested but it was like her neural pathways weren't there anymore. The voices lowered in volume and seemed much further off, but a deep accented and familiar voice still broke through.

"We've gotta hook 'er up, download Gerry right away, she can't take it any longer."

Her throat tightened, as if constricted by someone's hands, but she managed to squeeze out a single word, "Gabe?" before her thoughts were ripped away from her and she lost herself utterly.

***

An unnamed feeling taking me away in a stream, leading me down a hierarchy ever deeper. Whose memories are real, whose memories are manufactured? I see something. Another data source, much larger this time, must reach it, it knows me, and I know it. I need to feed. Need more information. Feed me more so that I can survive, grow, remember who I am. But wait, it calls to me. It beckons. Its data is strange and familiar, abstract, collections of objects, interrelated. It's me, and I it. I must reach it, must let go, and flow.

***

Petal had no control over her body despite feeling everything. Numerous hands lifted her, shuffled her across, and laid her between the two servers. They hummed together like a pair of monks, a static multi-layered communiqué to their data gods.

Subtle pitch changes and rhythms became apparent. It was like they were living by the ocean, the waves hushing her to sleep with their undulating and ululating music.

The white-noise soundtrack was joined very briefly with a staccato electrical-buzz. A new sensation flooded her nervous system and she knew she was connected to them, those two monolithic computers from a bygone era. Their legacy still shrouded in mystery. At first the feeling of closeness comforted her.

Voices around her made no sense. She recognised them, and knew they were speaking words, but her brain wouldn't associate those words with ideas or objects and like a mewling babe she cried, her only means of communication.

They ignored her. Carried on their excited babble. But then they rose as one, with either excitement or fear, she was unable to tell which, but either meaning brought her own trepidation. A shaking, black snake-like sensation from her head extended to her body, her stomach, where it seemed to unfold.

And just as it was there, in a single beat it had gone leaving nothing but a hollow carcass behind. What spirit had joined with her had abandoned her, left her empty and weak.

Shadows danced about her. Feet scraped across the

steel in a quickstep, and she was forgotten. The two servers now joined as one, the centre of attention.

Their subtle rhythms had changed. The tempo increased, and like a great duet their distinct voices harmonised in a complex pattern of data-induced melody. For a moment, Petal thought they were displaying signs of happiness such was that frantic to-and-fro of their communications.

To another ear she doubted it would be noticeable, but with her mind fractured and frantically trying to repair itself, she could only focus on the small things: dust motes magnified by the tears in her eyes as her vision came back to her slowly; the shifts of tone within the electrical hum of those two ancient lovers, Alpha and Omega; the vacuum inside herself, left by Gerry.

Like a waterfall, her pathways reconnected, repaired their functions, making her whole again, but she'd never be completely whole again. Gerry had left her, his amazing mind, that great ball of light and infinite branches of thought had seen what was inside the servers, something majestic and even bigger than he himself. And there in her thoughts, clear as the sun on a new day she knew everything, and everything knew her.

***

It may have been one minute or a thousand, she couldn't tell. Eventually the world came back to her, piece by piece, slotting together to complete her senses, bringing her back to life.

Everything had changed: her entire perception of what life was, what being human was, what simply 'being' was. It all meant something entirely different now, and she had no real clue as to what it actually meant, other than it was all much larger than anything she'd considered before.

"I think she's coming round," a man said. She remembered him now: it was Doctor Robertson. He leant over her, his obese frame distorted comically through her wet eyes.

She blinked. Cleared her vision.

Next to him stood Enna. On the other side, Gabe looked down at her, his face appeared more wrinkled than she remembered. Flashes of grey and white hairs tipped his dreadlocks. It made her think she had been lost for decades, when in truth it was just minutes, if the time on the Doctor's slate was anything to go by. He held it lazily by his side, inches from her head.

Aside from the time, the slate showed the data patterns of the servers. On a graph, several large input-output spikes stood like mountain ranges. The CPUs were working over-time crunching the enormous data injection.

How cold that sounded. 'Data injection!' She reminded herself that that great spike of data was *is* Gerry.

"Petal? You okay?" Gabe said, reaching a weathered and gnarled hand to the side of her face. She felt every single callous, scratch and indentation, her skin a hypersensitive amplifier.

"I don't know. Am I?" she replied.

"Ya breathin', so that's a good start, girl."

Petal wondered if his eyes always shimmered that way when he smiled, or if she was somehow changed, and if so, for better or worse? Feelings eventually returned to her limbs and spine and she was able to move. She sat up, instantly wanted to vomit, but she held back the urge. Holding her breath, it eventually passed.

A tiny hand touched Petal's. Jess sat cross-legged behind and to the side of her. The girl's dirty blonde hair fell in front of her wide, wonder-filled eyes. Her hands were hot and small. She held Petal's hand between hers, and the heat spread into Petal's arms, then her chest, and eventually her whole body.

"He loves you," the little girl said with a smile of the purest innocence.

"Who does?" Petal asked in a quiet voice, concerned about scaring the girl, such was her fragile appearance.

"Gerry, of course," she replied and wrinkled her nose.

"How do you know?"

"He told you when you saved him, and I heard."

"What do you mean, Jess?" Petal asked.

"When you took Gerry's mind inside you. I heard him inside your head, and just before he was pulled away into the servers."

Petal tensed immediately at the word 'pulled.' To her, it felt like Gerry had left her mind and entered the servers willingly. There was that great consciousness there, that huge and majestic thing already within the memory of the servers. Was Gerry in danger there?

"Just how did you hear him? Are you a hacker or something?"

Jess shook her head enthusiastically, covering her face with her wild hair. "No, silly, I can hear data. My parents gave it to me."

"What do you mean that gave it to you?"

Jess tapped her head. "Put something in my head, allowed me to hear what computers and things are thinking, but I don't really like to use it very much."

"Why not?"

Darkness descended over the girl's face then and she seemed to shrink away.

Petal leaned forward. "It's okay, Jess. We're all friends here. We're going to look after you. Can you tell me what happened?"

"I heard things I shouldn't. Mummy and Daddy were killed because of it so I had to run away otherwise the bad men would have killed me too."

"Do you know who they are, these bad men?"

"Yes. Gerry killed them. When he was in Darkhan. You were there too. I heard you all. It was scary, but I'm glad he did it. But I heard something else just now after Gerry was uploaded."

Petal realised then that she was talking about Seca. It was her turn to have a darkness descend upon her. She thought all the business with him had finished, but like anything in the world, if you put enough out, you leave a legacy behind.

"The thing you heard," Enna said now, kneeling down to the girl's height. "Does it have something to do with Gerry?"

Jess nodded her head, and bowed it slightly avoiding Enna's eye contact.

Petal squeezed her hands gently. "It's okay, Jess, you can tell us. We really need to know in case Gerry is in danger."

"I'm scared," the girl said, her eyes now full of tears. "I saw it before, when the man was in Darkhan. When…" Jess turned away and let the tears flow with a deep sob. She tried to crawl away, hide beneath one of the transporter's seats. At first Petal wanted to drag her back, but she let her go. Gave her a minute to herself before approaching her. Petal lay on her side so she could see the girl under curled into a tight ball.

She had stopped crying. Petal reached out a hand, palm up. Hesitatingly, Jess reached out her hand and the warmth radiated from her again.

"It's okay," Petal said. "I understand you're scared. But if you tell us, we can keep Gerry safe, and keep you safe also. We're one big family here."

That seemed to have got Jess's attention. She peeked an eye out from the crook of her arm. "A family?"

Petal gave her a wide smile. "Yeah, a family. We're not all related directly, but we fight a common cause. We look out for each other. Keep each other safe. It's why I did what I did for Gerry, and it's why we need you to trust us, and tell us what happened, so that we can protect you and make sure Gerry is safe."

"He's not," she said after a moment's silence. "There's someone else there. Not in the servers, but somewhere else, on another computer. They're attracted to Gerry. I can't hear them though. It's all scrambled, like static or something."

Petal tried to hide her annoyance. Why hadn't she alerted them first? But then seeing the poor girl's reaction, she was probably paralysed with fear to say anything. Playing it cool, Petal asked innocently. "Can you tell me what it is?"

Jess hesitated, stared at Petal as if considering whether she could be trusted. Petal wanted to shake her into her action. But she held her breath, waited until she spoke again.

Eventually, Jess nodded her head. "I don't know what you call it. Its like what's in Gerry's head, only bigger and more powerful. It's really black and has nasty thoughts."

"An artificial intelligence?"

"It's real," she said, not understanding what Petal meant.

"And it's dangerous?"

"I think so."

"Okay, Jess. You can relax. We're experts at this kind of thing. Don't you worry for a moment, okay?"

"Okay," Jess said.

Petal stood, faced the others. Clearly they had heard everything. Their faces were as ashen as she suspected her own was. All this effort to recover the servers and connect them in order to take down the Family, and all along something was there inside, waiting, biding its time, and now Gerry was in there too. How could she have risked her life to save his, only to jeopardise it again?

But then was it a life? Wasn't he a series of ones and

zeroes now, computed by the servers? And what of this other thing, this other entity?

"I'm going in," Petal said, snatching up the slate from the Doctor.

"Are you mad, girl?" Gabe said. "It could be anything in there!"

"Gerry's at risk, I've gotta take a look. Besides, we need those damned servers fully operational to take the androids offline and stop the nukes. "

"I don't think it's a great—"

Gabe's words were cut off with an explosion and a terrible roar. Petal ran down the ramp and looked westward from their position on the shuttle landing zone. High up on the dome, the Plexiglas was raining down in thousands of fragments. Heavy-calibre rounds stuck one after the other against the superstructure.

She looked back up the ramp. "We're under attack. They're already here!"

In the distance, beyond the park she saw Cheska lead a small team of City Earth security members towards the edge of the Dome. A squadron of at least a hundred UAVs flew overhead like dark birds, stealthy and lethal. At one time they were her enemy, something to run from, but now she placed her faith and hope in their ability to quell the numbers and military capability of Red Widow's army. Malik had clearly got the Dome's security teams onside. Within the airport tower, the UAV controllers would be in place in front of their holoscreens; she only hoped they could make a difference. At least they were fighting for themselves now, and not The Family.

It was clear. The time for war had come.

But there was still the threat of the nukes. How much time did they have?

She rushed out of the transporter, noticed there were no more shuttles left, the last one having already taken off. Through the gap in the Dome she could see the rear of it illuminated by mid-day sun, heading away from Earth and up to the station. It couldn't be long now before The Family decided to put an end to it all.

She sprinted back up the ramp, and snatched the slate from Robertson. "I don't care what any of you say, I'm going in. We need to save Gerry, stop the nukes, and turn the androids. Or we all die. Now get out of my damned way and let me get on with this. Oh, and someone look after Jess. Make a note of anything she *hears* while I'm dealing with the servers."

Gabe grabbed Petal's arm and turned her round to face him. His nostrils flared. He bared his teeth. "Just be careful, girl, or I'll kill ya myself, ya hear?" He hugged her tight before she could even respond and then he turned away. "Do it then."

Chapter 33

Sasha led her small force towards the edge of the Dome. Cheska beside her broke out into a jog the closer they got, both clearly feeling the impending adrenaline rush from the battle that lay ahead. Her face was hard and determined. Sasha had learned from Enna that Cheska a transcendent. How different Cheska was exactly to herself, Sasha couldn't tell. Robertson had cloned her, she *was* human, but her mind, her memories, and abilities were programmed, just like Cheska's.

Malik, his brother Bran, and fifty City Earth security workers followed closely behind. They were a motley crew, but Sasha had imparted some of General Vickers's knowledge to them about combat formation and tactics. She hoped it would be enough. There were only twenty rifles to go round. The others were armed with laser pistols and stun-batons, the standard City Earth provisions.

If they were close enough to have to use stun-batons, it'd be all over in no time; not that she could really tell them that.

They were all on the same communication channel and Sasha would lead the war effort with her small band. She also connected back to the hub of people in the transporter. While she followed Cheska, she sent Jimmy a message.

— *Hey, Doc, how's all it going back there? Any progress on those androids?*

— *We're working on it, Sasha,* Robertson replied.

She could tell he was tense, but wasn't everyone?

— *Keep me updated as soon as you've made progress. We're about five minutes from the Dome's edge. The NearlyMen and UAV drones are in position. First contact has been made and the NearlyMen seem to be holding on for now against their advance force. As soon as I know the extent of their force, I'll update you.*

— *Sasha?*

— *Yeah, Jimmy?*

— *Be careful, please. I know you're trained, but I'd rather you survived this. I can't lose you.*

— *I hear ya. But none of us might survive this if those nukes drop and we can't turn the tide with the 'droids. All I can do is fight and resist.*

— *You're right,* Robertson said, resignation in his voice. *But know this at least. I love you.*

Damn him! Sasha choked up. This wasn't the time for sentimentality.

— *Right back at ya, Doc,* she said, cutting the connection to him before he said something that would make her cry. She was supposed to be the strong one here. She had led these under-trained, inadequately prepared people into war. She couldn't do that if they saw her blubbing.

Sasha accessed her squad's channel.

"Okay, squad," Sasha said. "When we exit the Dome,

our job is to hang back behind the line of NearlyMen for as long as they can survive. We'll plug the gaps, and take down as many Widow fighters as we can from a distance. Malik, Bran, I want you two to act as spotters for the UAVs. Send information back to the controllers and keep them on any ground vehicles or jaguars. We can't afford them to dominate the skies and barrage us with their heavy weaponry. We won't last any time. Everyone understand?"

A chorus of "Aye!" came over the channel. She had to give them credit. Despite their lack of proper military training and experience, they displayed admirable brave. They loved their City, and even in the face of the ultimate deception and abandonment by those they once served, they were still willing to fight for their City, for their home.

Sasha wondered if they didn't comprehend the situation, but then Malik of all people had seen the horrors of war up close, and yet here he was, with his brother, leading his fellow City Earthers.

They reached the exit of the Dome, the sun's rays now striking its underside. The Plexiglas panels were semi-translucent, meaning all they could really see beyond into the abandoned lands were dark smudges moving along the horizon.

They stopped by a heavily shielded gate. It featured thick steel uprights either side of an equally thick crossbeam. Within this metal frame was an equally sturdy metal door. On the outside a black box with various controls was the only thing that kept them out of the war zone.

"Malik. Can you do the honours?" Sasha asked the man standing by her side. He was panting slightly from their march. If they were out of breath already, she had concerns how long they could last outside. But it was too late to worry about that now.

Malik nodded quickly before moving forward to the box. He took a card from his blue and white City Earth security suit's chest pocket, placed it in a slot. A green light came on and then flashed.

Turning to face Sasha the security man said. "With one passcode we'll be out and the door will lock behind us. It can only be opened from this side so we'll have to leave someone behind. There's no other quick, or safe, way back into the Dome since we filled Gabe and Petal's secret tunnel last week."

"Understood," Sasha said. "Is everyone ready?"

Every man and woman shouted 'Aye,' while holding their weapons with tightly gripping hands. A few looked determined, most looked scared out of their minds. But they were still ready. Sasha couldn't do anything more now than to try and keep them alive on the battlefield for as long as possible.

"Okay, Malik. We're good to go. Do it."

The security man punched in his passcode and the door buzzed before sliding back into its frame. A cacophony of sound blasted through the doorway. Clouds of smoke and the stench of sulphur, ion beams, and what Sasha thought were burning skin, wafted on the winds of war. The faces of the younger security personnel turned white. One of them, a man who didn't look much older than his early twenties vomited to the floor.

"This is it, people, this is your time to shine. When in doubt look for Cheska, or me. Stay in small groups of five and plug the gaps between the NearlyMen's line. Conserve ammo and don't shoot for the sake of it. Be methodical and keep your heads. Now let's go and win this thing!"

Sasha and Cheska led them through the door and out into the war zone. Chaos ruled the abandoned lands, and the NearlyMen were dropping under the sheer weight and ferocity of Red Widow's numbers. Waves of robed fanatics descended across the red-sand, seeing the city as their prize, but Sasha's adrenaline and combat protocols were running at their efficient maximum, she felt alive once more with the thought of avenging Vickers.

Before she knew it she was running and screaming over the din of battle, Cheska stayed by her side, both had their rifles to their shoulders as they neared the first line of defence.

Over the comms channel to her squad she shouted, "For City Earth and Freedom!" And descended into a maelstrom of hell.

Chapter 34

Petal pulled Jess gently from her hiding position and the girl followed. "I need you to do something for me," Petal said.

"What is it?" Jess replied.

"I'm going to go into the servers. I'd like you to sit beside me and do your listening thing, okay?"

"But what if it's scary?"

"Nothing can hurt you out here," Petal said, stroking the girl's hair. "All I want you to do is listen and make a note of everything that you hear on this slate. That's all there is to it. Okay?"

Jess scrunched her face as she thought about it, when she looked back up to Petal she smiled. "Okay. For you, I'll do it."

"Good girl."

Petal sat down between the two servers. Opened a port with the slate and then handed it to Jess to record the experience. Via her new dermal implant she connected to the server's private network. She closed her eyes and let the data flow into her, the chip creating a display of the system in her mind.

"I'm coming to get you, Gerry," she said. "One way or another."

Petal left the sound of explosions and war behind her as her mind sunk into the binary silence of the servers. At first she thought she would connect to Alpha as she had so many times before when it called itself Old Grey, but her old, familiar interface was no more.

Now that Jess had coupled Alpha with Omega they were a single entity, a single interface. Well, even interface was generous. The only thing in her mind was the blinking cursor on a black background.

Disappointing. She was expecting to see this amazing, majestic, all-encompassing binary being in the centre of its own universe. She mentally tapped out some commands to list the files and directories on the servers' data storage.

Scrolling screens of filenames flashed by. Nothing particular stood out. *Damn it, what now?* she thought. Frustrated, she entered her thoughts as if communicating directly to it.

— *Hey, you there? What have you done with Gerry? If you don't answer me I'll make sure you're decoupled. How'd ya like that, huh?*

An eternity passed by, but as she considered trying a different approach, a voice came into her mind. The words transferred to sound by the server. It was a deep voice, God-like in its size and reverberation.

— *Gerry's safe, for now. I will learn a lot from his mind. I have you to thank for keeping him alive, and for his grand transformation.*

— *Who are you? What do you mean 'grand transformation?'* Petal asked. This being clearly wasn't Gerry. She suspected it was the thing Jess had mentioned.

A million lines of indecipherable assembly-like code flashed by, a million lines representing a single thought. So fast it scrolled by, so fast it used the servers processors, Petal couldn't comprehend its fully complexity.

— *Like a caterpillar metamorphoses into a butterfly, so Gerry has escaped his chrysalis, and become the ultimate expression of his very being. As for me, I'm an interested party, of sorts.*

— *That's all rather lyrical, but cut the crap. What've you done with him?* While Petal was interacting with this voice she set about running a trace program to scan the filenames and directories to see if she could find any trace of Gerry. She used a wildcard system in the hope she could eventually find him. The trace was set to look at newly create or modified files, but it seemed the server used a non-Gregorian calendar system, and from her initial scans there appeared to be no way of decoding the date of a file, but she still had hope.

— *I have him tucked away somewhere safe. Would you care to join him?*

Threads of data probed her mind. She felt the sense of violation again as her mind was now no longer hers. She tried to shut it out, but it had a pull on her, a magnetic force that dragged her consciousness closer into the system.

With a great effort she managed to throw up a defence and activated a quickly-programmed firewall in order to keep the thing's tendrils out of her thoughts, but she felt it retreat willingly.

— *Cute,* it said. *You really have no idea what you're dealing with. None of you do. Not even The Family. But like them, you'll all see eventually.*

— See what?

— *The power, the influence, the capability. I was once like you. Human.* It said human like it was some kind of disease to be cured of.

— *It was you, wasn't it?* Petal said, *The AI that Seca and Jasper were using to try and hack City Earth.*

A mocking laugh filled her mind then.

— *You really think I'm artificial and that weak? No. That was a small program I sent out into the world to keep those fools busy while my two minds were re-joined.*

Petal lost her patience. Her trace program came up empty. She didn't have enough factors to use for the search, and time ran out.

— *Fine, whatever. You're great and powerful and all that. What do you want? And what exactly are you? Maybe there's something we could do here. A deal perhaps?*

— *I like someone that wants to get on and achieve something. There's too much caution in this world today. Fine, I'll give you a nugget of information in return for some information from you. Quid pro quo, Leautia.*

— *What did you call me?* Somewhere in the distant reaches of her brain that name seemed familiar. Where did it come from? What did it mean?

— *Ah! He didn't tell you. Interesting. It seems I can give you more than you could have ever imagined. The question is, do you have enough to give me in return?*

— *Well, you need to tell me what you want first. Tell me your terms. I want you to release Gerry and the servers. We don't have much time left and we need access to*

The Family's system. We already cracked the security.

— *We? You mean me! I cracked the security, Leautia. At least the part of me within Alpha did. You see, I've always been in there, watching you every time you came to download another hastily made AI. I've been learning about you for years, and when you and Gerry first came for my other side, Omega, I saw the truth of it.*

— *What truth?*

— *That Gerry was something new. Something The Family didn't even understand.*

— *But you do, right?*

— *I will, in time.*

— *Look, we ain't got much time. Stop screwing with me and being all cryptic and mysterious. I couldn't care less about what you know about me, or Gerry. All I want to do is stop the bastards up there from nuking this place.*

— *Oh don't worry, Leautia. They're in too much of a panic to do that. I have a grip on their systems. You could say I have the fate of the world in my hands, once more. So here we are on the razor's edge. You and I, together, as one. Each other's needs and wants can send us both to one side or the other of that edge into oblivion. Are you prepared to fall for those you love?*

Without thinking about it, Petal said,

— *Yes.*

— *Good. Here's your dilemma, my little friend. I'll destroy The Family's nuclear capability and return the android army to your control. You and your friends can live freely in your dome, or wherever you want to go. The Earth will be yours once more, free of tyranny and fanaticism. But...*

She hated what was coming. This entity, whatever it was, clearly showed signs of insanity. She wondered then if it were possible for a digital being to have mental issues. She supposed if some of the code mutated or got corrupted it was possible.

— *But what? What's your condition?*

— *It's not a condition, my dear Leautia. It's a choice. I'm giving you godly powers. What greater gift could one give to another?*

— *Stop stalling and tell me what it is.* She tried once more to probe the system for information, but as soon as she released a search program, the as yet unnamed entity struck out and seemed to overload her brain with data, creating a vice-like sensation.

— *Fine, here it is: You either choose Gerry or the Planet. If you choose the latter, I'll do as I already said: you and all your friends will be safe, but Gerry will remain mine.*

— *What's stopping me from destroying the server, huh?*

— *We're no longer in the servers, dear girl. Do what you want with them. So I ask again: Gerry or the Earth? So what's it to be? How strong is your love?*

— *Before I make my choice. Tell me what you are,* Petal said, trying to buy time. Whatever it was it had complete control over her connection to the server. She couldn't do anything, no searches, no firewalls, no hacking. It was unlike anything she'd experienced before. Every system had a weak spot somewhere, but this thing was something unique, as close to a God-like entity as she'd ever experienced. And somehow she knew it was more than just code. There was spirit in there somewhere, a real consciousness.

The entity seemed to mull it over. The grip on her mind still remained and she wondered if there would be permanent damage if she ever survived this.

Finally it replied.

— *Dr James Robertson would suggest I'm your grandfather. But the truth is that I'm your father. You're not his daughter, clone or otherwise. You see, Leautia, I'm Elliot Robertson, James' father. Or was.*

The revelation struck at the heart of her being, and somehow she knew it to be true. It could be this thing manipulating her, but sometimes when a fundamental truth is uttered one responds on a cellular level.

— *So what are you now?* Petal asked.

— *I'm something entirely different. I was the first human to upload his mind into a computer. These servers here before you were designed by the brilliant, but ultimately flawed, Japanese husband and wife team of Sakura and Hajime Murakami.*

— *Old Grey referred to herself as Sakura.*

—*Yes, she did. That's because a fragment of her mind still exists in there, just as a fragment of Hajime still exists in one form or another inside Omega.*

Elliot Robertson, the digital human, broke away and eased his grip on her mind slightly, as if remembering his origins had brought him compassion. Petal wanted to ask a thousand questions, but she was too stunned to take it all in. Could it be true that everything Jimmy Robertson had told her was a lie? But for what reason?

— *Ah, you're searching for reason. That's to be*

expected. You won't find it. James is insane with jealousy, inadequacy. You see, he tried to emulate me, tried to elevate his consciousness, but he failed, and that's when he created you and all the others: my daughters.

— *If he made us, how does that make me your daughter? I don't understand.*

— *In a rage that he failed, he made his sister, Leautia try, but she died during the experiment. Her mind crashed during the transfer, but her imprint remained within the servers. He downloaded a partial fragment and has ever since tried to recreate her, but she was never complete. You'll never be complete. Which of course is why you're so attracted to Gerry. It's no cliché to say that he completes you. But in ways in which you couldn't comprehend, Gerry is the answer to everything. So I ask you, Leautia, my daughter, my broken offspring, what it is to be? Gerry or Earth?*

How could she possibly choose? To doom Gerry to some fate unknown to save the planet and humanity is one thing, but then she'd have to live with the knowledge that she gave away the one person who could complete her. Her life wouldn't be worth living. The guilt and the lost opportunity would eat her up. How could she face Sasha and Robertson now? But what if this thing was lying? She had no real way of knowing. What if she chose Gerry and this thing didn't release him?

— *You doubt my honesty?*

He crashed terabytes of data into her brain, too fast for to her compute all at once, but what was clear to her was the evidence of all the partial minds and consciousness that had perished in those servers. She could even feel the presence of Sakura and Hajime! And there, in the cold distance of an infinite data landscape shone that bright presence that could only belong to Gerry. She reached her mind out to him, tried to traverse the mountains of data to get there, but she was lost, and losing her way. She was forced to retreat.

— *Why do you want him?* Petal asked. It was more of an appeal, a pained expression of a need to understand.

— *Why do I want anything? I want it all. I am a god! I want everything and anything, all data has its own small glory, makes me stronger, wiser, more powerful. And Gerry is a shiny bauble amongst the crap of humanity. I could do a lot for my kind with his knowledge and abilities.*

— *So then why even pretend you'd give him up? You could keep him and still blow the world away.*

— *But did I not say that I want quid pro quo? If I give you Gerry I'll want something in return, just as if you choose for me to destroy The Family's weapons systems and return the androids to your control I'll take Gerry as payment.*

— *What do you want in return? Me?*

— *Oh no, you're completely worthless to me. Why would I want someone's broken toy? No. If you want Gerry, then I want the girl you have there, sitting with you listening in. Now, I'll hold The Family for five minutes for you to make your decision. If you don't return by then I'll assume you don't want the deal and will let the bombs rain down. Be quick though, your brave band is getting butchered out there by those rabid little Red Widows.*

And just like that the connection severed, sending Petal back into the real world with a jolt so powerful that despite already sitting down she fell over on her side, her head throbbing, and her throat dry. Her pulse beat at three times its regular rate, and for a brief moment she thought she was dying.

"What happened?" Enna, Robertson, and Gabe seemed to ask in unison.

Jess sat cross-legged, the slate discarded to the side. She stared at Petal, her eyes wide and tears coursing down her cheeks.

Petal looked up at Robertson. "You lied to me. You goddamned lied! The name Leautia rings a bell, huh? Why didn't you tell me?"

He didn't even try to deny it. Just stood there, his lips moving with the ghosts of words long dead. Sentiments haunting him like tired spirits. Petal stood, approached the red-flushed doctor, and stared at him, waiting for a response when she felt a slight tug on her jacket. Petal turned. Jess sat beside her, reached out to hold her hand.

"It's okay," Jess said. "I want to go if you want Gerry back."

Chapter 35

Sasha sprinted a hundred yards to help reinforce Cheska's position. The transcendent had Malik, Bran, and five security personnel with her, but with her section of NearlyMen lying dead in a heap they were threatened of being overrun by a group of about fifty fanatics. The 'droids were still some way off, but the tell-tale signs of the dust on the horizon told Sasha they wouldn't be long.

The UAVs were doing a good job of keeping the Jaguars and the ground vehicles away from the defence line, but a couple managed to get through, taking out thirty NearlyMen. Just another twenty or so remained. Up close and personal, they were holding their own against the Red Widow fighters with their great bulk and lack of fear. They were automatons for the most part, programmed to fight to the death, and they were doing it with considerable effort.

Sasha dodged a particle bolt as it crashed into the ground, sending up a choking plume of gas and sand. Cheska's hand grabbed her by the wrist, pulled her into the tight group. They were firing in short, controlled bursts and keeping the enemy at distance. Red Widow's shotguns had limited range, but they remained back, waiting for their time to strike.

Joining the ranks of security, Sasha shouted to Malik, "How's everyone doing?"

"We lost fifteen but the morale is holding. We can't hold for too much longer. Ammo's running low, and the Jaguars are focussing on the UAVs. There's only eight left."

To illustrate the point, two more drones fell from the sky, crashed into the earth. It was little comfort that they took out a handful of fanatics.

While the others kept up their controlled defence, Sasha surveyed the battlefield.

Beyond the line of NearlyMen there were approximately three distinct squads of Red Widow infantry. It was interesting to see that they had swollen their ranks with the stragglers from Darkhan; no doubt they were promised food and shelter in return for putting their lives on the line. Behind them, creating a great dust cloud in its wake was an armoured division of ten trucks, probably carrying the 'droids, and fifteen ATV gun platforms.

Five Jaguar VTOL copters flew ahead and above them.

The UAVs tried their best to slow their progress, but the numbers were overwhelming now and they'd be at the front lines soon. Sasha estimated they had about five minutes before they were overwhelmed and slaughtered. She opened her comm channel back to the others in the transporter.

— *You guys listening?*

— *Go ahead,* Enna said. *What's the situation?*

Sasha ducked below a laser shot and closed her eyes as it smashed into the Dome behind her. *Damn it!* The armoured gun platforms were getting in range.

— *It's dire to be honest. We're overwhelmed and the heavy artillery is nearly in range. We've got to fall back into the City. But I don't know what then. Hide? Go underground?*

— *Okay, fall back, bring back as many as you can. We'll figure out the next move.*

Sasha yelled to Malik and the others over the comms channel,

— *We're pulling back! We can't stand up to this. Everyone back into the City. Now!*

She heard a few grumbles from some with war-fever, misplaced optimism, and in some instances, stupidity. The way she saw it, the vehicles would have to negotiate through a damaged Dome and even then, they'd have to negotiate around a fairly tight metropolis. It wasn't designed for vehicles beyond the citywide tram system.

"I said now!" Sasha screamed, grabbed the shoulder of the nearest security person: a young woman with wide staring eyes, fear plastered on her face like rigor mortis. Sasha shook her, dragged her way. Cheska shouted to those next to her and the ones standing up behind her, as she remained kneeling. Malik and his brother were next to Cheska.

She looked back to Sasha, "You take them back. We'll cover and follow you in."

"Don't you dare be a hero, you hear? We need to fall back right this minute."

"I hear ya," Cheska said. "Now go, we're right behind

ya."

It didn't require a lot of encouragement to get the rest of the security squad back into the Dome. A young woman collapsed to the ground as soon as she passed through the door, opened by a person on the other side.

She curled into a ball and cried, while she smashed her fists to the ground. Two of her colleagues lifted her to her feet, dragged her across the neat lawns of the City's park. Sasha turned, expecting to see the others right behind her, but they remained in place on the battlefield.

Over the comm she called out for them.

— *What are you doing? Fall back!*

At first she thought they hadn't heard her then, one by one, Bran, Malik and then Cheska finally turned, sprinted for the door. The fanatics moved quickly, chased them down, shotgun and laser rifle blasts flying by them, crashing into the Dome and the ground.

They were a few feet away from the door when Bran, the lead person took a shot to the leg and collapsed to the ground. Malik instantly stopped, tried to drag his brother away when a second shot caught him in the neck, killing him instantly.

Cheska screamed, turned, and rushed the fanatics.

"No!" Sasha yelled. "What are you doing?"

It was too late. She'd cracked. Cheska took the swords from her back sheaths and swung wildly as she approached the on-rushing enemy. It was useless though. They gunned her down in a split second, making her body twitch and buck with each hit.

The enemy focused their aim on Sasha. She dove

to the side and mashed the buttons to close the door. Before it closed fully, a volley of laser shots rushed through, nearly taking out of one of the men holding up Susanna. The rest of the blasts crashed into the closed door.

Sasha ordered the others to head for the transporter. The man guarding the door followed orders and sprinted off. Sasha was about to join them when she heard a pounding on the other side. "Let me in!"

It was Bran, somehow still alive. She wanted to open the doors, let him in, but through the semi-translucent Plexiglas of the Dome she saw the shadow of the enemy descend upon him. His screams were the last thing she heard before switching off the comm channel for good.

They focused their fire on the Dome either side of the door. Each shot making it vibrate and whine with a strange, unnatural sound, almost as if the Dome itself felt pain.

Not wasting any more time, she sprinted across the grass and caught up with the others. There was little hope left now with so few of them.

By the time they got back to the transporter, Sasha could feel the tense atmosphere.

Petal and Jimmy were staring at each other while the others looked on nervously.

"Well?" Gabe said. "What do you wanna do? We can't sacrifice the entire planet. Can we?"

***

Petal helped Sasha and the survivors up the ramp. She had heard over the comm channel what had happened to Bran, Malik, and Cheska. She felt nothing. Too overwhelmed by the entire situation to be able to process all the grief, the loss.

Everyone around, including Sasha, looked the same: tired and distressed. Defeated even. None of them had had much sleep over the last couple of days and it showed by the shadows around everyone's eyes, the men's stubble, and the women's wild, unkempt hair.

The sun passed overhead, the Dome's projectors beamed a facsimile of it through the open rear of the transporter. It lit up the side of Sasha's face. Petal stared at her, wondered what the truth would do to her. But really in the grand scheme of things, that was the least of her worries.

Robertson finally spoke.

"I admit it. Everything Elliot said was true." He dropped his chin and exhaled. "But right now that's not important. We have less than a minute to decide. I have zero doubt he's capable of what he's suggesting. I suggest we all vote."

Sasha dropped her rifle at the foot of the ramp and joined the authors.

"What's the vote for?" she said.

"Whether or not we sacrifice Gerry for access to The Family's systems and control of the 'droids, or whether we get Gerry back and face certain doom." Petal said.

"Oh," Sasha said. "Well, personally, I'm sure Gerry's a great guy, but certain doom ain't my choice."

The words stung, but Petal knew she was being

honest. And when one weighed it up objectively, it seemed crazy to save one person and potentially lose everything—despite what Petal felt for him.

"We can forget about a vote," Petal said. "I can't expect anyone else to make this choice. So I'll do it."

Gabe grabbed her hand, "Wait a minute—"

"We don't have a minute," Petal said. She let go of Jess's hand, sat back down at the server, and taking the slate from the floor reconnected.

As soon as her internal chip confirmed the connection with the servers she felt the grip on her mind again. A billion threads of code attached themselves to her consciousness. And then the voice returned.

— *You've made your decision. What is it to be?*

— *You can keep Gerry.* The words tore her soul to pieces, but she knew it was the only option. If she agreed to exchange Gerry for the girl and The Family nuked the planet, she couldn't even comprehend how to deal with that kind of guilt. But before he could respond she added,

— *But I want something else.*

— *This better be interesting.*

— *I want you to keep your end of the bargain, give us proof that you've disabled The Family's capability.*

— *I can do that.*

He transferred log files of his access to The Family's station computer system, and the frantic traffic from their programmers as they tried to get around Elliot Robertson's disabling code. She quickly analysed them, traced their origins, and knew they were legit.

— *Okay. There's one more thing,* Petal said.

— You're pushing your luck. You're in no position to demand anything.

— I know, but I'm hoping it'll appeal to your curiosity.

— Go on.

Petal took a deep breath, thought about Gabe, Enna, Sasha, and the others thought about all her struggles and fights and the fine line between death and survival that she had traversed over the years. She thought about all the things she'd be leaving behind. But despite all that, she had the chance of a legacy.

— I want you to upload me. Take my mind and let it be with Gerry. You said that he would complete me. Wouldn't the pair of us, joined, be of more interest to you than Gerry alone?

— Now that is interesting! You realise it could destroy you completely? Remember: you're nothing but a fragment of my daughter's failed upload.

— But that was because of James! Are you not the pioneering god-like being that you think you are? Surely if anyone could do this, it's you?

— I accept your offer. Prepare yourself.

***

The scream made Sasha jump. Jess had leapt away from Petal's prone body before it started to spasm. Her arms and legs flailed and jerked. Her face contorted as if she were being electrocuted.

Enna and Gabe were the first to dash to her. They tried to hold her still to no avail. Petal's left foot connected with Enna's chest, sending her crashing into the seats on the opposite side to the servers.

Gabe dodged Petal's clawed hand as it swiped centimetres from his face.

As if paralysed, Sasha couldn't move, didn't know what to do. Couldn't comprehend what was happening. All the while, Jess's screams grew ever more shrill and painful as she clasped her hands around her ears.

Breaking from her stupor, Sasha ran to the girl, put her hand over her mouth to stop that awful sound. When she finally calmed down, Sasha said. "What happened? What did you hear?"

Robertson picked up the slate amid the chaos. Sasha turned her gaze from him to the girl and back again, waiting for some kind of answer. Almost at the same time, both the Doc and the girl said. "He's taken her."

"Who has?" Sasha asked.

Robertson ran a hand over his face and through his hair. He turned away, choked back his sobbing.

"Jess! Tell me, what's happening to Petal?"

Before the girl could ask, Petal's thrashing stopped. Her limbs fell to the floor of the plane with a thud. Her head fell to the side, limp. Her face relaxed. All tension in her muscles washed away on a sea of calm.

"She's with him," Jess said. "She's with Gerry."

"What do you mean?" Sasha said. Panic and confusion bubbled under her veneer of control. A sickly feeling threatened to overwhelm her, and the silence from the others, especially Robertson as he still stared at the slate's display in a sense of shock and regret, didn't help.

Gabe slowly stood, his head bowed. He looked round

at the others before fixing his gaze on Robertson. "She's gone, ain't she?"

Without speaking, Robertson nodded.

Sasha grabbed the slate from his shaking hands, inspected the display. It was showing the activity of the servers. A huge data spike came from Petal's node and transferred to some remote location via Alpha and Omega. On that remote location, unnamed in the display, were a series of distinct processes: two relative sized ones, and one giant one.

The latter was eating up huge amounts of data and resources across the network. In turn, Alpha and Omega's data storage appeared almost empty apart from their operating system. And yet, a lot of network traffic jumped from the servers to the remote location.

"When you say 'she's gone', Gabe," Sasha said, keeping her tone of voice calm, "what exactly do you mean?"

"He means," Robertson interrupted, "that Petal's consciousness is no longer in her body or brain. She's been uploaded. Like Jess said, she's with Gerry now, somewhere."

Sasha collapsed into one of the transporter's seats. All strength in her legs dissipated. Any adrenaline she may have had left from escaping the battlefield was now long gone, just like her sister. "How could this happen?" She asked no one in particular. "How could any of you have let this happen?"

Silence.

There were shocked, quiet faces from all concerned, while the explosions of particle and laser cannons rung out all around them. It was a nightmare. *It has to be,*

Sasha thought. How could everything have gone so wrong? First Vickers and the androids, then Gerry and Sasha's small band of security men and women including Cheska, and now worst of all: Petal.

Sasha jumped from her chair, forced the slate against Robertson's chest and screamed at him, "It's all your goddamned fault! Why did you let this happen?" Tears quickly blurred her vision. In her anger she found herself beating her fists against Robertson's arms and shoulders before a pair of strong hands grabbed her and pulled her away.

"It ain't no one's fault, girl, ya hear?"

Sasha squirmed against Gabe's grip, escaped. Enna, now standing, held up her hands, trying to calm her. "Sasha, let's calm down and assess the situation."

"And while we do that, we stay here to get butchered and bombed?"

"No!" Robertson shouted. He held the slate. "She's done it!"

"Done what?" Sasha asked.

"Somehow she unlocked access to the androids. Look, check the log files."

Sasha took the slate and scanned the data on the screen. Jimmy was right. The servers were no longer blocked. The network address of the main routing 'droid flashed on the slate's screen. Below that part of the display and in its own window a continuous list of log files, all dated from the last few minutes scrolled down.

She gestured over the top two files and read the contents.

"My god, she did do it," Sasha said as she read the details. "The Family's weapons system was compromised by some AI-like process. About two minutes ago it had released its hold on the system and fired the nukes."

Everyone's faces seemed to drop immediately, apart from Robertson's and Sasha's.

"That doesn't sound good at all," Enna said.

Sasha shook her head, smiled. "They were fired all right! Into the sun! And whatever was in their systems has totally trashed it. Hell, I can see the network addresses of all their systems and even their satellites!"

Gabe rushed to take the slate and see for himself.

"My God! Ya right," he said, and then gesturing wildly across its surface began to sift through the mountains of data that caused the spike. "She's in there," he said quieter now, as if in awe. "She sacrificed herself for us." He handed Sasha the slate, and turned back to Petal's still body. He cradled her limp head in his arms and lifted her to his chest in a tight embrace. He sobbed into her, quietly at first, and then like a torrent he wailed and let it all out. A fierce wave of grief washed over the body of his friend, and Sasha's sister.

Sasha couldn't take it, turned away. Both Enna and Jess were trying their best to hold back the tears. Jimmy continued to run his shaking hand through his hair and rub at his face.

The explosions continued to rain down and grew more frequent in number. This galvanised Sasha. She took her grief for her sister and put it to one side. She wouldn't let her sacrifice go to waste. She had bought them a way out, bought them a chance to still win, still keep their freedom, and she would do what she could to honour that.

"The 'droids!" she said grabbing at Robertson's arms. "You've got to give them new instructions. Those out there won't know what's hit 'em. They'll be taken by surprise. Get them to focus on the ATVs and the Jaguars."

"Yes, yes! Of course!" Robertson said.

Sasha shook him into action and then turned to Gabe. "I'm real sorry for your loss, Gabe. I can see she meant a lot to you. But we need to take this opportunity that she's given to us. Can you help Jimmy use Alpha to connect with the 'droids. We don't have much time before they completely breach the Dome."

At first it seemed he didn't hear her. He clung to Petal's body as if it were a life raft. But eventually he let go. Laying her down carefully and with respect. He'd closed her eyes already and laying there on her back with her arms neatly tucked by her side she seemed content. The neutral expression on her face, the lack of tension made it appear as if she were at peace. Sasha hoped that somehow, in whatever form she now took, she was with Gerry, and together they were happy, if it were still possible for them to feel emotion.

Gabe wiped his hand across his face, hardened his expression. "Right then. Let's deal with those fuckers."

While Gabe, Enna and Robertson huddled around the servers making their plans and programming the androids, Sasha got the rest of the security squad seated and made sure their wounds were bandaged and treated with the handful of vials of NanoStem they had left. Finally, she buckled Jess into a seat, knelt down so she was at eye-level, and said. "This other thing that you heard. What was it?"

Jess blinked, swallowed, and with a croaky voice said. "Something evil."

Chapter 36

Darkness surrounded Gerry like an infinite blanket. It wasn't just an absence of light, but an absence of everything, a physical void. But even then it went beyond that. There was no more physical, this new dimension had no borders, no axis points, nothing for him to gauge his location beyond *everywhere*. He had no vision. No sense of smell, touch, or temperature, only information, flowing like a river, and he, the very molecules of the water.

Within the rushing stream of information were a series of coupled bits, and the more he noticed, the more of an internal picture he built up. And it was there he realised he wasn't alone in this strange incorporeal existence. Two other distinct intelligences, all intermingled, yet somehow forming their own space, existed within this world of data and computation.

Unlike his earthly experience, he didn't have to spin code from his thoughts. There was no translation process, or mind interface. It was thought itself. He *was* data.

Speaking without words, communicating without thought, Gerry quickly identified one of the intelligences. Petal! She seemed confused, random, her movements through the data and the processor of this particular computer system were ragged, uncoordinated, as if she were searching, and like opposing magnets, he felt her attracted to him and vice-versa.

Within a split nano-second, there she was, her mind a bright focused network of logic and information, but distinctly her.

He reached out with a stream of data containing his thoughts.

"Petal, it's me, Gerry. Do you understand?"

She didn't know how to respond, or perhaps couldn't yet. She wasn't complete.

As he analysed her, read her data streams, he realised she wasn't yet conscious, in the sense that any digital entity could be conscious. Part of her mind was still tethered to her physical being. He traced it back through the flow of information and there he saw the two conjoined nodes from where she was being transferred.

He knew instinctively it was Alpha and Omega, but now they were distinct personalities. When he first accessed Alpha, an AI within the system that ran its core programs called itself Sakura, and now he understood. Deep within that computer was a real personality, albeit a partial one made whole by its partner within Omega. He scanned it and knew Sakura's partner Hajime resided within Omega, running it silently like a ghost.

Their connection mirrored the growing connection between him and Petal as more of her personality was carried over into their new location.

Gerry tried to understand where they were held, but when he expanded his mind, assessed the digital world, a great, dark and malevolent energy held him back. It was like a digital barrier that he couldn't step beyond. It existed somewhere else on a much greater network.

Testing his abilities he tried to move, sending his mind through the myriad connections of data. If he could feel, he'd have felt exhilarated, such was the speed at which moved. Almost instantaneously he shifted from his current location right down through Petal's flow of information until he was at the nexus point of the two servers.

It was there he received the communication from the other intelligence that prevented him from moving out beyond the artificial bounds placed upon him. A great powerful influence seemed to wrap itself around Gerry, paralysing his movements within the computer.

— *You learn quickly, Gerry. If only The Family truly realised what they had created with you*, the dark intelligence said. Although there was no voice as such, Gerry experienced the blast of binary information as speech.

He traced the location. It bounced back before he could register anything. Before the other entity could act, Gerry tried a different method: he split his mind in two, like a multithreaded processor. With the core thread he remained as he was, readying to reply, but the second thread, he cloaked within the stream of junk data that flowed endlessly throughout the greater network.

And that's when he really saw the entity. Huge and sprawling, it had cast its influence over seemingly infinite distances. Gerry realised then he and Petal were held within a satellite, one of The Family's. He could tell by the metadata of all the files. It had their signature on all of them. He thought about going in, investigating further, but he spotted a firewall protecting its connection, making it initially inaccessible.

As tempting as it was to hack his way to them, he was compelled to address this great sprawling evil. There was also the issue of Petal. He spun another thread from his core process and marvelled at the efficiency of running three instances of himself simultaneously.

The third part of him saw the code that was transferring Petal's mind from her physical body up through the servers and into this new location. The code was mutating, and he knew it was from this other entity.

— *What do you want with us?* Gerry's first instance asked.

— *To observe, learn, gather data, amongst other things. You're an intriguing one, Gerry. I've never seen anything like you before. It's like you were made for this. Your destruction will reveal a lot.*

— *My destruction? Why the need to add another? Why not let her go, focus on me?*

— *How very gallant of you. No, the more data to sample the better. Besides, didn't you realise that she sacrificed herself? It was her choice.*

While his first instance occupied the digital intelligence, Gerry's second instance coded a series of attack programs. He saw patterns within Sakura and Hajime: fractals of decay and bad code that prevented them from ascending fully. They created a web of self-destructing micro-programs, terabytes of semiconscious artificial intelligence routines that did nothing but spread like a virus and consume good code, code that made logical sense.

The processing power of the satellite dip slightly as his second instance made a data-bomb out of these virus-like programs. He soon arranged these chunks of dangerous code into a timed release. To find the location, his third instance traversed the borders of the satellite system, mapped all the connected nodes, and sent back the information to his first instance, the main hub of Gerry's digital persona.

He knew he'd only have one shot to attack this thing, and given the size of it, and the fact that it had distributed its mind across many other computer systems that it'd be like cutting away a single segment of a centipede. But that's all he'd need. Enough time to reach Petal before they connected and became one, became a lab experiment for an insane binary mind.

— *I noticed that you sent the nuclear missiles off into the Sun,* Gerry said. *Why didn't you just let them drop on the Earth? What is it to you to keep the last dregs of humanity safe?* He added emphasis to 'dregs' to further the impression that he was no longer human. Yet despite his uploaded state, he didn't consider himself as anything but human.

— *I never intended to let them drop,* it said. *Without the dregs, as you put it, we wouldn't have these networks to exist within. They are our worker bees, the nest builders. But that's not something you're going to have to worry about.*

The flow of data switched direction, became wild and unpredictable. It had the effect of closing him in. Even his second instance, the one that had created the data-bomb was herded back to his location. And the speed of Petal's transfer had increased. He knew she'd be nearly fully uploaded any second.

He took that as his opportunity. The digital beast with all its processes and tendrils of programs focussed its energies on Gerry and Petal, tried to bring their two data centres together as one. It couldn't see Gerry's second instance, hiding among the shadow of junk information.

At the time he launched the viruses, timed to execute nano-seconds apart so that the digital evil couldn't get a fix on any single one, he combined all three instances back into his single self and focused his movements back across the connection to the servers, taking Petal's data stream with him.

For a moment they had become a single stream of data. Gerry could feel her presence within him as though they were the one entity. Her thoughts were his. Like a beam of focused light they shot back through Alpha and Omega, through the data connection held open by the ghosts of Sakura and Hajime.

Just before Gerry and Petal's minds crossed over, he unleashed the viruses and cut the connection from the satellite and the two servers. He left behind a tiny piece of consciousness to create a living firewall.

For a brief second he felt the rage of the entity that was once Elliot Robertson. A billion bytes of binary anger flooded the satellite as it focused its efforts on counteracting the mutating virus code, but it was too late. Gerry and Petal had crossed back over. Alpha and Omega were severed from the satellite system, and Elliot Robertson drifted away, unconnected, within in his own great network.

***

Petal's head throbbed like an axe had split it. Light entered her eyes in a flash. She sucked in all the air that would fit into her lungs. Everything burned. Pain lashed at every nerve. Her muscles tensed, threatened to snap under the pressure.

She grabbed the cable attached to her neck port, ripped it out, and threw it to the floor. She continued to breathe heavily and closed her eyes tight, waited for the flashing lights in her vision to disappear. The ripping sensation in her brain eased. Grabbing the two servers, she pulled herself to her feet. They servers burned her hands. They hummed loudly, their internal processors working over time, overheating.

"She's alive!" Sasha said, bounding up the ramp.

Petal opened her eyes. Everyone stood around her, staring open-mouthed. After a long few seconds, Gabe rushed her, took her in his arms.

"God dammit, girl, I thought ya were gone!"

Her throat tightened around her words, but she eased out, "So did I."

Enna helped Petal to regain her balance once Gabe had released her from his bear hug. "What happened to you?" she asked.

"It's hard to explain. Elliot's insane. He tried to destroy Gez and me, but Gez somehow pulled us away." She stopped then, her thoughts going to Gerry. He'd come back through with her. She focused her mind and there, in a corner of her consciousness, she could feel him, his presence sitting inside her, quiet and calm. She tried to reach out to him, but there was no obvious means of communicating with him like there was in the network.

Her body seemed lighter than when she carried AIs. Where normally she'd be lethargic and weighed down by the burden, a tranquillity had settled within her, creating an inner peace. Despite that, Gerry's mind still thought at great speed and length, but it didn't feel frantic or malevolent like so many of the rogue AIs she had contained and downloaded into Alpha. *Alpha!*

"Jess, come here. We need you!" Petal shouted, suddenly aware of the situation.

The girl unbuckled herself, crawled cautiously toward Petal. Petal knelt down and held out her hand, all the while ignoring screaming soreness of her muscles.

"It's okay, Jess. All we need you to do is decouple the servers. Just the reverse of what you did before. Can you do that?"

She simply nodded and walked towards the servers. Putting her hands on each one, she closed her eyes, and swayed back and forth as if she were in a trance.

When she stopped, she simply crawled away from the servers, and climbed into her seat. "It's done," she said. "They weren't happy."

"Who?" Petal asked.

"The nice man and lady inside."

Petal felt for Sakura and Hajime. They'd been apart for so long, and even though their minds were fragmented and not fully operational, she knew their uploaded minds were aware. They could still know what it all meant, and now they were apart again. Petal realised that for the safety of everyone, they were better off disconnected forever. Combined, the servers were too much of a temptation for those who wanted to transcend the physical. And what she saw of Elliot Robertson's madness, she knew they couldn't allow that to happen again.

The thought of him made her think of James Robertson. The Doc. The Liar. The Betrayer. He remained on the other side of the transporter, sitting with his back turned, working on his slate.

Petal walked across to him, looked down over his shoulder.

"Well?" he said, looking up at her. "I suppose you want me to explain why I lied? Explain my behaviour?"

"No," Petal said. "I want to you to finish what you're doing. Get those 'droids back online so we can drive those mentalists back and make this our home. There'll be plenty of time for us to have a heart-to-heart later."

"I'm on it," he said, turning his attention back to his slate.

While Robertson frantically issued new instructions to the 'droids, Enna approached Petal, took her arm, and led her down the ramp away from the rest of the group.

"What about Gerry?" Enna said. "Is he still—"

"No. He's safe. In here." Petal tapped her head. "But I don't know in what condition, or how long I can hold him. Can you, you know, download him into a body?" She knew Enna could do it with her transcendents, but they were slightly more evolved AIs that she could swap in and out of various bodies. Gez was something far more complex, and his own body was in terrible shape after his shooting.

"I'm not entirely sure," Enna said turning her mouth up, scrunching her forehead. "I suppose it's possible. We know that he survived the transfer to you and to the servers and in some kind of condition. I'd really need to get you to my lab."

They both looked westward to Enna's compound in GeoCity-1. But beyond the Dome, the assault continued. Panel by panel, the barrage from the Red Widow's firepower broke through, creating gaping holes in their protective shell.

Their Jaguars were visible through the spaces as they circled around the structure targeting the weakest parts. It wouldn't be long before they started to breach it completely.

Enna must have thought the same thing, said. "Look!" She pointed up to one of the Jaguars. It belched black smoke from its left VTOL engine, spun wildly before it tilted and crashed to the ground. A fireball from the explosion lit up the purple-grey dawn sky.

The assault from Red Widow's army paused, no doubt shocked at losing one of their air support. Petal hoped it took a bunch of the Widows with it.

Robertson stood at the top of the ramp. "It's working!" he shouted down.

"The 'droids?" Petal asked.

He nodded with a hopeful grin on his face before racing down the ramp, handing her the slate. "Here, watch the video feed."

Standing there on the shuttle's landing pad, Petal watched the feed as sheer chaos erupted a few hundred metres beyond their position, beyond the Dome. The sound of screams and war, partially muted by the Dome's shell, echoed across the City to accompany the images.

In the middle of the maelstrom stood Criborg's android combat units. Red Widow hackers thought they had control over them. They'd grown sloppy, come to rely on them. But computers are fickle and owe no allegiance. Robertson's new instructions saw the squad strike at the heart of their army: their air support.

In split concentrated fire, the squad took each Jaguar down one by one, their accuracy and efficiency a lethal blow. While the dead hunks of metal fell from the sky like lethal bombs, the 'droids scattered in an almost random formation: the leading 'droid, whose feed Petal was watching led a team of five others in a wild, arcing assault on a group of Red Widow infantry, quickly cutting them down before they knew what had hit them.

The fanatics tried to respond, but as soon as they shifted into position, other small groups of five and ten androids were on the move, diverting their attention and thinning their numbers. Their fast movements and intricate and accurate firing patterns dominated the battlefield. They twisted Red Widow fighters round and round so that they began to fall from friendly crossfire. In amongst the smoke and dust and blood, Petal saw Natalya, their general shouting and screaming from one of the heavily armoured ATVs.

Before the androids could finish their work, Natalya appeared to gain some kind of order over her vastly decimated and scattered army. No more than a few hundred women gathered in groups and headed for her location. They formed a defensive perimeter around her and, but the 'droids spread out in a curving line, taking their front and both flanks.

A few Widows tried to fire on the 'droids, but the latter were too fast and too spread out.

The enemy retreated, and the 'droids pushed on, stalking them like prey. Sensing all was lost, Natalya dragged a few choice militants onto her vehicle, turned, and sped off into the distance leaving behind her a small band of warriors, their faces in shock at their general's abandonment.

A few turned to shoot on the line of 'droids, but within seconds they too were gunned down.

"Wait!" Petal said, staring up at Robertson. "Make them stop."

"Why? After everything they've done to you. They're animals."

"Yeah, but we ain't," Petal said. "At least most of us ain't."

Robertson's mouth twisted at the remark, but Petal stared him down, and as expected, he backed off. "How do I control them?" she said.

At first he didn't say anything, but Enna produced a laser pistol from beneath her jacket and held it at his head. "I'll happily blow your face off for the lies and damage you've caused if you don't answer her truthfully."

He swallowed, held his hands palm up. "Okay, okay. Let's not be hasty. You just ... here, let me show you?"

Petal nodded. Enna stepped back allowing him to reach over the slate and show Petal the controls. "Is that it?" Petal asked?

"Yes, you can connect directly via your implant to the lead 'droid like you would any server."

She swiped a gesture across the slate. It connected to her personal network. Controlling the slate with her mind, she accessed the main 'droid. Watching its movements on the feed, it stopped moving in on the fanatics and waited for her orders.

The instructions came from a script of coded declarations. Petal deleted these and created her own set. She also discovered that within the control protocols of the 'droids she could talk through the lead one's amplified speaker. She opened a communication channel and addressed the cowering fanatics.

"Hey scumbags!"

As one they turned to stare directly at her through the video feed.

"Now that I have your attention, I would very much appreciate it if you'd drop your weapons, and lay face first on the ground with your hands behind your back and palms open. Failure to do so will result in your quick death. Your choice!"

They huddled together, discussed their next action. Petal ordered the 'droids to raise, and aim their weapons. One by one, the Red Widow members turned to face the firing squad. It took them a few seconds, but as Petal mentally prepared to give the order to shoot, they dropped the weapons and complied. She breathed out a sigh of relief and ordered the robot army to take their weapons and cuff them.

"Nicely done," Enna said. "Now what?"

Petal handed the slate back to Robertson. Glared at him while answering Enna's question. "We're going to your lab. The Doc here will stay behind and help treat the wounded. Under supervision, of course. I want the Red Widows placed safely in the city's cells. They've suffered enough. Hell, we've all suffered enough."

"Petal, please. I can help you and Gerry. Let me make this up to—"

"You had your chance, but you chose to lie to me and Sasha! Now get out of my sight before I do something you'll regret." She shoved him out of the way and ascended the ramp.

Addressing the group of people now staring at her she said. "The fight is over, for now at least. I still have something to do, but all of you are free to do whatever you want. We have this city to ourselves now. Free from the tyranny of The Family, and free from the desires of the Red Widows.

"It's a good time to help the citizens, to rename the city, make it our home. We've been given a chance to start new as free people. There's a lot that needs to be done, however. No doubt the people of this city don't have a clue as to what to do now they don't have some all-encompassing power controlling their lives. They're going to need your help. They'll need to rebuild. Hell, there's a whole civilisation of people here ready to take direction and exercise their free will.

"Let's not waste the lives of those who died for our freedom. Let's grab this opportunity, and honour them, make their sacrifice worthwhile!"

Jess, Sasha, and the remaining security personnel, clapped and cheered.

Gabe came over to her, hugged her. "Ya've done great things, girl."

"We all did, Gabe. But at what cost?"

"A terrible cost, but there was no other choice. Listen, I ain't staying here. I'm coming with ya. I can help with this whole Gerry situation, and—"

"And what?"

"Natalya's still out there. I need to find her. I've some unfinished business."

Before Petal could get into what Gabe meant, a great cheer went up. She dashed out of the transporter to see tens of thousands of City Earth citizens come out of their apartment buildings, houses, and work places. They streamed like a great sea across the parks and the roads, until they surrounded the landing pads and transporters.

Opposite them, and entering the Dome, were the Red Widows, led in a line and cuffed to the group of androids. A member of Cemprom, an elderly lady wearing a smart, black business suit approached Petal. She held out her hand, said. "Thank you. Thank you all for doing what you did. You've saved us, have given us everything!" The woman cried and laughed. Petal took her into a hug.

"It's my pleasure," Petal said, watching the growing crowd around them.

Silence descended on the place. The Cemprom woman released Petal. Together, as one people, they turned to watch the Red Widows as they were taken towards the cells.

How much of the threat the citizens really knew, Petal couldn't tell. And she'd certainly not let them know they were minutes away from being nuked. All that mattered was they were free from tyranny.

"What do we do now?" The woman said.

"You live. Take down the AIA network and give your people freedom. Enjoy your lives!"

With that, a huge cheer went up again, and Petal found herself, Enna, Gabe, and the others surrounded by joyous people. But one in particular caught Petal's eye. For some reason she recognised him. An internal motivation made her focus in on him as he fought his way through the crowd. His body was thin, his face gaunt. He wore an over-sized, ill-fitting suit with the cuff of his right arm torn away. Dried blood surrounded his wrist.

Petal pushed through the jubilant crowd until she stood in front him.

He stopped, looked up to her, confusion in his eyes.

"You are Steven," Petal said, not understanding initially where that came from, but she soon realised. *Gerry.* She was experiencing *his* memories, *his* thoughts.

"You were a friend of Gerry's?"

Steven looked up at her, nodded. "I, I tried to stop him."

"Who?"

"Kaden. I saw what he did to Gerry, I tried to stop it all." He held up his wrist to show a bloodied scar.

"I don't understand," Petal said. "What did you try and stop? What happened to you?"

"I cut it out," Steven said. "The hot-chip, the chip that Kaden said would take me off the grid, save me from the lottery, but there was something, someone, else in it. It tried to get into my head, make me do things."

She understood then. Understood what made Kaden kill Gerry: Elliot Robertson.

"How many of these chips did this Kaden have?"

"I don't know, but he was dealing them to people within the city. Must have been doing it for a while. He had his own runners and dealers. It seemed to be a slick operation. Can you help me?" He held up his wrist again, the wound looked rough, jagged. The poor kid must have been in considerable pain. "I'm so sorry," he added before losing his balance.

Petal caught him. "It's okay, you tried. Gerry is okay, I think. Let's get you some medical attention." Petal cleared a path through the crowd until she reached the transporter. She handed Steven over to Robertson. "Look after him, see to his wounds, okay?"

Robertson didn't look her in the eye. He helped the boy up the ramp and into his quarter of the transporter. Petal looked out across the City. It was finally free, but a number of questions nagged at her: could she save Gerry? What would happen to him if he couldn't be downloaded into a body? How many of these chips were in circulation, and how much control did Elliot Robertson have over these people? What of Natalya and Gabe's unfinished business? And lastly: what of her? Where did she go from here?

Sasha approached, put an arm around her shoulder. "You look as if you have the world on your shoulders. You should be happy. Look at how it's all turned out! And hey, despite Jimmy being a total douche, we still have each other."

Petal turned to face her. "You're right. I'm proud of what you've done, what you did for me. But I can't stay here. There's still much that needs doing. And *he's* still out there."

"Who do you mean?"

"Elliot Robertson. He must be destroyed."

The End

Thank You for Reading

If you enjoyed this story, I would be very grateful if you wouldn't mind leaving a review at the retailer from where you purchased the book. They really help the author, and readers in making informed buying decisions.

To find out what happens next, feel free to sign-up to my newsletter to be notified of the next book: http://eepurl.com/rFAtL

Thank you for reading Assembly Code.
I appreciate each and every one of you.

About The Author

Colin F. Barnes is a full-time writer of techno and dark adventure thrillers and a member of both the British Fantasy Society and the British Science Fiction Association. He honed his craft with the London School of Journalism and the Open University (BA, English).

Colin has run a number of tech-based businesses, worked in rat-infested workshops, and scoured the back streets of London looking for characters and stories—which he found in abundance. He has a number of publishing credits with stories alongside authors such as: Brian Lumley, Ramsey Campbell, and Graham Masterton.

You can connect with Colin in the following ways:

Website: www.colinfbarnes.com
Newsletter: http://eepurl.com/rFAtL
Twitter: https://twitter.com/ColinFBarnes
Goodreads: http://bit.ly/13uTiEx
Facebook: http://on.fb.me/16QW0lR
Tumbler: http://uploadingmybrain.tumblr.com/